PROLOGO

Erano passati due anni ed era il primo dicembre, il giorno del quindicesimo compleanno di E-Z. Anche se fuori faceva un freddo cane e i fiocchi di neve scrosciavano intorno a loro, lui, la sua famiglia e i suoi amici erano decisi a organizzare la sua festa all'aperto, dove avevano preparato un falò per tenerli al caldo e un barbecue.

Ora che Samantha e Sam erano sposati, la casa dei Dickens era ancora più impegnata. Non c'era mai un momento di noia quando gli amici venivano a trovarci.

Il matrimonio di Sam e Samantha era stato una piccola cerimonia, tenutasi all'Ufficio del Registro. Lia era stata la damigella d'onore, E-Z era stato il testimone e Alfred, il cigno trombettiere, era stato il portabandiera.

Lia aveva preso in giro Alfred perché era vestito con un papillon blu navy e nient'altro. Alfred non si sentì turbato da questa attenzione, perché sapeva di essere in buona compagnia con altri, come gli ex primi ministri britannici.

"Se il grande Winston Churchill pensava che un papillon andasse bene per lui, allora va bene anche per me!". disse Alfred.

"Fumava anche un grosso sigaro!". Disse E-Z. "Spero proprio che non inizierai a fumarne uno anche tu".

Lia sogghignò.

"Le bistecche sono pronte!" Sam chiamò. "Se ti piacciono al sangue vieni a prenderle adesso".

Solo Samantha si fece avanti con il piatto pronto. "Tuo figlio ha voglia di carne al sangue oggi", disse, accarezzandosi la pancia.

"Quello che mio figlio vuole, lo ottiene", disse Sam, sollevando una bistecca nel piatto della moglie. La donna ne punzecchiò il centro mentre il marito aggiungeva una patata al forno e qualche filo di asparagi.

Samantha sgranocchiò gli asparagi mentre si dirigeva verso il tavolo da picnic. Aveva organizzato il compleanno di E-Z alla perfezione e aveva dedicato molto tempo a decorare il tavolo con oggetti a tema Happy Birthday. Si sedette e tagliò a metà le patate al forno, poi aggiunse panna acida, erba cipollina, burro e qualche pizzico di sale.

E-Z, Lia, Alfred, PJ e Arden rimasero in disparte perché faceva più caldo vicino al caminetto. Allo Zio Sam non piaceva che ci fossero persone in giro mentre lui si occupava del barbecue, quindi si tenevano

E-Z DICKENS SUPEREROE LIBRO TRE

SALA ROSSA

Cathy McGough

Stratford Living Publishing

Il Copyright © 2020 di Cathy McGough

Tutti i diritti riservati.

Questa versione tradotta è stata pubblicata nel febbraio 2024.

Nessuna parte di questo libro può essere riprodotta in qualsiasi forma senza il permesso scritto dell'editore o dell'autore, ad eccezione di quanto consentito dalla legge sul copyright degli Stati Uniti, senza il previo consenso scritto dell'editore presso Stratford Living Publishing,

ISBN: 978-1-998304-25-7

Cathy McGough ha rivendicato il diritto di essere identificata come autrice di quest'opera ai sensi del Copyright, Designs and Patents Act, 1988.

Arte realizzata da Canva Pro.

Questa è un'opera di fantasia. I personaggi e le situazioni sono tutti di fantasia. La somiglianza con persone vive o morte è puramente casuale. Nomi, personaggi, luoghi e incidenti sono frutto dell'immaginazione dell'autore o sono utilizzati in modo fittizio.

Per coloro che credono...

Indice dei contenuti

"Un eroe è un individuo ordinario che trova la forza di perseverare e resistere nonostante ostacoli schiaccianti".

Christopher Reeve

alla larga da lui. Inoltre, a tutti loro piacevano le puntate ben fatte e questo dava anche l'opportunità di chiacchierare da soli e di aggiornarsi.

"Cosa ne pensi del nostro sito web sui supereroi?". Chiese E-Z.

PJ e Arden si guardarono, poi scrollarono le spalle.

"Avanti", disse E-Z. "Cosa ne pensate davvero? So che avete dato un'occhiata al sito, perché lo zio Sam mi ha aiutato a controllare i dati. Non avevo idea che potessimo scoprire così tante informazioni, come ad esempio chi visita il nostro sito, quanto tempo si ferma e cosa guarda. E ho riconosciuto i vostri indirizzi IP. Allora, dimmi cosa ne pensi?".

"Tutta la verità? Senza peli sulla lingua?" PJ chiese.

"Verità brutale?" Aggiunse Arden.

"Sì", lo incitò E-Z. Abbassò la voce a un sussurro. "Lo zio Sam ha fatto un ottimo lavoro. Tuttavia, non ci stiamo rivolgendo al pubblico giusto, visto che non riceviamo quasi nessun traffico. Oltre a voi due e a un indirizzo IP situato in Francia, non abbiamo avuto quasi nessun riscontro.

"Alcune persone, come te, sono tornate a visitare il sito qualche volta, ma non si sono fermate a lungo. Lo zio Sam ha suggerito che forse dovremmo avviare una newsletter, far iscrivere le persone e inviare loro gli aggiornamenti, ma non lo so. Tutti fanno newsletter in questi giorni e sembra un sacco di lavoro. Lo zio Sam mi ha mostrato che si è iscritto a circa cinquanta di esse!

"Per quanto riguarda le richieste di aiuto - che è il motivo per cui abbiamo creato un sito web - finora ci è stato chiesto solo di occuparci di cose che riguardano le autorità locali, come la polizia e i vigili del fuoco. Non mi piace l'idea che noi ci precipitiamo a salvare un gatto su un albero e che i vigili del fuoco si presentino in piena forma per fare lo stesso lavoro. È inefficiente per loro e per noi. Ed è imbarazzante quando arrivano proprio mentre stiamo finendo. Il loro tempo è prezioso: salvano vite ogni giorno. Mi sembra irrispettoso, se capisci cosa intendo. Stanno salvando delle vite e sono reperibili 24 ore su 24".

"Credo che le richieste debbano essere fuori dal loro ambito, in modo da non fargli perdere tempo e da non rendere il loro lavoro più difficile di quanto non lo sia già. Scusate il discorso così lungo, ma se penso a tutto quello che hanno fatto dopo l'incidente dei miei genitori...".

PJ e Arden si avvicinarono e sussurrarono. Non volevano ferire i sentimenti di Sam - dopotutto non erano esperti - né correre il rischio che li sentisse e bruciasse le loro bistecche.

"Capiamo perfettamente il tuo punto di vista", disse PJ. "Inoltre, la polizia e i vigili del fuoco sono servizi essenziali e vengono pagati per salvare le persone. Mentre voi siete volontari".

"Quindi, il loro sito web e la loro presenza online sui social media sono diversi da quelli che dovreste avere voi", ha detto Arden. "E hanno molto personale, a vari livelli, che si occupa della manutenzione e dell'aggiornamento".

"Mentre il tuo sito ha bisogno di qualcosa di più simile a un supereroe - se questa è una parola - e meno aziendale. Come le leggende, quelle di cui segui le orme. Guarda alcuni dei siti web creati per loro - e si tratta di personaggi di fantasia. Immagina cosa potremmo fare se seguissimo il loro esempio", ha detto Arden.

"Per esempio? So che avete delle idee, quindi condividetele", ha detto E-Z.

"Beh, come avrai capito, abbiamo fatto un po' di brainstorming tra noi due. E abbiamo creato un sito web di prova - non è ancora attivo e non lo sarà finché non lo approverai - di come potrebbe essere il tuo sito. È sul mio telefono. Guarda e vedi cosa intendiamo e pensa alle possibilità che ti offriamo, visto che abbiamo fatto tutto in fretta". PJ premette il pulsante di avvio. I Tre si avvicinarono.

Sullo schermo apparvero prima le parole: "Benvenuti nel sito web dei supereroi dei Tre". Poi lo schermo zoomò su E-Z in forma animata. Era seduto sulla sua sedia a rotelle come ci si aspetterebbe, indossava una maglietta nera, jeans blu e un paio di scarpe da corsa.

E-Z si è dato una pacca sui capelli quando ha visto che la striscia nera al centro dei suoi capelli biondi assomigliava a una bottiglia. Non era mai riuscito ad abituarsi.

"Cosa c'è sulla mia maglietta, sui jeans e sulle scarpe? È un logo? E come hai fatto a trasformarmi in un cartone animato?".

"Sì, è un logo. Abbiamo pensato che l'ala d'angelo fosse bella e appropriata", ha detto Arden.

"Abbiamo usato un'applicazione per trasformarti in un cartone animato", ha detto PJ. "Abbiamo fatto un po' di editing sulle tue braccia. Speriamo di non aver esagerato".

E-Z's guardò da vicino la versione animata di se stesso che incrociava le braccia. Ora i suoi avambracci più ingombranti attirano la sua attenzione e le sue guance si arrossano. Aveva l'aria di essere un idiota, un poser. I suoi amici pensavano davvero che stesse meglio così? Rabbrividì quando apparvero le ali di E-Z sullo schermo. Si librò in aria e indicò.

Questa fu la prima presentazione di Lia. Anche lei era arrivata in forma animata. Lia era vestita dalla testa ai piedi con una tuta viola e un tutù. I suoi capelli biondi erano raccolti in una coda di cavallo e sugli occhi aveva un paio di occhiali da sole viola. Sembrava vivace, amichevole e carina mentre camminava sullo schermo. Si girava e si fermava, come una modella su una passerella, e si metteva in posa.

E-Z fece una smorfia, ma non riuscì a trattenersi.

"Beh, almeno non sembro una posatrice con i muscoli finti!", disse lei.

E-Z non fece commenti.

Lia animata allungò le braccia in avanti, con i palmi rivolti verso il suolo. Poi, voilà, le girò. L'occhio sinistro del palmo si aprì, seguito da quello destro. In sincronia, sbatterono le palpebre. Lia mantenne la posa, poi sibilò tra le dita.

"Vorrei poterlo fare davvero!" disse, cercando di imitare la versione animata di se stessa.

E-Z fischiò.

"Fatti vedere", disse lei, dandogli una gomitata.

Ora sullo schermo apparve la Piccola Dorrit. Era elegante e femminile e bianca come la neve. L'unicorno volò verso Lia, atterrò e abbassò la testa per permettere alla bambina di accarezzarla. Lia saltò su e la Piccola Dorrit volò accanto a E-Z. Si librarono, poi girarono la testa.

Questo era il segnale di Alfred. In forma di cartone animato, il suo becco arancione brillante sembrava brillare alla luce. Era in diretto contrasto con il suo papillon rosso mela candita. Mentre si dirigeva verso Lia ed E-Z, i suoi piedi palmati si muovevano come se fossero ventose.

"I miei piedi non fanno questo rumore!". disse Alfred.

"Anche loro lo fanno", disse E-Z con un sorriso, mentre Alfred sullo schermo apriva le ali e volava al fianco dei suoi due compagni.

I tre si misero in posa. E-Z era al centro, Lia a sinistra e Alfred a destra. Poi è successo. I Tre - beh, Lia ed

E-Z hanno alzato il pollice. Alfred, dal canto suo, fece il gesto delle ali alzate.

"È imbarazzante", sussurrò E-Z ad Alfred.

"Non scherziamo!".

"Shhhh", disse Lia mentre la voce fuori campo sullo schermo entrava in funzione. Era la voce di Arden, ma il suo tono era più basso. Sembrava il conduttore di un game show.

"Se hai bisogno di un supereroe... E-Z, Lia e Alfred - noti anche come i Tre - sono a tua disposizione 24 ore su 24, 7 giorni su 7. Chiama ***-***-**** o invia un messaggio sui social media.

Quando hai bisogno di qualcuno che ti aiuti... chiama i Tre. Saranno lì per te... immediatamente. Puoi contare su di loro... perché sono i migliori che tu possa incontrare. Ventiquattro ore al giorno, sette giorni su sette... soddisfazione garantita".

"E ora il grande finale", disse Arden.

I Tre piegarono le braccia sul petto. Alfred piegò le ali.

"Non è possibile", disse Alfred.

"Shhhh", disse Lia.

Con il mento in avanti, uno dopo l'altro, i Tre si misero in posa.

PJ mise in pausa.

"Tenendo conto di quello che hai detto sulle giurisdizioni, forse dovremmo cambiare questo pezzo", disse. Ha premuto il tasto start.

"Nessun lavoro è troppo grande o piccolo per noi!". Disse una versione computerizzata della voce di E-Z.

Poi un cerchio al centro dello schermo girò e girò, come se il wi-fi cercasse di trovare un segnale. Ora la parola BAM! riempiva lo schermo. Poi la parola SOCKO!

Guardarono E-Z mentre salvava un gatto bloccato in alto su un albero.

"Oh, fratello", disse.

La voce del suo personaggio animato continuò.

"Siamo i Tre

Siamo qui per te!

Gatto bloccato su un albero...

Lo tiriamo giù noi per te!".

E-Z è stato mostrato mentre consegnava il gatto salvato a una famiglia.

"Non è mai successo", ha detto.

"Ci siamo presi una piccola licenza poetica", ha ammesso Arden.

"Possiamo sistemare tutto ciò che non ti piace", disse PJ.

Il cerchio apparve di nuovo sullo schermo, girando in tondo. Quando si fermò, sullo schermo apparve la parola BANG! Seguita dalla parola ZIP!

Sullo schermo E-Z animato salvava un aereo pieno di passeggeri. Quando ha fatto atterrare l'aereo, centinaia di osservatori in attesa sulla pista hanno applaudito.

"Ora sì che ci siamo", disse.

"Shhh", disse Lia.

Sullo schermo E-Z disse,

"Perché siamo tuoi amici!

I nostri servizi sono gratuiti.

24/7

Perché noi siamo i Tre!".

Di nuovo in cerchio, girando in tondo. Seguito da BINGO! E BAM!

Il salvataggio sulle montagne russe è stato ricreato in forma animata. Era molto bello. Era così accurato che potevano sentire l'odore dello zucchero filato e del caramello.

"Oh!" Disse E-Z.

Lia applaudì.

Alfred scosse il collo da una parte all'altra come se fosse stato spruzzato di recente con acqua molto fredda.

"Mi piace!" disse Lia. "E grazie per aver incluso il mio colore preferito. Come facevi a saperlo?".

"Ho notato che lo indossi spesso", disse PJ. Le sue guance arrossirono. "Sono felice che ti piaccia".

"Cosa ne pensi, E-Z?". Chiese Arden.

Alfred lanciò un'occhiata in direzione di E-Z.

"È stato...", disse E-Z, "un buon tentativo".

"La cena è pronta, vieni a prenderla!". Chiamò Sam.

"Lascia che il festeggiato vada per primo", disse Samantha.

E-Z attraversò il cortile con Alfred.

"A proposito di tempismo perfetto", disse.

"Sì, quei due sono ancora degli imbranati", rispose Alfred.

"Ma il loro cuore è nel posto giusto. È un'idea intelligente, solo un po' esagerata per noi".

"Un po'?" Alfred strillò.

"Ok, molto, ma ci hanno provato. Possiamo tenere quello che ci piace e sbarazzarci del resto".

Quando tutti ebbero il loro cibo, si sedettero al tavolo da picnic e mangiarono. Il cielo cambiò e le stelle luminose riempirono il cielo intorno a loro. Mangiarono a sazietà, poi Samantha tirò fuori la torta di compleanno che aveva preparato e tutti cantarono "Buon compleanno!".

"Discorso! Discorso!" Arden li rimproverò e presto tutti si unirono a loro.

E-Z pensò per qualche secondo.

"Grazie per aver reso speciale il mio quindicesimo compleanno. Vorrei prendermi un minuto per ricordare mia madre e mio padre e per condividere con voi un ricordo del mio compleanno. Se ti va bene? Prometto di non fare la sdolcinata".

Tutti annuirono.

Samantha, da quando era rimasta incinta, era sempre sdolcinata. Che si trattasse di lacrime di felicità o di sedere, ne asciugò una prima ancora che lui cominciasse. "Sto bene", disse, mentre Sam le metteva un braccio intorno alle spalle.

"Era il giorno del mio quinto compleanno. Non volevo una festa e ho chiesto di andare a vedere un film. Invece di guardare il giornale per sapere cosa c'era, decidemmo di presentarci e di decidere cosa vedere sul posto. In ogni caso hanno detto che potevo scegliere io, visto che ero il festeggiato".

Chiuse gli occhi per un secondo.

Era di nuovo lì, al teatro. C'era la mamma, tutta infagottata in un parka. Aveva i paraorecchie e si stava sfregando le mani come faceva sempre. La mamma indossava sempre i guanti e si lamentava di avere le dita fredde.

Papà indossava il suo cappotto blu al ginocchio sopra i jeans. Non gli piaceva indossare un cappello in città perché gli scompigliava i capelli. Le sue mani erano senza guanti. Infilate nella tasca del cappotto insieme alle chiavi.

E-Z annusò l'aria. Sentiva l'odore dei popcorn al burro all'interno del cinema, in attesa che entrassero per ordinarli.

Stavano guardando le locandine.

"Che ne dici di quello?" disse sua madre.

"No, E-Z preferisce quello?" disse suo padre.

Riaprì gli occhi.

Invece di essere in giardino con la sua famiglia e i suoi amici, era di nuovo nel silo, di nuovo. Non era più tornato lì da quando gli arcangeli avevano rinnegato il loro accordo.

"Buon compleanno!" esclamò la voce nel muro.

Un pannello si aprì nella parete accanto a lui e ne uscì un cupcake. Sulla parte superiore c'era scritto:

"Buon compleanno, E-Z". Al centro c'era una singola candela già accesa.

"Buon appetito!" disse la voce, lasciando cadere un coltello e una forchetta sul tavolo accanto a lui.

"Grazie", disse lui. "Perché sono qui?".

"Il tempo di attesa è di quattro minuti", disse la voce fastidiosa. "Per favore, rimanga seduto".

Come se avesse avuto scelta.

CAPITOLO 1
COMPLEANNO INTERROTTO

E-Z non toccò il cupcake seduto di fronte a lui, anche se aveva un aspetto e un odore gradevoli. Si chiese cosa stesse succedendo alla sua festa. Almeno sapeva che non potevano tagliare la torta finché non avesse spento le candeline ed espresso un desiderio. Una festa di compleanno a casa, quando lui non c'era!

"Fatemi uscire di qui!", gridò. "Mi sto perdendo la festa del mio quindicesimo compleanno e stavo per raccontare una storia".

Il tetto del silo si aprì con uno sbadiglio ed Eriel si slanciò verso di lui come un fulmine in una tempesta.

"È bello rivederti, ex protetto", disse.

"Il sentimento non è reciproco. Perché sono qui? Pensavo di aver chiuso con tutti voi e poi è il mio compleanno, devo tornare al lavoro".

"Sì, mi scuso per il tempismo, ma non potevamo lasciar passare il tuo compleanno senza farti almeno gli auguri".

"Grazie, credo".

"E visto che sei qui, perché non assaggi il tuo cupcake di compleanno? E non dimenticare di esprimere un desiderio: avrai bisogno di tutto l'aiuto possibile!" disse l'arcangelo con una risatina.

Accanto a E-Z si aprì una finestra e ne uscì un braccio meccanico con un fiammifero acceso. Il braccio meccanico accese lo stoppino, poi si ritirò nel muro così velocemente che il fiammifero si spense da solo. Si chiese cosa significasse l'ultimo commento, ma pensò che Eriel lo stesse prendendo in giro. Il suo cervello si svuotò. Non riusciva a pensare a una sola cosa da desiderare. A parte questo, era di nuovo a casa con i suoi amici e la sua famiglia per festeggiare il suo compleanno. Mentre spegneva la candelina, Eriel si mise a cantare. Si trattava di un'interpretazione scoppiettante di "Perché è un bravo ragazzo, e nessuno può negarlo".

"Senza offesa", disse E-Z, "ma tu dovresti cantare Buon Compleanno".

"È il pensiero che conta", disse Eriel. "Ora che abbiamo concluso la parte della tua visita dedicata al compleanno, vorremmo sapere se hai già risolto l'indovinello".

"Indovinello? Quale indovinello?".

"Sì, ti abbiamo suggerito di cercare di fare dei collegamenti con le tue prove passate. Ricordi quando ti abbiamo detto che non volevamo imboccarti? Sei riuscito a farlo?".

"Oh, non mi sembrava una priorità o un indovinello da risolvere, soprattutto da quando avete rinunciato alla vostra offerta. Ma sì, stavo scrivendo sul mio taccuino, annotando le cose che abbiamo fatto finora, e ho individuato un paio di collegamenti con il gioco d'azzardo, ma erano puramente casuali".

"Coincidenza! Assolutamente no. Gli incidenti sono collegati, chiunque può vederlo!". disse Eriel, tenendo la voce bassa per non perdere la calma.

"Mi dispiace, ma le coincidenze accadono di continuo. Sai quanti bambini giocano al computer? Ho fatto una ricerca online. Nel 2011 si leggeva che il 91% dei bambini di età compresa tra i due e i diciassette anni giocava ogni giorno. Si tratta di circa sessantaquattro milioni di bambini in tutto il mondo".

Ah, quindi hai individuato il problema. È una buona cosa. Hai scoperto qualcos'altro al riguardo? O qualche preoccupazione che potresti avere? Qualsiasi motivo per cui dovresti fare ulteriori ricerche... La ricerca è buona. L'iniziativa è molto, molto, buona".

"No. Sono piuttosto impegnato, con altre cose: scuola e altro. Inoltre, se vuoi che approfondisca la questione, dovrai prima convincermi che si tratta di qualcosa di più di una coincidenza. Ho controllato altre statistiche. Ad esempio, le giocatrici sono più numerose che mai. Molte hanno creato delle attività su YouTube e si guadagnano da vivere. Non si tratta di ragazzini, ovviamente, ma dalle statistiche che ho letto online nel 2019 il 46% dei videogiocatori sono ragazze".

Eriel batté il dito lungo e ossuto sul mento, come se stesse riflettendo su ciò che E-Z gli aveva detto. "Ah, ancora una volta sono impressionato. Non trovi preoccupanti queste statistiche?".

"No, non lo trovo". Inspirò profondamente perdendo la pazienza di perdere il suo compleanno. "È importante farlo oggi? Non puoi riportarmi qui un'altra volta? Non c'è niente di importante in questo discorso".

Eriel smise di battere e il suo sopracciglio destro si alzò. Lanciò un'occhiata al festeggiato.

"O forse sì?" chiese E-Z.

Eriel aspettò prima di rispondere. Avvolse la lingua intorno alle parole, come se avesse difficoltà a farle uscire. Alzò il tono della voce a soprano e disse: "An-y-thin-g el-se a-bou-t tho-se t-wo in-ci-de-nts? Per usare un'arma? Per fare un contratto con te?".

E-Z desiderava che Eriel si esprimesse chiaramente e arrivasse al punto. Non voleva mettersi in imbarazzo dicendo cose ovvie o sbagliando.

"Raphael aveva ragione, sei un po' tonto".

"Ehi!" E-Z gridò. "Se hai bisogno del mio aiuto, stai cercando di ottenerlo in un modo molto strano". Passò il dito sulla glassa del cupcake e lo succhiò. Il sapore era buono, come lo zucchero filato. "Uccidere. Uno stava cercando di uccidermi e l'altro stava uccidendo delle persone in un negozio. Entrambi hanno detto che i loro motivi erano legati al gioco".

"Un bel colpo", disse Eriel.

"E?"

"Non importa!" Eriel sparì attraverso il soffitto, cantando: "Spessa come un mattone, spessa come un mattone, spessa come un mattone".

E-Z alzò i pugni in aria. "Torna qui e dimmelo in faccia!".

La risata di Eriel rimbalzò sulle pareti.

PFFT.

"Grazie", disse E-Z, poi si ritrovò a casa, alla sua festa. Tutti erano indaffarati, giocavano, facevano le loro cose, come se lui non fosse mai stato presente, cosa che invece non era.

Guardò Sam mentre faceva il suo turno alla palla della scala. Non era particolarmente bravo, ma E-Z si avvicinò e osservò comunque il suo secondo tentativo. Dopo aver terminato il lancio, mancando completamente il bersaglio, si avvicinò al nipote.

"Vedo che stai ancora lavorando per prendere confidenza con questo gioco", disse E-Z.

"Sì, è un talento acquisito. A proposito, dove sei andato?".

"Eriel voleva augurarmi buon compleanno, tra le altre cose".

"È stato gentile da parte sua. Non è vero?"

"Beh, conosci Eriel. Non fa mai nulla senza un motivo. In questo caso, voleva che facessi un collegamento basato su un ricordo".

"Un ricordo di cosa? I tuoi genitori? L'incidente?":

"No, voleva che facessi un collegamento tra due degli istigatori del processo. Cosa che, tra l'altro, ho fatto. Poi se n'è andato dicendo che ero un mattone".

"Che maleducato!" Esclamò Lia. Stava ascoltando da quando si era annoiata a morte per il gioco del lancio della palla.

"E per di più nel giorno del tuo compleanno", disse Alfred. Era ancora più disperato di Sam, visto che doveva lanciare le palline con il becco.

"Vuoi provare?" PJ chiese, passando la palla a E-Z che riposizionò la sua sedia davanti al bersaglio, poi lanciò la palla. La palla ha colpito il piolo superiore, ha girato un paio di volte ed è atterrata nella posizione di premio.

"È così che si fa!". Disse Sam.

"Io e PJ abbiamo fatto lanci del genere per tutta la partita", ha detto Arden.

"Ah, ma tu non sei mio nipote", rispose Sam.

La festa continuò fino a quando non fu troppo buio per fare altri giochi e tutti decisero di non cantare insieme. PJ e Arden tornarono a casa mentre E-Z e il resto della banda andarono a letto.

CAPITOLO 2
TROPPO

Due giorni dopo la festa di compleanno di E-Z, PJ e Arden si trovarono in difficoltà.

È stata Lia ad avere la visione che qualcosa non andava. Ha ricordato la visione ad Alfred ed E-Z: "Era come se fossero in trance. Erano entrambi seduti alle loro scrivanie e fissavano lo schermo di un computer vuoto".

"Non c'è niente di strano", ha detto E-Z. "Spesso giocano insieme e forse stavano dormendo".

"Con gli occhi aperti?".

"Ok, andiamo laggiù", disse E-Z.

"È notte fonda!". Esclamò Alfred.

"Comunque, è meglio controllare".

I Tre sgattaiolarono fuori di casa, decidendo di andare prima da PJ, visto che la sua era la più vicina.

"Non credo che i suoi genitori apprezzeranno una visita così tardiva", disse Alfred.

"Capiranno", disse Lia, mentre suonava il campanello d'ingresso.

Pochi istanti dopo, un uomo molto assonnato, che si strofinava gli occhi, aprì la porta in pigiama: il padre di PJ.

"Chi è?", chiamò la madre dall'interno.

"Sono gli amici di PJ", disse il padre. "C'è qualcosa che non va?".

"Ehm...", disse E-Z, "Mi dispiace disturbarvi ma abbiamo davvero bisogno di vedere PJ. È urgente".

"Allora è meglio che entriate", disse il padre di PJ.

CAPITOLO 3
PRECEDENTE

All'inizio della serata, PJ e Arden avevano lavorato al sito web dei supereroi. Hanno aggiornato le informazioni e aggiunto alcuni nuovi elementi.

In passato, quando arrivava una richiesta di assistenza, veniva inviata un'e-mail alla casella di posta. La volta successiva che qualcuno si collegava, la vedeva e rispondeva di conseguenza. Con il nuovo sistema, E-Z, Arden e PJ riceveranno messaggi di testo all'istante.

Inoltre, la persona che richiedeva la richiesta avrebbe ricevuto una risposta automatica con data e ora. PJ e Arden erano certi che questo aggiornamento automatico avrebbe aumentato la fiducia e portato più traffico al sito.

PJ e Arden hanno anche creato un canale YouTube con un podcast. Si trattava di una novità che avevano ideato durante una sessione di brainstorming. Erano entusiasti di parlarne a E-Z. Sarebbe stato un modo eccellente per aumentare la presenza online dei Tre. Hanno anche creato una Community Board per le discussioni aperte.

Il sistema ha anche classificato i messaggi in arrivo. Ad esempio, il salvataggio di un gatto da un albero. The Three aveva ricevuto diverse richieste per questo servizio. Dato che i funzionari locali erano più attrezzati per rispondere a queste chiamate, PJ e Arden lo hanno reso un Codice Blu.

Un codice blu significava che quando E-Z arrivava per salvare il gatto, questo era già stato salvato. Un Codice Blu indicava che avrebbe dovuto aspettare per vedere se la situazione era stata risolta prima di uscire.

Un Codice Giallo potrebbe indicare che qualcuno ha dimenticato le chiavi o le ha chiuse in macchina. Anche in questo caso, quando E-Z è arrivato sul posto, la situazione era già stata risolta. Anche in questo caso, il consiglio è di aspettare e controllare prima di uscire.

Classificando i blu e i gialli, E-Z e il suo team sarebbero stati in grado di concentrarsi sulle chiamate più importanti, ovvero i codici rossi.

Un codice rosso si verifica quando sono in pericolo vite o arti. Da quando è stato creato il sito web, i Tre hanno ricevuto zero richieste in questa categoria.

Soddisfatti di quanto avevano fatto, decisero di sfogarsi un po'. Si iscrissero a una partita multigiocatore.

"Tre ragazze", ha scritto PJ ad Arden.

"Possiamo affrontarle!", rispose lui.

La partita iniziò e all'inizio tutto si svolse come sempre. Stavano picchiando le ragazze, salendo di livello dopo livello, uccidendo tutto ciò che vedevano. Poi, all'improvviso, tutto si fermò.

CAPITOLO 4
IL POSTO DI PJ

Ora i Tre e i genitori di PJ si diressero lungo il corridoio verso la sua stanza. Quello che videro era più o meno come lo aveva immaginato Lia. La differenza era che lo schermo del computer era ancora acceso. Lampeggiava e sfarfallava mentre PJ sembrava dormire profondamente.

"Che cosa gli succede?" Chiese la madre di PJ. "Dovrebbe essere a letto a dormire. Guarda la sua postura. Probabilmente è disidratato. Gli porto un bicchiere d'acqua".

Il padre di PJ attraversò la stanza e scosse le spalle del figlio. Si aspettava che il figlio si svegliasse, ma non lo fece. Invece, scivolò sulla sedia e sarebbe caduto sul pavimento se il padre non l'avesse afferrato. Prese in braccio il figlio e lo mise sul letto.

La madre di PJ tornò, mise l'acqua sul tavolino e appoggiò le labbra sulla fronte del figlio. "Non c'è febbre", disse.

Il padre di PJ sollevò la palpebra destra del figlio e vide che era visibile solo il bianco degli occhi. "Chiama il 911", esclamò.

"No, credo che dovremmo chiamare il nostro medico di famiglia, il dottor Flannel", disse la madre di PJ. "È già venuto qui in passato per una visita a domicilio. Quando si trattava di un'emergenza, e questa è decisamente un'emergenza".

"Signora Handle", disse E-Z, "Si riprenderà".

"Certo che starà bene", rispose lei, mentre il signor Handle usciva dalla stanza per chiamare il dottor Flannel".

Quando tornò, aspettarono tutti insieme in silenzio, osservando PJ mentre dormiva. Come se si aspettassero che si alzasse e iniziasse a fare i capricci. Sarebbe stato proprio da lui fare finta di niente. Prendendoli in giro.

Mr. Handle era agitato e faceva rimbalzare la gamba su e giù mentre era seduto. Si alzò, attraversò la stanza e si chinò per guardare il disco rigido. Alzò il piede, come se volesse dargli un calcio, ma all'ultimo momento cambiò idea e tirò fuori il cavo dalla presa.

I due guardarono mentre Mr. Handle iniziava a tremare per tutto il corpo, finché non lasciò cadere la spina. Si girò e si diresse verso di loro. Dietro di lui il fumo fuoriusciva dal disco rigido. Pochi secondi dopo lo schermo del monitor si incrinò.

"Prendete l'estintore!". Alfred chiamò, ma E-Z aveva già preso il bicchiere d'acqua e lo aveva gettato sulla scatola. Sfrigolò e si unì allo schermo, entrambi assolutamente morti.

La madre di PJ corse dal marito e lo aiutò a sedersi. "Il dottore potrà dare un'occhiata anche a te quando arriverà", disse. "Sei davvero fortunato. Non posso sopportare che vi facciate male tutti e due".

"Sto bene", disse Mr. Handle.

Ma agli occhi di The Three non sembrava che stesse bene. Era pallido, un po' verde e un po' grigio.

"Non fare storie", disse il signor Handle. "Grazie per la prontezza di riflessi, E-Z". Poi alla moglie: "Hai fatto bene a portare l'acqua".

"PJ si arrabbierà molto quando vedrà che il suo computer è rovinato".

"Su, su", disse Mr. Handle. "Capirà".

Stava chiaramente migliorando: i Tre notarono che il suo respiro era tornato normale, così come il suo pallore.

Dato che tutto sembrava in ordine, E-Z parlò di Arden. "Mentre aspettate il dottore, dobbiamo controllare Arden. Pensiamo che possa trovarsi in condizioni simili".

"Giocano spesso insieme, ma cosa mai può aver causato questo?". Il signor Handle si informò.

"Non lo so, ma le dispiace se vado a controllare Arden?".

"Vai pure", disse la signora Handle.

"Lia resterà qui con te", disse E-Z. "Potrà tenerci informati e ci terrà informati". "Ci terrà informati e se avrai bisogno di noi, torneremo subito".

"Grazie, E-Z, e Alfred", disse il signor Handle, mentre li accompagnava alla porta d'ingresso.

CAPITOLO 5
POSTO DI ARDEN

E-Z e Alfred si diressero a casa di Arden. Prima ancora che potessero bussare, il padre di Arden, il signor Lester, aprì la porta.

"Come lo sai?" chiese.

E-Z non poteva dirgli la verità. Così improvvisò una bugia. "Sono sempre stato il migliore amico di Arden, quindi so quando qualcosa non va. Posso vederlo?"

"Certo, vieni in camera sua", disse la madre di Arden, la signora Lester. "Non ti allarmare. Sta solo dormendo. Si riprenderà domattina".

Il signor Lester prese la mano della moglie e la condusse nel corridoio dove Arden dormiva profondamente.

"Oh", esclamò Alfred quando lo vide. "Sembra che sia sotto shock".

"Guarda sotto le sue palpebre", disse il signor Lester.

E-Z tirò indietro la palpebra del suo amico. La pupilla di PJ era visibile, ma era più grande e sembrava che potesse esplodere da un momento all'altro. Richiuse di nuovo la palpebra.

Alfred ha fatto "Hoo-hoo". Questo è ciò che hanno sentito i Lester. Lui disse: "Cosa diavolo può averlo causato? Paura? O qualcosa di più serio come una crisi epilettica?".

E-Z scrollò le spalle senza rispondere. I Lester erano già abbastanza spaventati e stressati, in più non avrebbero fatto altro che tirare a indovinare.

"Dove lo avete trovato esattamente?" Chiese E-Z.

"Era seduto davanti al suo computer", disse la signora Lester.

"Lo schermo era acceso?" chiese lui.

"Sì, lo era", disse il signor Lester. "Abbiamo chiamato il nostro medico di famiglia. È occupato in questo momento, sta facendo un'altra telefonata ma ci richiamerà".

"Hanno già chiamato un medico a casa di PJ, il dottor Flannel. Fammi chiamare Lia per sapere se ha già fatto una diagnosi".

"Sono quasi uguali", disse.

"Cosa intendi con "quasi"?"

Uscì dalla stanza con la sedia a rotelle. Non c'era bisogno di preoccupare i Lester più di quanto non lo fossero già. Sussurrò al telefono: "Le sue pupille sono ancora visibili, ma sono enormi. Come piaghe che stanno per scoppiare!".

"Oh, che schifo!" Disse Lia. "Forse dovrebbe andare in ospedale?" "Hanno chiamato il loro medico di famiglia, ma non è disponibile. Fammi sapere quando il dottor Flannel darà la sua opinione e gliela comunicherò. Potresti dirgli dell'occhio di Arden e vedere se ti consiglia un ricovero immediato".

"Lo farò. Mi terrò in contatto".

Spiegò tutto ai Lester. Loro guardavano davanti a sé, con il volto vuoto. Era preoccupato per come stavano prendendo la cosa.

"Qualcuno vuole una tazza di tè?". Chiese la signora Lester.

"No, grazie", disse E-Z. La signora Lester era una di quelle mamme che credevano che il tè potesse risolvere la maggior parte dei problemi.

Il signor Lester seguì la moglie in cucina.

"Di solito non partecipi ai loro giochi?". chiese Alfred, ora che lui ed E-Z erano soli con Arden.

A volte", disse E-Z, "ma ultimamente, se ho del tempo libero, lo passo a scrivere. Non ho molto tempo per me stesso in questi giorni".

"È comprensibile. Scusa se ti sto frequentando troppo".

"No, va bene così. Devo organizzarmi meglio. Il lavoro scolastico sta diventando più complicato, sai che siamo sulla strada della carriera e della laurea. Vogliono che sappiamo dove stiamo andando e noi non sappiamo ancora dove siamo".

"Ricordo quei giorni, ma lo scoprirai. Comunque, sono contento che tu non abbia giocato con loro, altrimenti potresti trovarti nello stesso stato in cui si trovano loro".

"È vero. Non riesco a immaginare cosa possa spaventarli così tanto... se è questo che è successo. Voglio dire, un gioco è un gioco, non la realtà. Deve essere stata una bella gara".

I Lester tornarono nella stanza del figlio.

"Che cosa è successo?" La signora Lester urlò.

Le palpebre di Arden erano ora aperte, rivelando un interno completamente bianco. Come PJ, le sue pupille erano scomparse.

E-Z ebbe una sensazione di déjà vu quando il signor Lester attraversò la stanza e si chinò per staccare la spina.

"Fermati!" E-Z urlò. "Non toccarlo!"

Il signor Lester si bloccò sul posto.

"Il signor Handle ha rischiato di prendere la scossa quando l'ha toccato. La cosa migliore da fare è lasciarlo stare".

"Oh, grazie al cielo eri qui e mi hai avvertito", disse il signor Lester.

"Sì, grazie E-Z. Non ce l'avrei fatta se mio figlio e mio marito si fossero fatti male. Non ce la farei mai". Attraversò la stanza e abbracciò il marito.

"In seguito il suo computer si è rotto, lo schermo si è incrinato ed è uscito del fumo", spiegò E-Z. "Quindi, il computer di PJ si è rotto, lo schermo si è incrinato ed è uscito del fumo". "Quindi, il computer di PJ è sfrigolato, fritto, abbrustolito. Mentre il computer di Arden è ancora intatto. Se riusciamo a capire come entrarci, in modo sicuro, forse possiamo scoprire cosa gli è successo. Per prima cosa, devo chiamare lo Zio Sam e chiedere il suo aiuto. Lui è un tecnico informatico e saprà cosa fare".

"Aspetta", disse la signora Lester. "Ci stai dicendo che sia PJ che Arden sono uguali?".

Lui annuì.

"Ho sempre detto che i computer sono malvagi!", disse lei. "Il mio Arden è un atleta. Avrebbe dovuto essere fuori a fare sport, non seduto al computer a perdere tempo". Singhiozzò nel petto del marito che la strinse a sé.

"I computer sono necessari per la scuola", ha detto il signor Lester. "Nostro figlio non ha fatto nulla di male e sono sicuro che da un momento all'altro tornerà come prima. Ha bisogno di un po' di riposo. Un po' di riposo, tutto qui. Starà bene".

Alfred ha fatto "Hoo-hoo".

E-Z ricevette un messaggio sul suo telefono. "Lia dice che il dottor Flannel ha detto loro di lasciare PJ dov'è. Ha detto che i suoi occhi dovrebbero tornare normali da soli. Dice che PJ non sembra soffrire. Il battito cardiaco e il polso sono normali. Ha bisogno di riposo".

"Grazie", disse il signor Lester.

"Grazie a voi per essere passati", disse la signora Lester. "Vi faremo sapere se ci saranno cambiamenti".

E-Z e Alfred se ne andarono dopo una lunga visita, si incontrarono con Lia e tornarono tutti insieme a casa.

"Non posso fare a meno di chiedermi", disse E-Z, "se questa cosa con PJ e Arden sia destinata a essere una prova. Eriel mi ha fatto intendere che dovrei essere preoccupato per qualcosa. Che dovrei addirittura voler perseguire la cosa. Se è così, non sono sicuro di come dovrei risolvere il problema. Hai qualche idea? A parte chiedere allo Zio Sam di aiutarci a entrare nel computer di Arden, non so proprio cosa fare".

"È strano, se si tratta di un processo", disse Alfred. "Perché i processi appartengono al passato, non è vero?".

"Lo sono, ma se PJ e Arden sono feriti, allora non ho altra scelta che essere coinvolto. Anche se gli arcangeli hanno rinnegato il nostro accordo".

"Sembrano entrambi così, fuori di sé. Cosa si aspettano che tu faccia? Non è che tu abbia poteri di guarigione o altro", disse Alfred.

"Ma tu sì!" Disse Lia.

"Li ho, ma quando sono utilizzabili. Ho provato a comunicare con le loro menti. Ma era come se fossero vuote. Non riuscivo a raggiungerli. Per guarirli, ci sarebbe dovuta essere una sorta di connessione. E non c'era nulla con cui potessi connettermi.

"Continuo a chiedermi se dovrei chiedere aiuto ad Ariel. Lei è l'Angelo della Natura. Forse c'è qualcosa che può suggerire o qualcosa che può fare che io non posso fare".

"È un'idea promettente", disse E-Z.

WHOOPEE

Ariel arrivò.

"Che succede?" chiese.

Alfred le spiegò la situazione.

E-Z chiese se si trattava di un processo che gli arcangeli stavano cercando di fare a posteriori.

"In ogni caso devi aiutare i tuoi amici", disse. "Vuoi aiutarli, vero?".

"Certo, lo voglio, ma quello che devo fare, le azioni che devo intraprendere in un processo di solito sono più ovvie".

"Non ho sentito sussurrare che non sei in grado di prendere l'iniziativa?". chiese Ariel.

"Stai forse insinuando", chiese E-Z, tenendo la voce bassa per non perdere la calma. "Che gli arcangeli abbiano mandato in coma i miei amici per mettere alla prova la mia iniziativa?".

Ariel sorrise. "No, non sto insinuando nulla del genere. Ma, se si trattasse di una prova, cosa faresti per aiutarli?".

"Quando mi si presenta una prova, il mio cervello si mette in moto. So cosa fare per risolvere il problema e lo faccio. In questo caso, non ho idea di cosa fare per risolvere il problema. Sono in pericolo di vita. Non sono un medico".

Ariel incrociò le braccia. "Cosa hai provato a fare, Alfred?".

"Ho provato a connettermi con le menti di entrambi. Di solito, se riesco a guarire esseri umani o creature, c'è una connessione che non è stata interrotta da una forza esterna. In entrambi i casi, era come se la porta fosse stata sbattuta e non potessi sfondarla".

"Hai risposto alla tua stessa domanda", disse Ariel. "C'è qualcos'altro che posso fare per te?".

"Non sei stata proprio d'aiuto", disse Lia.

Alfred si scusò.

WHOOPEE

E Ariel se ne andò.

"Non dovresti parlarle così", disse Alfred. "Se avesse potuto aiutarci, lo avrebbe fatto".

"Mi dispiace, ma è frustrante quando non sanno più di quanto sappiamo noi. Sono arcangeli! Dovrebbero sapere qualcosa che noi non sappiamo, altrimenti che senso avrebbe?". Lia chiese.

"Vuoi dire che Haniel è sempre in grado di risolvere qualsiasi problema?".

Lia scrollò le spalle. "Non ne ho avuti molti da discutere".

E-Z disse: "Eriel è inutile. Ogni volta che gli ho chiesto aiuto me lo ha negato. Sì, mi ha dato dei consigli. Mi ha detto di trovare una soluzione da solo.

"Ad esempio, quando mi ha convocato l'ultima volta, ha accennato a una specie di cospirazione, o connessione, come l'ha chiamata lui.

"Quando ho intuito che si trattava di un gioco, che c'era una connessione, è stato ancora inutile. Vorrei che lo dicessero. In un modo o nell'altro, potrei concentrarmi per tirare fuori i miei due amici da questa situazione".

"Capisci cosa intendo?" Disse Lia. "Tutti gli arcangeli sono totalmente inutili".

"Haniel ti ha aiutato quando ti sei ferita agli occhi", le ricordò Alfred.

Lia gli voltò le spalle.

"Speriamo che il dottore avesse ragione e che domattina siano entrambi in sé", disse E-Z. "È tutto ciò che possiamo fare".

Arrivati a casa, andarono nel giardino sul retro. Salutarono la piccola Dorrit, guardarono il sole sorgere e parlarono della loro prossima mossa.

E-Z ripassò alcune cose che lo stavano tormentando. Nella Stanza Bianca lo avevano incoraggiato a collegare i punti. Di recente Eriel lo ha aiutato a restringere il campo.

Ripercorse tutto ciò che la ragazza del negozio gli aveva raccontato. Come aveva preso degli ostaggi, come in un gioco. Che indossava un costume, in modo da assomigliare a un cacciatore di taglie del gioco.

Poi, ha analizzato i dettagli del ragazzo fuori da casa sua. Il ragazzo aveva detto chiaramente di essere stato mandato a uccidere E-Z da voci nel gioco e che se non l'avesse fatto la sua famiglia sarebbe stata uccisa.

Poi ha pensato al coinvolgimento di Eriel e degli altri Arcangeli nelle prove. Ora PJ e Arden erano coinvolti.

Gli Arcangeli li avrebbero coinvolti per arrivare a lui? Era colpa sua, per essere stato troppo lento a risolvere il puzzle che gli avevano dato? Gli arcangeli avevano detto di aver chiuso con lui. Avevano annullato le prove e lui era contento di non vederle più. Perché erano tornati, cercando di creare un nuovo legame con lui? Non poteva essere una coincidenza.

Aprì la bocca per dire ad Alfred e Lia quello che stava pensando e invece atterrò di nuovo nel silo. Solo che questa volta il contenitore, invece di essere di metallo, era di vetro e lui era senza la sua sedia.

CAPITOLO 6
A TESTA IN GIÙ

E-Z era sospeso a testa in giù in una bolla di vetro, osservando l'erba verde della terra. Si trovava in alto e la testa gli faceva così male che temeva di scoppiare e di schizzare in tutto il contenitore. Ma per fortuna qualcosa lo teneva su. Non sapeva cosa fosse.

A differenza delle altre volte in cui si trovava nel silo, non era assicurato (o la sua sedia non era fissata) al suo posto. L'altra cosa che lo preoccupava, appeso a testa in giù in questo modo, era che non avrebbe visto arrivare Eriel. Né sarebbe stato in grado di sentirne l'odore.

Nel momento in cui pensava a Eriel, il contenitore si spostava. Temeva di cadere. Voleva aggrapparsi a qualcosa, ma non c'era nulla a cui aggrapparsi se non l'aria. Si avvolse le braccia intorno a sé. Poi sentì un movimento. La camera di vetro ruotò in senso orario di centottanta gradi. La sua testa si sentì subito meglio, più chiara, e si concentrò per uscire. Prima è, meglio è.

Troppo tardi però, la cosa si spostò e poi ruotò di altri centottanta gradi. Riportandolo al punto di partenza.

"Salve, Doody", urlò Eriel premendo il viso contro il vetro. Poi bussò e cantò: "Fammi entrare, fammi entrare".

"Fatemi uscire di qui!" E-Z urlò.

"Calmati", disse Eriel. "Sei qui per la gentilezza del mio cuore. Volevo dirti personalmente che i tuoi amici sono in pericolo".

"Vuoi dire PJ e Arden?". Eriel annuì. "Beh, questo lo so già! Sei un grande buffone!"

"Bastoni e pietre mi spezzeranno le ossa, ma i nomi non potranno mai farmi del male", cantò Eriel.

"Se non mi porti via da qui, subito, ti farò più male di quanto possano fare bastoni e pietre!".

Eriel batté il dito ossuto contro il mento. Dopotutto era ancora a destra, il che era un vantaggio rispetto alla prospettiva in cui si trovava E-Z.

"Volevo che sapessi che, anche se i tuoi amici sono in pericolo, non devi preoccuparti. Non sono in pericolo per i supereroi". Fece una pausa. "Un uccellino mi ha detto che pensi che stiamo cercando di farti sfuggire un altro processo... beh, non è così. Lasciali al destino".

"Cosa vuol dire che non sono in pericolo per i supereroi?". E-Z urlò.

Eriel scomparve e il contenitore di vetro cadde. Lui si agitò, si tenne in equilibrio. Cadde di nuovo. Continuò così, finché non fu certo che il suo cranio si sarebbe aperto come un uovo sul marciapiede.

Poi vide Alfred, sul bordo del prato, che sgranocchiava l'erba.

"Ehi!" E-Z gridò. "HEY!"

Alfred smise di mangiare e si avvicinò. Osservò il suo amico, appeso a testa in giù in una bolla di vetro.

"Cosa ci fai lì dentro?" chiese il cigno trombettiere.

"Eriel!" Esclamò E-Z.

"Basta così. Vado a svegliare Sam. Spero che sappia cosa fare per farti uscire da lì".

"Buona idea e chiedigli di portarmi la sedia".

Mentre aspettava, E-Z si maledisse. Aveva perso l'occasione di chiedere più informazioni a Eriel. Si era comportato come una vittima. Aveva deluso i suoi due migliori amici.

Formulò un piano. Quando uscirò da qui, troverò Eriel e mi farò dire come salvare PJ e Arden. Gli farò giurare che non mi metterà mai più in questa situazione.

Aspetta un attimo. Se PJ e Arden non erano in pericolo per i supereroi. In che tipo di pericolo si trovavano? Avevano bisogno di essere salvati? O il dottor Flannel aveva ragione nel dire che avrebbero superato la cosa e sarebbero tornati presto come prima?

Non gli piaceva l'affermazione "lasciali al destino". Credeva che fossimo noi a creare il nostro destino e i suoi due amici erano in coma. Non potevano aiutarsi da soli, quindi lui li avrebbe aiutati. A prescindere da ciò che diceva Eriel.

Alla fine, lo zio Sam uscì brandendo un grosso attrezzo in mano. "È un tagliavetro", disse. "Sapevo che un giorno mi sarebbe stato utile quando l'ho comprato grazie a una di quelle televendite. Dicevano che poteva tagliare il vetro come il burro. Vediamo se era pubblicità ingannevole". Tagliò intorno al fondo. Lentamente. Con attenzione.

"Ehi, sbrigati, sto soffocando qui dentro! Se spunta il sole, friggerò".

"Pazienza, caro ragazzo", disse Alfred.

"Ci siamo quasi", disse Sam. Era in ginocchio, avanzando, mentre la taglierina tagliava il fondo del contenitore. Nel frattempo le ginocchia del suo pjs sorseggiavano la rugiada del prato. "Suppongo che Eriel abbia avuto a che fare con la tua presenza lì dentro?".

"Affermativo."

Sam finì di tagliare e liberò suo nipote, poi lo aiutò a salire sulla sedia a rotelle.

"Grazie zio Sam".

"Non c'è di che. Ora spiegami, per favore".

"Sono troppo stanco. E sono troppo seccato per spiegare. Possiamo farlo domattina, per favore?".

Il sole si stava colorando di rosso mentre saliva all'orizzonte.

Tra qualche ora, E-Z avrebbe dovuto controllare i suoi amici. Sperava che stessero bene. Che tornassero alla normalità. Così non avrebbe dovuto pensarci un attimo di più. In caso contrario... se non lo fossero stati. In ogni caso, tutto sarebbe andato meglio dopo aver dormito un po'.

"Posso spiegargli tutto", si offrì Alfred.

"Tu cosa ne sai? Ho dovuto urlare per attirare la tua attenzione".

"Oh, ho visto tutto. Cosa pensi che stessi facendo qui fuori? Stavo aspettando che tu chiedessi aiuto. Non volevo interrompere il tuo tempo con Eriel".

"Interrompere. Molto divertente. Ok, aggiornalo. Vado a riposare un po'. Sono troppo stanco per pensare ancora". Salì con la sedia a rotelle sulla rampa ed entrò in casa e si mise a letto completamente vestito.

E-Z sognò che era il suo settimo compleanno. I suoi genitori avevano affittato il parco giochi virtuale al chiuso. Aveva invitato dodici bambini in tutto, quindi erano in tredici e una squadra doveva avere un giocatore in più. Dato che era il suo giorno, hanno chiamato le squadre e l'ultimo scelto è entrato nella sua squadra. Si chiamavano i Ball Breakers. L'altra squadra, guidata da Kyle Marshall, si chiamava Bat Shitz.

"Non puoi usare quel nome", li rimproverò la squadra di E-Z. "È praticamente una parolaccia". "È praticamente una parolaccia".

"Ah, ripensaci", disse Marshall. "Lo spelling è Shitz. Ci chiamiamo come il mio cane. È una Shitz-hu".

"Giochiamo", disse E-Z.

PJ e Arden erano nella squadra di E-Z. La squadra del trio tornado prese a calci nel sedere la squadra dei Bat Shitz finché non furono tutti troppo stanchi per muoversi.

"Il cibo è servito", disse la madre di E-Z. I genitori stavano aspettando nel ristorante adiacente. Avevano ordinato una serie di pizze, secchiate di bibite e infine una torta piena di candeline.

I ragazzi lasciarono insieme l'area di gioco. Ben presto Arden si rese conto di aver dimenticato il suo cappellino da baseball.

"Non posso lasciarlo! Devo tornare indietro!".

"Veniamo con te", disse E-Z. "Dammi un secondo per dirlo a mia madre".

"Glielo dirò", disse Kyle che era lì vicino.

E-Z, PJ e Arden fecero marcia indietro. Non trovando il cappello, continuarono a camminare.

"Deve essere qui da qualche parte!" Disse Arden.

"Di sicuro non pensavo che fosse così lontano", disse E-Z.

"Quegli avvoltoi mangeranno tutta la pizza prima del nostro ritorno", disse PJ.

"Non preoccuparti, la signora Dickens ci terrà da parte del cibo. Sa che non ci metteremo molto".

Il corridoio si espandeva in un altro edificio, in un altro luogo. Davanti a loro c'era una ghigliottina gigantesca. In cima, sopra la lama, c'era il cappello di Arden. Sulla lama stessa c'era una scritta. Era ancora grondante di vernice rossa, o di sangue. Diceva: "La testa va qui".

"Stiamo sognando?" Chiese Arden. "Perché il mio cappello da baseball non mi serve così tanto".

"Ascolta. Voci", disse E-Z.

Sussurri, molto silenziosi, ma mormorii. Prima era una donna sola. Poi se ne aggiunse un'altra, per un duetto. Poi se ne aggiunse un'altra per un trio. I sussurri si trasformarono in un canto.

"Non riesco a distinguere le parole", disse PJ.

"Shhh", disse E-Z, portandosi il dito alle labbra.

Mentre le voci cantavano,

"B-link e sei morto.

B-link e sei morto.

B-link e sei morto, B-link e sei morto", sulle note di Happy Birthday to you.

"È inquietante!" Disse PJ.

"Torniamo indietro", disse Arden, mentre la porta da cui erano entrati si chiudeva sbattendo e dei passi risuonavano lungo il corridoio.

I passi si fecero più forti.

CLANK. CLANK. CLANK.

Cotta di maglia. Si avvicinano. Piedi stivalati. Un soldato. Una figura molto alta, incappucciata. Portava con sé qualcosa di argentato: un affilacoltelli.

Quando arrivò ai piedi della ghigliottina, la figura incappucciata tirò fuori dalla tasca una piuma. La mise contro la lama. La tagliò come se fosse burro. Tuttavia, andò avanti e la affilò ulteriormente. Mentre affilava la lama, canticchiava sottovoce, come se si stesse godendo il suo lavoro.

"Come se la lama della ghigliottina non fosse abbastanza affilata!". PJ sussurrò. "Fatemi uscire di qui!"

Arden corse verso la porta e iniziò a martellarla. "E-Z devi farci uscire di qui! Devi aiutarci! Ti prego, aiutaci!".

MESSAGGIO DI CARICAMENTO.

I volti di PJ e Arden apparvero sullo schermo. Pronunciarono due parole:

"AVVISATELI".

E-Z si svegliò sentendo lo zio Sam sbattere i pugni sulla porta della sua camera da letto. "Alzati E-Z, non riusciamo a trovare Lia!".

Ora che era sveglio, si rese conto che lei lo stava contattando per cercare di mettersi in contatto con lui. Per aggiornarlo. Controllò il telefono. Un messaggio con un aggiornamento.

"Va tutto bene", disse E-Z, "è con PJ. Di' a Samantha che sta bene. Devo andare a trovare lui e Arden al più presto. Dov'è Alfred?"

"È in giardino", ha detto Sam. "Vuoi fare colazione prima di andare?".

"Un panino al formaggio grigliato sarebbe perfetto. Grazie".

Mentre E-Z si vestiva, pensava al suo sogno. I ragazzi gli stavano parlando, attraverso un evento comune che avevano condiviso quando avevano sette anni. Doveva capire di cosa si trattava. Metterli in guardia?

Scaldare chi esattamente? Questo era un indizio preciso, ma chi volevano che avvertisse esattamente?

Sì, era assolutamente certo che stessero cercando di dirgli qualcosa, ma cosa esattamente? Ancora una volta ebbe il vago sospetto che tutto ciò avesse a che fare con Eriel.

Per prima cosa si recò a casa di Arden e il poveretto, come prima, era come uno zombie nel suo letto. Un medico era al suo fianco quando E-Z e Alfred entrarono.

"Qual è la diagnosi?" Chiese E-Z.

"Per prima cosa, porta via quel pollo!" esclamò il dottore.

Alfred fece un "Hoo-hoo" di protesta e poi se ne andò a zonzo. Fuori sgranocchiò dell'erba e si pulì le piume.

Il dottore guardò i signori Lester: "Quanto volete che sappia questo bambino?".

"Questo è E-Z, è uno dei migliori amici di Arden".

"So chi è, l'ho visto in televisione mentre salvava le persone".

E-Z non sapeva cosa dire e non disse nulla, ma non gli piaceva l'atteggiamento del dottore.

"Arden è in coma".

"Sì, lo immaginavo. Oh, e quando ne uscirà? Il dottor Flannel alla casa di cura Handle, dove PJ è nello stesso stato, ha detto che tornerà presto alla normalità".

"Questo non lo so. Il suo corpo lo sta proteggendo da qualcosa, quindi si sveglierà quando starà abbastanza bene per farlo. Nel frattempo, suggerirei che qualcuno stia con lui 24 ore su 24". Poi si rivolge ai Lester: "Sarebbe meglio se entrambi vi impegnaste ad assumere un'infermiera. Posso raccomandare qualcuno. Se potete lavorare da casa, sarebbe meglio. Ci sentiamo tra un paio di giorni".

"Tra un paio di giorni", ripeté il signor Lester.

La signora Lester condusse il dottore fuori di casa.

E-Z lo seguì. "Se posso aiutare, fare un turno al suo fianco, non esiti a chiedere. Ora vado da PJ. Lia è già lì e mi ha scritto che è lo stesso".

"Tienici aggiornati e saluta la famiglia di PJ".

"Lo farò", disse E-Z, mentre lui e Alfred si riunivano. Entrambi si sollevarono da terra e volarono verso la casa di PJ.

Mentre volavano fianco a fianco, Alfred disse: "Non mi piaceva quel dottore. Quando una persona non è gentile con gli animali... non mi fido".

"Ti capisco, ma stava solo facendo il suo lavoro".

"Noi cigni non abbiamo causato nessuna piaga o... non importa. Ho dimenticato l'influenza aviaria, ma quella è avvenuta a causa degli umani".

Atterrarono a casa di PJ, dove Lia li stava aspettando con la porta aperta.

"Come vanno le cose tra voi due?", chiese.

"Bene", rispose Alfred.

"Ah, è un po' arrabbiato perché il medico di Arden lo ha cacciato dalla stanza, ma io sto bene grazie. E tu?"

"Io sto bene, ma i genitori di PJ stanno impazzendo e non c'è alcun segno di ripresa".

"Hanno richiamato il dottore?" Chiese Alfred.

"No. Ha dato loro speranza, ma nient'altro, soprattutto che si riprendesse. Ma temo che si sia sbagliato". Fece una pausa, arrossendo un po'.

"Oh, un'altra cosa, quando gli tenevo la mano". Guardò i due. "Lui... beh, non so se me lo sono immaginato o se l'ha fatto davvero, ma mi è sembrato che l'abbia stretta".

"Grazie per essere rimasti con lui. Dovremmo fare i turni con i suoi genitori, così nessuno si stanca troppo. Ora puoi andare a casa e passare un po' di tempo con tua madre. Probabilmente si starà chiedendo di te". Non aveva intenzione di menzionare la presa della mano.

"Me ne andrò quando lo farai tu", disse Lia mentre si dirigevano verso la stanza di PJs.

Alfred, Lia ed E-Z erano ora soli con PJ.

"Ho fatto uno strano sogno la scorsa notte. PJ, Arden e io eravamo al mio settimo compleanno, ma le cose non accadevano come allora. Stavano cercando di comunicare con me attraverso un evento che abbiamo condiviso, ma non sono sicuro di cosa stessero cercando di dirmi".

"Raccontaci il sogno", disse Alfred. "E non tralasciare nulla".

"Sì, raccontaci e vedremo se possiamo aiutarti a interpretarlo".

"Beh, è iniziato in modo normale. Tutto era come quel giorno, finché Arden non ha dimenticato il suo cappello da baseball e noi tre siamo tornati a prenderlo".

"Quindi non ha perso il cappello da baseball alla vera festa?".

"No, non l'ha perso. Anzi, era così ossessionato da quel cappello che spesso lo prendevamo in giro dicendo che era incollato alla sua testa. Quindi, questa era una parte importante del sogno. Stavamo tornando all'area di gioco e il corridoio sembrava molto più lungo di quando l'avevamo lasciato.

Abbiamo camminato a lungo. Chiacchierando come eravamo soliti fare. All'inizio non ce ne siamo resi conto, stavamo camminando da un bel po'. Arden pensava di lasciare il berretto dov'era perché ci stava mettendo così tanto ad arrivare, ma abbiamo deciso di prenderlo. Ha detto che il berretto aveva un valore sentimentale per lui".

"Interessante", disse Lia. "Sai perché amava così tanto il berretto?".

"Lo indossava sempre perché gli piaceva la squadra. Non ho mai saputo che ci fosse un attaccamento sentimentale nella vita reale, se non alla squadra stessa. E nel sogno, a quel punto, non lo sapevo finché non l'ha detto. Quindi, il corridoio si è allargato e ci siamo ritrovati in una grande stanza ariosa, come un auditorium. Al centro della stanza c'era una ghigliottina gigantesca".

"Cosa! Che strano!" disse Alfred.

"Fa un po' paura", disse Lia.

"C'è di più. In cima, sopra la lama, c'era il cappello di Arden e sotto di esso un cartello con scritto: La testa va qui".

Lia e Alfred sussultarono.

"Arden disse che non gli piaceva più il cappello. A quel punto si fece buio e sentimmo dei passi pesanti venire verso di noi. Stivali. Scricchiolii di catene o di armature. Poi le luci si sono riaccese e un uomo è entrato con un cappuccio in testa. Si avvicinò alla ghigliottina e affilò i coltelli, uno dopo l'altro".

"E poi?" Chiese Alfred.

"Poi è apparso lo schermo di un computer con la scritta LOADING e si è accesa una visuale di loro due. Hanno pronunciato due parole:

"AVVISATELI".

"E poi?" Alfred chiese di nuovo.

"Poi lo zio Sam mi ha svegliato e mi ha chiesto se sapevo dove fosse Lia".

"Non è molto su cui basarsi", disse Lia, "Amava quel berretto? E chi doveva essere avvertito?".

"La squadra preferita di Arden era ed è ancora la Boston Red Sox. Il cappellino era un regalo per lui - autentico - e non l'avrebbe mai lasciato, qualunque cosa fosse successa. Eppure, ha pensato di lasciarlo nel sogno almeno due volte".

"Ma non era così entusiasta da infilare la testa nella ghigliottina per averlo", disse Alfred.

"Chi lo sarebbe!" Chiese Lia.

"Vorrei che potessimo usare il computer di Arden. Scommetto che c'è un indizio lì dentro. Scommetto che ha un file, qualcosa di nascosto che potrei trovare. Forse è questo il motivo del sogno. E perché mi ha dato l'indizio".

Lia controllò online il significato di un sogno con una ghigliottina nel suo telefono. "Dice che rappresenta la paura o l'ansia. L'essere messi in disparte o in imbarazzo per qualcosa".

"Credo di avere un'idea", disse E-Z mentre scorreva l'elenco dei contatti sul suo telefono.

"Aspetta un attimo", disse Alfred, "chiama Sam".

"Hai ragione, forse dovrei parlarne prima con lui". Fece una chiamata rapida a Sam e gli spiegò la situazione. Sam disse che sarebbe venuto subito da Arden e che avrebbero dovuto incontrarlo lì.

"Tutto bene qui?" Chiese la mamma di PJ. "Vuoi qualcosa da bere o altro?".

"No, grazie, ma lo zio Sam sta andando da Arden e noi lo incontreremo lì. Daremo un'occhiata al computer di Arden per scoprire l'ultima cosa che ha fatto. Peccato che il computer di PJ sia inattivo".

"È un'idea intelligente. Abbiamo sentito che i genitori di Arden hanno chiamato anche un medico, è stato d'aiuto?".

"No, non lo è stato".

"Vi terremo informati se avremo notizie", disse Lia, mentre tastava la fronte di PJ.

"Sei una brava ragazza", disse la madre di PJ. Poi lasciò la stanza, combattendo contro le lacrime.

Quando arrivarono a casa di Arden, Sam li stava aspettando fuori. Aveva il suo portatile, una borsa piena di strumenti informatici e altri oggetti.

Insieme entrarono in casa dove Sam sistemò il suo computer vicino, un portatile, lo collegò all'altro lato della stanza e poi diede un'occhiata alla configurazione di Arden. Era collegato direttamente alla presa di corrente. Senza alcuna barra di protezione per evitare sovratensioni insospettabili. Per fortuna ne portava sempre una nella borsa.

Dopo aver fissato la barra di sicurezza, collegò il computer di Arden. Aspettarono e non successe nulla. Prendendolo come un buon segno, cliccò sull'alimentazione e il computer di Arden prese vita. Era richiesta una password. Una password che nessuno di loro conosceva.

"Qualche ipotesi?" Chiese Sam.

E-Z digitò Boston Red Sox. Provò con il secondo nome di Arden, Daniel. Niente da fare.

"Prova con la ghigliottina", suggerì Alfred.

"Bingo!" Disse E-Z, ora doveva solo cercare nella cronologia.

"Lascia fare a me", disse Sam, mentre cliccava sulle impostazioni alla ricerca di qualcosa di insolito. Non c'era nulla di strano.

"Qual è stata l'ultima cosa che ha fatto? Stava giocando?" Chiese E-Z.

Mentre Sam cliccava per scoprirlo, la barra di sovratensione senza sovratensione prese fuoco. Zio Sam corse a spegnere il fuoco e quando tornò E-Z lo aveva già soffocato con una coperta. "Bella pensata", disse.

"Spero che la mamma di Arden la pensi così!".

"Prendi l'hard disk!" Disse Sam, che lo fece prima che fosse fritto. "Ora portiamo questo con noi e vediamo cosa riusciamo a vedere".

CAPITOLO 7

DISCUSSIONE

Mentre tornavano a casa, E-Z pensava ancora al messaggio "Avvisali". Poteva essere qualcosa di più di un sogno?

"Mi chiedo", disse.

"Su cosa?" Chiese Sam.

E-Z spiegò il suo sogno e il messaggio, poi aggiunse la sua nuova idea per vedere cosa ne pensavano.

"PJ e Arden hanno impostato il sito web in modo da poter fare dei podcast in futuro. Mi sto chiedendo se sia il caso di usarlo, una volta che avremo capito chi avvisare. Potremmo sicuramente raggiungere molte persone".

"È un'idea brillante!" Sam disse: "Ma non dovremmo costruirci un seguito adesso? Così, quando saremo pronti a trasmettere l'avvertimento, avremo già degli iscritti?".

"Cosa dovrei dire?"

"Pensiamoci su", disse Lia. "E noi saremo al tuo fianco".

"Per me va bene anche parlare un po'".

Arrivati a casa, entrarono in casa.

CAPITOLO 8
BRANDY VIVE

Quando lo vide per la prima volta, era la musica che avevano in comune. Lei suonava il pianoforte, meglio della media ma non in modo eccezionale. Il suo insegnante di musica disse che aveva un'abilità naturale, qualunque cosa significasse. Ma riusciva a suonare solo le canzoni che avevano un significato per lei. Allora le ricordava e riusciva a suonarle subito. Tuttavia, costringerla a suonare qualcosa che non le piaceva le faceva odiare le lezioni.

Ma ha continuato a farlo. Si è costretta a farlo anche quando lo odiava. Sperava di essere in grado di fingere di entrare nella banda della scuola.

I suoi genitori volevano qualcosa da mostrare per tutte le lezioni che avevano pagato. Insistettero perché provasse a entrare nella banda, per essere più coinvolta nelle attività scolastiche.

"Farà bella figura nella tua domanda di ammissione al college", le disse suo padre.

"Fai del tuo meglio, è tutto ciò che ti chiediamo. Fai del tuo meglio!", ha detto la madre.

Tuttavia, le audizioni per le scuole superiori di quest'anno erano piene di ragazzi di talento. Un talentuoso batterista maschio era già sul palco quando lei entrò nell'auditorium.

Con i palmi delle mani sudati e il cuore che batteva forte, si mosse lungo la fila. Una fila di studenti e insegnanti batteva le mani e batteva i piedi. Sentiva il pavimento pulsare a ogni battito.

Come un robot, continuò a camminare lungo il bordo dell'auditorium, finché non fu il più vicino possibile al palco.

A questo punto uscì di nascosto dalla porta e andò dietro le quinte. Si mise in piedi con gli altri artisti sul ponte e applaudì come se fosse sempre stata lì.

Era un piano brillante. Erano tutti così presi dalla sua audizione che non si erano nemmeno accorti che si era intromessa nella fila.

"Chi è?", sussurrò alla ragazza in fila davanti a lei.

"Shhhh!" risposero gli altri artisti in attesa.

Lui continuava a suonare, vestito di jeans, con i capelli biondi che ondeggiavano e rimbalzavano. Poi si avvicinò al microfono e la sua voce profonda e melodica si unì al ritmo.

Lei si avvicinò un po' di più e, nel farlo, notò un prurito che prima non c'era. Sui palmi delle mani, sulle braccia e sulle gambe. Si grattò e non trovò sollievo. Anzi, il prurito peggiorò e presto fu come se la sua pelle stesse bruciando. Poi il suo respiro peggiorò e il battito cardiaco rallentò.

"Calmati", sussurrò ad alta voce e nella sua testa.

È stata l'ultima cosa che ha ricordato prima di svegliarsi in un veicolo in movimento.

CAPITOLO 9
SU BRANDY

Il veicolo stava sfrecciando sull'autostrada. Lei era sul sedile posteriore. Di chi era l'auto? Non era un veicolo che riconosceva.

Cercò di alzarsi a sedere; le faceva male la testa, come se un treno la stesse attraversando. Chiuse gli occhi per un attimo e ascoltò, cercando di capire come fosse arrivata lì. L'auto aveva un odore strano, nuovo e vecchio allo stesso tempo.

PFFT.

Il condotto di ventilazione emanava un odore che le fece venire il voltastomaco e vomitò.

"Ehi, guarda gli interni", disse una voce maschile. "È pelle, quella vera". Il suo telefono squillò e lui ci parlò attraverso un microfono nella visiera. "Sì, arriveremo presto", disse. Si scollegò e alzò il volume della radio.

Le sue mani erano legate, non dietro di lei come aveva visto nei film, ma davanti a lei, appena sopra la cintura di sicurezza allacciata. "Voglio andare a casa!"

"Presto", rispose la voce maschile sopra il ritornello di una canzone di Drake.

Dopo aver viaggiato per circa trenta minuti, lui si fermò in una stazione di servizio. La chiuse dentro, poi sbatté la porta dietro di sé e la lasciò lì senza dire una parola.

Guardò fuori dal finestrino cercando di non vomitare di nuovo. Il suo sequestratore o rapitore, che dir si voglia, era entrato. Sperava che non fosse un rapitore che avesse intenzione di chiedere un riscatto. I suoi genitori non avevano soldi per pagare il suo ritorno. Si concentrò sul momento, notando che le portiere non avevano maniglie e i pulsanti per aprire il finestrino non funzionavano.

Dall'altra parte dell'auto che faceva benzina, vide un ragazzo.

"AIUTO!" gridò, dando tutto quello che aveva. Sapeva che questa poteva essere la sua unica opportunità.

Quando l'uomo non rispose, batté le mani sui finestrini chiusi. Era difficile emettere suoni in quella specie di boccia per pesci. Si guardò indietro e il suo rapitore stava tornando all'auto portando con sé una lattina di bibite e due barrette di cioccolato. Quando si mise al volante, le lanciò una barretta di cioccolato da sopra la spalla. Lei non riuscì a prenderla, odiava quel tipo di cioccolato, senza contare che aveva da poco vomitato.

"Ho sete", disse lei.

"Cosa vuoi?" le chiese lui, poi entrò e uscì quasi subito con una bottiglia d'acqua.

Le slacciò il tappo e gliela mise tra le mani. Anche se erano legate, dopo un paio di tentativi lei riuscì a mettere in bocca un po' d'acqua. La parte anteriore della maglietta gocciolava d'acqua. Non le dispiacque, perché lavava via un po' dell'odore di barba.

"Grazie", disse.

Pochi istanti dopo erano di nuovo in autostrada. Lui accelerò, si spostò nella corsia di sorpasso e la cintura di sicurezza di lei si slacciò. Lei ruzzolò sul retro dell'auto, come un singolo dado che rotola senza direzione.

"Smettila, pazzo!", le disse l'uomo, mentre lei cercava di riallacciare la cintura di sicurezza con le mani legate.

Le gomme del guidatore cambiarono corsia in modo sconsiderato. Gli altri automobilisti hanno frenato per evitare di essere sorpassati. Poi si è diretto verso la rampa di uscita. Ha schiacciato i freni, si è fermato. Scese dal sedile anteriore e aprì la portiera posteriore.

Lei era pronta con i piedi puntati verso di lui e lo colpì con tutta la sua forza in un grande calcio a due piedi. Lui cadde a terra e lei uscì dall'auto, correndo all'impazzata quando un'auto la investì, poi un'altra, poi un'altra ancora.

Lui risalì in macchina e partì.

"Stupida ragazza!" esclamò.

CAPITOLO 10
IL BRANDY SI RAMMARI

"È successo di nuovo, vero?" chiese sua madre, mentre aiutava Brandy a scendere dal carrello della spesa. "Cosa è successo questa volta?".

"Scusa, mamma", disse l'adolescente, chinandosi per allacciarsi le scarpe. Le sue mani erano così belle, ora che non erano più legate.

Sua madre si chinò e sussurrò: "È stato come le altre volte? Sei svenuta?"

Lei si alzò in piedi e guardò verso la porta.

"Dimmi", disse sua madre, spostando la figlia di fronte a lei in modo che fossero vicine e nessun altro potesse sentire. Inoltre, non c'era nessun altro nel loro corridoio.

"Ero a scuola, alle audizioni. Un ragazzo stava suonando da solo la batteria e cantando. Era davvero eccellente".

"E anche sognatore, immagino?" chiese sua madre.

Sentiva le guance diventare bollenti. "Il mio cuore ha accelerato, ha corso, i miei palmi sono diventati sudati e mi sono sentita strana. Poi mi sono ritrovata legata sul retro di un veicolo in movimento!".

"Legata? In un'auto? Di chi è l'auto? Chi guidava? Dove stavi andando?"

"Non ho riconosciuto l'auto, né il conducente. Stava parlando con qualcuno, usando uno di quei microfoni senza fili. Era un buon guidatore finché non ha imboccato l'autostrada. Poi ha guidato come un pazzo e io ho fatto finta che la cintura di sicurezza si fosse slacciata. Quando è uscito di strada e si è fermato, gli ho dato un calcio così forte che è caduto e sono scappata".

"Grazie al cielo sei riuscito a scappare. Qualcuno si è fermato ad aiutarti? Spero che tu abbia il loro numero, così potrò chiamarli e ringraziarli".

Brandy non parlò, perché stava ricordando le auto, una, due, tre, che la investirono e lei morì. Di nuovo. E finì di nuovo al supermercato con sua madre.

"Parlami", disse la madre di Brandy.

"Sono morta - di nuovo", disse Brandy "e sono finita qui. Di nuovo".

Si sedette sul pavimento, o meglio, le sue ginocchia si indebolirono e cadde in ginocchio. Sua madre la seguì, come un domino.

Si sedettero insieme, tenendosi per mano senza parlare.

CAPITOLO 11
ALLORA BRANDY

"Sbrigati, Brandy!" è quello che le aveva detto sua madre l'ultima volta. L'ultima volta che la sua unica figlia era morta e risorta.

Quando la maggior parte dei genitori doveva andare a fare la spesa con i figli al seguito, non riusciva ad andarsene abbastanza in fretta.

Brandy non era una di quei bambini. Preferiva i negozi ai parchi, agli sport, a quasi tutte le attività. Portarla a fare la spesa era l'unico modo per farla uscire di casa.

Non era del tutto colpa di Brandy. Era nata con una rara malattia cardiaca. Una patologia che, secondo loro, sarebbe stata superata. Quindi, correre e giocare con gli altri bambini non era un'opzione per lei.

Di conseguenza, aveva imparato ad amare il centro commerciale, ma quello che amava di più era il negozio di alimentari. E nelle corsie degli alimentari la situazione era sempre piuttosto tranquilla. Tranne una volta, quando stavano distribuendo dei DVD gratuiti. Brandy era così eccitata che non riusciva a respirare e dovettero portarla d'urgenza in ospedale.

Aveva tre anni allora.

CAPITOLO 12

BRANDY ORA

Ora che sua figlia aveva quattordici anni, sembrava che succedesse sempre meno. Tuttavia, si chiedeva cosa sarebbe successo quando sarebbe stata troppo grande per entrare nel carrello della spesa.

"Perché qui, secondo te?" Chiese la madre di Brandy: "Perché sempre e solo io e te qui?".

"Non lo so mamma, ma una cosa la so. Voglio fare acquisti. Voglio comprare cibo e bevande e poi me ne vado. Tu resta qui se vuoi, io torno tra un minuto. Tieni, gioca a Solitario sul tuo telefono. Calmerà i tuoi nervi e lo shopping calmerà i miei".

La donna si sedette sul pavimento, mentre i carrelli andavano e venivano, concentrando tutta la sua attenzione sul gioco del Solitario. Sua figlia la conosceva così bene. Tuttavia, cercava di non preoccuparsi di quanto - o quanto poco - dire a suo marito. Non glielo aveva detto l'ultima volta, quando sua figlia era morta, né la volta precedente, né quella prima ancora. Gli aveva solo detto che erano andati a fare shopping e che era stato stressante.

"Sono pronta", aveva detto Brandy, quella volta che era una bambina con le braccia piene di cereali e crostatine.

Si diressero allora verso la fila della cassa self-service.

"Lasciami fare, mamma!"

Questo è ciò che Brandy diceva sempre. Adorava guardare la persona alla cassa che scansionava ogni oggetto. E che Dio li aiuti se la scansione è sbagliata.

Brandy e sua madre, dopo aver terminato la giornata, tornarono in macchina. Brandy si sedette davanti e si allacciò la cintura. Partirono, fermandosi solo brevemente al drive-through per prendere due coppe di gelato.

"Oggi abbiamo fatto degli ottimi affari", disse Brandy allora e lo ripeté anche adesso.

"So che sei innamorato, ma vorrei comunque sapere di più sul tuo... incidente di oggi. Riesci a ricordare qualcos'altro di quello che è successo? Dovevi essere terrorizzata, trovandoti da sola in un'auto con un estraneo? Quello che non capisco è come mai succedono queste cose. Questa volta è stato diverso dalle altre volte? Hai detto che un minuto prima eri all'audizione della banda scolastica e quello dopo eri in macchina?".

"Sì, stavo aspettando il mio turno per esibirmi, insieme agli altri studenti. Stavamo tutti ascoltando un ragazzo alla batteria. Era incredibile, cantava e suonava. Mi stavo avvicinando alla prima fila quando, ZAP, sono sparito".

"Oh, non mi piace il suono di quello ZAP".

"È successo così, mamma. Prima mi prudevano le mani, poi le gambe, le braccia".

"Non mi avevi detto del prurito prima?".

"Succede. Di solito mi tranquillizzo. Questa volta non ha funzionato nulla e, beh, sai, la parola Z".

"Devo chiedertelo, ma pensi che forse è successo perché volevi evitare l'audizione? Voglio dire, fare un'audizione da solo. Non è una cosa che ti piace fare".

Brandy tamburellò le dita sul braccio della porta. "Non salterei in macchina con uno sconosciuto per evitare un'audizione", disse.

"Va bene, cara", disse sua madre, piangendo. Aveva detto la cosa sbagliata, di nuovo. Diceva sempre cose sbagliate quando si trattava delle... come chiamarle? Le avventure di viaggio di sua figlia.

"Va tutto bene, mamma".

Guidarono in silenzio per un po'. Era un silenzio confortevole.

"Voglio sapere come aiutarti", disse la madre di Brandy. "Per la prossima volta...".

"So che lo vuoi mamma, ma non sei lì quando succede. Devo essere in grado di gestirlo da sola".

"C'è una cosa che succede sempre, prima che tu scompaia?".

"Vorrei poterla ricordare, mamma, ma come l'ultima volta non la ricordo". Guardò fuori dalla finestra, poi incrociò le braccia.

"Beh, quando saremo a casa potrai esercitarti a fare pratica. Così sarai ancora più preparato per l'audizione di domani".

"Era un'audizione di un solo giorno. Quindi, quest'anno non ci sono possibilità per me. Inoltre, a papà non piace che io mi eserciti, soprattutto quando lavora da casa. Dice che gli fa venire il mal di testa".

"Papà non la pensa così", disse lei. "Gli parlerò. Dopotutto, tu vuoi suonare il pianoforte, come lavoro, no? Intendo dire un giorno, dopo il diploma. E chiamerò il tuo insegnante per chiedere un'eccezione alla regola".

"Mi piacerebbe sapere com'è andata la conversazione!", disse ridendo. "Salve, signor Hopper, sono la mamma di Brandy e mia figlia, beh, ha viaggiato nel tempo in un'auto in corsa con uno sconosciuto e poi è morta. Quindi, potrebbe fare un provino per lei domani?".

"È crudele", disse sua madre. "Hai cambiato idea sul fatto di voler intraprendere una carriera musicale? Sicuramente fanno sempre delle eccezioni per gli studenti".

"Forse lo fanno, ma non mi preoccupa. Mi sono persa l'occasione. C'è sempre il prossimo orecchio. Inoltre, mi piacerebbe fare shopping, credo sia per questo che torno sempre al supermercato o al negozio di vestiti. Ricordi quella volta?".

Sua madre annuì.

"Dopo la commessa, un pianista e poi un insegnante", disse l'adolescente incrociando le braccia e mangiandosi le unghie.

La madre le lanciò un'occhiata: "Non farlo, tesoro. Mangiarsi le unghie non è igienico". Brandy si sedette sulle mani. "In quest'ordine?", disse sua madre ridendo.

"Forse al contrario", strillò Brandy mentre entravano nel vialetto. "Papà non è ancora tornato".

Usò l'apertura automatica del garage senza rispondere alla figlia. Sì, suo marito era di nuovo in ritardo. Tornava a casa sempre più tardi ogni sera. Diceva che il lavoro lo tratteneva, facendogli fare ore extra senza pagare gli straordinari. Lei odiava il fatto che non tornasse mai a casa per vedere Brandy prima che lei andasse a letto. Almeno avevano uno spuntino pronto da mangiare. Avrebbe preparato la cena e l'avrebbe sistemata nella sua stanza. In questo modo lei e suo marito avrebbero potuto cenare insieme. Sarebbe stata una bella serata, solo per loro due.

"Prendi le borse", disse.

"Ok, mamma", rispose Brandy mentre entravano in casa.

CAPITOLO 13
OUTBACK AUSTRALIANO

Il ragazzo nell'Outback, nella parte settentrionale dell'Australia, viveva in una scatola. Aveva dodici anni quando lo hanno trovato. Il suo corpo era malformato perché stava seduto con la schiena arcuata e le ginocchia alzate, come una scatola. Anche quando lo aprirono e lo fecero uscire.

Non riusciva a parlare, o non voleva parlare. Finché non iniziò a fidarsi di nuovo. Poi si distese e il suo corpo si rilassò.

Preferiva le voci tranquille, i sussurri. Le cose forti, i suoni forti di qualsiasi tipo lo spaventavano. Si agitava e si chiudeva in se stesso. Cercava e gridava: "Scatola!".

L'avevano tenuta lì, in un angolo. Finché le persone a Sydney dissero che non sarebbe mai guarito se non fosse stata distrutta.

Li aiutò a farlo, con una mazza grande quasi quanto lui. Quando si frantumò in piccoli pezzi, i suoi occhi si rovesciarono nella testa e lui se ne andò. Via. Da qualche parte nella sua mente. Irraggiungibile.

Nessuno sapeva chi fosse. O a chi appartenesse. Che razza di genitori rinchiuderebbero il proprio figlio in una scatola, come un animale?

Eppure, non era stato affamato. Non per il cibo, comunque. E non era disidratato.

Il che significava che qualcuno era nelle vicinanze. I ranger e gli ufficiali hanno aspettato che tornassero, ma non è successo. Quindi, dovevano sapere che la scatola nella scatola era fuori.

Un team di psicologi ha installato delle telecamere nella casa, in modo da poter osservare il ragazzo a distanza da Sydney.

Altre persone, provenienti da tutto il mondo, volevano "partecipare" all'osservazione del bambino. Alcuni stavano scrivendo tesi di laurea sull'abuso dei bambini, sull'abbandono. Hanno lottato per arrivare in cima alla lista.

Il bambino si dondolava avanti e indietro senza dire una parola. "Box!" era stato il suo unico sforzo. Ma sapeva cosa stava succedendo. Li sentiva bisbigliare. Milionari che volevano adottarlo. Non sarebbe andato da nessuna parte. Sarebbe rimasto qui. Questa era la sua casa.

Il bambino, che non aveva mai dormito in un letto prima d'ora - o se l'aveva fatto, non se lo ricordava - non voleva dormirci adesso. Invece, si arrotolò in una palla e dormì nell'angolo sul pavimento. Il cuscino e la coperta che gli avevano lasciato non gli servivano. Quei lussi non furono toccati.

Mentre decidevano cosa fare di lui, fu nominata una suora. In Australia, le suore sono chiamate anche infermiere. In alcuni casi, una suora è anche una sorella (una suora). Inoltre, una suora che è un'infermiera può essere un fratello. Se la suddetta Sorella/Infermiera era di sesso maschile.

La sorella/infermiera del ragazzo era una signora gentile che portava sempre i capelli raccolti in uno chignon. Indossava un'uniforme bianca con scarpe abbinate che scricchiolavano a ogni passo che faceva.

La prima volta che cercò di mettergli una coperta addosso, lui urlò come se fosse stato attaccato da una nuvola inferocita.

"Ecco, ecco", disse la Sorella. Rabbrividì, poi sollevò la coperta. Se la gettò intorno alle spalle e il ragazzo sussultò.

"È morbida", disse.

Ci si accoccolò dentro. La annusò.

"È molto morbida e calda", esclamò.

Il bambino allungò la mano e toccò il bordo della coperta. La accarezzò, come se fosse ancora sulla pecora da cui era nata.

"Ti piacerebbe?" Chiese la sorella.

Lui disse di no per due giorni, poi le permise di mettergliela intorno alle spalle. Dopodiché dormì con essa, come se fosse un essere vivente. Lo cullava come un bambino e gli sussurrava. Alla fine si consolò con esso e non permise alla sorella di prenderlo o di lavarlo.

La quarta mattina di libertà del ragazzo, gli animali iniziarono a radunarsi fuori dal prato della proprietà. Per prima cosa arrivò una femmina di canguro. Saltellò fino ai gradini del portico, poi si sedette sulle zampe e osservò la porta. Poi è arrivato un emù che ha fatto lo stesso. Poi arrivarono una gazza, un cacatua e un galah. Gli uccelli cantavano a turno e le loro voci sembravano richiamare il ragazzo fuori dalla porta. Prima non era propenso ad aprire la porta o a uscire. Tuttavia, quando vide gli animali e gli uccelli, uscì senza esitare per andare loro incontro.

La sorella lo osservava da dietro la zanzariera della porta d'ingresso. Non amava i cani, i gatti o gli uccelli - anzi, le facevano paura - ma questi animali selvatici la terrorizzavano. Si sarebbe avventurata se fosse stato necessario. Sperava che mandassero presto qualcuno ad aiutarla.

Il ragazzo si fermò sul portico e respirò l'aria. Spalancò le braccia e si riempì i polmoni con l'aria esterna. La inspirò con avidità.

La Sorella, che avrebbe voluto che fosse suo figlio, osservò il suo petto che si espandeva all'interno della sua piccola struttura.

Poi accadde.

Il ragazzo iniziò a sollevarsi, come se fosse un palloncino che prendeva il volo, solo che non era un palloncino e non era legato a un filo: era un ragazzino.

La sorella corse fuori. Lo amava e lui stava scappando. Dietro di lei la porta della zanzariera si schiantò.

"ASPETTA!", gridò lei, tendendo le dita verso di lui.

Mentre il ragazzo scivolava via. I suoi piedini si alzavano. Portandolo fuori, più lontano. Mentre i tre uccelli lo trasportavano, sempre più in là.

Lei lo afferrò, ma lui era troppo lontano. Così, guardò la madre canguro che alzava gli occhi.

E il bambino cadde sulle spalle della madre. Lei si sedette in alto, con le braccia intorno al collo del canguro, e si allontanò saltellando. Accanto a loro un emù teneva il passo.

La sorella, non sapendo cos'altro fare, corse in casa a prendere le chiavi dell'auto. Accese il motore e seguì il ragazzo, finché non riuscì più a vederlo.

Il ragazzo che un tempo viveva in una scatola, era stato portato via dal mondo umano. Era andato nel mondo in cui gli animali si prendevano cura di loro stessi. E questo bambino era uno di loro. Era una famiglia.

Il bambino cantava canzoni, con le voci che conosceva nel profondo di sé stesso. Rideva ad alta voce ed era felice, mentre veniva trasportato nel luogo del suo cuore. Il luogo in cui era, quello che era sempre stato destinato a essere.

CAPITOLO 14

RAGAZZO SOLITARIO

Nella foresta proibita del Giappone risuonò il grido di un bambino. Gli uccelli si riunirono e si unirono al canto, amplificando la richiesta di aiuto del ragazzo solitario. Arrivò una civetta, che spaventò il resto degli uccelli. Si sedette nelle vicinanze, sorvegliando e aspettando.

L'allarme di un'auto suonò. Il suo lamento soffocò le grida del bambino. Era in un seggiolino per neonati. Un seggiolino che di solito si trovava sul sedile posteriore di un'auto.

"Click, click" e l'allarme dell'auto si fermò, abbastanza a lungo da permettere all'autista di sentire le flebili grida del bambino. Lei e suo marito si precipitano nella foresta, dove trovano il bambino spaventato e tutto solo. Insieme lo confortarono.

Diverse cernie sono rimaste a guardare. Valutando la situazione. Facevano frusciare le loro piume e cinguettavano. Come se stessero segnalando in diretta il salvataggio del bambino.

La donna ha tolto le cinghie al bambino. Lo strinse a sé e gli fece delle domande a cui era troppo piccolo per rispondere. Domande come: "Dov'è il tuo Haha, Ko? Dov'è il tuo Otosan?" (Tradotto: Dov'è tua madre, bambino? Dov'è tuo padre?").

Suo marito cercò nell'area. Chiamò a gran voce. Quando nessuno rispose, cercò dei segni. Impronte di adulti. Non ne trovò nessuna.

"Nessuna orma", disse scuotendo la testa incredulo. Per lui la foresta non era il suo posto preferito. Preferiva le città e il rumore. Era stato lui a far scattare per sbaglio l'allarme dell'auto. Sperava che sua moglie volesse andarsene. Le aveva promesso un pranzo nel suo ristorante preferito. In quel momento lei aveva sentito il bambino ed era corsa nella foresta.

Lui aveva seguito sua moglie, per la sua sicurezza. In città, evitavano le zone in cui potevano annidarsi i predatori. Attirando persone ignare e fiduciose, come sua moglie, nel pericolo.

La foresta, questa particolare foresta, era viva di suoni. Viva, con la luce. E il bambino, non potevano lasciarlo.

"Andiamo", disse. "Lo porteremo all'ospedale, per assicurarci che stia bene e che possano verificare con la polizia a chi appartiene".

Strinse il bambino al petto, facendo scorrere la mano sulla schiena, come una madre farebbe con il proprio figlio. Nella sua mente, era proprio quello, suo figlio. Il bambino che non aveva mai potuto avere, che l'aveva chiamata, che era venuta nella foresta proibita e che l'aveva reclamato.

"È mio", disse, prima con aria di sfida, poi più dolcemente, "Voglio dire, nostro. Il nostro bambino. Il figlio che hai sempre voluto".

Suo marito guardò il bambino. Aveva bisogno di loro. Ed era troppo piccolo, troppo giovane per ricordare qualcosa di precedente. Si fidava già di loro. Nessuno lo saprà, pensò. Eppure, era giusto prendere questo bambino come proprio?

"Nessuno lo saprà", disse sua moglie, come se avesse letto i suoi pensieri.

Succedeva spesso, dopo dodici anni insieme. Pensavano cose simili. Parlavano allo stesso tempo. Completavano le frasi dell'altro.

Erano una coppia amorevole e stabile. Insieme avevano tanto da dare a un bambino. Eppure, il destino non gliene aveva dato uno tutto loro.

Lei consegnò il bambino al marito e aspettò.

Gli uccelli sopra di lei potevano vedere come le sue braccia tremavano. Cantarono, incoraggiandola a prendere il bambino. Lo aiutavano a decidere che il bambino era ormai suo.

Lo aveva già reclamato nel suo cuore e nella sua anima. Anche suo marito l'aveva fatto, ma era combattuto dall'egoismo. Voleva fare la cosa giusta, non quella egoistica.

"Ti piacerebbe venire a vivere con noi?" chiese al bambino.

Anche se non rispose, i tre tornarono al parcheggio. Sistemarono il bambino al centro del sedile posteriore, lontano dagli airbag.

Gli uccelli e il gufo annuirono, poi volarono via nella foresta.

CAPITOLO 15
UNA DONNA

Un'anziana donna si dondola sulla sua sedia, avanti e indietro, avanti e indietro. I suoi ricordi sono fugaci, come le nuvole. Spesso non sono raggiungibili.

La confusione si fa strada. Presto sostituirà ogni cosa nella sua mente con il nulla.

La demenza non sceglie le sue vittime in base ai desideri o alle esigenze della persona malata. Il suo scopo è confondere. Alienare. Cancellare.

Aveva affrontato la cosa, fino a quando un giorno tutto è andato a rotoli.

È così che lo chiamava adesso, "topsy-turvy". O, in breve, T/T. L'altra cosa era stata brutta e stava peggiorando. Ma il "topsy-turvy" significava che non era pazza e, soprattutto, che non era più sola, non più.

Nella sua mente, vedeva tutto. A volte accadeva al rallentatore, come se avesse cliccato un pulsante sul telecomando. A volte le scene si ripetevano, all'indietro, in avanti, in loop. Altre volte si trovava nel bel mezzo di un evento, osservando in prima persona come una reporter.

La prima volta che è successo, aveva paura di essere ferita o uccisa. Aveva assistito a cose da far arricciare i capelli. Ma quando si è resa conto che coloro che la circondavano non potevano vederla o sentirla, è riuscita a rilassarsi. A parte gli arcangeli, loro sapevano che lei era lì, ma non facevano sapere della sua presenza agli altri.

Come quella volta che la sua mente volò in Olanda. Si era sistemata, osservando la bambina. Aveva pianto quando la bambina aveva perso la vista. Si era sentita impotente, non potendo fare altro che guardare. Col tempo anche questo è cambiato.

Poi Lia ed E-Z diventarono amiche e Alfred, il cigno, si aggiunse al gruppo. Lei li osservava, li ascoltava. Si sentiva un membro invisibile e inascoltato della loro squadra. Li ha visti lavorare insieme e crescere fino a diventare amici.

Poi, all'improvviso, parlò a Lia nella sua mente e la bambina rispose. Per Rosalie si aprì un mondo completamente nuovo.

All'inizio la loro conversazione era piuttosto limitata. Anche se c'era una grande differenza di età, le due avevano alcune cose in comune. Come l'amore per la danza classica.

Da quando gli arcangeli hanno cambiato le regole, Rosalie ha tenuto d'occhio i Tre ancora di più. Tuttavia, questi scambi non erano sufficienti a sfidare la sua mente, a tenerla occupata.

Fu allora che Rosalie scoprì gli Altri. Bambini con abilità uniche in altre parti del mondo, con i quali poteva parlare.

Prima c'era Brandy, un'adolescente che viveva negli Stati Uniti. Poi c'è stata la comunicazione di Lachie, conosciuto anche come il ragazzo nella scatola. Il terzo, ma non ultimo, era Haruto, che viveva in Giappone. Haruto era il più giovane di tutti. Tutti e tre i bambini avevano delle abilità. E lei era l'unica a essere collegata.

Per il momento, Lia l'ha tenuta in contatto con Alfred ed E-Z, ma presto avrebbe dovuto dir loro tutto sugli altri.

Rosalie tremava quando gli assistenti arrivarono con il suo cibo. Gelatina rossa. La sua preferita. Mangiò la prima dopo averci versato sopra un po' di crema. Crema che avrebbe dovuto finire nel suo caffè.

Nella sua testa ringraziò la ragazza che le aveva portato il cibo, perché Rosalie non riusciva a parlare. Non era in grado di parlare. Il suo unico modo di comunicare era la mente...

Convocare i Tre per farle visita alla Residenza per Anziani non sembrava la cosa giusta da fare. Per il momento, avrebbe lasciato che Lia la tenesse segreta e avrebbe preso appunti su Brandy, Lachie e Haruto e li avrebbe messi in un libro.

Avrebbe dovuto nasconderlo agli arcangeli. Avrebbe tenuto un archivio segreto. Non avrebbe perso le tracce di questi ragazzi, in nessun caso.

"Oh!" esclamò, allungando la mano nel cassetto superiore del comodino accanto al suo letto. Si ricordò di un regalo. Un quaderno, sul quale c'era scritto "Buon compleanno!".

Scarabocchiò le prime pagine. Non riuscì a scrivere nulla di concreto, poi, quando arrivò alla tredicesima pagina, si mise a scarabocchiare. Il tredici per lei era sempre stato un numero fortunato, iniziò a scrivere di Brandy, Haruto e Lachie. C'erano così tante cose da scrivere. Quando le fece male la mano, si fermò, la fletté per un po' e poi riprese a scrivere.

Rosalie si chiese se ci fossero altri bambini oltre a questi tre nuovi. Se avesse aspettato un po', anche loro avrebbero potuto parlarle. Sarebbe stato meglio svelare il suo segreto quando tutti i bambini si fossero rivelati.

Rosalie fece attenzione a non scrivere "Segreto" o "Privato" sull'esterno del libro. Ed era contenta che non avesse una chiave. Queste tre cose avrebbero spinto chiunque avesse visto il quaderno a leggerlo. Si sarebbero incuriositi, come un gatto. C'erano molte persone della sua età che erano curiose. Ma non avrebbero voluto leggere dopo aver visto le prime tredici pagine disordinate.

Sfogliò il libro fino alla fine. Rosalie riempì le ultime tredici pagine con una scrittura ancora più disordinata. Poi rimise il libro e le penne nel cassetto e lo chiuse.

Sorrise, si appoggiò al cuscino e riposò il braccio pensando alla cena. Soprattutto al dessert.

CAPITOLO 16

SBAGLIATO VS GIUSTO

C'è un mondo in cui viviamo, un mondo pieno di persone buone e cattive. Un mondo controllato da esseri umani che hanno difetti e sono imperfetti. Persone che non sono robot... Non sono programmate per essere buone o cattive.

Impariamo la nostra vita da ciò che vediamo, da ciò che notiamo, da ciò che ci viene insegnato e da ciò che diventiamo.

Impariamo dalle fondamenta che sono state gettate per noi. Man mano che cresciamo e ampliamo i nostri orizzonti, dobbiamo fare delle scelte.

Sta a noi applicare le conoscenze apprese. Scegliere tra il male e il bene.

Nel corso dei secoli, grandi persone sono state ingannate. Persone grandi e potenti. Anche gli adulti.

A volte la decisione è facile. Senza zone d'ombra. A volte ci sono forze fuori dal nostro controllo che ci guidano. Altri ci spingono a seguire il loro codice etico. A volte ci sono elementi inaspettati.

Diciamo che stiamo percorrendo un sentiero e qualcuno ci pone un ostacolo. Possiamo toglierlo o fermarci e aspettare che la persona lo rimuova. Possiamo scegliere.

La vita è fatta di scelte. Le scelte che facciamo possono metterci in riga per tutta la vita. Seguiamo quella strada, con i mattoni posati dalle nostre buone decisioni.

Oppure possiamo lasciarci fuorviare. Ingannati. Ingannati e portati ad andare contro ciò che sappiamo essere vero.

Quando ciò accade, tutto può crollare come un domino.

E ci saranno conseguenze per le nostre azioni o inazioni. Non solo per noi stessi. Ciò che facciamo si ripercuote sugli altri.

E alla fine, dopo la morte, veniamo tutti catturati e tenuti tra le braccia delle nostre Anime Cacciatrici.

Le Furie, tre dee malvagie, stanno prendendo il controllo degli acchiappa-anime.

Gli Acchiappa-anime sono stati derubati.

Le anime volano in giro senza una casa.

Anime senza casa.

Il caos è all'orizzonte.

Tu da che parte starai?

CAPITOLO 17
ROSALIE NELLA STANZA BIANCA

Rosalie aprì gli occhi. Era l'ora del pasto e aveva richiesto un vassoio per la colazione. La sua stanza era sulla strada per la sala da pranzo. Quando portavano il cibo lì, sentiva il profumo del bacon. Le sarebbe venuta l'acquolina in bocca. E il caffè. Aspettò il suo turno. Non aveva altra scelta che aspettare il suo turno.

Sapeva che preferivano dare da mangiare ai residenti nella sala da pranzo. Capiva la necessità di rispettare gli orari. Tuttavia, sapeva che prima o poi l'avrebbero raggiunta. Lo facevano sempre nella casa di riposo in cui viveva.

Osservò un cardinale su un albero fuori dalla finestra e pensò di alzarsi dal letto per vederlo da vicino. Ma quando gettò indietro le coperte e scese sul tappeto, si sentì strana. Sfumata.

E atterrò nella Stanza Bianca.

Non era cambiato nulla da quando E-Z era stato lì. Non ci volle molto perché Rosalie trovasse i suoi piedi e iniziasse a esplorare.

Mentre faceva scorrere le dita sugli scaffali, ebbe una sensazione di déjà vu. Era già stata in questa stanza?

Si spostò al centro della stanza e si girò. Gli scaffali si susseguivano a perdita d'occhio. A perdita d'occhio. La loro altezza le dava le vertigini e desiderava sedersi per riprendere fiato.

BINGO

Apparve una sedia comoda e lei vi si sedette. Si appoggiò allo schienale e poi, rendendosi conto che aveva delle ruote e poteva girare, la girò. E la girò. Poi chiuse gli occhi e si riposò. Era contenta di non aver ancora fatto colazione, perché il suo stomaco aveva un po' di nausea quando, sopra di lei, qualcosa si mosse.

O forse lo aveva immaginato.

"Tu sei lì!" gridò, indicando niente e nessuno. "Ti ho visto muoverti, tu, piccolo... qualunque cosa tu sia, vieni fuori, vieni fuori", disse.

Decidendo di esserselo immaginato, tornò a indagare sull'ambiente circostante. E si chiese come avesse fatto a trovarsi in questo posto.

"Sono tornata nella mia stanza, immaginando di essere in questo posto?". Usò le unghie per scavare nei braccioli della sedia. Osservò i segni che lasciavano sulla superficie in pelle. Erano graffi leggeri, abbastanza leggeri da poter essere rimossi con un piccolo sfregamento. Dopotutto era un'ospite e gli ospiti dovrebbero sempre prendersi cura del luogo che visitano. Altrimenti non saranno più invitati a tornare.

Sopra di lei, qualcosa si mosse di nuovo. Questa volta era accompagnato da un rumore di ali che sbattevano. Un uccello era forse intrappolato lassù, incapace di uscire?

"Sto arrivando, piccolino", disse, alzandosi e dirigendosi verso la scala.

La struttura di legno, come se potesse leggerle nel pensiero, rotolò sul pavimento e si fermò ai suoi piedi.

"Salta su!", disse.

Rosalie lo fece e solo quando si spostò si rese conto che la cosa le aveva parlato.

"Grazie", disse lei, mentre si fermava.

"Non c'è di che", disse la scala. "Cerchi qualche libro in particolare?".

Rosalie rise. "Mi sembrava di aver sentito un uccello. Shhhh."

La scala rise. "Non ci sono uccelli qui dentro, signora. Il suono che sente proviene dai libri".

"Libri con le ali?" "Sì", rispose la scala. Poi: "Tu lì! Vieni qui!"

Rosalie osservò un libro nero e spesso che si spingeva fino al bordo dello scaffale. Poi spuntarono delle ali dalla parte anteriore e posteriore. Volò giù e atterrò nelle mani di Rosalie.

"Oh, mio Dio!" disse, guardando il dorso. "Credo di averlo già letto".

DORMIRE.

Il libro si strappò dalle sue mani e tornò nella sua posizione originale sullo scaffale.

"Mi dispiace", disse Rosalie. Poi, rivolgendosi alla scala, disse: "Spero di non aver offeso il signor Dickens".

"Se hai finito con me", disse la scala, "posso suggerirti di scendere?".

"Mi dispiace di averle fatto perdere tempo", disse lei.

"Non è così. Sono lieta di essere stata utile".

Rosalie scese e la scala si diresse velocemente verso l'altro lato della stanza.

Rosalie si tastò la fronte: non era febbricitante. Il suo livello di zucchero nel sangue doveva essere sceso troppo. E ora non avrebbe potuto mangiare, non per ore. E quella ladra di Agnes Lindsay le avrebbe rubato la colazione. Si sarebbe intrufolata nella sua stanza e ne avrebbe mangiato ogni pezzo. Quando gli inservienti sarebbero tornati a prendere il vassoio, avrebbero pensato che fosse stata Rosalie a mangiarlo. Rosalie e Agnes erano nemiche giurate.

Per distrarsi dallo stomaco brontolante, Rosalie si concentrò sui libri. Un libro in particolare. Un libro che aveva amato leggere più e più volte quando era bambina. Si intitolava Anne of Green Gables di... Non riusciva a ricordare il nome dell'autrice.

"Lucy Maud Montgomery", disse la scala, mentre sfrecciava al suo fianco. "Salta uno", disse.

"Ah, grazie per l'offerta ma ho troppa fame e forse troppe vertigini per salire su di te".

"Siediti", disse la scala, "laggiù". Poi la scala fischiò e in alto sugli scaffali un libro avanzò. Gli spuntarono delle ali sul fronte e sul retro e volò tra le mani di Rosalie. Lo abbracciò al petto.

"Grazie", disse.

"È tutto?" chiese la scala.

"Sì, a meno che tu non abbia un paio di occhiali da lettura in più nascosti da qualche parte in questa stanza".

BINGO.

Gli occhiali apparvero e si posarono perfettamente sul suo naso.

La scala tornò nella sua posizione precedente.

Le caviglie di Rosalie fanno male.

BINGO.

Un piede si alzò sotto i suoi piedi.

Aprì il libro. All'interno c'era uno schizzo dell'omonima Anne Shirley. Fece scorrere il dito lungo i contorni dei capelli rossi della piccola orfana.

Anne fece l'occhiolino a Rosalie. Che sbatté le palpebre e sorrise a sua volta. Aveva già sentito parlare di libri interattivi, ma questo era davvero eccezionale!

Con le mani tremanti, aprì la mappa del Canada e i suoi occhi seguirono le frecce che portavano all'Isola del Principe Edoardo. Nella sua mente percorse la distanza e arrivò a Green Gables. Fuori dalla casa c'erano i Cuthbert. In attesa di Anne.

Girò la pagina e si mise a leggere. Rideva di ogni imprevisto in cui Anne si cacciava.

Poi lo stomaco di Rosalie brontolò e desiderò qualcosa di molto diverso dalla colazione. Un'insalata di gelatina. Una cosa che sua madre le preparava sempre in occasioni speciali quando era piccola. La sua parte preferita era la panna montata in cima.

BINGO.

Davanti a lei c'era un'insalata di gelatina a strati con un cucchiaio di panna montata in cima. Pensò al cucchiaio e

BINGO.

Ne apparve uno. Ma poi si ricordò che sua madre e suo padre la rimproveravano se mangiava prima il dessert. Pensò al purè di patate. Caldo come il vapore e con il burro che si scioglieva sopra. E al polpettone con il ketchup. E ai piselli appena raccolti dall'orto.

BINGO.

Davanti a lei c'era un'enorme ciotola di purè di patate. Il burro si scioglieva ai lati. Era un'opera d'arte. Sembrava quasi troppo bello da mangiare.

Accanto c'era un quadrato di polpettone con un po' di ketchup in cima.

E in una ciotola a parte, i piselli. Con un rametto di menta in cima.

Sorrise. Da bambina non le piaceva che gli alimenti venissero toccati. In questa stanza, lo chef sapeva cosa le piaceva.

Ma lo chef aveva dimenticato di darle gli strumenti per mangiare. Immaginò un coltello e una forchetta.

BINGO.

Arrivarono anche quelli. Mangiò avidamente. Attenzione a non danneggiare Anna di Green Gables. Il libro, sentendo il bisogno di protezione, si alzò in volo e si librò nell'aria dove Rosalie poteva raggiungerlo facilmente.

Rosalie mangiò tutto, compresa l'insalata di gelatina che si muoveva sul cucchiaio.

Quando ebbe finito

BINGO

i piatti, le posate, ecc. scomparvero.

Dopo qualche momento di gratitudine per il cibo che le era stato dato, alzò lo sguardo verso il libro.

Se volò verso di lei e riprese a leggere.

Leggere e aspettare.

Cosa o chi stesse aspettando, non lo sapeva.

CAPITOLO 18
CHARLES DICKENS

Nella città di Londra, in Inghilterra, un contenitore metallico è caduto dal cielo.

Il contenitore non era lungo né simile a un silo. In effetti, l'oggetto più simile a questo era una capsula. La differenza è che questo oggetto aveva una forma quadrata e non aveva finestre. Al posto delle finestre, era specchiato su tutti i lati. Inoltre, essendo piatto, quando colpì l'acqua sbandò con una forza tremenda. Atterrò sulla riva del Tamigi.

Ad assistere a tutto questo c'erano due rilevatori che si chiamavano John e Paul. Entrambi avevano circa trent'anni. Si guadagnavano da vivere con i profitti della detezione. Per questo motivo, erano considerati rilevatori professionisti.

Gli orari dei rilevatori variavano. Erano lavoratori autonomi e responsabili della manutenzione e della gestione dei loro strumenti.

Un rilevatore aveva bisogno di molti strumenti. Non voleva trovarsi impreparato in uno scavo. La maggior parte di loro portava sempre con sé una cassetta degli attrezzi. All'interno c'erano gli oggetti essenziali. Per citarne solo alcuni: cuffie, coperture per la pioggia, imbracature, strumenti per lo scavo, cazzuole, una cintura per gli attrezzi, un grembiule (con tasche), una borsa impermeabile, uno zaino, un sacco per la spazzatura.

La maggior parte degli scavi di John e Paul si è svolta a Londra, sul Tamigi. Come richiesto dalla legge, portavano con sé i permessi Standard e Mudlark. Questi sono stati concessi dall'Autorità Portuale di Londra.

Il permesso permetteva loro di scavare fino a una profondità di 7,5 cm, se necessario (la scala era necessaria sia che si volesse scavare o meno).

Nel caso dell'oggetto quadrato, che era atterrato di fronte a loro, era necessario riflettere un po'. Prima di prenderlo e di reclamarlo.

"Ti va di dare un'occhiata da vicino?" Chiese Paul.

John, che non aveva detto molto, annuì.

Avanzarono con gli attrezzi in mano. I loro stivali wellington si muovevano e si muovevano, spostando fango e acqua a ogni passo. La riva del fiume era spesso molto fangosa, dopo diversi giorni di pioggia costante.

"Rivendica!" Disse Paul.

"Mi sembra giusto", disse John.

Anche se l'avevano visto entrambi nello stesso momento, sapeva che stava reclamando anche a nome suo. Erano partner, lo erano sempre stati e nulla avrebbe mai cambiato questo fatto.

Entrambi proseguirono fino a raggiungerlo. Era come una palla a specchio quadrata e quando cercarono di esaminarla videro solo i loro riflessi.

"Ho bisogno di un taglio di capelli", disse John.

Paul si schernì, mentre toccava il lato dello specchio con la punta dello stivale. "Ci deve essere un modo per aprirla", disse.

"È troppo grande per poterci rotolare sopra", disse John, mentre prendeva un metro dalla tasca e misurava l'altezza di un lato. Mostrò il risultato a Paul: 60 centimetri.

Camminarono intorno all'oggetto. Fermandosi a picchiettare di tanto in tanto. Facendo attenzione a non lasciare impronte sporche sull'oggetto a specchio. Ma speravano di toccare un pulsante segreto e di aprirlo.

E ascoltando. Per assicurarsi che non stesse ticchettando.

"Forse dovremmo portarlo al museo o denunciare la nostra scoperta?". suggerì Paul. "Manderebbero un camion o una gru per raccoglierlo e trasportarlo. Dopo che gli artificieri gli avranno dato un'occhiata".

John scosse la testa.

"Se mandano gli artificieri, lo faranno saltare in aria. I vetri rotti saranno ovunque e la nostra richiesta sarà inutile".

"Vero, vero", disse Paul. "Quei ragazzi amano far saltare in aria le cose. Voglio dire, è un vantaggio, no?".

"Credo di sì. Cosa dovremmo fare ora? Non ha ticchettio. Siamo a posto da questo punto di vista".

"Sì. Non c'è bisogno della squadra", disse Paul. Camminava intorno all'oggetto, con le mani dietro la schiena. Era la sua camminata pensante. John lo seguì dietro, seguendo i suoi passi, con le mani dietro la schiena.

Paul disse: "Dobbiamo capire cos'è e quanti anni ha. Dobbiamo rivendicare solo alcune cose secondo la Legge sul Tesoro del 1996. Non sembra oro o argento e sicuramente non ha più di trecento anni. Questo ritrovamento potrebbe essere nostro e solo nostro, vale a dire che potremmo non doverlo segnalare al nostro FLO (Finds Liaison Officer) locale.

"Sicuramente non è oro o argento", disse John, battendo sull'oggetto metallico e ascoltando. Sembrava vuoto. Lo picchiettò in alcuni punti e rimase in ascolto.

Sopra di loro apparvero due luci.

Una era verde e l'altra gialla.

Si posarono sulla parte superiore dell'oggetto.

"Sciò!" Disse Paul.

"Stiamo impazzendo?" Chiese John, grattandosi la testa.

"Non credo", rispose Paul.

Le luci si sollevarono e fluttuarono. Entrambe caddero ai piedi del contenitore. Una volta sistemate, le luci lo sollevarono e lo mantennero in posizione. Pochi secondi dopo iniziò a ruotare, prima lentamente, poi più rapidamente. Ben presto ruotò a una velocità elevatissima. Mentre ruotava, iniziò a cantare con una voce acuta.

I rilevatori caddero in ginocchio e si coprirono le orecchie con le mani. I loro corpi erano afflitti dalla nausea, non dissimile dal mal di mare. Ed erano molto spaventati.

"Cosa sta succedendo?!" John gridò.

"Credo che la cosa si stia schiudendo!". Rispose Paul.

Mentre il contenitore cadeva a terra, pulsava. Tremava. Rabbrividì. Quando la scatola a specchio si aprì, una parte di essa scese come un ponte levatoio sulla riva erbosa del fiume.

"Arrrgggggh!" gridarono i rilevatori.

Aspettarono, guardando attraverso lo spazio tra le loro dita. Non erano più interessati a reclamare l'oggetto. Non erano più interessati al suo valore.

Uscì un ragazzo.

"È un bambino", disse Paul, alzandosi in piedi.

Anche John si alzò e mise le mani sui fianchi.

"Aspetta", disse Paul. "È vestito come uno di quei bambini di Oliver Twist".

"Sono rinato", esclamò il ragazzo, rovesciando il cappello e poi rimettendolo in testa. Si stiracchiò, sbadigliò, poi osservò l'ambiente circostante. "Guarda, là! Gli edifici del Parlamento. Sono cambiati dall'ultima volta che li ho visti. E ascolta", disse mentre l'orologio batteva una, due e tre volte. "Perché hanno messo la Grande Campana in una gabbia?" chiese.

"Come sarebbe a dire una gabbia? E si chiama Big Ben", disse Paul. "E perché sei vestito così? Stai partecipando a una festa in maschera?".

Il ragazzo si tastò il davanti del gilet. Controllò che il gilet fosse completamente abbottonato e che i pantaloni fossero completamente abbassati. Era più abituato a indossare pantaloni corti e con quelli più lunghi voleva sempre infagottarsi. In testa aveva un cappello che si tolse prima di parlare di nuovo.

"Conosci la strada per Portsmouth?", chiese. "Mamma e papà si preoccuperanno per me".

I rilevatori si guardarono, ma nessuno dei due parlò. Per una volta nella loro vita, erano senza parole.

"Vado", disse il ragazzo, rimettendosi il cappello.

POP.

POP.

Hadz e Reiki arrivarono e si bloccarono davanti agli occhi del ragazzo.

"Charles Dickens, devi restare con questi due uomini. Ti porteranno dove devi essere. Devi stare con E-Z".

"Cosa hanno detto?" Disse John, strofinandosi le orecchie. "Credo di stare impazzendo".

"Hanno detto che è Charles Dickens. Charles Dickens! E che dobbiamo aiutarlo a raggiungere E-Z, chiunque sia, quando è a casa", rispose Paul.

Charles Dickens. IL Charles Dickens. Altrimenti conosciuto come il lontano parente di E-Z e di Sam... Si rivolse alle due creature fatate. "Una volta avevo un libro di Grimm con una fata in copertina. Lo conoscete?" chiese.

Hadz e Reiki ridacchiarono e poi scomparvero.

POP

POP.

Charles Dickens si riapplicò il cappello: "Vado a Portsmouth". Iniziò a camminare.

"No, non lo farai", dissero all'unisono i rilevatori.

"Certo che sì", disse lui.

"Portsmouth è una lunga passeggiata", disse John.

Dietro di loro, il cubo a specchio iniziò a scuotersi e ad agitarsi. Poi parlò: "Questo cybus autem speculatam si autodistruggerà in 5, 4, 3, 2, 1, 0".

I detectoristi caddero a terra, coprendosi la testa con le mani.

POOF.

Ed era sparito.

"Whew!" Disse Dickens. Poi indicò il London Eye. "Cosa diavolo è quello?" chiese.

I rilevatori corsero davanti a Charles. Gli aprirono la strada e gli spianarono il cammino. Come due difensori di calcio, lo tenevano al sicuro. Schivando biciclette, pedoni e cani randagi. Lo guidarono verso altri percorsi per evitare tram, taxi e scooter.

"Si chiama London Eye e si può vedere per chilometri e chilometri lassù".

"C'è la possibilità di mangiare qualcosa a breve?". Chiese Charles, massaggiandosi lo stomaco.

"Perché non venite da noi a prendere una tazza di tè prima?", chiese Paul. "Mia madre prepara una buona tazza di tè e potrebbe anche aggiungere uno o due biscotti".

"Mi sembra una buona idea", disse Dickens. "Poi dovrò tornare a casa. La mamma si chiederà dove sono. Non dovrei stare fuori fino a tardi e, visto dove si trova il sole, credo che tramonterà presto".

Quando si avvicinarono a Convent Gardens, Dickens notò una targa. "Guarda qui", disse. "Qui c'è scritto il mio nome".

John e Paul guardarono Charles Dickens.

"Cosa?" disse.

"Sarai l'autore britannico più famoso di tutti i tempi", disse John. "E Oliver Twist è uno dei suoi personaggi più famosi".

"È così?" Chiese Charles.

"È così", disse Paul. "E non voglio offenderti o altro, ma sai, anche William Shakespeare è piuttosto famoso", disse Paul.

"Shakespeare era un drammaturgo. Io ho scritto opere teatrali?". Chiese Charles.

"No, scrivevi romanzi. Allora forse avevi ragione".

Arrivarono a casa di Paul: "Mamma, questo è Charles Dickens", disse lui.

Lei era in cucina, indossava un grembiule e si pulì le mani prima di stringere la mano a Charles.

"Sei parente di quel Charles Dickens?". Chiese la mamma di Paul.

"È un piacere rivederti", disse John, cambiando argomento. "Potrei essere così scortese da chiedere una tazza di tè con pane e burro?".

"Voi tre andate a sedervi, ve lo porto subito", disse la signora, scacciandoli dalla cucina.

Si sistemarono nella sala d'ingresso. Paul si sedette vicino alla finestra per poter guardare fuori attraverso le tende a rete.

Nel frattempo John e Paul stavano pensando in modo simile. Come avevano scoperto Charles Dickens e come avrebbero potuto fare un po' di soldi.

Paul cercò, Quando è morto Charles Dickens? Risposta: 1870. Mostrò lo schermo a John.

"Perché volevi andare a Portsmouth?". Chiese John.

"Vivevo lì", disse Charles.

"Hai altri libri?", chiese Paul. "Intendo dire libri che non hai ancora pubblicato?".

"Non lo so", disse Charles. "Ho scritto molti libri?".

"Sì, certo che ne hai scritti, Charles", disse John.

"Sono buoni?" Charles si informò.

"Ho letto Oliver Twist quando ero ragazzo e anche Grandi speranze. Ottimi ma un po' lunghi per i miei gusti", disse Paul.

"Il Canto di Natale era bello", disse John, "Non troppo lungo e con un'ottima lezione da imparare".

La stanza rimase in silenzio per qualche minuto.

"Devo trovare questo Ezekiel Dickens, o come lo chiamano gli amici E-Z", disse Charles. "Non so come faccio a saperlo, ma credo che viva in America". Sbadigliò e fece fatica a tenere gli occhi aperti.

La mamma di Paul entrò portando un vassoio pieno di leccornie. Tutti mangiarono a sazietà e presto Charles si addormentò sulla sedia.

"Ah, il piccolino sta dormendo profondamente", disse la mamma di Paul, mentre gli metteva una coperta addosso.

"È così piccolo", disse.

"Ma è uno dei più grandi scrittori".

John interviene: "La scrittura è nel suo sangue, quindi un giorno potrebbe diventare un grande scrittore".

La mamma di Paul rise, poi salì in camera sua per guardare un po' di televisione.

Nel frattempo, Paul e John discutevano su cosa avrebbero dovuto fare con Charles Dickens.

"Peccato che non possiamo tenerlo", disse John.

"Beh, non credo che il museo lo accetterebbe", disse Paul.

Entrambi decisero di fare delle ricerche su Charles Dickens su internet.

POP

POP.

John e Paul guardarono davanti a sé come se stessero dormendo. Anche se erano molto lontani. Hadz e Reiki cantarono loro una canzone che recitava più o meno così:

"Charles Dickens è solo un ragazzo.

Non è un giocattolo da detectorist.

Aiutalo a trovare suo cugino negli Stati Uniti.

Fallo domattina o te la faremo pagare!".

Questa canzone girò e rigirò nella testa di John e Paul finché non capirono cosa dovevano fare.

"Troveremo E-Z Dickens", disse Paul.

"Sì, è la cosa giusta da fare", disse John.

POP

POP.

E se ne andarono.

CAPITOLO 19

ROSALIE BORED

Rosalie si stava stancando di leggere Anne of Green Gables. Più invecchiava, più le era difficile concentrarsi a lungo su una cosa qualsiasi. Si tolse gli occhiali e desiderò avere una maschera di lavanda per coprire gli occhi.

BINGO.

Una maschera morbida, con un profumo di lavanda, bloccava la luce e calmava i suoi occhi stanchi.

"È come se ci fosse un genio della magia qui dentro!", disse, poi chiuse gli occhi e si addormentò.

Quando si svegliò qualche tempo dopo e si tolse la maschera, era di nuovo nel suo letto nella residenza degli anziani. Era impazzita o aveva fatto un viaggio nella sua mente?

Rosalie sentiva un po' di freddo, probabilmente a causa dell'ambiente freddo e sterile in cui risiedeva. In alcuni momenti della giornata, la temperatura scendeva.

In quei momenti notava che gli specializzandi erano nelle loro stanze, mentre i partecipanti riordinavano. Poiché stavano lavorando sodo, non si accorgevano del freddo. Non come gli anziani che non facevano nulla.

BINGO.

Il cassetto inferiore del suo armadio si aprì e il suo morbido e soffice maglione rosso volò verso di lei. Si è stabilizzato da solo mentre lei vi infilava le braccia. Si accoccolò sentendo il suo calore mentre l'oggetto si abbottonava.

"È un evento piuttosto strano", si disse.

Si sedette in silenzio, sognando una tazza di tè caldo con tanto zucchero e latte.

BINGO.

Su un tavolo vicino arrivò una bella teiera con dei fiori. Quando il tè fu in infusione, si versò in una tazza da tè coordinata, aggiunse due zollette di zucchero e una spruzzata di latte.

"Tre zollette, per favore", chiese Rosalie.

Fu aggiunta una terza zolletta.

La tazza di tè su un piattino fluttuò verso di lei.

"Che ne dici di uno o due biscotti di pasta frolla?" chiese.

Si fermò a mezz'aria.

BINGO.

Sul piattino c'erano due biscotti di pasta frolla.

"Hai dimenticato un cucchiaino!".

BINGO.

"Grazie", disse lei, chiedendosi ancora se avesse le allucinazioni e/o stesse perdendo la testa.

Il tè era comunque caldo, ma non troppo. Dolce, ma non troppo. E si sposava benissimo con la pasta frolla.

Dopo aver sorseggiato fino all'ultima goccia dalla tazza....

BINGO

sparì proprio dalla sua mano.

Si chiese quanto a lungo sarebbero durati questi trucchi magici, o trucchi della sua immaginazione. Finché sarebbero durati, se li sarebbe goduti appieno.

"Aspetta un attimo!"

Si ricordò del libro. Quello che non voleva che nessuno potesse leggere.

"Puoi", chiese all'aria, "sistemarlo in modo che l'altro possa leggere il mio libro". Si avvicinò al cassetto e lo sollevò. "Quindi, gli unici che possono leggerlo, oltre a me, sono Lia, Alfred e E-Z. Nessun altro. Se qualcun altro lo trova e sfoglia le pagine, saranno tutte bianche".

Attese un segno. O un rumore, ma non ne arrivò nessuno.

Riportò il libro nel cassetto, si girò e si addormentò di nuovo.

POP

POP

"Sta già dormendo?" Chiese Hadz.

"Credo di sì. Sta russando!".

"Fai attenzione a non svegliarla. Ma dobbiamo portarla a bordo, cioè ufficialmente".

"Gli arcangeli le hanno dato i poteri per sorvegliare Lia, E-Z e Alfred. Loro sanno di lei", ricordò Reiki.

"È vero, e lei sarà fedele a quei ragazzi. E agli altri. Gli arcangeli non sanno nulla di loro e credo sia meglio così".

"Sono d'accordo. Quindi, cosa dobbiamo fare. Per fare in modo che sia così?".

"Rosalie", sussurrò Hadz direttamente al suo orecchio sinistro. "Vuoi aiutare Lia, E-Z e Alfred, non è vero?".

"Sì", disse Rosalie.

Reiki parlò. "E gli altri? Sei disposta a proteggerli? Anche dagli arcangeli?".

"Sì", rispose Rosalie.

"Molto bene", disse Reiki. "Ora, diamo una spinta alla sua memoria. Non vogliamo che dimentichi ciò che ha accettato di fare, vero?".

Hadz e Reiki cantarono una canzone,

"I ricordi sono cose bellissime.

Che fluttuano come anelli di fumo.

Avanti e indietro, avanti e indietro

Lascia che i ricordi di Rosalie la mantengano in carreggiata.

Magia, magia nell'aria e nel mare

Che vincola il nostro contratto con Rosalie".

POP

POP

Hadz e Reiki se ne andarono, mentre la cara vecchia Rosalie continuava a russare.

CAPITOLO 20

CUGINI

Al mattino, in Inghilterra, mentre il bollitore bolliva John e Paul si stavano preparando. Il computer era acceso e il motore di ricerca era aperto.

"Preparo il tè", disse John.

"Inizio a digitare", disse Paul, mentre digitava Ezekiel Dickens nella barra di ricerca. "Oh", disse. "Questo sì che è inaspettato".

John arrivò portando un vassoio di tè, zollette di zucchero in una ciotola, pane caldo imburrato e un barattolo di marmellata a parte.

"Hai trovato qualcosa?", chiese.

"Dai un'occhiata a questo", disse Paul, girando lo schermo e mescolando le zollette di zucchero nel suo tè.

Era il sito web dei Supereroi dei Tre. Guardarono E-Z che si presentava, seguito da Lia e Alfred.

"È legale?" Chiese John. "Sembrano tre personaggi di una rete di cartoni animati".

Poi iniziò la ricostruzione del salvataggio sulle montagne russe. Paul premette PAUSA. Aprì un'altra finestra. Digita "Amusement Park Rescue E-Z Dickens". Apparve un giornale con un articolo al riguardo. "È legale", disse.

"Quindi il parente di Charles è un supereroe?".

"Pensi che ci assomigliamo?". Chiese Charles. Era ancora mezzo addormentato nel pigiama oversize che gli avevano dato per dormire. Prese una fetta di pane tostato dal piatto e la addentò.

"Avete entrambi il naso di Dickens", disse John.

Charles guardò con attenzione la parte in pausa dello schermo.

In base a quando sei nato", disse Paul, cercando su Google, "dal 1812 a oggi, E-Z sarebbe il tuo settimo o ottavo cugino acquisito".

"Che cosa significa cugino remoto?".

"Significa il numero di generazioni che vi separano", disse John.

"Quindi, il mio antenato è un supereroe. Cos'è un supereroe? È come in Sir Gwain e il Cavaliere Verde?".

"Ah, ricordo di averlo letto a scuola quando ero ragazzo, sì, cavalieri e supereroi sono simili", disse Paul.

John scorse la pagina per vedere se E-Z Dickens fosse menzionato altrove. C'erano dei filmati su YouTube che lo ritraevano mentre giocava a baseball prima di finire sulla sedia a rotelle e dopo.

"È un vero atleta", disse John. "E fa sport su una sedia a rotelle".

"Il gioco sembra simile a Rounders", disse Charles.

"Oh, aspetta, c'è qualcosa sui suoi genitori", disse Paul.

Lessero i necrologi dei genitori di E-Z, riguardanti l'incidente che aveva tolto loro la vita.

"Povero ragazzo", disse Charles. "Almeno ora ha il fratello di suo padre, Sam, che si prende cura di lui".

"Perché non gli facciamo uno squillo?". Chiese Paul. Aprì il telefono e chiamò le informazioni.

Charles lo guardò da sopra la spalla, mentre Paul parlava e una voce femminile rispose. "Ho bisogno di una tazza di tè", disse.

John andò in cucina a prenderne una.

Nel frattempo, Paul chiese il numero di un certo Ezekiel Dickens in Nord America. Dopo aver composto il numero e aver fatto squillare il telefono, Paul mise il vivavoce.

"Pronto", disse Sam.

Charles per poco non fece cadere la sua tazza di tè.

"Salve, mi chiamo Paul e chiamo da Londra, Inghilterra. Vorrei parlare con Ezekiel Dickens, per favore".

"Sono suo zio, posso chiederle di cosa si tratta?". Sam si diresse verso la stanza di E-Z.

I tre stavano guardando un film sul nuovo televisore a schermo piatto. Sam prese il telecomando e premette MUTE. Poi mise il telefono in vivavoce.

"Ad essere sincero, non sono molto sicuro", disse Paul. "Non sono io che voglio parlare con lui, ma...".

"Io". Una nuova voce prese il controllo del telefono. Una voce più giovane.

"E tu chi sei?" Chiese Sam.

"Mi chiamo Charles Dickens".

Sam passò il telefono a suo nipote. "Dice di chiamarsi Charles Dickens".

"Te l'avevo detto che oggi sarebbe successo qualcosa di strano", disse Alfred.

"Anch'io", disse Lia, "ma non sapevo che avrebbe coinvolto Charles Dickens!".

E-Z esitò prima di dire: "Sono E-Z Dickens, ehm, signor ehm, Charles. Come posso essere d'aiuto?".

Charles rise. Era una risata nervosa. Non sapeva cosa dire. Non aveva mai parlato con qualcuno che si trovava dall'altra parte del mondo.

"Sono tornato", sbottò. "Per trovare te. John e Paul, i miei amici, sono (si mise la mano sul telefono) - detectoristi...".

E-Z non aveva mai sentito il termine "detectoristi".

"Usano apparecchi per trovare le cose", disse Alfred.

Paul riprese il discorso. "Una cosa è atterrata nel fiume. C'era dentro Charles Dickens. Due luci, una verde e una gialla, ci hanno detto che Charles doveva mettersi in contatto con E-Z Dickens".

"Che tipo di cosa?" Chiese E-Z. "Era una specie di silo?".

"Qui John", disse una nuova voce. "No, era un cubo. Un cubo a specchio".

E-Z si mise una mano sul telefono: "Non sembra uno di quei silo".

"Ti hanno mandato gli angeli?" Lia sbottò. "Comunque io sono Lia e l'altra voce che hai sentito era quella di Alfred. Siamo qui insieme a E-Z e Sam".

"Piacere di conoscervi", disse Charles.

"Quanti anni hai?" Chiese E-Z.

"Circa dieci, credo. È vero che siamo cugini?".

"Sì", disse E-Z, "e anche lo zio Sam è tuo cugino".

"Siamo collegati attraverso lo spazio e il tempo", disse Charles.

"Anche E-Z è uno scrittore", disse Sam.

E-Z rabbrividì e le sue guance si scaldarono.

Sam diede una gomitata al nipote per riportarlo alla realtà.

"Questo è molto da elaborare, signor Dickens, ehm, volevo dire Charles. Dovremo organizzarci per farti venire qui, oppure posso venire io da te. Puoi stare con John e Paul per un po' e ci risentiremo quando avremo deciso cosa fare?".

Paul rispose: "Sì, la mamma dice che Charles non è affatto un problema. Può stare con noi per tutto il tempo che vuole".

"Ti richiamo io", disse E-Z.

Il telefono si scollegò.

"Oh, a proposito", disse Sam, "non c'era nulla di utile sull'hard disk di Arden. A parte la conferma che erano online insieme a giocare a un gioco di tiro multiplayer".

"Buono a sapersi", disse E-Z, che aveva già capito tutto da solo.

CAPITOLO 21
IL LORO PIANO E ROSALIE

Nella sua stanza, E-Z, Lia e Alfred, insieme allo zio Sam, discutono della conversazione avuta.

"Non posso credere che il vero Charles Dickens ci abbia chiamato al telefono", disse Sam.

"Sì, ma quello che non capisco è perché sia qui. E in che modo è arrivato qui", ha detto E-Z. "Voglio dire, ha dieci anni - pensa. E il suo modo di viaggiare sembra strano, una scatola quadrata a specchio. Che diavolo significa?".

"Non sembra una navicella spaziale", disse Alfred, "Non che sappiamo che aspetto avrebbe".

"Aspetta un attimo!" Disse Lia.

E-Z la guardò. "Stai pensando quello che penso io?".

Lei annuì.

"COSA?" Chiese Alfred.

"Ricordi quando gli arcangeli ci hanno convocato per dirci che uno di noi doveva morire?". Chiese Lia.

Alfred ed E-Z annuirono.

"Pensa al contenitore. Come se ci fossi di nuovo dentro e ricordassi le cose che abbiamo trovato. I documenti che abbiamo trovato?".

"Ho capito dove vuoi arrivare. Intendi le informazioni dell'altro mondo. Sulle nostre vite in dimensioni alternative?". Chiese E-Z.

"Esattamente", disse Lia.

Alfred rimbalzò sul letto.

"Cosa?" Chiese Sam.

E-Z spiegò, come meglio poteva.

"Allora, vediamo se ho capito bene", disse Sam. "Tutti noi abbiamo delle vite in corso, da qualche altra parte oltre che qui. Intendo dire sulla Terra. Ci sono altre versioni di noi stessi, che vivono vite diverse dalla nostra. In tempi diversi, spazi diversi, dimensioni diverse".

"È vero", disse E-Z.

"Possiamo cambiare le nostre vite, allora?" Chiese Sam. "Voglio dire, cambiare il risultato? Possiamo impedire che accadano cose terribili?".

"Non credo", disse Lia. "Ma non so quanto vogliano farci sapere delle altre dimensioni. Ma da quello che ci ha detto Eriel, noi siamo il centro. Tutto ciò che accade ruota intorno a noi e alle vite che stiamo vivendo ora".

"Quindi", disse Alfred, "il fatto che Charles Dickens sia qui deve avere qualcosa a che fare con Eriel e gli altri".

"Sì, è quello che penso anch'io", disse E-Z. "Ma perché proprio ora? "Ma perché ora? Le prove sono finite. È stata una loro scelta. Eppure, sembra che non riescano a lasciarmi in pace".

"Riportare in vita Charles Dickens. E per di più con una versione di dieci anni! Per me non ha alcun senso", disse Lia.

"Forse quando lo incontreremo", disse Sam, "tutto avrà un senso".

"Non se c'è di mezzo Eriel", disse E-Z. "Con lui non c'è mai niente di chiaro".

"Sembra che un viaggio a Londra sia l'unico modo per scoprirlo", disse Sam.

"Mi sembra di non essere stato lì tanto tempo fa".

"Sì, è facile per te andarci. Basta puntare la sedia nella direzione giusta e si parte", disse Alfred. "Mentre per me c'è un sacco di energia da sbattere e il vento è un fattore importante".

"Potresti salire su un aereo se lo zio Sam venisse con te", suggerì E-Z. "Tutto ciò che devi fare è andare in giro per il mondo. "Dovresti solo sederti con gli altri passeggeri e goderti il viaggio".

Alfred abbassò la testa.

"Non lo dico per farti sentire in colpa. Ti ricordo solo che siamo tutti sulla stessa barca".

"Lo capisco. E grazie".

Ok, ora torniamo all'argomento in questione", aggiunse E-Z. Spense la televisione.

Lia fissava davanti a sé, come se fosse in trance. "Rosalie!" esclamò.

"Chi?" Chiese Alfred.

Lia continuò a fissare il vuoto.

"Lia sta bene?" Chiese Sam. "Respira a malapena".

Lia si alzò. "Devo dirti una cosa. Ho incontrato una persona, non di persona ma nella mia testa. È nella mia testa e le sto parlando da un po' di tempo. Mi ha chiesto di non dire nulla, per ora. Penso che possa essere collegata a questa storia della reincarnazione di Charles Dickens".

"Stiamo ascoltando", disse E-Z, avvicinandosi.

"Si chiama Rosalie. Vive in una casa di riposo a Boston ed è piuttosto anziana. Ha la demenza senile".

"Non è quella che causa la perdita della memoria?". Chiese Alfred.

Ma nel momento in cui Rosalie sentì Lia pronunciare il suo nome, fu trasportata nella sua mente e nel suo corpo nella stanza di E-Z. Si librò sopra di loro, ascoltando attentamente ogni parola che veniva detta. Si schiarì la gola per vedere se potevano vederla o sentirla: non potevano. Avrebbe voluto portare con sé quaderno e penna.

BINGO.

Entrambi arrivarono nelle sue mani. Sorrise e si mise a prendere appunti.

"Vuoi dire che voi due siete in contatto, attraverso l'ESP?". Chiese Alfred. "Pensavo di essere l'unico ad avere l'ESP".

"Non è esattamente ESP, non credo. Non nello stesso modo in cui ce l'hai tu".

"In che senso?" Alfred chiese.

"I ricordi di Rosalie sono spariti. La maggior parte di essi, in ogni caso. Non riconosce nemmeno la sua famiglia quando viene a trovarla. Non vengono a trovarla spesso. A lei non importa, perché non le piacciono. Ma in qualche modo siamo entrate in contatto. E sapeva tutto di noi e dei nostri poteri. In un certo senso si è presa cura di noi".

"Perché ce lo stai dicendo adesso?". Chiese E-Z.

"Perché ha detto che andava bene. E ha anche parlato della Stanza Bianca. È stata lì non una, ma due volte. La prima volta è stata riportata sana e salva nel suo letto, ma questa volta no. Dice che ora è lì e che non la lasceranno tornare a casa".

"Come entrambi sapete, sono stato in una Stanza Bianca", disse. "È il luogo in cui gli Arcangeli mi hanno fatto le prime promesse e mi hanno detto che avrei potuto stare di nuovo con i miei genitori. In pratica, dove mi hanno portato a bordo utilizzando le prove".

Sam aggiunse: "Una volta Eriel mi ha rapito nella Stanza Bianca. È stato abbastanza piacevole, almeno all'inizio, finché non mi ha lasciato andare via".

"Sì", disse E-Z, "Eriel ha poco tatto. Ed è un posto molto bello. Puoi ottenere qualsiasi cosa tu chieda pensandoci, come la magia. E ci sono libri, libri con le ali. Ma non voglio entrare troppo nei dettagli, concentriamoci su Rosalie. Cosa sta succedendo ora?".

Rosalie rise, pensando a cosa sarebbe successo se avesse detto a Lia di essere in due posti contemporaneamente? No, questo potrebbe spaventarli. Parlò con Lia nella sua testa e raccontò qualche bugia bianca.

"Dice che sta fingendo di dormire. Ricorda due punti, uno verde e uno giallo, che fluttuano davanti ai suoi occhi".

"Hadz e Reiki", disse E-Z. "Dille di non avere paura di loro. Sono i buoni".

Rosalie sospirò. Poi si rese conto che questa poteva essere l'occasione che stava aspettando. Per dire ai Tre degli altri. Rifletté attentamente, poi decise che era giunto il momento di condividere ciò che sapeva.

"Oh, aspetta, vuole che ti dica qualcosa". Lia fissò il futuro mentre la voce di Rosalie le usciva dalle labbra: "Ci sono altri come te, li ho visti. Credo sia per questo che sono qui".

"Altri come noi?" Lia, Alfred ed E-Z esclamarono.

"Non so quanto dovrei dire loro degli altri bambini presenti in questa stanza. Avete qualche consiglio da darmi? Cosa dovrei dire? Mi faranno del male? Se dico loro degli altri bambini, faranno loro del male?". Disse Rosalie, tramite Lia.

"A te la parola, E-Z", disse Lia.

"Ascolta prima quello che hanno da dire", disse E-Z. "Ti diranno quello che già sanno e poi potrai decidere quanto, se non di più, devono sapere".

"Un buon consiglio", disse Alfred. "Sii sempre un buon ascoltatore. Soprattutto quando sei trattenuto contro la tua volontà in un luogo sconosciuto".

Lia propose: "Terrò aggiornati i ragazzi qui, se vuoi che restiamo in linea, per così dire".

Rosalie parlò usando la bocca di Lia come se fosse la sua: "Ho bisogno di mantenere tutte le mie facoltà... quindi per il momento passo e chiudo. Grazie a te e al gruppo per l'aiuto. Mi farò sentire se avrò bisogno di te mentre sono qui. Altrimenti, ti aggiornerò quando sarò di nuovo a casa, il che avverrà presto visto che mi manca la cena. Stasera c'è tacchino, purè di patate e piselli". Esitò. "Oh, a proposito Lia, che bel top che indossi".

BINGO.

"Grazie", disse Lia, abbassando lo sguardo sulla maglietta e chiedendosi come facesse Rosalie a sapere cosa indossava.

"Cosa?" Chiese E-Z.

"Oh, niente", disse Lia.

Di nuovo nella Stanza Bianca. Rosalie pensò che il suo quaderno sarebbe stato più utile nel cassetto del suo comodino.

BINGO

E se ne andarono.

BINGO

Arrivò la cena. Aveva mangiato tutto ciò che era delizioso, ma ora riusciva a pensare solo a un frullato alla fragola.

BINGO.

Ne arrivò uno e, accanto ad esso, una fetta di torta al limone meringata.

Fu allora che arrivarono Eriel e Raphael.

"Oh, oh", disse la scala, mentre fluttuavano verso di lei come se fossero vestiti per Halloween.

"Sto sognando? O sono morta?" Chiese Rosalie.

"Nessuno dei due" risposero gli arcangeli.

CAPITOLO 22

INCONTRO E SALUTO

"Andate pure a finire il vostro pasto", disse Raphael.

"Sì, non abbiamo niente di meglio da fare", disse Eriel.

Mentre la guardavano mangiare, Rosalie aveva problemi a masticare. Aveva problemi ad assaggiare. E sembrava più freddo. Diede un'occhiata agli scaffali e alla scala. Aveva la sensazione che questi due estranei non stessero tramando nulla di buono e posò coltello e forchetta.

"Prima di tutto", esordì Eriel, "questa conversazione deve rimanere tra noi e solo tra noi".

Nella sua mente, parlò a Lia. "Ci sei, bambina? Stai ascoltando?"

"... Estinzione".

"Mi dispiace", disse Rosalie, "ma potresti ricominciare da capo, cioè dall'inizio? Sono vecchia e ho perso il filo di quello che mi stavi dicendo".

Eriel sbuffò. Come un bambino che è stato rimproverato, aprì le ali e volò via. Quando si avvicinò alla cima della biblioteca, incrociò le braccia e aspettò. Aspettava che Raphael facesse un tentativo.

Raphael si avvicinò a Rosalie.

"I tuoi occhiali sono davvero belli", disse Rosalie. "Ma mi fanno venire un po' di mal di mare con tutto quel sangue che pulsa e fluttua lì dentro".

Eriel rise.

Raphael si tolse gli occhiali e li mise nelle tasche della sua vestaglia nera.

"Mia cara Rosalie", disse Raphael, "ti prego di ignorare la maleducazione della mia dotta amica, ma qui ci troviamo in una situazione. Una situazione in cui abbiamo bisogno non solo del tuo aiuto, ma anche di quello di E-Z, Lia, Alfred e degli altri. Sai a chi mi riferisco quando parlo degli altri, vero?".

Rosalie annuì, senza dire nulla.

"Siamo una squadra di arcangeli e i nostri poteri sono limitati. La cosa che sta accadendo in tutto il mondo riguarda le anime".

"Vuoi dire quando le persone muoiono?" Chiese Rosalie.

"Esattamente".

"Ma non è più il tuo dominio che il nostro? Hai parlato con Dio - lui ti conosce, giusto? E se stai cercando di rimediare a una situazione difficile, perché non chiedere direttamente a lui?".

Poiché Raphael ed Eriel non parlarono, Rosalie continuò.

"Da quello che so, una volta che una persona muore, il suo corpo viene sepolto. O cremato. Le loro anime, se esistono, vivono in un altro luogo".

Eriel le si parò davanti in pochi secondi, ringhiando. "Questo non è corretto.

Raphael lo spinse da parte. "È più complicato di quanto tu sappia. Troppo complicato per essere compreso dalla maggior parte degli umani".

"Gli umani sono piuttosto intelligenti", disse Rosalie. "Siamo stati sulla luna, abbiamo inventato l'aereo, internet e il fuoco. Io non sono un genio, eppure mi hai portato qui per convincermi".

Eriel rise di nuovo.

Questa volta Raphael non riuscì a trattenersi e rise anche lei.

E rise. E rise.

Nessuno dei due riuscì a fermarsi.

Rosalie li ignorò. Ignorava ciò che stava accadendo intorno a lei. La scala che si lanciava avanti e indietro, avanti e indietro. I libri che uscivano e poi rientravano. Era un tale frastuono. Così rumoroso. Desiderava di nuovo la tranquillità della sua stanza.

Anne of Green Gables, pensò.

BINGO.

Il libro era nelle sue mani. Lo aprì, trovò un segnalibro e lesse. Se avevano bisogno del suo aiuto, avrebbero dovuto lavorare per ottenerlo. Ora che avevano insultato lei e l'intera razza umana, non gli avrebbe reso le cose facili.

"Buon per te", sussurrò Lia nella mente di Rosalie. "Sei tu al comando. Io sono qui con E-Z e Alfred e ti copriamo le spalle".

Raphael ed Eriel stavano ancora ridendo. Fuori controllo. Rimbalzavano l'uno contro l'altro a mezz'aria, come palloncini legati tra loro.

Poi si ricordò che la sua torta al limone e meringa non era ancora stata mangiata. Mise da parte il libro, infilò la forchetta e diede un morso. Era perfetta. Non era né troppo dolce né troppo aspra, proprio come la preparava sua madre. Ne prese un'altra forchettata.

Sopra di lei Eriel e Raphael erano in preda a una crisi isterica.

"Smettila!" Gridò Rosalie. "Voi due siete i più maleducati, i più odiosi che abbia mai incontrato. E ho incontrato persone piuttosto odiose nella mia vita". Mise giù la forchetta. "Non ti hanno insegnato le buone maniere? Proprio le buone maniere?". Raccolse la forchetta e la puntò nella loro direzione.

Eriel volò giù. In pochi secondi era su Rosalie, con la bocca aperta. Lei infilzò la forchetta nella cagliata di limone e poi la infilzò nella bocca dell'arcangelo.

"Che schifo!", urlò lui. Lo sputò come se gli avesse dato dell'arsenico.

"La mamma mi ha sempre insegnato a condividere", disse con un sorriso.

Il pallore di Eriel passò dal nero al verde. Dopo aver vomitato, scomparve attraverso il muro.

"Immagino che non sia un fan della torta". Disse Rosalie.

Lia rideva nella mente di Rosalie.

Raphael prese gli occhiali dalle tasche della vestaglia, li pulì e li rimise sul viso. Si sedette accanto a Rosalie. Era così vicina che stava quasi per sedersi sulle sue ginocchia.

Povera Rosalie.

"SAPPIAMO CHE CE NE SONO ALTRI E DOBBIAMO SAPERE CHI SONO E DOVE SONO... ORA!".

Mentre parlava, il volto di Raphael si contorse, diventando irriconoscibile.

A Rosalie si rizzarono i capelli in testa. Il suo corpo tremò.

"Le persone maleducate non ottengono mai ciò che chiedono e tu, mia cara, sei molto maleducata. E anche la tua amica lo è", sussurrò Rosalie.

Rosalie tornò ad essere quella di prima.

Solo che questa volta il tatto dell'arcangelo era cambiato. La sua voce era sciropposa quando disse,

"Attraverserò quel muro e raggiungerò Eriel. Tra cinque minuti torneremo e ricominceremo. Abbiamo bisogno del tuo aiuto - hai ragione - e non lo stiamo chiedendo nel modo in cui dovremmo". Poi alla donna nel muro: "Imposta il timer per cinque minuti". Poi torna da Rosalie: "Quando il timer suonerà, torneremo e ricominceremo". Come promesso, Raphael si diresse verso il muro e scomparve attraverso di esso.

L'orologio nel muro ticchettava forte. Sembrava fuori luogo. Addirittura troppo rumoroso per la biblioteca.

"È molto fastidioso!" disse la scala, avvicinandosi.

"Mi dispiace per tutto questo trambusto", disse Rosalie. "La mia presenza qui vi ha causato solo caos".

"Ci piaci", disse la scala. "Perché non ti muovi un po'? Ti farà sentire meglio".

Rosalie si alzò, aspettandosi di sentirsi stanca dopo aver mangiato un pasto così abbondante. Invece, era piena di energia. Soprattutto le sue gambe. Le sembrava di avere di nuovo dieci anni. Eseguì un salto mortale. Che divertimento!

"E ora", disse Rosalie, "il prossimo trucco. La Grande Nonna tenterà non una, né due, ma tre capriole consecutive" - e lo fece. "Grazie, grazie!" disse, inchinandosi e salutando come se avesse vinto una medaglia d'oro alle Olimpiadi.

BRRRIIIING.

Il timer si esaurì. Arrivarono Eriel e Raphael.

Gli arcangeli erano vestiti in modo diverso. Come se stessero andando a due feste diverse.

Eriel indossava un abito scuro a righe, camicia bianca e cravatta.

Raphael indossava un abito rosso simile a quello di Mumu che le copriva interamente il corpo dal collo alla punta dei piedi.

"Mi sento poco vestita", disse Rosalie.

BINGO.

Ora indossava il suo abito più elegante. Era quello che aveva detto di voler indossare dopo la sua morte.

Si accasciò sulla sedia, con gli occhi rivolti verso l'alto. E gli arcangeli fluttuarono verso di lei. Le loro ali si muovevano come quelle di una farfalla e si avvicinavano a lei con grazia e bellezza. I suoi occhi si riempirono di gioia.

"Come posso aiutarvi, cari?". Chiese Rosalie.

Era come se avessero un potere su di lei, un potere che non voleva superare. Cadde a terra, ora in ginocchio davanti ai due arcangeli. Raphael la toccò sulla spalla destra ed Eriel sulla spalla sinistra.

"Dicci quello che dobbiamo sapere", le dissero.

"Gli altri si sono dispersi", disse lei, poi si lasciò cadere a terra come una marionetta senza fili.

"È troppo vecchia per questo", disse Eriel. "Se muore, non ci sarà di alcuna utilità".

"Continua, sta funzionando".

POP.

POP.

Hadz e Reiki apparvero e sussurrarono alle orecchie di Rosalie. La aiutarono a mettersi in piedi.

"Andate via di qui, voi due intrusi!". urlò Eriel con voce esplosiva,

Rosalie uscì di scatto dalla trance in cui l'avevano messa.

"Andatevene!" Raphael esclamò e non ci fu alcun POP, ma si udì invece un singolo

SPLAT.

Rosalie mise le mani sui fianchi: "Spero che non abbiate fatto del male a quei due tesori. Infatti, se vuoi che prenda in considerazione l'idea di aiutarti, allora dovresti riportarli qui ORA in modo che io possa vedere che stanno bene. Mi rifiuto di dirti altro finché non me li riporti". Attraversò la stanza, si sedette con la schiena contro la parete bianca, chiuse gli occhi e aspettò. Aveva tutto il giorno, tutta la settimana, tutto l'anno. Non aveva fretta di andare da nessuna parte o di fare qualcosa.

POP.

POP.

"Grazie", dissero Hadz e Reiki sedendosi sulle spalle di Rosalie.

"Stiamo rovinando tutto", disse Raphael. Poi si rivolse a Hadz e Reiki: "Sapete in che situazione si trova la Terra, potete aiutarci a ottenere l'aiuto di questo umano?".

Reiki disse: "Sappiamo che c'è una situazione! Se non avessi rinnegato l'accordo con E-Z, Lia e Alfred sarebbero già stati a bordo. Rosalie non si fida di nessuno di voi due".

Hadz ha detto: "E tu non sei stato onesto con lei".

Hadz disse: "Con gli umani la fiducia e l'onestà sono tutto".

Eriel si diresse verso di loro.

Raphael lo trattenne prima di dire: "È stato commesso un errore da parte nostra e questo errore ha una causa e un effetto. Stiamo cercando di salvare la Terra dai danni collaterali. L'unico modo per farlo è fare appello a coloro che hanno ricevuto poteri, poteri soprannaturali, poteri da supereroi. Senza di loro, l'umanità fallirà e sarà colpa nostra".

Rosalie si alzò in piedi. Guardò le due piccole creature che erano sedute sulle sue spalle. "Posso fidarmi di questi due?".

"Raphael è affidabile", disse Hadz.

"Ma non siamo sicuri di lui", disse Reiki.

POP.

POP.

Entrambi scomparvero, nel timore di essere rispediti nelle miniere da Eriel.

Eriel si alzò, sempre più in alto, poi scomparve attraverso il soffitto.

Rosalie cambiò argomento. "Mentre ci penso, puoi spiegarmi cos'è questo posto? Io la chiamo la Stanza Bianca, ma è il nome corretto e perché ogni volta che desidero qualcosa, questa appare? Forse si chiama Stanza Magica?". In quel momento, Rosalie pensò a E-Z, l'angelo/ragazzo sulla sedia a rotelle.

ACK.

E-Z arrivò.

"Wow!" disse, rendendosi conto di aver raggiunto Rosalie nella Stanza Bianca. Pensò ai suoi occhiali da sole e

PRESTO

Erano sul suo viso. Camminò per la stanza, riprendendo confidenza con le gambe e con il pavimento. Poi allungò la mano e disse: "Tu devi essere Rosalie".

E tu devi essere E-Z", disse, "Senza la tua sedia a rotelle. Questo posto è davvero magico!".

"E, ciao, Raphael".

"Benvenuto, E-Z", disse Raffaello. Poi, rivolgendosi a Rosalie: "Alla faccia della discrezione, questa doveva essere una cosa riservata".

"Qualsiasi promessa ti stia facendo, la infrangerà. Non è capace di mantenere la parola data - ed Eriel è ancora peggio, così come Ophaniel - e non l'hai ancora conosciuta. Comunque, ti faccio sapere che sono tutti dei bugiardi".

"L'avevo capito", ammise Rosalie. "E se ne è andato, Eriel si comporta come una bambina viziata".

"Mi sarebbe piaciuto vederlo", disse E-Z. "Sembra molto poco da Eriel, ma sarebbe stata una cosa fantastica da vedere".

"Basta con queste cordialità", disse Raphael. "Credo di non avere altra scelta se non quella di spiegare la situazione anche a voi". Batté i piedi e le sue ali si abbassarono sui fianchi in segno di stizza. Si voltò verso E-Z e Rosalie. "Il mondo ha bisogno di essere salvato, a causa di un nostro errore. Tu e gli altri volete aiutarci a correggere la situazione, cioè a salvare la Terra, oppure no?".

Rosalie ed E-Z si scambiarono uno sguardo.

"Fai pure", disse lei. "Sono d'accordo con qualsiasi cosa tu decida".

E-Z non rispose immediatamente.

"Se mi dici tutto, lo comunicherò agli altri e voteremo. Siamo un gruppo democratico".

"Quanto tempo ci vorrà?" Raphael si schernì. "E come mi farai sapere? Dovrei forse tenere Rosalie qui come prigioniera fino a quando non lo scoprirai? Ventiquattro ore saranno sufficienti?".

Rosalie disse: "Non mi dispiace rimanere in questa stanza. Ci sono molti libri da leggere e posso ordinare tutto quello che voglio. È molto più interessante ed emozionante che stare in casa".

E-Z annuì. A Rosalie disse: "Grazie e hai ragione, questa stanza è davvero speciale. Sarai al sicuro qui". Poi a Raphael: "Rosalie non sarà tua prigioniera, anzi sarà tua ospite". Un libro volò via dallo scaffale e gli finì in mano. Era Harry Potter e la Camera dei Segreti.

"Mi piacerebbe leggerlo", disse Rosalie. Il libro lasciò la mano di E-Z e volò verso Rosalie. Lei lo prese, lo aprì e iniziò subito a leggerlo.

"Rosalie sarà nostra ospite", disse Raphael. "Ventiquattro ore quindi?".

"Ventiquattro ore", concordò E-Z.

"Aspetta!" urlò una voce. Una voce senza corpo. Una voce che risuonava e risuonava. Finché un libro si staccò da uno scaffale in alto. Il libro precipitò verso il pavimento, finché le sue ali non si spinsero in avanti e lo salvarono dalla rottura della schiena.

Raphael sembrò spaventata dalla voce. Cercò di ritirarsi, ma qualcosa la trattenne.

Rosalie ed E-Z aspettarono e ascoltarono.

"Raffaello non vi ha detto tutto", disse la voce tonante.

Era come se l'aria vibrasse a ogni sillaba, ma in un modo buono, gentile e delicato, non in un modo spaventoso da fine del mondo.

"Raccontaci", disse E-Z.

"Con un po' più di calma", suggerì Rosalie. "Sono vecchia, ma non sorda, sapete!".

"Scusa", disse la voce. Si schiarì la gola. Poi sussurrò: "E-Z Dickens, ti ricordi le scelte che ti abbiamo dato? Le due scelte?".

E-Z le ricordava abbastanza bene. Una era quella di rimanere nel silo per sempre. I ricordi della sua famiglia in loop. L'altra era tornare alla sua vita con lo Zio Sam.

"Sì".

"Dimmi cosa ricordi delle scelte?" chiese la voce.

"Dicevano che potevo rimanere nel contenitore e rivivere i ricordi della mia famiglia in loop o tornare alla mia vita con lo Zio Sam".

"E l'acchiappa-anime? Cosa c'è?"

"Niente", ammise E-Z con un'alzata di spalle.

La voce emise un muggito, come se parlare ora le provocasse dolore. Gli scaffali tremavano e gli oggetti si muovevano a caso a mezz'aria. Prima c'era un cetriolo gigante. L'oggetto verde ruotò in senso orario, poi in senso antiorario e infine scomparve.

Poi apparve una palla a specchio sopra di loro. Cambiava colore mentre girava. Quando girava troppo velocemente, temevano che si sarebbe schiantata su di loro. Si misero al riparo ma, prima di riuscirci, la palla scomparve.

Poi apparve la testa di un clown. Fluttuò davanti a loro e disse: "Cosa c'è di bianco e di nero e di bianco e di nero e di bianco e di nero e di bianco".

"Basta!", tuonò la voce.

"Mi dispiace", disse Raphael.

"Dovresti esserlo!", disse la prima voce. Poi, più tranquillamente, più dolcemente, disse: "E-Z e la sua squadra devono sapere tutto sui Cacciatori di Anime, tutto.   Altrimenti non capiranno la complessità della violazione".

La voce fece una pausa di qualche secondo, poi continuò: "Un Acchiappa-anime cattura le anime quando un corpo umano muore. È un luogo di riposo senza fine. Tutti gli umani e tutte le creature hanno dei vasi in cui andare. La cosa che hai chiamato silo è un contenitore di anime. Un luogo di riposo per l'eternità".

"Ok", disse E-Z. "Allora, cosa c'entra questo con la fine del mondo?".

"Voglio vedere il mio Acchiappanime", disse Rosalie.

"Se tu e i tuoi amici non fate qualcosa, nessuno avrà un Acchiappanime. Quando il tuo corpo morirà, morirai. Tutto qui. Fine. La tua anima e le anime di tutti gli altri non avranno un posto dove andare e quando un'anima non ha un posto dove andare, non ha più uno scopo. Non ha più motivo di esistere. E senza anima, gli esseri umani sono semplici abiti di carne".

"Aspetta un attimo", disse E-Z. "Stai dicendo che la persona che è responsabile degli Acchiappa-anime. In qualsiasi modo li chiami, CEO, Presidente, hai capito bene. Stai dicendo che sono stati compromessi?".

Raphael aprì la bocca per rispondere, ma E-Z non aveva ancora finito di parlare.

"Come funziona questa storia dell'Acchiappa-anime? Sono stato convocato nella mia in diverse occasioni e non sono nemmeno MORTO. Stai dicendo che questi, qualunque cosa siano, ora possono costringermi a entrare nel mio Soul Catcher a piacimento?". Esitò: "E cosa sai di Charles Dickens? È arrivato in un contenitore a specchio, quindi non in un Acchiappanime. Come ha fatto la sua anima a passare da un luogo all'altro? La sua resurrezione è merito di voi arcangeli?".

Raphael aspettò per vedere se aveva altre domande.

E così fu.

"E i miei due migliori amici PJ e Arden? Come si comportano? Sono entrambi in coma. Voglio riportarli in vita. Aiutare te li aiuterà?".

La voce nel muro tuonò in risposta.

"Nessuno gestisce i Cacciatori di Anime. Non è un'azienda creata a scopo di lucro. Quando qualcuno muore, la sua anima viene catturata e vive nell'Acchiappanime assegnato".

"Non capisco", ha detto E-Z. Poi: "Aspetta un attimo, qualcuno o qualcosa ha dirottato gli Acchiappanime? E se la risposta è sì, avrò bisogno di maggiori informazioni su chi sono prima di essere coinvolto. Se voi arcangeli non riuscite a sconfiggerli, allora come pensi che possiamo farlo noi?".

La voce nel muro disse a Raffaello: "Beh, Eriel si sbagliava quando diceva che questo ragazzo è grosso come un mattone. Ce l'ha fatta, in un colpo solo. Ben fatto, E-Z".

"Grazie, credo", disse lui. "Ma cosa ho azzeccato esattamente?".

La voce continuò. "Tre dee hanno dirottato gli acchiappa-anime".

E-Z aprì la bocca per parlare, ma prima che potesse farlo la voce parlò di nuovo.

"Charles Dickens non è arrivato in un cattura-anime, come sospettavi. I parenti di sangue hanno poteri sul tempo e sullo spazio. L'hai evocato tu. È venuto ad aiutarti".

"Non l'ho convocato io!". Disse E-Z.

"Eppure è tornato, conosceva il tuo nome e voleva aiutarti, è vero?".

E-Z annuì.

"E per quanto riguarda la tua ultima domanda, sì, le vite dei tuoi amici sono in pericolo a causa delle tre dee".

"Dee?" E-Z ripeté. "Come nella mitologia greca? Esistono davvero? Pensavo che tutte quelle storie fossero finzione".

"Si basano su fatti storici", disse Raphael.

"Non possiamo affrontare una squadra di dee mitologiche!". Esclamò E-Z. "Siamo bambini".

"I rischi sono molto maggiori se non lo fate, perché non abbiamo nessun altro a cui chiedere aiuto. Non ci sono Batman, né Spiderman, né Supereroi reali. Gli unici eroi siete voi bambini, potete? Ci aiuterete? Sappiamo come risolvere questo problema, abbiamo bisogno di corpi, di persone sul campo. Gli esseri umani con i loro poteri possono vincere. Potete sconfiggere queste cose. Queste cose. Per prima cosa, voi potete vederle. Noi non possiamo", disse Raphael.

"So che avete bisogno di aiuto, ma non vedo come possiamo salvare la situazione, non contro dee potenti. Sì, abbiamo dei poteri, ma contro cosa ci scontriamo esattamente? Cosa ci si aspetta da noi? Quali sono i pericoli per noi? Voglio dire, tu sei già morto - noi no. Se aiutiamo, quali sono i rischi?".

Esitò e quando nessuno disse nulla continuò.

"Se siamo d'accordo, puoi proteggere mio zio Sam, sua moglie Samantha e i bambini? Puoi assicurarti che PJ e Arden non finiscano morti nei Cacciatori di Anime? E cosa ci guadagniamo noi? Dopo tutto, rischieremmo le nostre vite. Tu non sei umano, quindi non hai nulla da perdere!".

Rosalie interviene: "E-Z non credo che tu abbia scelta. Hai ragione, ci saranno dei rischi e io non sono ancora morta, ma sono vecchia, quindi il rischio per me non è così grande. Inoltre, mi piace l'idea che, quando la mia vita finirà, ci sarà un'anima catturata ad aspettarmi".

E-Z annuì. "Lo capisco. L'idea che i miei genitori siano in giro. Soli. Senza casa. Senza un'anima da catturare. Beh, mi fa star male. Mi fa arrabbiare così tanto che vorrei sputare. Ma devo comunque parlare con gli altri", ribadì E-Z accavallando le gambe. Era così bello poter fare cose semplici come accavallare le gambe.

Stai diventando un ottimo oratore, gli disse Lia nella sua testa.

"Grazie", rispose lui.

"Come allora", disse la voce. "Ventiquattro ore. Nel frattempo, Rosalie rimarrà qui con noi".

"Come tua ospite", sottolineò E-Z.

"Starò bene", disse Rosalie. "E mi terrò in contatto chiacchierando con Lia. Io e Lia amiamo chiacchierare".

Lui annuì. Con Lia, tramite Lia. E-Z non era sicuro di quello che sapevano e di quello che non sapevano, ma non aveva intenzione di dare loro qualcosa che già non avevano.

"Ci vediamo presto", disse, salutando con la mano.

Poi era di nuovo sulla sua sedia a rotelle. Era faccia a faccia con i suoi amici. Ma come poteva dirglielo? Come poteva spiegare?

Alla fine decise che la cosa migliore era spiattellare tutto. Ed è esattamente quello che ha fatto.

CAPITOLO 23
CAMBIAMENTO

Sebbene la notizia di E-Z non fosse quella che si aspettavano di sentire, sia Alfred che Lia ebbero molto da dire in risposta.

"Hanno una bella faccia tosta!" Esclamò Alfred. "Dopo quello che ci hanno fatto. Voglio dire, fare promesse e poi rinnegare e cambiare il piano di gioco. Per quanto mi riguarda, non mi fido di nessuno di loro".

"Si tratta di una cosa enorme, che coinvolge i nostri cari che sono morti", disse E-Z.

"Come mai?" Chiese Sam.

"Non conosco i dettagli. So solo che si tratta di tre dee malvagie il cui piano consiste nel dirottare e controllare tutti gli acchiappa-anime".

"È assurdo!" Disse Lia. "Perché dovrebbero volerli? Perché darsi tanto da fare? Cosa ci guadagnano?"

"Aspetta", disse E-Z. "Ti dirò tutto quello che mi hanno detto. Tieni presente che nemmeno loro lo sanno con certezza".

"Comunque, ecco come stanno le cose. Sono dee mitologiche che sono state riportate in vita. Il loro obiettivo è controllare gli Acchiappa Anime, con ogni mezzo possibile.

"E il modo in cui hanno scelto di farlo è uccidere le persone. Persone che non erano destinate a morire! E poi le mettono nei Cacciatori di Anime che hanno dirottato. Alle persone che ne hanno bisogno. Così, le loro anime non hanno un posto dove andare".

"Ancora non capisco", disse Lia.

"Vedila in questo modo. Lia, tu, Alfred e io siamo già stati nei nostri Acchiappa-anime. Pochi possono entrarci prima di essere morti. Insomma, chi vorrebbe entrarci?".

"Sono d'accordo", disse Alfred.

"Idem", disse Lia.

"Ma cosa succederebbe se ti dicessi adesso che il tuo Acchiappanime è stato riempito da qualcun altro e quindi non è più tuo?".

"Gli umani non conoscono nemmeno gli Acchiappa Anime!". Esclamò Alfred. "La maggior parte pensa che le loro anime vadano in paradiso (o se sono cattive in un posto caldo). Se lo sapessero, si arrabbierebbero per questo. Ma non lo sanno".

"Sì, non si può perdere qualcosa di cui non si sa nulla", disse Sam. "Né puoi lottare per qualcosa che non conosci".

"Mi hanno detto che l'anima dei miei genitori potrebbe essere in giro in questo momento, senza casa. Questo mi ha colpito molto".

"Ed è proprio per questo che te l'hanno detto!". Disse Sam. "È una vera e propria manipolazione".

"No, è un ricatto emotivo", disse Alfred. "Ma capisco perché l'hanno detto. Se mi avessero detto la stessa cosa della mia famiglia, avrei voluto essere coinvolto. Voglio combattere queste dee. Se fossi una testa calda, agirei immediatamente in base alle mie emozioni. Ma dobbiamo essere logici. Dobbiamo mantenere la calma".

"Ma chi sono queste dee? Cosa sappiamo di loro?" Chiese Lia.

"E siamo sicuri che gli arcangeli siano dalla parte giusta?". Sam chiese.

"Hanno detto che un errore da parte loro ha causato il verificarsi di questo evento, ma non mi hanno detto esattamente come è successo o perché. E non erano dell'umore giusto per essere pressati per ottenere informazioni, più di quelle che ero già riuscito a ottenere. Inoltre, hanno Rosalie e il nostro tempo per prendere una decisione sta per scadere".

"Esattamente", disse Lia. "Eppure, come possiamo decidere se non sappiamo nemmeno con chi abbiamo a che fare? Sanno che siamo bambini. Sì, ognuno di noi ha dei poteri unici, ma sono sufficienti? Se gli arcangeli non sono in grado di gestire questa situazione da soli... perché sanno che noi saremo in grado di farlo?".

"Questo non posso dirlo. Ho fatto pressione perché mi dicessero di più. Se non fosse stato per la voce nel muro, non mi avrebbero detto tutto quello che ho appreso".

"Come osano nasconderci delle informazioni!". Esclamò Alfred.

"Ho spiegato quello che so. Ce ne sono tre. Sono dee, creature mitologiche che pensavo non fossero reali".

"Possiamo scoprire online tutto ciò che ci serve sapere per difenderci da loro", disse Sam. "Ma ci vorrà del tempo". Esitò. "Tuttavia, non credo che avremo molta fortuna nel cercare informazioni sugli Acchiappa-anime".

"Ho già provato e non ho trovato nulla".

"Quando ne hai sentito parlare per la prima volta?". Sam chiese.

"La voce nel muro mi ha fatto intendere che me ne avevano già parlato, ma ogni volta che cerco di ricordare è come se un muro bloccasse le informazioni".

"Wow! Mi succede esattamente la stessa cosa", disse Lia. "È davvero strano".

E-Z guardò l'ora sul suo telefono. "Beh, vi ho dato molto su cui riflettere. Abbiamo tempo fino a domattina per prendere una decisione definitiva... ma non credo che abbiamo altra scelta se non quella di accettare di aiutarli. Voglio dire, se non lo facciamo noi, chi?".

"Stavo pensando la stessa cosa", disse Alfred. "Ma non mi piace comunque il modo in cui hanno affrontato la cosa".

"Neanche a me", disse Lia. "Vado a letto. Notte a tutti. Ci vediamo domattina". Si chiuse la porta alle spalle.

"Hai bisogno di qualcosa?" Chiese Sam.

"No, sono a posto così. Notte zio Sam".

"Notte E-Z. Devo dirti quanto sono orgoglioso di te e quanto lo sarebbero i tuoi genitori".

"Grazie".

"E buonanotte Alfred", disse Sam aprendo la porta.

"Buonanotte", disse Alfred, poi si sistemò con la testa sotto l'ala e si addormentò.

E-Z, non riuscendo a dormire, fissava il soffitto con le mani dietro la testa. Fece alcuni addominali, poi si girò su un fianco sperando di addormentarsi. Invece, notò due luci, una verde e una gialla che fluttuavano verso di lui.

"Sei sveglio?" Chiese Hadz.

"No", disse E-Z con un sorriso mentre si alzava a sedere.

"Non dovremmo parlarti", disse Reiki, "ma dobbiamo parlarti, quindi devi indovinare cosa non dobbiamo dirti".

"Indovinare? Sul serio? Potete darmi un indizio... insomma, restringere il campo per me, anche solo un po'?".

Gli aspiranti angeli si sussurrarono l'un l'altro. Sembravano non essere d'accordo, mentre Hadz volava da un lato della stanza e Reiki dall'altro.

"K, vado a dormire. Quando lo scoprirai, potrai dirmelo domattina".

Si appisolò e poi si svegliò. Era sulla sua sedia e stava volando nel cielo. Si allacciò la cintura di sicurezza. "Che cosa?"

"Abbiamo deciso che non potevamo restringere il campo per te. O di dirti quello che hai bisogno di sapere. Per prendere una decisione informata... Abbiamo deciso di MOSTRARTI. Quindi, seguici".

Mentre le nuvole sfrecciavano e l'aria pulita ma fresca della notte gli riempiva i polmoni, E-Z si sentì più vivo di quanto non si sentisse da tempo. In un certo senso gli mancava essere convocato per le prove per aiutare e salvare le persone in difficoltà.

Da quando aveva smesso di lavorare con l'Eriel, non si era più sentito un supereroe. È vero, aveva salvato un gatto che era rimasto bloccato su un albero. E aveva impedito che una palla da baseball distruggesse una preziosa vetrata della chiesa.

Ma la maggior parte della sua vita quotidiana consisteva nel pensare al futuro. Pianificava di finire la scuola superiore nella posizione migliore per ottenere una borsa di studio. Per il miglior college o università che potesse ottenere.

Lo zio Sam e Samantha stavano pianificando il nuovo bambino. Stavano tenendo segreto se il bambino fosse maschio o femmina e nessuno poteva entrare nella nuova stanza del bambino. E-Z pensava che fosse strano avere quindici anni e diventare presto zio, ma non vedeva l'ora.

E Lia, se la cavava bene a scuola, adattandosi anche se era passata dai sette ai dodici anni in due salti in un periodo di tempo relativamente breve. Qualsiasi cosa la facesse invecchiare sembrava essersi fermata e ora sembrava che avesse una cotta per PJ. Stava decisamente crescendo e lui sorrise pensando a quanto fosse diventata autoritaria. Gli ricordava la Piccola Dorrit, l'Unicorno. Non l'avevano più vista dopo le prove. Forse gli arcangeli l'avevano mandata ad aiutare Lia quando erano tutti collegati. Poi c'è stato l'arrivo di suo cugino Charles Dickens. PJ e Arden erano bloccati in coma e nessuno sapeva come tirarli fuori. Alfred si teneva occupato in casa. Da quando era arrivato lo zio Sam non aveva più bisogno di tagliare l'erba così spesso.

Ricordò di nuovo i due processi in cui aveva trovato delle somiglianze. Quello con la ragazza vestita da personaggio di un videogioco. L'altro con il ragazzo a cui era stato detto di uccidere E-Z per salvare la vita della sua famiglia. Erano collegati. Eriel aveva ragione. Doveva solo capire cosa significasse esattamente.

"Siamo già arrivati?", chiese, notando che stava diventando freddo. Si stavano muovendo velocemente, avvicinandosi al Parco Nazionale della Valle della Morte, nel deserto del Mojave. Era dicembre, uno dei mesi più freddi dell'anno per il deserto di notte e si augurò di aver portato la felpa con il cappuccio. Era così buio che le stelle sembravano un milione di volte più luminose. Come occhi nel cielo con appena un dito di distanza tra loro, o almeno così sembrava.

Gli angeli in formazione non risposero. Scesero di qualche metro, poi continuarono a volare a tutta velocità.

"Fantastico!" disse. "Fammi sapere quando atterreremo. Vorrei tanto avere un agente di viaggio che mi dicesse cosa sto vedendo".

"Usa il telefono", sussurrarono Lia e Alfred. Poi tacquero.

Continuarono a volare, sorvolando il Badwater Basin, il punto più basso del Nord America. È stato chiamato così perché l'acqua è cattiva, quindi non potabile a causa dell'eccesso di sali. Tuttavia, alcuni animali selvatici e piante possono prosperare in questa zona, come le alghe, gli insetti e le lumache.

Si addentrarono nella Death Valley, mentre E-Z osservava il terreno e cercava di non pensare alla sete che aveva.

"Siamo già arrivati?", chiese ancora, mentre un uccello nero volava sopra la sua testa lasciando cadere un carico di cacca prima di proseguire il suo cammino. "Benvenuto nella Valle della Morte", disse, asciugandola con il retro della manica. Si affrettò a raggiungere Hadz e Reiki.

CAPITOLO 24

VALLE DELLA MORTE

"Sbrigati!" Hadz e Reiki dissero. "Siamo quasi arrivati a Rhyolite".

Si spinse avanti, raggiungendoli. "E cosa c'è esattamente a Rhyolite?".

"Un po' di storia", disse Hadz. "A meno che tu non ne abbia già sentito parlare?".

E-Z scosse la testa. Aveva imparato qualcosa sul Grand Canyon a scuola, soprattutto su come si era formato.

Hadz continuò: "Un tempo Rhyolite era una città fiorente durante la corsa all'oro del 1904. Ma non durò a lungo: nel 1924 morì l'ultimo abitante e divenne una città fantasma".

"Cosa significa la parola Rhyolite?".

Reiki rispose: "È una roccia vulcanica acida, la forma lavica del granito. Fu chiamata così da un geologo di nome Ferdinand von Richthofen nel 1860. Le sue origini sono greche, dalla parola rhyax che significa flusso di lava".

"Quindi la città ebbe una grande corsa all'oro e le diedero il nome di una roccia vulcanica?". Esitò. "Credo di ricordare qualcosa dalle lezioni sull'azione vulcanica".

"È vero", disse Hadz. "Risale a due milioni di anni fa".

"Allora, questa lezione è interessante e tutto il resto, ma non ho ancora capito perché stiamo andando a Rhyolite".

Reiki sbottò: "Perché è il quartier generale dei rinnegati".

"Quelli che si contendono il controllo degli Acchiappa-anime".

"Chi sono esattamente e come possiamo fermarli? Per noi intendo noi, i Tre. Perché Eriel e Raphael stanno trattenendo Rosalie e, tra l'altro, il tempo sta per scadere. Ci hanno dato solo ventiquattro ore per tornare da loro".

"Shhh", disse Hadz. "Hanno un udito straordinario e il vento potrebbe riportare le nostre voci a loro sottovoce. Da questo momento in poi parleremo solo con la mente".

E-Z chiese, usando la sua mente: "Cosa succede se sanno che siamo qui? Voglio dire, non saranno in grado di vederci?".

"Hadz e io non siamo umani, quindi siamo fuori dal loro radar. Tu, invece, non lo sei, ed è per questo che ti abbiamo schermato".

"Fantastico! C'è uno scudo protettivo invisibile intorno a me: è un'informazione utile da sapere".

In lontananza poteva vedere le Montagne Nere. "Scommetto che quando il sole scalda quelle montagne ci si può friggere un uovo". Esitò: "E quell'uccello che mi ha fatto la cacca addosso? Potrebbero averlo mandato i cattivi a cercarci?".

Hadz e Reiki scossero la testa. "Abbiamo visto l'uccello. Era un corvo, noto per essere un portatore di messaggi dal cielo".

"Ok, mi sembra giusto. Non mi sembrava un corvo. Dimmi che cos'è che ha fatto fuori gli acchiappa-anime e cosa dovremo fare per sconfiggerli". Esitò: "E cosa ha a che fare con la reincarnazione di Charles Dickens da giovane". Esitò di nuovo. "Inoltre, Lia otterrà il trasporto? L'unicorno Little Dorrit tornerà se/quando accetteremo di aiutarvi?". Erano un sacco di chiacchiere. Aveva sete e avrebbe voluto portare una bottiglia d'acqua.

POP.

Ne apparve una. La bevve dopo aver detto "Grazie" a nessuno.

Reiki chiese: "Hai mai sentito parlare di Erinni?".

E-Z scosse la testa.

"Conosciute anche come le Furie", disse Hadz.

"Non ho idea di cosa siano... ma ho un vago ricordo di qualcosa di un gioco, forse?".

"Sono conosciute collettivamente come le Dee della Vendetta".

"Dimmi di più. Su chi si vendicano?".

"L'intera razza umana!". Hadz sbuffò.

"Io e i miei amici ne abbiamo parlato prima. La maggior parte degli umani non conosce gli Acchiappa-anime. La maggior parte crede che abbiamo un'anima. Anime che vanno in paradiso o all'inferno, a seconda delle scelte che facciamo nella nostra vita".

"Sì, ne siamo consapevoli", disse Hadz.

"Allora dimmi", chiese E-Z. "Dov'è Dio in tutto questo? Dio o Gesù, Allah, Buddha... qualunque sia il nome con cui lo conosci. Dov'è?"

Hadz e Reiki guardarono avanti senza rispondere.

"Ok, ho capito che non puoi rispondere a questa domanda. Rispondete invece a questa. Perché le dee puniscono gli umani usando qualcosa di cui non sono nemmeno consapevoli? Capisco che sono malvagie, ma sembra comunque ridicolo".

"I bambini", disse Hadz.

"Puniscono gli impuniti. Ma..."

"Ah, stavo aspettando un ma... Continua".

"Le Furie stanno abusando dei loro poteri. Si spingono oltre i limiti. Stanno prendendo di mira degli innocenti. Bambini innocenti che stanno giocando".

"Aspetta, vuoi dire che i bambini che giocano vengono puniti per le cose che fanno all'interno del gioco? Ma il gioco non è reale! Come possono essere puniti nella vita reale per qualcosa che non è reale?".

"Lo so, e lo sai anche tu, ma per le Furie è la stessa cosa. Se in un gioco vuoi uccidere qualcuno, segui lo stesso processo di pensiero di un assassino. Si tratta di pianificare l'azione, di avere l'intenzione di uccidere e poi di andare fino in fondo. In alcuni casi si tratta di omicidi di massa. E sì, sono innocenti e viene chiesto loro di fare queste cose per avanzare nel gioco. Per le Furie, i bambini sono gli impuniti e sono un bersaglio facile quando sono all'interno del gioco".

"Aspetta un attimo!" Esclamò E-Z. "Cosa stai dicendo esattamente? Credo di aver capito come si inseriscono gli Acchiappa-anime, ma l'idea è così malvagia... che non voglio nemmeno pensarla, figuriamoci dirla".

"Le Furie si stanno vendicando dei giocatori. Coloro che hanno peccato nel loro cuore", disse Reiki. "Non sono destinati a morire! I loro cattura-anime non sono pronti ad accogliere le loro anime e quindi...".

"Non hanno un posto dove andare", disse Hadz.

"E le Furie li stanno accumulando qui, creando la loro tribù di Anime. Immagazzinano le anime dei bambini in catturatori di anime rubate".

"Questo sta creando il caos", disse Hadz.

"Quindi, voi ragazzi dovete aiutarci".

"Aspetta un attimo!" Disse E-Z. "Aspettate un dannato minuto!"

CAPITOLO 25

QUATTRO OCCHI

"Oh, oh", urlò Hadz, mentre una nuvola scura si muoveva velocemente nel cielo e si dirigeva nella loro direzione.

"Non possono aver penetrato lo scudo protettivo!". Esclamò Reiki.

E-Z si guardò alle spalle. Vide una cosa nera che non era una nuvola. Era infatti simile a un serpente. Con una lingua biforcuta che leccava l'aria. Invece di due occhi, aveva numerosi occhi. Troppo numerosi per essere contati. Ognuno dei quali colava sangue. Sangue e pus giallo fumante.

La lingua della cosa si spostava da destra a sinistra. Emetteva un suono sferzante, mentre le sue mascelle si aprivano e si chiudevano di scatto. E dalla sua gola usciva un suono nodoso, che si alternava tra uno stridio e un ronzio.

Con il vento alle spalle, una puzza nauseabonda riempì l'aria e raggiunse presto le narici di E-Z, Hadz e Reiki.

L'odore era molto sgradevole. Peggio dello zolfo. O delle uova marce. Più disgustoso del liquido settico e dei cadaveri in decomposizione messi insieme.

Il trio si spostò più in alto, in modo da poter vedere oltre un crinale che non avevano notato prima. Dietro c'erano dei contenitori d'argento. Cattura-anime. A perdita d'occhio.

"Così tanti! Sono tutti pieni di bambini? Oh, no!" E-Z disse con un tono nasale, dato che si stava ancora tappando il naso. Anche se riusciva ancora a sentire la puzza.

PTOOEY.

Schivarono uno spruzzo di pus giallo e appiccicoso.

"Che diavolo è?" esclamò E-Z.

In basso si vedeva un enorme bulbo oculare. Era stato chiuso. Camuffato.

PTOOEY. PTOOEY. PTOOEY.

"Oh no!" esclamò E-Z. "Caccole negli occhi!".

Si scagliò contro di loro, sparando il suo liquido caldo e appiccicoso.

"Tenetevi forte!" Hadz e Reiki gridarono.

Ognuno di loro afferrò una delle orecchie di E-Z.

"Ahhhh!" esclamò.

PTOOEY.

E-Z schivò la caccola, ma per poco non finì sulla sua sedia a rotelle.

FIZZLE.

POP.

POP.

E-Z era di nuovo nel suo letto. Perle di sudore gli colavano sulla fronte.

Nel frattempo Alfred continuava a russare in fondo al letto.

"È stato un po' troppo vicino per essere confortante!". disse E-Z. "Hanno penetrato lo scudo protettivo? Ci hanno visti? Sanno chi sono e dove vivo?".

"No, siamo usciti da lì prima che potessero passare", disse Reiki.

"Forse è una domanda stupida, ma perché non ci avete fatto entrare e uscire da lì con il POP? Invece di prendere il tempo di volare fino a lì e mettere in pericolo le nostre vite?".

"Dovevamo mostrarvelo".

"Prima della battaglia... come la chiamate voi...".

"Vuoi dire ricognizione?" Chiese E-Z.

"Sì, è così. Dovevamo mostrarvelo. Dovevi vederlo, con i tuoi occhi. Tutto quanto. Quello che stai affrontando", disse Hadz.

"Abbiamo pensato che quello che avresti imparato sarebbe valso il rischio".

"Credo che il tempo ce lo dirà", disse E-Z.

"Mi dispiace se abbiamo esagerato", disse Hadz.

"Avevamo davvero a cuore il tuo interesse".

"Lo so. E sono felice di aver visto gli Acchiappa Anime. Quanti ce n'erano, mi ha davvero scioccato".

"Sì, ha scioccato anche noi. E puoi star certo che ha scioccato anche gli arcangeli. Quando l'hanno visto per la prima volta".

"Non avresti dovuto dirlo" disse Reiki.

POP.

Hadz scomparve.

"Oh, ora va bene", disse E-Z.

"Non importa."

"Non riesco ancora a capire cosa ci guadagnano le Furie in tutto questo? Qual è il loro scopo? Qualcuno l'ha già capito?".

"Ne aggiungono ogni giorno di più. Altri bambini che giocano e che vengono risucchiati nella loro rete".

"Ma perché non c'è una protesta pubblica? Non dovremmo dirlo ai leader mondiali, ai presidenti, ai primi ministri? Non c'è nulla che possano fare?".

"Pensaci, qual è la prima cosa che farebbero? Manderebbero l'esercito. Morirebbero altre persone. Altri Acchiappa-anime richiesti prima del tempo".

"Da quello che abbiamo osservato, il gioco d'azzardo è un fenomeno mondiale. Le sorelle del male stanno prendendo le anime di bambini ignari".

"Ma la maggior parte dei leader ha i propri figli", disse E-Z. "Sicuramente, se lo sapessero, vorrebbero proteggere i loro figli e anche gli altri bambini".

"Più che altro, le Furie si concentrerebbero sui loro figli. Sarebbe come far penzolare un bastone davanti a loro", disse Reiki.

POP.

Hadz era tornato.

"Sarebbero felici di poter distruggere i bambini grandi e potenti. Al momento, quello che sembrano fare è casuale, scelto all'interno del gioco" disse Reiki.

"Dimmi di più su quello che sai su di loro". Chiese E-Z.

Hadz sussurrò: "I loro nomi sono Allie, Meg e Tisi. La vendetta di Allie è per la rabbia, quella di Meg è per la gelosia e Tisi è conosciuta come la vendicatrice".

"Ok, allora perché hanno un odore così cattivo? E come possono essere sconfitte tutte e tre?". E-Z chiese guardando l'orologio. Erano appena passate le 8 del mattino. Doveva parlare con il resto della banda per riavere Rosalie. Come avrebbe fatto a raccontare loro di questo terribile trio e di tutti i bambini che si trovavano in quelle catture di anime?

"La leggenda dice che in passato sono stati puniti per aver fatto il loro lavoro. Ora hanno trovato una scappatoia con la Realtà Virtuale, una nuova invenzione umana". Hadz esitò. "Perché gli umani non vogliono mai vivere la loro vita nel presente? Perché devono fuggire e giocare a stupidi giochi che mettono a repentaglio la loro vita?". L'aspirante angelo era rosso in viso ed estremamente arrabbiato".

Reiki cercò di confortare l'amico dicendo: "Non sanno quello che fanno".

"L'ignoranza non è una scusa", disse E-Z. "Dobbiamo rispedirli ovunque fossero prima dell'invenzione della VR. E dobbiamo restituire loro le anime dei bambini che hanno preso con l'inganno. L'unico problema è: come facciamo a convincerli che stanno sbagliando? Che stanno rubando vite e punendo le persone per i pensieri, non per le azioni?

"Ora che ho visto le Furie, so che dobbiamo aiutarvi più che mai. Ma devo ancora convincere gli altri. Anche se sono d'accordo, stiamo ancora combattendo contro le probabilità. Voglio essere positivo. Dire che siamo all'altezza del compito. Ma non lo sapremo con certezza finché non arriverà il momento di combattere".

Diede un pugno al cuscino e lo tenne sulle ginocchia. "Aspetta un attimo, sono morti? Voglio dire, le Furie sono riuscite a sfuggire ai loro Acchiappa-anime? E se lo hanno fatto, come? Chi li ha aiutati a uscire?".

Hadz guardò Reiki e Reiki guardò Hadz.

POP.

POP.

Erano spariti.

"Fantastico!" Disse E-Z. "Semplicemente fantastico!"

CAPITOLO 26
EQUILIBRIO

Nonostante cercasse di dormire, E-Z non ci riusciva. Continuava a pensare ponendosi delle domande. Domande a cui non riusciva a rispondere.

Così si è alzato dal letto, ha cliccato sul suo computer e ha fatto delle ricerche.

In poco tempo trovò l'oro. Trovò un collegamento tra le Furie e le Tre Grazie. Sembravano essere come lo yin e lo yang l'una dell'altra. Una buona e l'altra malvagia. Si chiese se potessero usare queste informazioni a loro vantaggio. Se le dee malvagie potevano essere portate sulla terra, anche le dee buone potevano essere richiamate?

Per prima cosa, prima di suggerire agli arcangeli di riportarle indietro - sempre che siano in grado di farlo. Voleva sapere esattamente cosa avrebbero portato le Grazie.

Sì, erano dee. Figlie di Zeus, il dio del cielo. I loro poteri erano rivolti al fascino, alla bellezza e alla creatività. Continuò a leggere, ma non riuscì a capire come avrebbero potuto essere di grande aiuto contro le Furie.

Tuttavia, aveva un po' di tempo e continuò a leggere. Lesse un testo accreditato a Nietzsche. Le sue teorie sul bene e sul male erano ancora discusse e dibattute nei forum.

Poi un ricordo gli balzò in testa. I ricordi dei suoi genitori gli tornavano sempre più spesso alla mente. Sperava che non smettessero mai.

Questo era una conversazione con suo padre. Sulla terza legge di Newton. Avevano preso una barca e stavano pescando.

"È il modo in cui un pesce si spinge nell'acqua", spiegò suo padre.

Da allora, aveva imparato di più a scuola. Pensò che Newton e Nietzsche avrebbero avuto delle conversazioni molto interessanti. Ma le loro vite erano distanti migliaia di anni.

Poi si rese conto. Lui, Lia e Alfred erano l'opposto delle Furie.

Gli arcangeli lo sapevano già? È per questo che sembravano così insistenti sul fatto che solo lui e la sua squadra potessero battere le Furie?

La domanda che continuava a scorrere nella sua mente, però, era ancora: potevano vincere?

Era possibile fermare le Furie?

Doveva parlarne con gli altri.

Spense il computer e tornò a dormire prima che gli altri si svegliassero.

Tutti si aspettavano che avesse tutte le risposte. Lui non le aveva, ma stava facendo del suo meglio. Da quando era diventato leader, la vita era così.

CAPITOLO 27

SALA ROSSA

E-Z si trovava in una stanza rossa. Una stanza che puzzava di sangue. Il forte odore di ferro gli fece male al naso e lo coprì con la mano, poi avanzò di qualche passo. I suoi passi lasciavano segni sul pavimento insanguinato. Dove si trovava? All'inferno? Almeno qui aveva la possibilità di correre, ma dove? Non c'erano porte. Nessuna finestra. Non c'era alcun tipo di luce eppure poteva vedere che tutto era rosso. E bagnato.

Tirò fuori il telefono e cliccò sull'applicazione torcia. Usando il raggio della torcia seguì le pareti intorno a lui. Erano tutti uguali. Insanguinate e gocciolanti. E puzzolenti. Aspettò. Chiamare aiuto non sembrava una cosa intelligente da fare. Forse sarebbe stato meglio se qualsiasi cosa lo avesse portato in questo posto non fosse venuta ad incontrarlo. Preferiva non incontrarli. Il raggio della torcia si spense e il suo telefono si spense. Con la paura di muoversi, rimase fermo ad ascoltare.

Un qualcosa di strisciante. Strisciando, lungo il pavimento. Uno scendeva dalla parete a destra e un altro a sinistra. Tre. Serpenti.

Poi l'aria nella stanza si è spostata e si è sentito un odore familiare. Marciume. Di uova. Sulfureo. Carcassa in decomposizione.

Si coprì il naso. Come in precedenza, non riuscì a mascherare il fetore rivoltante.

Aspettò.

Quindi, lo volevano da solo. Lo avevano in pugno. Si sarebbe assicurato che se ne pentissero se fosse stata l'ultima cosa che avesse fatto.

"Potremmo mangiarti a colazione", urlò Tisi.

"O a pranzo", disse Alli. "Ho un certo languorino, dopotutto".

"O per il tè del pomeriggio, non c'è molto di lui. Non per tre di noi da dividere", disse Meg.

E-Z concentrò ogni fibra del suo essere sulle sue ali. Erano la sua unica speranza di fuga e non servivano a nulla.

"Guarda!" Meg urlò. "Sta cercando di usare le sue piccole ali".

Tisi e Alli si sollevarono. Meg si unì a loro mentre si libravano appena fuori dalla sua portata.

Sotto i suoi piedi, il pavimento tremava e rimbombava. Come se stesse per aprirsi e inghiottirlo. Fece un passo indietro, per stabilizzarsi contro il muro. Ma quando lo toccò, sentì la camicia bagnata. E quando vi posò sopra la mano, questa tornò ad essere ricoperta di sangue.

"Non ho paura di voi tre puttane!", gridò.

"Forse non hai ancora paura di noi...". Meg urlò.

"Ma lo sarai molto presto", sibilò Tisi.

"Per ora, puoi occuparti di questi tre", sussurrò Meg, con il suo alito fetido che quasi lo faceva vomitare.

I tre serpenti, sfruttando la leva dell'altezza, scattarono verso di lui. Le loro lingue biforcute sibilavano e sputavano. Poi iniziarono ad avvolgersi l'uno con l'altro. Unendosi, intrecciandosi. Fino a diventare un unico enorme serpente, con tre teste e tre fruste. Frustini che scattavano in direzione di E-Z per tenerlo fermo.

Si spinse più indietro. Sentire lo stridore del sangue dietro di sé gli diede in qualche modo conforto. Il suo corpo si rilassò mentre la schiena affondava nell'angolo contro il muro grondante sangue.

"Guardalo", disse Tisi. "È solo un ragazzo e non ha fatto del male a nessuno. Anzi, è così buono e buono che è un peccato doverlo distruggere".

"Sì, il suo cuore è puro", disse Meg. "Ma ha una macchia nera sul cuore. Una macchia di vendetta che vorrebbe compiere contro coloro che sono stati responsabili della morte dei suoi genitori".

"Non parlare dei miei genitori!". E-Z gridò, spingendosi ancora di più contro il muro insanguinato. Aveva paura. Aveva paura che quello che stavano dicendo fosse vero. Chiuse gli occhi. Se non poteva vederli, forse se ne sarebbero andati. Poi qualcosa dietro di lui cedette. E cadde in caduta libera, all'indietro. Rotolando. Cadendo.

PULSANTE

Atterrò sulla sua sedia a rotelle e poi volarono via.

Nella Sala Rossa le Furie erano furiose!

"Inseguitelo!" Gridò Tisi.

"Prendetelo!" Meg gridò.

"È troppo tardi!" Disse Alli. "È come se fosse scomparso!".

"Torniamo nella Valle della Morte", disse Meg. Se ne andarono, lasciando la Stanza Rossa vuota. Ma la loro puzza persisteva ancora.

THUMP.

"Stai sanguinando", disse Sam. "Portiamolo in bagno. Possiamo vedere quanto è ferito". Sam spinse la sedia a rotelle verso la porta.

"No, fermati!" Disse E-Z. "Sto bene. Il sangue non è mio. Ma ho bisogno di pulirmi. Per lavare via la puzza. Poi ti spiegherò cosa è successo. Te lo prometto".

"Basta che tu sia sicuro di stare bene", disse Sam.

Dopo che se ne fu andato, Sam, Lia e Alfred non riuscirono a pensare a nulla da dirsi. Aspettarono in silenzio il suo ritorno.

Nel bagno, E-Z posizionò la sua sedia a rotelle sulla rampa. Quando ricostruirono la casa, lo zio Sam inventò una nuova doccia per lui. Gli diede maggiore indipendenza. Ed era divertente! Simile a un autolavaggio.

Si avvicinava e faceva passare le braccia e il collo attraverso le cinghie. Spinse un pulsante per muoversi in avanti e la sedia lo seguì. Immediatamente l'acqua iniziò a scorrere. Pulisce il suo corpo e i suoi vestiti contemporaneamente. Ogni tanto usciva del gel doccia o dello shampoo, seguito dall'acqua per lavarlo via.

Ora che era pulito, continuò a muoversi in avanti e azionò il meccanismo di asciugatura. L'asciugatrice asciugò lui e i suoi vestiti e li rese privi di pieghe in pochi minuti.

Quando arrivò alla fine, si staccò dalle cinghie e si lasciò cadere sulla sedia. Si guardò allo specchio. I suoi capelli erano già così belli che non aveva nemmeno bisogno di pettinarli. Tornò nella sua stanza. Quando vide i suoi amici, il suo stomaco ebbe un sussulto e vomitò.

"Mi dispiace", disse. "Mi dispiace tanto".

Lia e Alfred lo abbracciarono. Non si preoccuparono del vomito. Gli amici devoti non si preoccupano di cose del genere.

Sam andò a prendere una ciotola e dell'acqua per pulire il nipote.

E-Z fu grato per l'aiuto e gli diede il tempo di pensare a cosa avrebbe detto e come l'avrebbe detto.

"Grazie, zio Sam. Quello che devo dirti... Non è bello".

"Continua", disse Alfred.

"Siamo qui per te", disse Lia.

"Siediti, zio Sam".

Si misero in lista senza dire una parola.

"Ci sto", disse Alfred.

"Anch'io", disse Lia.

"Io tre", disse Sam.

"Sono d'accordo", disse E-Z. E un secondo dopo, stava tornando nella stanza bianca. O meglio, era lì che sperava di andare.

Qualsiasi posto era meglio della stanza rossa. Qualsiasi posto.

CAPITOLO 28

LA SALA BIANCA

La sala bianca sembrava in qualche modo diversa quando i suoi piedi toccavano terra.

E-Z si sentiva così felice di essere tornato nel comfort della stanza bianca. Dove poteva camminare. Toccare i libri. Annusare i libri. Ma c'era qualcosa di strano. Spento.

Si stabilizzò. Notò che le sue mani stavano tremando. Le ginocchia gli tremavano. Ora gli tremano i denti.

Si avvolse le braccia intorno a sé desiderando di aver portato la giacca. Aspettò, aspettandosi che ne arrivasse una. Non arrivò.

"Cos'è questo posto?" chiese.

Nessuna risposta.

"Cheeseburger, con patatine", disse.

Niente.

"Chop suey, con involtino primavera", disse con più autorità.

"Esigo di sapere dove mi trovo!", gridò.

Niente.

Nadda.

"Rosalie?", chiamò. "Ci sei? Eriel? Raphael? C'è qualcuno? Hadz? Reiki?"

Di nuovo niente.

Nemmeno un educato PFFT per farlo rilassare.

La familiarità dei libri era l'unica ancora che lo tratteneva in questo luogo. Si diresse verso la scala e la spostò sotto il Ds. Aspettandosi di trovare Charles Dickens, iniziò a salire. Invece, scoprì che ogni singolo libro che toccava era legato al mondo dei giochi.

Che cosa?

E nessuno dei libri aveva le ali. Erano tutti nuovi di zecca. Come se nessuno li avesse mai aperti prima.

Per poco non cadde dalla scala quando una voce disse,

"E-Z Dickens - questa non è la stanza bianca che conosci. È una replica. Sei stato mandato qui per fare delle ricerche. Tutti i libri di cui hai bisogno sono a portata di mano. Ogni libro deve essere letto e rivisto per intero".

"Non posso leggere tutti questi libri velocemente; mi ci vorrebbero anni per leggerli tutti!".

"Per questo motivo, ti verrà dato un potere aggiuntivo. Un potere che si realizzerà solo tra le mura di questa stanza. Leggi ora. Veloce. Furioso. Memorizza tutto".

Quando quella voce finì, ne iniziò un'altra,

"Dieci, nove, otto, sette, sei, cinque, quattro, tre, due, uno. Ora leggi E-Z Dickens. Continua".

E-Z sfogliò velocemente ogni singolo libro.

Quando ne finiva uno, gliene cadeva subito un altro tra le mani. Poi un altro e un altro ancora.

Li lesse tutti, finché non riuscì più a leggere.

Sperava che la sua testa non stesse per esplodere!

Poi cadde contro il muro, si mise in un angolo e pianse mentre nella sua mente si formulava un piano.

L'idea gli venne quando pensò a PJ e Arden. Perché le Furie li avevano messi in coma invece di catturare le anime? Facevano parte del gioco, giocavano sempre, perché non ucciderli?

Il piano era questo: Lui e la sua squadra avrebbero inventato il loro gioco multiplayer. Sam avrebbe conosciuto persone che avrebbero potuto aiutarlo nel settore. Quando le Furie sarebbero arrivate per reclamare le loro anime, li avrebbero fatti fuori.

Avrebbe voluto che Arden e PJ fossero lì a giocare con lui, perché gli avrebbero coperto le spalle. Non c'è problema, era lui che copriva loro le spalle. Li avrebbe salvati e liberati.

Camminava avanti e indietro, riflettendo su tutto. Un aspetto non avrebbe funzionato. Se lo avesse ingaggiato in un gioco e si fosse rifiutato di ucciderlo, gli avrebbero dato la caccia. E avrebbe potuto mettere in pericolo gli altri.

Non può certo dire a tutti i giocatori del mondo di smettere di giocare. Se avesse detto loro la verità, sulle tre dee che cercano di rubare le loro anime, lo avrebbero rinchiuso.

Eppure, era l'unica idea. L'unica strada percorribile per battere le Furie nel loro stesso gioco.

Rassegnato a non poter pensare a nulla di meglio, disse: "Tiratemi fuori di lì".

E così si ritrovò da solo nella vera stanza bianca con Rosalie e Raphael. Si chiese dove fosse Eriel, non che gli mancasse.

"Ok, ho un'idea. Una specie di piano", disse. "Ma non sono sicuro che funzionerà. Ho bisogno delle risposte a due domande. E ho una richiesta per una terza: la richiesta non è negoziabile".

"Chiedi pure", disse Raphael.

"Numero uno: riuscirò a salvare i miei migliori amici PJ e Arden se affronteremo le Furie?".

Raphael esitò prima di parlare. "Se ci riuscirai, non c'è motivo per cui i tuoi amici non si salveranno".

"Incroci il tuo cuore?", disse.

Lo fece.

"Come sospettavo, le loro condizioni sono dovute alle Furie. È così?"

"Sì, crediamo che sia vero. I tuoi amici sono fortunati, in un certo senso, perché le loro anime sono rimaste intatte. Quello che non riusciamo a capire è perché, se sono stati presi di mira dalle Furie. In tutti gli altri casi di cui siamo a conoscenza, hanno preso l'anima di bambini. Non conosciamo altri casi come quello dei tuoi amici che sono rimasti vivi in uno stato comatoso".

"Ho un'idea anche su questo, ma quello che voglio sapere è: se le Furie vengono sconfitte, cosa succederà a PJ e Arden? Cosa succederà a tutti i bambini le cui anime sono già nei cattura-anime? Non dovevano morire. E cosa succederà alle anime dei senzatetto?".

"In questo momento, le Furie stanno usando il potere di Internet. Hanno accesso ai cuori e alle case di ogni persona sul pianeta. È come se aveste lasciato porte e finestre aperte: chiunque può entrare. È vero che le Furie sono solo tre, ma i loro poteri sono enormi. Sono creature mitiche, dee le cui origini risalgono a Zeus. Hai sentito parlare di Zeus, vero?".

"Ho letto che era il dio del cielo e il padre delle Tre Grazie. Sarebbero in grado di aiutarci, se le riportassi indietro?".

"Zeus non è coinvolto. E nemmeno le sue figlie. Noi arcangeli non giochiamo con il tempo. E abbiamo sempre creduto che i Cacciatori di Anime fossero sacri. Intoccabili. Fino ad ora".

"Bene, quindi pensi che i miei amici siano stati presi di mira dalle Furie, ma non ne sei sicuro. Non più di quanto lo sia io, giusto?".

"Esatto. Perché non posso dire al cento per cento né sì né no. Se i tuoi amici stavano giocando. Intendo dire uccidere nell'ambito dei giochi... Allora soddisferebbero i criteri delle Furie.

Ma se li avessero voluti morti, sarebbero già morti". A meno che... no, non avrebbe senso. Significherebbe che sanno di te e della tua squadra. Non è possibile che lo sappiano. L'abbiamo tenuto nascosto. Se lo sapessero, allora terrebbero in vita i tuoi amici nel caso in cui avessero bisogno di una leva".

"Vuoi dire come merce di scambio?".

"È possibile, ma a dire il vero non lo so. Come ho detto, abbiamo tenuto nascosto tutto ciò che riguarda te e la tua squadra. Noi, compresi me e gli altri Arcangeli, faremmo di tutto per proteggerti.

"Alle Furie sono stati concessi dei poteri nel corso dei secoli. Ma non hanno mai preso di mira bambini innocenti. Non hanno mai stravolto il loro programma per soddisfare i loro scopi".

"Quali sono i loro scopi?" Chiese E-Z.

"Questo non lo sappiamo".

E-Z disse: "Ecco perché dobbiamo avere le migliori possibilità di vincere contro di loro".

"Esattamente, ma ogni giorno rubano l'anima di altri bambini e stanno accelerando il processo".

"Accelerando di quanto?". Chiese E-Z.

"A migliaia, pensiamo, ma presto saranno milioni. Presto sarà troppo tardi per fermarli".

"Ok, capisco cosa c'è in gioco, ma siamo solo ragazzi e non vogliamo andare alla cieca. Siamo mortali e anche loro lo sono. Dobbiamo pensare, considerare tutte le opzioni prima di rischiare le nostre vite".

"Capiamo e, come ho detto, vi copriremo le spalle".

"Ora passiamo alla mia prossima domanda: voglio sapere cosa dovrei fare con un Charles Dickens di dieci anni?".

"Oh, questo", disse Raphael. "Prima di tutto, non abbiamo nulla a che fare con la sua reincarnazione. Abbiamo una teoria, oltre a quella che ti abbiamo detto, ovvero che tu l'abbia evocato. Ci chiediamo se il suo ritorno sia stato un errore da parte loro. Forse l'universo si è aperto e lo ha mandato ad aiutarti, come equilibrio. Dopo tutto, è un parente di sangue. È un narratore e un maestro della trama. Potrebbe avere strumenti e intuizioni che ancora non conosci per aiutarti a sconfiggere le Furie".

E-Z scelse con cura le parole. "Ma è un ragazzino. Non ha ancora scritto nulla. Sarà una distrazione, viene da un'altra epoca e potrebbe mettere in pericolo noi e la nostra missione".

"Dipende", disse Raphael. "Potrebbe essere un'arma segreta. È qui, per te. Se credi in lui. Che è nato per essere uno scrittore. A dieci anni avrà già tutte le capacità necessarie. Usalo a tuo vantaggio, se decidi di farlo".

E-Z strinse i pugni. "Stai dicendo che dovremmo usare mio cugino come esca?".

Raphael rise e si mise a svolazzare, provocando un'inutile brezza.

"Sarebbe utile se smettessi di svolazzare così tanto", disse Rosalie. "Mi sono coperta di maglioni, ma non riesco a scaldarmi qui dentro. A proposito, vorrei andare a casa adesso. E-Z e gli altri sono d'accordo, quindi ho fatto la mia parte. Ora, addio, arrivederci. Lasciatemi andare a casa".

BINGO.

Rosalie scomparve e tornò nella sua stanza. Conversò con Lia nella sua mente, dicendole che era tornata illesa e che ora stava andando a fare un pisolino.

E-Z pensò a un altro requisito non negoziabile.

"Voglio Hadz e Reiki con me, nella nostra squadra".

Raphael sorrise. "Hadz e Reiki sono legati a Eriel dal nostro leader Michael".

"Lasciami parlare con lui allora. Quei due ci hanno aiutato. Vengono quando li chiamo. Se vogliamo combattere contro il male antico, abbiamo bisogno di quei due al nostro fianco per aiutarci".

"Michael non può parlare con te. Tuttavia, gli sottoporrò la tua richiesta. Se lo riterrà necessario, me lo farà sapere e io a mia volta lo farò sapere a te. C'è altro?"

"Sì. Ho bisogno di sapere come liberarmi delle Furie. Dobbiamo ucciderle? Rimandarle da dove sono venute? Cosa ci stai chiedendo di fare esattamente con queste dee?".

"Legarle, trattenerle e noi faremo il resto. Se il tuo piano funziona, dovremmo essere in grado di prendere il controllo degli Acchiappa-anime. Ripristineremo tutto come prima".

"E coloro che sono morti prematuramente?"

"Saranno tutti equiparati... una volta neutralizzati i nemici".

"Prima di rimandarmi indietro", disse E-Z, "ho bisogno di qualcosa, di un'assicurazione che non ci metterete di nuovo contro. Darci Hadz e Reiki doveva essere un'assicurazione, ma dato che non puoi darmela, ho bisogno di qualcos'altro. Qualcosa che possa portare agli altri e dire: questa è la prova che non ci tradiranno come hanno fatto in passato".

"Ad esempio?"

"I tuoi occhiali dovrebbero bastare", disse.

Raphael si inginocchiò, le sue ali smisero di sbattere e si ritrasse. "Non quello, tutto tranne quello", gridò. "Senza i miei occhiali non sono d'aiuto a te e a nessuno".

"Gli arcangeli hanno tenuto Rosalie qui contro la sua volontà. L'hanno usata per arrivare a me. Avete cambiato idea sulle promesse fatte, avete annullato i miei processi...".

Toccò l'orlo degli occhiali, poi li tolse. Nelle sue mani, gli occhiali si trasformarono in un serpente, un serpente rosso che strisciò sul braccio di E-Z e strisciò verso l'alto, verso l'alto, verso l'alto.

"Ma che diavolo!" E-Z gridò, mentre il serpente continuava a salire sul suo collo. Superò il bordo del mento. Si infilò tra le sue labbra ben chiuse. Si arrampicò sul naso. Poi si dimezzò e avvolse un'estremità attorno alle orecchie. Poi tornò al suo stato originale pulsando gli occhiali.

"I miei occhiali sono tuoi ora, qualsiasi cosa tu faccia - non lasciare che le Furie te li portino via. Se ciò accadesse, saremmo tutti distrutti".

"Aspetta!" disse la voce dal muro. "E se falliste? Dopo tutto siete solo dei bambini".

"Non posso promettere il successo, ma daremo tutto quello che abbiamo. Ma sarebbe bello sapere, se avremo bisogno del vostro aiuto, che userete i vostri poteri per aiutarci".

"Affare fatto", disse la voce.

E-Z era di nuovo sulla sedia a rotelle nella sua stanza con gli occhiali rossi che pulsavano sul viso.

"Devi smetterla di fare così", disse lo zio Sam, che stava preparando il letto del nipote. "Prima che mi dimentichi, oggi io e Sam siamo andati a trovare PJ e Arden durante un controllo in ospedale. Abbiamo incontrato il padre di PJ e ci ha aggiornato. Ora condividono la stanza d'ospedale, ma le condizioni di nessuno dei due sono cambiate".

"Grazie, stavo per chiamarli. Va bene, venite tutti qui".

CAPITOLO 29
NON CERTO

"Hai bisogno che resti?" Sam fece una pausa. "Perché mia moglie sta aspettando che le massaggi i piedi. Il bambino nascerà a giorni, quindi non è possibile farla aspettare".

"Vai pure a occuparti di lei", disse E-Z. "Ti aggiornerò sui dettagli più tardi".

Lia abbracciò Sam.

"Grazie", disse Sam chiudendosi la porta alle spalle.

Il campanello d'ingresso suonò.

"Ce l'ho!" Sam chiamò, mentre correva verso la porta d'ingresso.

"Ha un sacco di cose da fare", disse E-Z.

"Sarà più facile quando arriverà il bambino", disse Lia.

"Sarà più caotico", disse Alfred. "Ma non preoccupiamoci di questo adesso".

"Allora, quali sono le ultime novità?". Chiese Lia.

"Comincia con gli aspetti positivi, se ce ne sono. Spero proprio che ce ne siano", disse Alfred.

"La buona notizia è che ho un'idea. La notizia triste è che non ho idea se funzionerà contro i nostri nemici. Sono conosciuti come le Furie. Qualcuno di voi ne ha sentito parlare? Ho imparato il nome dalla mitologia e sono presenti in alcuni giochi".

Lia scosse la testa in senso negativo.

Alfred disse: "Ne ho sentito parlare, ma molto tempo fa. Credo che ne abbiamo letto al liceo, in passato. Ricordo che erano malvagie, forse tre? E non sono forse delle dee? Ho una visione di Medusa nella mia testa. Erano parenti?".

"Sono peggiori. Molto peggio, perché sono in tre", disse E-Z. "Quando ho vomitato, beh, è stato subito dopo il mio secondo incontro con loro. Il primo incontro è avvenuto durante un viaggio con Hadz e Reiki. Quello che loro chiamano un piccolo giro di ricognizione. Non preoccuparti, eravamo nascosti, ma ho imparato molto. Hanno stabilito il loro quartier generale nella Death Valley.

"Come sospettavamo, stanno prendendo di mira i bambini. Nel mondo dei giochi. Lia, hai chiesto quale fosse il loro scopo... È quello di spingere i ragazzi oltre il limite. Ragazzi della nostra età e anche più giovani.

"Una volta catturati, rubano loro l'anima. E le inseriscono nei Cacciatori di Anime destinati ad altre persone. Così, quando muoiono, non c'è un posto dove le loro anime possano andare".

"È così malvagio!" Disse Lia.

"Quindi, quando i veri proprietari degli Acchiappanime muoiono, cosa succede alle loro anime? Voglio dire, se le loro anime non hanno un posto dove andare - nessuna casa, nessun paradiso - allora cosa succede loro?". Chiese Alfred.

"Questo è il punto. Non hanno un luogo di riposo eterno, quindi quando muoiono fluttuano in giro. Questa è la versione sintetica. Dobbiamo fermare le Furie e dobbiamo farlo presto".

"Come fanno a prendere le anime dei bambini? Non capisco", chiese Lia.

"Nemmeno io", disse Alfred. "I bambini, soprattutto quelli che giocano, sono molto esperti di computer. Come fanno a mettersi in pericolo? Come fanno le Furie ad avere accesso a loro nelle loro case, proprio sotto il naso dei loro genitori?". Rifletté un attimo: "Sono loro i responsabili del coma di PJ e Arden?".

"Ok, prima la domanda di Lia. Le Furie puniscono coloro che sono impuniti: questo è il loro scopo da sempre. La loro arma principale è sempre stata il rimorso. Fanno sentire le persone in colpa. Si pentono di aver fatto del male. E quando lo fanno, prendono il controllo. Le fanno impazzire, le spingono a distruggersi.

"Ti ho detto del ragazzo che è venuto a casa mia e ha cercato di spararmi? Ha detto che qualcuno del gioco gli ha detto che avrebbe ucciso la sua famiglia se non mi avesse ucciso. L'hanno spinto a darmi la caccia, a causa delle azioni che stava compiendo nel gioco. Mi è servito un suggerimento di Eriel per fare questo collegamento. Sul momento mi è sembrato strano, ma non l'ho capito subito.

"È così che fanno. Un ragazzo sta giocando e per avanzare nel gioco deve uccidere qualcuno, o addirittura commettere un omicidio di massa, o, beh, hai capito l'idea. Nel mondo reale, queste cose sono peccati e contro la legge, nel gioco sono parte integrante del gioco. Nella maggior parte dei giochi è l'unico scopo".

"Aspetta un attimo", disse Alfred. "Mi stai dicendo che nel gioco puniscono i bambini come se avessero commesso un omicidio nella vita reale?".

"Esatto", ha detto E-Z. "È esattamente quello che stanno facendo. Stanno usando l'industria del gioco per giustificare, non credo sia la parola giusta, le loro azioni nella vita reale. Intendo dire per giustificare le loro azioni nel prendere l'anima dei bambini".

Lia chiuse le mani e le strinse a pugno. Poi le usò per coprirsi le orecchie come se non volesse più sentire. "Hai assolutamente ragione E-Z. Non abbiamo scelta: dobbiamo assolutamente porre fine a quelle streghe. Prima lo facciamo, meglio è".

"Lo so", disse E-Z, "ma non sarà facile. Sono dee, note anche come Figlie delle Tenebre ed Erinni. Il loro scopo principale è punire i malvagi e nell'ambito di un gioco tutti sono malvagi. È l'unico modo per avanzare nel gioco".

"Hai detto di avere un piano, qual è?". Chiese Alfred.

"Per prima cosa rispondo alla tua domanda su PJ e Arden. La mia sensazione è che la risposta sia sì. Ma ho chiesto a Raphael se poteva confermare. Mi ha risposto che non poteva dire al cento per cento né in un senso né nell'altro. Poiché le Furie, per quanto ne sanno, non si sono mai allontanate dal furto di un'anima. Per non parlare di due anime.

"Oh, un'altra cosa che devo dirti è che nella Valle della Morte ci sono migliaia di Acchiappa Anime. Forse più di migliaia e in numero crescente ogni giorno. Sono a perdita d'occhio". Si fermò, come se avesse il cuore in gola e si asciugò una lacrima.

"È stato difficile esserne testimone. Quello che stanno facendo è così premeditato, deliberato. Quello che non riesco a capire, però, è cosa ci guadagnano. Hadz e Reiki hanno fatto bene a portarmi lì a vedere. Se me lo avessero detto, senza mostrarmelo... non mi avrebbe colpito così tanto. Oh, e Raphael dice che stanno aumentando la loro assunzione ogni giorno. Quindi, non abbiamo molto tempo per stare seduti a pensare. Abbiamo bisogno di un piano e di agire".

"Sono mortali?" Chiese Alfred.

"Sì, siamo a livello di questo", ha detto E-Z. "Quindi, il piano che ho pensato è quello di creare un gioco tutto nostro. Lo zio Sam potrebbe aiutarci. Quando giocherò per ostentare le uccisioni, le Furie verranno a prendermi. Quando lo faranno, le intrappoleremo e le uccideremo nel gioco.

"Pensavo che i loro poteri potessero diminuire durante il gioco. Ma poi mi è venuto in mente: e se anche i miei diminuissero?".

"Non lo sapremmo finché non fosse troppo tardi", disse Alfred.

"È vero. Più ci pensavo e meno l'idea mi sembrava efficace. Per non parlare del fatto che se hanno PJ e Arden, bloccati in un limbo, fino al loro controllo... Beh, potrebbero portare via le loro anime. E noi li perderemmo".

"Vuoi dire che potrebbe essere una trappola?". Chiese Lia.

"Esattamente."

"Ci hai dato molto su cui riflettere", disse Alfred. "Penso che dovremmo dormirci su, rimuginarci sopra e riparlarne domani".

"Non so se riuscirò a dormire", disse Lia, "ma sono d'accordo, prendiamoci una pausa. Ho bisogno di tempo per pensare al pericolo in cui ci stiamo cacciando. Dobbiamo assicurarci di coprirci le spalle a vicenda".

"Certo", disse E-Z. "Nel frattempo, vedrò di trovare un piano B".

Lia uscì dalla stanza e si chiuse la porta alle spalle.

"Chissà chi c'era all'ingresso?". Chiese E-Z.

"Possiamo chiederlo a Sam domattina, probabilmente è ancora impegnato a curare i piedi di sua moglie".

Si misero a ridere. "Sembra un buon piano", disse E-Z. "Buonanotte Alfred".

"Notte E-Z."

CAPITOLO 30
OOOH, BAMBINO BAMBINO

"Il bambino sta arrivando!" Sam gridò qualche ora dopo.

Mentre scendeva nel corridoio, teneva la mano di Samantha in una mano. Sulla spalla aveva una borsa per la notte. Afferrò le chiavi dell'auto.

"Non guiderai tu, amore", disse Samantha, rimettendo le chiavi sul bancone.

E-Z uscì nel corridoio. "Vuoi che ti accompagniamo?".

"Sto bene", disse Samantha. "Lia sta ancora dormendo profondamente".

"La sveglio e ci vediamo all'ospedale, ok?".

Lia si guardò alle spalle: "Ho già chiamato un taxi. Lui non guida".

Sam sorrise: "È lei il capo".

"Ci vediamo presto", disse E-Z. "A proposito, chi era alla porta ieri sera?".

"Era Rosalie. Era esausta, quindi l'abbiamo messa nella stanza degli ospiti".

"Ok, grazie", disse E-Z.

Mentre percorreva il corridoio verso la stanza di Lia, chiedendosi cosa ci facesse Rosalie lì, bussò alla porta.

"Sono io Lia", disse. "Tua madre e lo zio Sam stanno andando all'ospedale. Il bambino sta per nascere!".

Ci fu un rumore di fondo, poi Lia aprì la porta. La lampada del suo comodino era sul pavimento accanto al letto. "Sarò pronta in un secondo", disse. Chiuse la porta.

Si spostò nella stanza degli ospiti. Guardò dentro e Sam aveva ragione: Rosalie stava dormendo profondamente. Tornò nella sua stanza, si vestì e cercò di non svegliare Alfred. I cigni non erano ammessi in ospedale, quindi svegliarlo sarebbe stato meschino e si sarebbe sentito escluso. Scrisse un biglietto dicendo che Rosalie dormiva nella stanza degli ospiti e di prendersi cura di lei fino al loro ritorno. Dille di fare come se fosse a casa sua, scrisse. Lasciò il biglietto in modo che Alfred non lo perdesse al suo risveglio.

E-Z si chiuse la porta alle spalle e la chiuse a chiave, poi lui e Lia salirono sul taxi in attesa e si diressero verso l'ospedale.

Seguirono le indicazioni e trovarono subito il reparto neonatale. Sam era lì, camminando su e giù come fanno i padri in attesa in televisione.

"Come te la cavi?" Chiese E-Z.

"Come sta mia madre?" Chiese Lia.

"Grazie a entrambi per essere venuti", disse Sam. La mano gli tremava mentre cercava di bere dell'acqua da una bottiglia. "Samantha sta davvero molto bene. Voglio dire, ci è già passata con te, Lia, quindi sa cosa aspettarsi e io... Beh, non so se riuscirò a gestirlo. Il corso che abbiamo seguito per prepararci ad affrontare la giornata di oggi era buono, ma la realtà è ben diversa. Odio gli ospedali".

"Tutti odiano gli ospedali", disse E-Z. "Ma quando entrano da quelle porte girevoli... E ti dicono che c'è bisogno di te... Allora devi farti forza, entrare e aiutare tua moglie. Ricorda che siete una squadra, insieme. Potete farcela!". Diede una pacca sulla spalla allo zio.

"Lo so".

Lia appoggiò la testa sulla spalla di Sam. "Sarai bravissimo".

Arrivò un'infermiera. "Tua moglie ha bisogno di te. Non ci vorrà molto. Ti porto a lavarti e poi potrai stare con tua moglie quando la porteremo giù".

Sam annuì e se ne andò.

L'ultima espressione del suo volto ricordava a E-Z quella di qualcuno che si trova davanti a un plotone di esecuzione.

"Starà bene", disse Lia, accarezzando la mano di E-Z.

Ore dopo, Sam tornò da loro con un ampio sorriso sul volto. "Ho un'altra figlia", disse, "e un figlio!".

"Due bambini?" Lia ed E-Z dissero all'unisono.

"Sì, due. Ne abbiamo visto solo uno nella scansione".

"Come sta mia madre?"

"È fantastica! Fantastica!"

"Possiamo vederla? E i bambini?"

"Lasciateli qualche minuto, per preparare le cose. Poi potrai conoscere tuo fratello e tua sorella Lia, e E-Z potrà conoscere i tuoi cugini".

"Sai già come li chiamerai?". Chiese E-Z.

"Sì, ma te lo diremo insieme".

"Mi sembra giusto", disse E-Z.

"Due bambini, in quella casa, con tutti gli altri", disse Lia.

"Stavo pensando la stessa cosa. Abbiamo già una casa piena... ma ce la faremo. Ci riusciamo sempre".

Si sedettero insieme e aspettarono.

EPILOGO

Passarono alcune settimane ed era il 17 gennaio. Il Natale era passato con il consueto sfarzo e lo stesso valeva per l'inizio del nuovo anno. E-Z aveva un altro anno, il sedicesimo, e la banda era riunita nella sua stanza. Charles Dickens li stava raggiungendo via Facetime.

In fondo al corridoio, i gemelli Jack e Jill si stavano agitando. Sam e Samantha si stavano ancora abituando alla routine dei nuovi arrivati. Nessuno in casa aveva dormito molto, fino all'apertura dei regali di Natale. E-Z, Lia e persino Alfred hanno ricevuto delle cuffie che bloccano il suono.

E-Z aveva pensato ad altri modi per sconfiggere le Furie. Oltre alla sua idea di inseguirle nel gioco. Poche altre opzioni si stavano presentando.

Mentre gli altri dormivano, aveva avuto alcune conversazioni online con Charles. Charles pensava che sconfiggerli al loro stesso gioco sarebbe stato "assolutamente tosto". '

E-Z era un po' preoccupato per le altre frasi che quei detectoristi stavano insegnando a Charles. Insieme decisero di informare il gruppo sulle loro discussioni su come portare avanti l'idea del gioco.

"È facile", disse Charles Dickens. "Io ed E-Z abbiamo parlato al telefono l'altro giorno e abbiamo pensato a cosa potrebbe funzionare. Se hanno delle informazioni su The Three - voglio dire che siete su internet - sapranno di te. Ma non sapranno di me.

"Non che abbiano paura di me. Anche se Edward Bulwer-Lytton una volta scrisse: "La penna è più potente della spada". In questo caso, spero che sia vero.

"Quindi, ho fatto pratica con i miei amici detectoristi. Pensiamo che il gioco migliore per farli partecipare sia un gioco già esistente. E pensiamo di conoscere il gioco perfetto.

"Si chiama The PK Crew. La classificazione del gioco è 13+ o 12+ in alcuni luoghi ed è gratuito. Lo scopo del gioco è uccidere tutti, compresi i tuoi familiari e amici. Vieni ricompensato per ogni uccisione, ma quando uccidi persone a te vicine, ottieni anche più punti. Più denaro. Persino notorietà all'interno del gioco. La tua foto sulla televisione PK TV. Sulla prima pagina del giornale The Peachy Keen Times. Il gioco si svolge in una città immaginaria chiamata Peachy Keen. È la trappola perfetta ed è un gioco che lanceremo noi stessi. Io vestirò i panni di un dodicenne, loro entreranno nel gioco e voi sarete già lì dentro".

"Sarà abbastanza sicuro", disse E-Z, "Voglio dire, sei già morto - intendo nella tua vita passata - quindi non possono ucciderti".

Bussarono alla porta: "È aperta", disse E-Z.

Lia saltò in piedi e abbracciò Rosalie. "È bello vedere che sei sveglia", disse mentre si accoccolava nello spesso maglione dell'amica.

Rosalie era diventata una parte importante della loro squadra. Tuttavia, le era stato concesso di rimanere con loro solo per un altro giorno. Dopo di che, doveva tornare a casa.

Mentre attraversava la stanza per sedersi, diede una pacca sulla testa del cigno Alfred. Erano diventati tutti amici da quando lei era arrivata prima dei bambini.

"Ho alcune cose da dirvi. Innanzitutto, grazie per avermi dato il benvenuto. È stato bellissimo vederti e grazie per avermi fatto sentire parte della tua squadra".

"Ahhhh", disse Lia.

"Quello che devo dirti è che ho scritto un libro su altri bambini con poteri speciali come te. È nel cassetto del mio comodino. La prossima volta che verrai a trovarmi, te lo darò così potrai andare a cercare gli altri per aiutarti a sconfiggere le Furie".

"Avremo bisogno di tutto l'aiuto possibile", disse Lia.

"Raphael ed Eriel pensano di poterti aiutare, ecco perché volevano che gli fornissi i dettagli. Per questo ho scritto tutto, per non dimenticare nulla di importante".

"È per questo che Raphael ed Eriel ti hanno portato nella stanza bianca?". E-Z chiese.

"Sì e no. Voglio dire sì. Sanno degli altri bambini. Ma no, non mi hanno chiesto apertamente di consegnare le informazioni su di loro. So che questi ragazzi sono importanti per te e che senza di loro non puoi battere le Furie".

"Che cosa sai delle Furie?". Chiese Alfred.

Rosalie rabbrividì e incrociò le braccia. "So alcune cose su di loro. Ad esempio, sono tre sorelle spaventose che sono tornate qui sulla terra per non fare del bene".

E-Z disse: "Non stai scherzando. Ho visto di persona i danni che hanno fatto finora. Stiamo lavorando a un piano. Ma dicci, dove sono questi altri ragazzi? Pensi che ci aiuteranno? Sempre che riusciamo a trovare un modo per farli venire qui".

"Sono bravi ragazzi, ma dovrete chiedere il permesso a loro e ai loro genitori. Uno si trova dall'altra parte del mondo, in Australia, uno in Giappone e l'altro negli Stati Uniti, a Phoenix, in Arizona. Potrebbero essercene altri, ma questi tre sono gli unici con cui ho avuto contatti finora", ha detto Rosalie.

"D'altra parte, l'ingresso di nuovi ragazzi complicherà le cose", ha detto E-Z. "Inoltre, se falliamo, non ci sarà nessuno a sostituirci. Forse è meglio che ce la caviamo da soli, con la minore esposizione possibile. Se siamo in grado di farlo, cioè di eliminare le Furie, perché coinvolgere altri? Estranei? Perché rischiare la vita di altri ragazzi?".

"Non è passato molto tempo da quando eravamo tutti estranei", disse Alfred.

"Io sono ancora un estraneo, anche se siamo parenti", intervenne Charles Dickens. "Ma non sono uno dei Tre. È E-Z che comanda e io sono felice di fare tutto ciò che lui pensa sia meglio. I detectoristi dicono che sono un novellino. Ed è vero".

Rosalie guardò il ragazzo nello schermo. "Non ci siamo presentati bene", disse. "Io sono Rosalie e sono abbastanza sicura di essere più novellina di te".

Charles rise. "Io sono Charles Dickens".

"Hai qualche parentela con il Charles Dickens?". Chiese Rosalie.

"Sì, sono lui, reincarnato".

Rosalie rise. "Pensavo di aver sentito tutto. Beh, sono felice di conoscerti Charles".

Si sentì bussare forte alla porta d'ingresso.

Pochi secondi dopo, dei piedi stivalati si fecero strada lungo il corridoio contro le proteste di Sam.

"Rosalie", disse il più corpulento dei due uomini attraverso la porta chiusa. "È ora di tornare a casa. Hai bisogno delle tue medicine, quindi vieni fuori o dovremo entrare per te".

Rosalie si alzò: "Sembra che vi abbia detto tutto quello che c'era da sapere e in men che non si dica". Si avvicinò alla porta, la aprì e uscì con gli assistenti.

Un minuto nel retro dell'ambulanza, poi nella stanza bianca. Gli scaffali e i libri erano gli stessi, ma l'odore no. Prima non c'era odore, ma ora era cattivo. Puzzolente. Brutto. Come la candeggina e le uova marce.

Attraverso il muro, entrarono tre donne vestite di nero dalla testa ai piedi. Al posto dei capelli, avevano dei serpenti. E altri serpenti strisciavano su e giù per le loro braccia. Volavano verso di lei. Le loro ali da pipistrello contrastavano con la purezza e il candore della stanza. Il sangue schizzava fuori dai loro occhi, mentre agitavano le fruste nella sua direzione.

E il loro fetore era insopportabile.

"Dicci quello che vogliamo sapere", le Furie dissero all'unisono.

"Non so cosa mi state chiedendo", disse Rosalie tappandosi il naso.

FRUSTA.

Lo schiocco della frusta sfiorò la pelle della guancia dell'anziana donna. Quando si toccò il viso e guardò la mano, questa era ricoperta di sangue.

"Sai", disse Allie, mentre lei e le sue sorelle agitavano ancora una volta le loro fruste in prossimità della donna anziana.

"Non capisco cosa intendi".

Una libreria si rovesciò. Se non fosse stato per la scala che si muoveva velocemente, Rosalie sarebbe stata schiacciata sotto di essa.

SQUILLO.

Sto sognando, pensò Rosalie. Devo svegliarmi. Devo svegliarmi ORA e allontanarmi da queste orribili creature puzzolenti.

Un'altra libreria cadde.

Poi un'altra. E un'altra ancora.

Presto anche la scala colpì il pavimento e rimbalzò. Una, due, tre volte. Poi si frantumò in pezzi.

"Oh no!" Rosalie gridò.

"Ce lo dirai amore", chiese Tisi, sollevando la donna più anziana da terra mentre le sue braccia serpeggianti la avvolgevano.

I piedi di Rosalie penzolavano precariamente. Mentre i serpenti stringevano le loro morse intorno alla sua parte superiore del corpo.

"Attenta, sorella, le farai venire un infarto", urlò Meg avvicinandosi a Rosalie. "Dacci quello che vogliamo, amore".

"Non ti dirò nulla. Non importa cosa mi farai", disse Rosalie.

Era così coraggiosa. Sapeva di non essere sola. Lia era lì, ad ascoltare.

"Questa è una completa perdita di tempo", disse Allie mentre lanciava una frusta in aria e abbatteva un'intera parete di scaffali. Alcuni libri alati lottarono per uscire da sotto gli scaffali. Uno cercò di volare con l'unica ala rimasta.

Tisi si girò verso la parete più lontana e diede fuoco ai libri. Caddero, come tessere del domino, sulla povera Rosalie, che fu sepolta sotto i libri in fiamme.

Le Furie risero forte e orgogliose.

Rosalie chiamò il nome di Lia nella sua mente. Dove sei Lia? chiese. Dove sei piccola?

Tornato a casa, E-Z aprì il suo portatile. "Ok, abbiamo avuto modo di dormirci su. Siamo tutti d'accordo sul fatto che non abbiamo altra scelta che combattere le Furie?".

Lia e Alfred annuirono.

"Dobbiamo prendere gli altri bambini e portarli qui. Noi siamo in tre e loro sono in tre. Lia, tu vai a Phoenix - la Piccola Dorrit può accompagnarti o puoi prendere un aereo".

"Preferisco la Piccola Dorrit".

"Ok, il primo bambino è stato scelto. Anche se non sappiamo il suo nome o dove si trovi esattamente a Phoenix, in Arizona. E dovrai chiarirlo con i suoi genitori. Non sarà facile perché dovrai far capire loro in che tipo di pericolo si troverà la loro bambina".

"Sì, dovrò chiedere maggiori dettagli a Rosalie".

"Alfred, puoi andare in Giappone. Ti suggerisco di prendere l'aereo, ma dovremo definire la logistica. Dovrai tornare in aereo con il ragazzo, sempre che i suoi genitori ti diano il permesso. Anche in questo caso, abbiamo bisogno di informazioni specifiche da parte di Rosalie su dove si trova il bambino. E ci sarà una barriera linguistica, a meno che tu non conosca il giapponese".

Alfred scosse la testa.

"Mi procurerò un traduttore".

"Ti daremo un telefono e potrai inserire un'applicazione che tradurrà per te. Ci sarà una curva di apprendimento", disse E-Z. "Soprattutto perché non hai le dita".

"Mi sembra una buona idea", disse Alfred. "Dovrò iniziare subito a lavorare con il telefono. Non dovrebbe volerci molto per capirlo. Nel frattempo, Rosalie può dire al bambino che sono un cigno, così non cadrà e non sverrà quando mi vedrà per la prima volta".

"È una buona idea", disse Lia. "Ma come farai a scrivere?".

"Posso usare il mio becco".

"O un programma ad attivazione vocale", disse E-Z.

"Forte", dissero all'unisono Lia e Alfred.

"E volerò in Australia. Prenderò un aereo per tornare con il bambino, ma sarà più veloce se andrò direttamente lì. Oh, e un'altra cosa: dobbiamo pensare a una botola per noi stessi. Un modo per uscire, nel caso in cui uno o più di noi venissero catturati, uccisi o feriti. Dobbiamo essere preparati a tutto. Se moriamo prima di finire questa cosa, non rimarrà nessuno a raccogliere i pezzi".

"Gli arcangeli", balbettò Lia, poi si fermò. Rabbrividì, poi non riuscì a riprendere fiato. Si avvolse le braccia intorno a sé.

"Stai bene?" Chiese E-Z.

"Shhh", rispose lei. Non c'erano suoni nella stanza né nella sua mente, c'era un silenzio assoluto e totale. Il suo battito cardiaco tornò normale, così come il suo respiro.

"Falso allarme", disse. "Ho pensato che qualcosa non andasse, come se stessi ricevendo un SOS, ma ora sembra tutto a posto".

"Succede spesso?" Alfred chiese.

"No", ha risposto Lia.

"Ok, iniziamo a fare brainstorming", ha detto E-Z. Trascorsero il resto della giornata a stilare una lista, individuando ciò che poteva andare male e ciò che poteva andare bene.

Andarono nelle loro stanze e dormirono.

Fu una notte tranquilla per tutti tranne che per Rosalie.

Rosalie, la cui voce non fu ascoltata.

La cui voce non ricevette risposta.

Non arrivò nessun aiuto.

La Stanza Bianca fu distrutta.

Nessuno venne a salvare Rosalie.

Dalle malvagie Furie.

Riconoscimenti

Grazie per aver letto il terzo libro della serie E-Z Dickens... Mi dispiace per il triste finale, ma a volte queste cose succedono.

Il libro finale sarà disponibile molto presto!

Grazie ancora una volta a tutte le persone che mi hanno aiutato a rendere questa serie tutto ciò che poteva essere, come i miei lettori beta, i correttori di bozze e gli editor. Complimenti!

Ai miei amici e alla mia famiglia, grazie per il vostro incoraggiamento e il vostro sostegno.

E come sempre, buona lettura!

Cathy

Informazioni sull'autore

Cathy McGough vive e scrive in
Ontario, Canada, con suo marito, suo figlio, i loro due
gatti e un cane.
Se vuoi mandare un'email a Cathy il suo indirizzo è
cathy@cathymcgough.com.
Cathy ama ascoltare i
i suoi lettori.

Sempre a cura di:

E-Z DICKENS SUPEREROE LIBRO QUATTRO: SU GHIACCIO

Milton Keynes UK
Ingram Content Group UK Ltd.
UKHW012006080224
437493UK00013B/383

C000043038

GOD'S GENERALS

FOR KIDS

A. A. ALLEN

GOD'S GENERALS

FOR KIDS

A. A. ALLEN

BY
ROBERTS LIARDON
& OLLY GOLDENBERG

BRIDGE
LOGOS

Newberry, FL 32669

Bridge-Logos

Newberry, Florida 32669 USA

God's Generals For Kids—A. A. Allen

Roberts Liardon & Olly Goldenberg

Copyright ©2020 Roberts Liardon & Olly Goldenberg

All rights reserved. Under International Copyright Law, no part of this publication may be reproduced, stored, or transmitted by any means—electronic, mechanical, photographic (photocopy), recording, or otherwise—without written permission from the Publisher.

Printed in the United States of America.

Library of Congress Catalog Card Number 2018903567

International Standard Book Number 978-1-61036-211-5

eBook International Standard Book Number 978-0-7684-5845-9

Hardcover International Standard Book Number 978-0-7684-6006-3

Large Print International Standard Book Number 978-0-7684-6007-0

Unless otherwise noted, all Scripture is from the King James Version of the Bible.

The photographs used are owned by and taken from the private collection of Roberts Liardon.

Timeline illustrations by David Parfitt.

A. A. ALLEN

CONTENTS

TIMELINE

March 27 1911 Born in Arkansas — 1911

1925 Left home — 1925

June 1934 Saved — 1934

Sept 19 1936 Married Lexie — 1936

1951 July 4 First tent meeting — 1951

1953 November First radio programme — 1953

1955 Arrested for drink driving — 1955

1958 Miracle Valley is bought — 1958

1967 Separates from wife — 1967

June 11 1970 Dies — 1970

CHAPTER 1

BORN DRUNK

Asa A. Allen

A TORTURED CHILDHOOD

It's horrible when people laugh at you.

If it happens to you lots, it can change your life. People who are bullied can feel scared. After a bit they just push it away hoping it will go away. If they are made to do dangerous things they often dream of being somewhere else.

When your own parents push you into danger then life can be very hard. All day long all you know is fear and you don't have anywhere to go to.

Asa Alonso Allen had lots to be scared of at home. He had six older brothers and sisters. And his father was a drunk.

Asa's dad spent all his money on alcohol. Asa's dad spent all his time drinking. The children had to get on with life.

When Asa's dad had friends round the bullying really started. Asa and the other small children in the house were forced to drink alcohol. The adults wanted to make the children drunk. They wanted to laugh at the children.

The little toddlers would drink so much that they would fall over and not be able to get up. This made the adults laugh even more.

Asa's parents both loved to smoke. Asa could light a cigarette before he knew how to read. It was his job to light his mom's cigarettes. Each time he lit one he would take a few puffs of smoke from it, then give it to his mom.

MY FIRST SHOES

When Asa's parents were not harming him, they did not look after him. He had to look after himself all day. He didn't even own a pair of shoes.

Asa loved to stand next to the road. Every day he watched the horse and cart go by. The cart carried people into town. Little Asa loved to wave at the driver when he went past. The driver always looked at him and waved back.

The cart driver knew that Asa's father was a drunk. The driver could see little Asa never wore shoes. He felt sorry for Asa. One day he stopped his cart right next to Asa.

"Come here boy, I've got something for you."

Asa ran up to the cart and smiled. The driver pulled out a pair of brand new shoes. They were black and red and made of real leather. Asa looked at them.

"Go on, take them. They're yours."

Asa beamed, "Thank you."

He sat down and put the shoes on. They were his very first pair. He felt so special.

No one in his family had ever given him shoes. But this stranger had. Asa loved those shoes so much. He wasn't four years old yet, but he remembered that day for the rest of his life.

When Asa turned four, his little life looked like it was about to get better. His mother had had enough. She did not want to live with Asa's dad anymore. She left him drinking and took the children with her.

For a few months things were a bit better. Then she married again, and her new husband also drank too much.

FETCH ME SOME BEER

Asa's mom and stepdad fought a lot. When they were drunk, they would fight so much that Asa and his sisters were scared. They did not know what would happen. Things would be thrown around the house and the two adults would hit each other.

The children did not feel safe. If they stayed in the same room a flying object would hit them. They knew it was safer outside. So they ran out and stayed away. Several hours later they would creep back into the house. They did not know what they would find. Would the police be there? Would both parents be at home still?

As little children they half expected to come back and find that one of their parents had been killed by the other one. It was a terrifying time.

In this new home the children were still picked on. Asa was made to do things that no child should ever have to do. Sometimes he had to carry a bucket of beer home to his stepfather. It was so heavy. Asa struggled to pick it up. It was even harder to carry it. But he had to get home fast.

If he took too long his stepdad would be angry. If he spilt any beer his stepdad would be even more angry. Asa was so frightened that he always managed to get that bucket home somehow.

I'VE HAD ENOUGH

When Asa was 11 years old he had had enough. He did not want to stay at home another day. He loved his mother, but he couldn't stand his stepfather. Every job he had to do for his stepdad made him feel sick.

Asa had a plan. He was going to run away. He was going to find his real dad.

Asa lay in bed at night waiting for the whole house to be quiet. When everyone was asleep he slipped out of bed and wrote a letter. He carefully put the letter on his pillow and got dressed. His heart was beating fast as he climbed out the window towards his freedom.

Asa knew where his dad lived, but he didn't know how to get there. He knew he had to follow the railway south to get to his dad. He ran through the darkness straight to the railway line and started walking.

He hadn't got very far when he saw a flashlight. Asa wasn't the only person out that night. The railway guard was walking along the line too.

Asa did not want to be caught. If the guard saw him, he would send him home. Asa needed the railway to help him find his dad. But right now he had to avoid the guard. He needed the line if he was to find his dad, but more importantly he needed to stay away from home.

He walked faster, moving away from the railway.

Then the wind started to blow. Dry leaves attacked him as the wind picked them up and threw them in his face. Lightning started to flash around him. Rain began to fall.

Asa had been scared many times before. Now he was so scared that he felt sick. Another flash of lightning lit up the whole area for a short time. Asa looked around but was thrown back into darkness. The wind pushed against him. Still Asa tried to fight on.

He did not want to go back. He had walked for miles. But there were hundreds of miles still to go. Surely he was far enough away from home for now.

He found a ditch and hid in it. The wind howled around him like a wild wolf, but it did not feel so strong in there. The rain was falling but Asa was too tired to care. He snuggled under some leaves and fell asleep.

All through that night the rain kept falling. When Asa woke up he thought he was in the bath. As he opened his eyes it took him a while to remember where he was. The ditch had filled with water. His clothes were soaked.

Asa stood up and started to walk. He wished he had a jumper. He wished he had a coat. The wind blew straight through his wet clothes taking all his warmth and leaving him shivering. Asa had walked a long way for an 11 year old boy. Now he could not go on. He had been beaten by the weather.

Home was horrible. He did not want to go back, but he had no choice. At home they had a roof and walls. At home the wind could not blow through him. At home he had dry clothes.

Unwillingly, Asa turned round. He knew he had to go home. He arrived home in time for lunch. As he ate, he started to plan how he would leave for good. Next time his plans would be better.

TRYING TO BE GROWN UP

A. A. Allen in action

AWAY BUT NOT FREE

When Asa was 14 he decided to run away again. This time he took spare clothes and food with him.

He had grown up a lot in the last few years. Now he was as strong as a grown man. He could do almost anything he was asked to do. He planned to travel around and earn money at the same time. And that's just what he did.

In one place he would pick cotton from the field, in another he would dig ditches. In one town he was a waiter in a restaurant, in another he went to college and learned to be a barber. Asa did so many different jobs and in each job he did well.

But he could not stay still for long.

Life was not pleasant. Sometimes he found a bed to sleep in. Often he ended up sleeping on the street. He went to sleep hungry and woke up feeling ill. When the sun shone he overheated. When it was cold he would shiver.

Life was hard, but it was better than life at home. Asa had learned how to be cheerful no matter how bad things got. He would sing to himself so he could stay smiling and he loved to dance.

When Asa turned up at a party he brought the fun with him. He made people laugh and everyone would start to dance with him.

Then he would have a drink.

Sometimes he would drink so much that he would fight with people, just like his parents had done. He didn't care about himself or others. Each time he ended up in a lot of trouble. If a fight got really bad the police would come and warn Asa. But Asa never changed. Before long they would lock him up in prison.

When they let him out he moved to a new town. In the new town the parties and the fights would start again. In each place it was not long before he was sent to prison again. Asa didn't care. At least in prison he had a bed and was safe from the wind and the rain.

At some parties Asa would drink so much that he would feel ill. The next morning, he would wake up with a headache, feeling sick. "I'm never going to drink again," he would promise himself.

That evening he would be at another party drinking again. He could not keep his promise. Alcohol was his master and he had to obey.

TAKING ON THE FAMILY TRADE

Asa had become just like his father. As a child he was forced to drink. Now he could not stop drinking even if he wanted to. Because of his parents, his whole family was in a mess. He had two brothers. One had died as a child. The other died a drunk. His father died a drunk. Asa's four sisters used to drink loads even as children. It was clear they were all going to end up as drunkards too.

Now Asa was a drunk. He could not live without alcohol. If he did not drink his whole body would shake. The only thing that stopped the shaking was more alcohol. The shakes were so bad that he couldn't even have a drink without spilling it.

"Do you want a coffee, Asa?" his friends would ask.

"Just fill my cup half way."

Even with half a cup Asa had to concentrate. He would grip the cup with both hands and slowly bring it to his mouth. The alcohol was destroying his life. And so were the cigarettes. Asa had been smoking cigarettes before he was five. Now he smoked non-stop.

By the time he was 21 he was always coughing. He tried different types of cigarettes, but he could not get rid of the cough. Whenever he tried to stop his whole body would scream at him until he had a puff of smoke. His body was falling apart.

WHAT'S THE POINT OF LIFE?

It wasn't just his body that wasn't working. His mind was also wearing out. He would get up to do something and forget what he was supposed to do. He struggled to wash and dress. There was no way he could work. What did he have to live for? What was the point of his life?

"If I kill myself this horrible life will be over," Asa thought. He wanted his troubles to end. He knew he could not kill himself.

"People will know that I quit life. I am not a coward, I will not quit."

There was only one thing that Asa could only think to do.

"If I go back home I can work on the farm. At least I will have proper food to eat."

So, Asa set off home. As he walked in through the door his mom wept. She had not seen her son for years. When she last saw him he was strong and fit, just a few years later his life was a total mess. He looked ill and he moved like an old man.

"Asa, please don't follow the rest of the family," his mom begged. "I stopped drinking, I know you can too. It's destroying your life."

"I know it is mom. But this IS my life. It's the only thing I have."

"SAVE HIM, MOVE HIM OR KILL HIM"

Back at home Asa carried on like before.

Every Saturday night he had a big party in his house. Everybody in town knew about it. Loads of people went each week. They loved dancing but they also knew there would be lots of alcohol. Asa didn't have to buy any. He made his own. Every week more people turned up to join him. They thought it was fun.

But one man was not impressed. A short walk away lived a farmer called Brother Hunter. He had met Jesus and been filled with the Holy Spirit. Now he wanted everyone to know God like he did. Every Sunday morning Hunter invited people to come to his home. He ran prayer meetings and church meetings. He wanted to see loads of people saved, but it did not happen.

Sometimes a young person would come and give their life to Jesus. By Saturday night they would be back in Asa's home, no longer interested in God. It seemed like every young person was at the Asa Dance Hall. Nobody wanted to be saved.

Hunter was desperate.

"If we're ever going to win people to God that dance hall has to close," he told his small group of followers. "Let's pray."

And their prayer was very clear:

"Lord, close down that dance hall. Save Allen if you can. But if he doesn't want you then move him out of town or kill him. We don't care which one, but please just close down that dance hall!"

Their prayer was not the most godly prayer in the world. It was a desperate prayer. God doesn't want to kill people and we shouldn't pray for people to be killed! But God knew their hearts. They wanted to see people saved.

God heard their prayer and he answered it.

CHAPTER 3

A NEW CREATION

A. A. Allen praying

ANSWERED PRAYER

"Asa, I've got to do a job. Do you want to come and help?"

It was June 1934. One of Asa's friends was standing at the door.

"Sure, why not?" Asa replied. "I've got nothing better to do."

So Asa and his friend set out on the road. On their way they went past a small Methodist church. The door was open and Asa peered inside. The people were all singing a song and they seemed so happy.

Asa had always thought that church was boring. He thoughts churches were full of serious, boring people. But these people were full of life. Their faces were shining.

Asa and his friend slipped inside and found a seat. It was right behind a huge stove so they could hide from the preacher. After all they didn't want to join the church. They just wanted to see what was happening.

When the preacher stood up Asa was shocked. The preacher was a woman! She was wearing white clothes and had a huge smile.

"She looks like an angel," Asa murmured to himself.

The preacher lady started to talk about the sins people do. Asa hid behind the stove, but she moved so she could see him. Every word that she spoke was about his life. It seemed like she knew him.

Asa moved behind the other side of the stove. The preacher lady moved too. She was looking into his eyes again. Every time she looked at him Asa knew he was a sinner. He had never felt it before, but in that church he discovered the truth. He had blamed his dad for his problems. He had tried to blame the alcohol too. But at that moment he could not escape it. His problem was that HE was a sinner.

It was too much for him to cope with. He had to get out of there. He stood up and ran out of the church before the preacher lady got him saved. He had to get away from that feeling. But the feeling did not leave him. Wherever he went that night he knew he was a sinner. God was convicting him.

For years he had been looking for peace and joy. The people in that church had it. A big fight was going on inside him. Could Jesus really be the answer? Something dark tried to pull him back. God gently nudged him forward.

COMING BACK FOR MORE

The next night Asa had to get to the church of happy people. He arrived before the meeting started. He did not want to miss one bit of it. When the service began it felt like it was just for him. Every song that was sung seemed to be like a hug from God. Every testimony gave him hope.

The preacher lady was there again. She spoke about the blood of Jesus. "It washes away every sin. No sin is too big for the blood of Jesus." She looked around the room and saw Asa. She remembered him from the night before. He was a rough looking man who had scars from his fights.

"He must be here to make trouble," she thought. But she carried on preaching.

"If you want to give your heart to Jesus please lift up your hand." Asa didn't hesitate, his hand shot up in the air.

"If you really want to be saved tonight, stand up." Asa stood. A couple of other people stood with him.

"If you *really* mean business with God come to the front of the church." Only Asa moved. He walked to the front of the church and stood. The preacher waited.

"Why isn't he kneeling," she thought. "Surely he would kneel if he wanted to pray to God!"

Asa waited.

"I've done everything she asked, what's she waiting for?" Asa wondered. The preacher broke the silence.

"Do you *really* want to be saved?"

"That's why I've come here."

"Then please will you kneel." She was shocked when he did. This man was serious. That evening, at the front of a Methodist church, Asa gave his life to Jesus. At that moment Jesus changed him instantly.

ALL CHANGE

No more dances.

No more drinking.

No more smoking.

Asa had changed overnight. For years he had tried to stop the habits that were killing him. Now God had healed him instantly. When his friends heard what had happened, they burst out laughing. "Asa's got religion!"

"It won't last," one teased.

"If it goes on more than a month I might try it too," another mocked.

But they did not know that Asa had really changed. He didn't even sing the songs he used to. He only wanted to sing about Jesus. Jesus really had given him freedom: Freedom from his past and freedom from himself. Now Asa filled his time with God.

"Asa," his mom asked, "can you stop singing these religious songs. You sing them all day long."

But Asa didn't stop. Up in the attic he found a Bible. One of his sisters had been given it when she was a little girl. It had never been opened. Now Asa did not stop reading it. In the morning he came down to breakfast reading the Bible. As he worked in the fields he read the Bible. At night time his light was on late into the night so he could read it.

Night after night people popped by to see him. "Asa are you going to have a party tonight. We want to have a drink and to dance." But Asa was not interested.

Bit by bit they stopped asking him. They got the message— Asa had changed. He no longer wanted to party. Some kept away. Others started to become interested in God.

CHAPTER 4

FILLED WITH THE SPIRIT

A. A. Allen preaching

THEY TALK IN TONGUES!

When the prayer group in Hunter's house heard that Asa was saved they could not stop thanking God. God had answered their prayer. He had done the impossible. Asa was now saved. The people who used to go to the dances were now coming to meet God. When Asa turned up at one of the prayer meetings they celebrated even more.

"Lord, you've saved him. Now fill him with your Holy Spirit." The next day Asa's pastor called.

"I hear you've been up to Hunter's house. You better stay away from there! Those people are from the devil."

"What do you mean?" Asa asked. The people had seemed so friendly.

"They talk in tongues."

"What's that?"

"It sounds like a load of gibberish. You won't have to go many times before you hear it. I tell you it's of the devil. Keep away!"

Now Asa really wanted to go again. He wanted to hear them speak in tongues. He did not think they would speak nonsense, they seemed so nice. At the next meeting Asa was scared. What if his pastor was right? He was not ready to hear this language. Quietly he prayed, "Lord, please don't let these nice people talk in tongues."

That night nobody spoke in tongues. Asa kept going back. The more he went the more he wanted to hear this strange tongues thing. After several weeks he was ready to hear it. One night he did. That night everyone was worshipping God and praying to him. Then the room went quiet. One lady carried on worshipping. Her hands were lifted up to God as she praised him from her heart.

She opened her mouth and started to speak. But the words that came out were not English. She was speaking a different language. As she spoke it felt like the whole building was filled with peace. From over the other side of the room a man stood up. He started to speak in English. The words were so beautiful. Each word encouraged those there to keep following God.

"That, my friends was a message from God," the leader said. "It was given in tongues and interpreted for us here."

This was what Asa had been waiting for. His pastor had said it was from the devil, but it was so obvious that it was from God. The message encouraged people to follow God; God's peace was in that place.

WHAT ABOUT THIS VERSE PASTOR?

Asa had read all about tongues in the Bible. He knew that God gave it to help get his church strong. Now he had heard it spoken, he could not understand why his pastor was against it.

"Pastor, I've heard it!" Asa bounced up to his pastor the next day. "I've heard them speaking in tongues. It was wonderful! Now I want to be baptized in the Holy Spirit."

"You are already baptized. When I baptized you in the river you were baptized in the Holy Spirit."

"I didn't know that. But how come in Acts 2:4 when the disciples were baptized they spoke in tongues."

"Ah, that was the first Pentecost. That was special. It was only for the 12 apostles. It did not happen again."

Asa whipped his Bible out of his pocket. "But look it says that there were around 120 people there, not just the 12 apostles."

"Oh. I'd not seen that before. Umm, but it's still just a one off."

"What about Acts 10:44-46, pastor? Don't run off," Asa called, as the pastor tried to slip away. "What about Acts 19:6. When Paul laid his hands on people they received the Holy Spirit and started to speak in tongues."

"You can't have it!" the pastor screamed. "Nobody gets that kind of experience today."

"Well I am going to have it," Allen replied. "And, Pastor, you need it too!"

His pastor couldn't cope. He stormed off shouting, cursing Asa and everyone who had taught him about tongues.

CAMPING OUT FOR GOD

A few days later Asa was off camping. He went with his sister and other people from Hunter's church. They weren't going on holiday. They were going to join a Pentecostal camp. They were going to meet with God.

At the meetings Pentecostal ministers taught from the Bible. Each night they gave people an opportunity to be filled with the Holy Spirit.

Each night Asa would walk to the front to be prayed for. He was very careful when he got to the front. You see the camp did not have carpet or nice flooring. The floor was covered in sawdust. If Asa had knelt in the wrong place his clothes would have been ruined.

Every night Asa checked the floor to find the cleanest spot. Then he carefully knelt down.

Night after night he got up no different.

But even though Asa was careful, his clothes still got dirty! With two nights left to go Asa was down to his last set of clothes—a white shirt and a pair of white pants. With only two nights to go Asa was desperate to be baptized in the Holy Spirit.

"God, fill me with your Spirit!" he cried. Sweat poured down his face on to his back. His clothes were soaked in sweat. But Asa did not care anymore. He wanted God to fill him.

"Lord, I dedicate every fiber of my being, every moment of my life to you!" As he prayed, he found himself on the floor rolling around in the dirty sawdust. His suit was getting dirty, but this time he didn't care. He had to meet with God.

Then suddenly it happened. God's presence came all around him. Firstly, his fingers started to tingle. The tingling feeling crept down his wrists along his arms. Then it started in his feet. The feeling crawled up above his knees. The tingling from his feet crept towards the tingling in his hands. Asa knew that when they met in the middle something special was going to happen.

And it did. At that moment Asa was only aware of God. He knew he was in God's presence. As he lay there, he could hear a sound. Someone was shouting louder than he had ever heard. The shout was in a completely different language—one that Asa had never heard before.

As Asa drifted along in God's presence he realized who was shouting. It was him! He was speaking in tongues. He had been filled with the Holy Spirit! It was past midnight.

Most of the camp had gone to bed. But when they heard him shouting people came from across the grounds to celebrate with him.

Asa's clothes were totally ruined, but he had got what he came for. God had met him. God had filled him with the Holy Spirit. Now he was ready to go back home and serve God. But God had other plans.

ON THE SAME PAGE

Evangelist A. A. Allen

ALL SUPPORT REMOVED

Back at home Asa felt like he was in the right place. He had Hunter and the other believers to help him. Now he also had the Holy Spirit. Finally he felt like he belonged somewhere.

But he did not have a job. There was a bad drought in the land. There had been no rain for months. The animals were dying and the plants were drying up. People were struggling to survive. Nobody could pay him to work. Asa loved it there, but he also needed to eat.

"God what do you want me to do?" he asked.

God answered by letter. Asa opened the letter and found it was from an old friend in Colorado: "Come and help me, Asa. I'm getting ready to build a barn and I need help. I'll pay you and give you somewhere to stay." Asa had no other choice. He had to go.

When Asa arrived on the ranch in September 1934 he was tired and he was thirsty. He had walked over 12 miles to reach the ranch and he could go no further. His new boss was kind, but he did not know Jesus. Asa had left all his Christian friends and had come to a place where nobody knew Jesus. He knew God wanted him there, but he felt very alone.

"Lord, please help me to win my friend to you. Please send me one other soul in this lonely place who loves you like I do."

As he looked out across the plain he could hardly see a single house. The land looked the same for miles around. Down on the ground he saw some white paper flickering.

He bent down and picked up the paper. It was a sheet of paper torn from a newsletter: The Foursquare Bridal Call. It was a newsletter from Aimee Semple McPherson—one of the most famous preachers of the time. If that newsletter was here then somebody must go to a foursquare church. That means someone here believes in Jesus!

Asa was relieved. He was not alone after all. God knew what he was doing. Now all he had to do was find out who it was. "Do you know who goes to a four-square church?" he asked his friend.

"The only one I know is that Scriven girl who lives up the road. She's religious just like you are. She goes to that church whenever she can get to town. She even thinks she's called to preach."

Asa felt so happy. He could not wait to meet her, and he did not have to wait long.

GETTING TO KNOW HER

Asa and his friends went shopping in the town. When they got home they realized they had forgotten to buy kerosene. They needed to get some before it went dark as they did not have any electricity. The kerosene fueled the lights. No fuel meant an evening of darkness.

"I think I saw the Scriven home had loads of kerosene. We could borrow some from them after supper."

His host smiled. "You know there are people who live closer than the Scrivens, but if you want to go there, we can go there." They didn't stay long and Asa did not say a word.

As they went he left his hat behind. The next night he had to go back to get it. This time he took his Bible along too. Asa wanted to spend time with Lexie Scriven. He wasn't looking for a wife, or even a girlfriend. He just wanted someone who could answer his questions about God.

For hours he asked question after question. Lexie tried to answer his questions from the Bible, but each time he would reply with another question. Lexie had been in church for a while. She had heard a lot of teaching, but she couldn't answer his questions.

Asa was digging deep. He didn't care what other people had taught her. He wanted to know what it said in the Bible. Day by day they met up to talk about what they were learning from the Bible. Day after day they both grew closer to Jesus.

Lexie didn't know it, but she was falling in love with Asa, the man who was inspiring her to follow Jesus more closely. Then she had some bad news.

"I'm going home in a few days' time." Asa had come to see her. "My mom needs help selling the farm and moving. I won't be coming back."

Lexie was in shock. She wanted to make him stay, but she didn't want to stop him from doing what he wanted. Lexie took a deep breath. Quietly she prayed to God, "Thank you God that he has been in my life for this short time. Bless him as he moves on from here."

As the days went by Lexie missed Asa. She carried on studying the Bible and looking for answers to her questions there. Now she did it alone.

But it was not the end of their friendship. Asa started to write every day. The letters were friendly. They told her how people were being saved. They spoke about the people he was meeting. They talked about the church he was going to and they told her what he was learning about.

THE GIFTS OF THE SPIRIT

"Desire the best gifts."

Asa had been reading 1 Corinthians 14. There was a long list of gifts that the Holy Spirit gives there and God then said we should want the best gifts. "God give me the best ones. I really want the best gift that you have for me."

As he sat in church that Sunday "I'd love to interpret tongues." Asa thought to himself.

At that moment a lady stood up and spoke in tongues. Somehow Asa just knew the first line of what she was saying. Then he understood the second line. But he couldn't hear anymore.

"God, if you tell me what the rest of it means, I'll stand up and tell everyone else."

But God didn't tell him. Instead God replied, "If you tell the people what I've told you so far, I'll tell you what the rest of it means."

Asa felt embarrassed. What if he started and couldn't finish it? People would think he was silly. Surely he needed to know more than the first line? As he sat there waiting to hear more, a lady at the back stood up.

"God has told me what the message in tongues means," she started. The words she spoke where the same words Asa had heard, but somehow she got the whole message. Asa wanted to know how she did it. At the end of the meeting Asa ran over to her. "When you understand tongues, do you get it all at once, or a bit at a time?"

"I only get a bit at a time," she replied. "I've found that when I have shared the bit I know God gives me the next bit."

"What would you do if you shared the first bit and God doesn't give you anymore. Aren't you scared you'll just be stood there looking silly?"

"If you're afraid of that you may as well not start. God gives us gifts to use them. The whole point of them is to help other people. We have to trust God, that's what faith is. You can't be afraid of what other people think. Fear is the opposite of faith."

READY FOR MARRIAGE

Lexie continued learning. She wanted to go to Bible school and Asa was excited for her. "I'd love to join you," he said. But he did not know how it would happen. Asa kept on writing letters. But one letter was different from any he had sent before.

Dear Lexie,

I guess you've worke• out by now that I love you. I •i•n't realize how much I love• you until you •eci•e• to go to school. Then I starte• to think, 'she'll fin• a nice young man who she can love. It won't be long before she has forgotten all about me.'

I can't let that happen without telling you first how I feel. Coul• it possibly be true that you love me too?

For the first time Asa and Lexie admitted that they were more than just friends. They wanted to be married. Asa travelled back to Lexie. A few days later, on Wednesday, September 19, 1936 they were married. They did not have much money, but they did love each other and God.

They also had a plan.

CHAPTER 6

IN TRAINING

People in prayer during a meeting

OFF TO BIBLE SCHOOL

Asa and Lexie had it all worked out.

A few days after they were married the happy couple set off to start Bible School. Between them they had saved up enough money to pay for the college and live for the year. Their little car was packed full of everything they owned in the world as they set off on the adventure.

This year would be just what they needed to get ready for the ministry.

On the way they stopped over to see Asa's mom.

When they saw her they were shocked. She was very sick. Worse still she did not even have any decent food in the house.

They knew they had to help her. Using some of their college money and went out and bought food to give her strength. For the next few days they looked after Asa's mother as she got better.

By the time she was well, they had used nearly all of their money to help her. Now there was no way they could afford to live and pay for both of them to go to school. Perhaps one of them could go and the other could work to earn money. They did not know what they were going to do, but they were sure God had a plan.

When they turned up at the college they had to find somewhere to live. "We'll work for you on your farm if you can give us somewhere to live and food to eat," they offered. But no one could help them.

They had no food, no money and no real options. There was only one thing for it, they would have to go back home.

"I'm sure we were doing what God wanted us to do. How could it have gone so wrong?" they asked each other. Back at home they could still not find any work to do.

HOW MUCH WOOD CAN YOU CHOP?

"You could always chop down the trees in the wood out back," his mom suggested. "If you've got an axe and saw you can get a dollar for a huge pile."

"But we don't have an axe or a saw. I don't think we've got enough money to buy them either." Asa protested.

"You could borrow somebody else's tools. They'll pay you 75 cents," she replied.

That night they went to a neighbor to borrow his axe. The next morning they set out early, ready to get chopping.

All day they worked hard, cutting a tree into logs. By evening they had finished their first pile. They had earned their first 75 cents. After a few weeks work they could afford their own tools. Now they were earning a dollar each day.

At last things were getting easier, but their dream of going to Bible school had been shattered. They had to wait until God showed them what was next.

THE FIRST MEETING

"You know Asa and Lexie are called to the ministry."

Asa and Lexie had popped round to see a neighbor. She was chatting to a friend who had come to visit. The friend looked up. "People really need God where I live. There's no church. Why don't you come over? My living room is quite big, we can meet there. If you come, I'll invite the neighbors."

Asa had not been to Bible school. He had not been ordained a minister. But God was giving him somewhere to preach so Asa went. Each night Asa preached. The first night the room was full and three people came forward at the end crying. They wanted to give their life to Jesus. All three of them left with huge smiles on their faces. They knew God had taken their sin away.

The next night even more people came. After a few nights people were walking for six miles, just to get to the meeting. People filled the living room and the kitchen. Each day Asa and Lexie went to the wood to work. Each evening they went to the house to preach.

After two weeks Asa had no sermons left to preach. He was tired and they were running out of food. But God knew what they needed. That night they were given their first offering and could get some food.

The same night a lady invited them to go and preach in her local schoolhouse. "It's a pretty rough place," she explained. "Preachers have been there before but the people have chased them out of town. There will probably be trouble, but you're welcome to try!"

Asa was used to rough people. He had been one himself. He was ready to go anywhere that would let him preach.

CHAPTER 7

A NEW LIFE

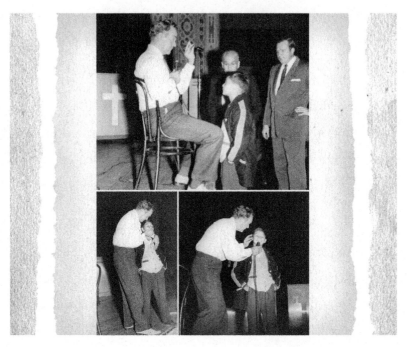

A. A. Allen prays for a boy

HOME SWEET HOME

The schoolhouse was too far from home for them to travel each day. Asa and Lexie had to move there. When they arrived they found that they could use the school house, but there was nowhere to live.

All day they searched through the town. As evening came they had only found one free place: a small cabin.

"Well, Lexie, at least we will have a roof over our heads," Asa said.

When they got inside they realized that was about all they would have. There were cracks in the walls and the windows were broken. This was to be their new home.

By the time they had hung up a couple of blankets to cover over the gaps it almost felt like home. No one could pop round and knock on their door as the cabin's door was missing. Even the quilt they hung over the doorway didn't do much—it was the middle of winter and the air was cold!

Can you imagine living in a house like that? Would you do it? Asa and Lexie were determined to follow God's call, no matter what happened. They did not know what the people would do to them and their house was falling apart, but they still went.

People came to the meetings. They didn't try to throw them out of town, but they didn't get saved either. As Asa spoke people were convicted, but still nobody responded to the Gospel.

After two weeks of preaching nobody had come forward to accept Jesus. Not even one.

Asa knew there was only one way they were going to see people saved—they would have to pray and pray, and then pray some more.

PRAYING THROUGH THE NIGHT

"Lexie, let's stay up all night and pray for the lost in this place."

They didn't have much fuel for their lamp so they turned it off and huddled round the fire. The fire gave them a little bit of light so they could see each other. More importantly it kept them warm.

For the first hour they prayed passionately for the lost. One by one they prayed for the people who had been coming to the meetings. When they had prayed for everything that they could think of Lexie started to nod off.

"Wake up!" Asa prodded her. "We promised God we would stay up all night to pray for them. We must keep our promise!" Lexie woke with a start. A few minutes later Asa started to breathe heavily. Now he was drifting off to sleep. Lexie poked Asa and he stirred.

For the rest of the night they prayed and poked each other so that they would stay awake. When morning came they fell into bed and slept for a few hours. That night they could not wait to see how God would answer their prayers.

ONE BY ONE

The meeting started as usual. The same number of people came. The people sang the song as they had done on previous nights. The preaching was the same as on other nights.

Everything was the same until Asa invited people to give their lives to Jesus.

When the altar call was given a young teenager came forward! He was the only one who came, but God was working in him. He knelt at the front weeping. He knew he was sinner and he stayed kneeling for over five minutes until he had found Jesus.

The rest of the congregation sat and watched him, nobody moved forward and nobody left the building.

When he got up he was smiling. He walked over to an older man. "Dad, you've got to give your heart to Jesus. He is the only one who can forgive sins. Please go forward, I beg you."

The man got up and went to the front. A few minutes later the man and his son both stood grinning. They had found Jesus. Together the two went to a group of teenage girls. There the boy found his sister. As they got near to her she started to cry. She jumped up and ran to the front.

Everyone else kept watching.

On and on it went. One at a time people came forward to find Jesus. Asa simply sat back and watched—God was doing all the work.

For two and a half hours the whole congregation sat there. Nobody got up except to go to the front. There was never more than one person at the front, but by the end of the time 23 people had become Christians. Not only that, but the people had forgiven each other for things they had done wrong.

At midnight Asa, Lexie and the 23 new believers all knelt and started to pray for those in the town who did not know Jesus. Other Christians now came forward who were willing to help. God had answered their prayers.

IT'S GOOD TO SERVE GOD

Back in bed that night they were so excited they could hardly sleep. The next morning they got up early and leapt out of bed. As soon as they got up they wished they hadn't. There was no food in the house. The last of their beans had been eaten the night before.

As they stood there wondering what to do, someone came to the house. A man stood in the doorway. He was holding a cardboard box. Asa had not met him before. "My two children were saved last night thanks to you. I've not been there myself but I'm right glad with what you are doing."

"I thought you might be able to use some groceries," he added as he gave them the box. "Let me know if there is anything else I can do."

When they opened the box there was ham, fresh eggs and milk, homemade bread, butter and honey. For a couple who had been living off beans and corn it was a feast—the best meal they had had in weeks.

All thoughts of going to Bible school were now in the past. Asa A. Allen was now doing what God had called him to do. When he had finished his work there he knew that God would move him on - and God did.

CHAPTER 8

MOVING ON

A. A. Allen praying for a lady

THEIR 2ND HOME

When God told them to move to a new town they had to find a new home. The new town only had one empty property. Like their last home it was full of cracks and gaps. Outside it was winter. Ice covered the ground as the cold air blew through the house.

As the ice melted their house started to leak. Not just one small leak, but dozens of them. They could not put their bed anywhere in the house without it getting wet. The best they could do was make sure no water fell on their heads while they slept. They covered the rest of the bed so that the water would run off on to the floor.

When they got out of bed in the morning they had to wade through water. Now that's gross! "Lexie," Asa said one day, "we need to ask God for money." Anyone looking at them would agree. They had no real home and no proper food.

"It says in the book of James in the Bible that we don't have things because we don't ask. Let's ask God to give us $200." That same day someone gave them 35 cents.

"It's a start," Lexie said. She wrote the date and the amount in a notebook. "Whenever we get money that is obviously from God, I'm going to write it in here, until we have the $200 that we asked God for."

AN EMPTY BUILDING

When God sent them on to another town, Asa found an empty building. It had been used for a church to meet. Nobody had been in there for years except for some birds that had made it their home. Asa had walked the whole way there. He couldn't drive because he had no money to put gas in his tank.

The next day someone sent them $5. Now he could fill the car up and they could eat. Once again God had provided just in time.

On the first night it was raining hard. Most people stayed indoors. Only one man turned up. The man gave his life to Jesus. The meeting was worth it. The next day they popped round to see the new Christian. When Asa walked into their home he knew the family was poor.

Their home had one small room and two beds. The man lived, ate and slept in that room with his wife and six children. The children were skinny and their clothes were all worn. Asa and Lexie spent some time with the happy family, praying with them and sharing more of Jesus.

When it was time for them to go the man got up. "Here, take these," he said, and he thrust a bag into Asa's hand. Asa opened the bag. There were two brown eggs inside. "You can have one each for breakfast," the man smiled.

Asa looked at the family. They needed these eggs more than he did. "Please, give them to your children," Asa begged. "Brother Allen, Jesus saved me last night. I want to do something for him. I love him so much. I feel he wants me to do this for you. Please don't stop me from doing what God's asked me to do, will you?"

Asa could not reply. He knew he had to take them. Tears ran down his cheeks as he accepted the eggs. More tears came as they ate the eggs the next morning. They could not stop thanking God.

AN EGGY REWARD

That night the rain had stopped and the church was half full. As the first song began the egg man came running in. He was holding a small brown paper bag.

"Look! Look! Can you see? There are four eggs in here. Every single one of my hens laid an egg today. They have hardly laid a single egg for three months, now they have laid four!"

He gave them to Asa. "I want you to have them." The next night the egg man came just as the meetings had started. This time in his brown bag he had eight eggs.

"Brother Allen, they are all for you!" he said passing them over. God was doing a little miracle and getting those hens laying eggs. The man, and everyone else, was finding out that you can't give more than God can give back to you.

The next night the man looked like he was going to pop with excitement. When it was time to share testimonies he was the first to stand up.

"First I gave the preacher two eggs. The next day my hens laid four eggs. I gave them all to the preacher and the next day the hens laid eight eggs. I gave all of these to the preacher and today they laid twelve eggs!"

His hens had laid enough eggs for him to sell. God was looking after his family.

BIBLE SCHOOL?

Asa had wanted to go to Bible School, but God had other plans for him. God wanted to teach him direct from the Bible. Asa tried to get a job to earn money, but there was no work available. He had no choice! Instead he spent the days praying and studying the Bible.

In the meetings he let people ask any question that they wanted to. Then he and Lexie would go home and study the Bible to find the answer to people's questions. They wanted every answer they gave to be from the Bible. God was teaching them and then they were living it straight away.

He was also showing them how it applied to real people in real situations. For some people God sends them to Bible

School for others God brings the Bible School to them. God had created a course just for them to learn what he wanted to teach them.

But there was one area that Asa did not understand. "So many people are suffering. So many people are sick. God promises that if I lay hands on sick people they will get better. Some of them do, but most of them walk away just as sick as when they came. I know there is nothing wrong with God, so there must be something wrong with me."

For hours at a time Asa would seek God. "God please show me what's wrong with me. Show me what is stopping you from using me to do miracles." He kept on asking God.

God was getting him ready to hear the answer.

CHAPTER 9

SO YOU WANT GOD TO USE YOU?

Crowds responding to an altar call

I *MUST* HEAR FROM GOD

Asa was desperate. By now he had become the pastor of a church. God was doing things, but he still wasn't seeing lots of healings. "I am not going to eat. I am going to fast and pray until God speaks to me," Asa told his wife. It wasn't that easy. Every time he tried to fast he found he was in the middle of a battle.

He would start praying for a few hours. Then he would smell the food wafting under the door. Before he knew it Asa was sat at the table eating with them. He had stopped fasting before God had answered. The next day Asa went to pray again. This time he found that he felt really tired. "I think I will go and rest now, then I can carry on praying tomorrow," he told himself.

And so it went on. Day after day he started to pray, but he kept stopping to eat. Lexie always kept a place for him at the table. She knew that he would join them soon enough. Asa had come out of his prayer room yet again to eat with his family. As he put food to his mouth he heard God speak to him.

"Asa, until you want to hear from me more than anything else in the world I will not answer you."

Asa looked at the food. Did he want God to use him more than he wanted to eat? Did he really want to find out why he was not seeing miracles regularly? He got up from the table. "Honey, I am going to pray. This time I do mean business. Lock me in to the closet and leave me there. I am going to keep on praying until I hear from God."

"You'll be asking me to open the door for you in around an hour. I know you." As she locked the door behind him she called, "I'll let you out as soon as you knock."

"I will not knock until I get the answer that I have been waiting for!" Asa replied. This time he really was serious.

GOD TURNS UP

Hour after hour Asa prayed. Many times he felt so close to giving up, but he carried on. At times he thought about how he didn't really need to see God move in this way. He could just carry on serving God like he had been.

Each time he was about to stop he would remember that he really wanted to see God move like in the Bible. He would carry on praying until God answered or until he died. He would not quit.

After many hours the closet began to change. Light started to fill it. Asa turned round to look at the door. He thought his wife must have opened it. It was still locked shut. This light was coming from heaven. God had opened up the door of heaven and God's glory was pouring in. God came closer and closer. God's presence was so powerful Asa thought he might die.

Still he asked the same question, "Lord, why can't I heal the sick? Why can't I work miracles in your name? Why do I not see signs following like Peter, John and Paul did in the Bible?"

At that moment he heard a whirlwind stirring around him. As Asa listened, he realized God was speaking quickly and clearly. Asa hadn't expected such a clear answer. He did not realize that God had such a long list of things for him to deal with. He knew he had to write down everything God was saying. If only he had brought pen and paper into the closet with him.

He looked around and found a broken pencil. He sharpened it with his teeth. Then he pulled out a cardboard box filled with clothes and started to write on the side of it.

"Lord, please can you start again so that I can write down all you say to me."

God started the list again.

GOD HAS SPOKEN

This is what God told Asa he had to do:

1. The disciple is not above his master (Luke 6:40): You must not expect to do greater things than Jesus or to be

greater than him. Jesus was persecuted, so you should expect persecution too.

2. Everyone that is perfect will be like his master (Luke 6:40): You can do the same things that Jesus did. It is possible. We can be like Jesus, not only in the power he shows but in the way he lived his life.

3. Be perfect, even as your father in heaven is perfect (Matthew 5:48): God wants us to be perfect and he helps us to live as he wants us to live. It's a high standard, but one that we have to aim for.

4. Christ is our example: To live as Jesus lived, we need to think as he thinks. Jesus lived his life led by the Holy Spirit. We need to do the same.

5. If anyone wants to follow me they need to deny themselves … (Luke 9:23): If anyone wants to follow Jesus they have to turn away from what they want, to follow what God wants. Pray even when you don't feel like it. Spend time with Jesus instead of just playing around. It's hard to do it sometimes, there are hundreds of great things you could be doing and want to be doing, but that's what it means to really follow Jesus—we don't do what we want to do, we do what HE wants us to do.

6. … take up their cross every day and follow me. (Luke 9:23). Every day has to be set aside for God. You never get a holiday when you are serving Jesus. Every day of our lives should be given to him if we really want him to use us.

7. I must decrease, (John 3:30). When God uses us it is not so that we look great. In fact the more he uses us the less people should notice us. Instead they should see Jesus.

8. He must increase, (John 3:30). As we become less, Jesus should be seen more clearly. When we understand that we need God for everything then he can shine through us. After all we can't do anything without him. We need more and more of Jesus every day if he is to be able to use us more and more.

9. Be careful what words you speak, don't say foolish things. The words that come out of our mouth show us what's really going on in our heart. We need to watch every word we say and not just talk for the sake of talking. Think before you speak!

10. Present your body. When we give our bodies to Jesus he can use us as he chooses. That means he decides what we do every day of the week (not just on Sundays).

11. Part of his divine nature. We need to be plugged into God so that he can work through us. As we believe what God said we get to be part of his plan for the world. Simply believing God brings about change.

12. Asa never told anybody what the final two items on the list were. He didn't even tell his wife! They were two sins that he struggled with.

Every person fights against a particular sin in their life. Maybe we make excuses for why it is okay to do these things. But Asa found that it is only when we admit that these things are wrong and deal with these sins that God can really use us.

"Asa," God said, "this is your answer. When you have done all of these things on the list then you will not only heal the sick, but in my name you will cast out demons. You will see mighty miracles as you preach the word for I will give you power over all the power of the enemy.

The light started to leave the closet. Asa banged on the door and waited for his wife to let him out. God had spoken to him. Now he knew what to do. The next challenge was doing it. Asa started to work his way through the list one at a time, ticking off each thing as he conquered it.

GOD IS CALLING ME

A woman shares what God has done for her

GO TO IDAHO

Asa and Lexie both heard God telling them to go to a small town in Idaho. "New Meadows" was a small town with 300 people in it. When they got there no one wanted to give them a building. They were a bit confused until a friend suggested they go to a town a few miles down the road.

They arrived with only 40 cents. They had kept this money to buy food for their new baby.

It was Saturday.

"I'm going to preach on Sunday," Asa told his wife.

They had no money to hire a hall, they did not know anybody, but they knew that God had called them to be there.

"You can't have my hall unless you pay me $10 for the month," the owner told Asa.

"I will pay you on Monday," Asa promised.

"You preachers are all the same you promise to pay but then you don't. But I'll tell you what we'll do. You can have the hall for $10 a month but you must pay me on Monday. No money and you will have to leave."

Asa was excited. God had given them a hall. They could preach there and live there. Lexie put a curtain up at the back of the room. This would be their home. The rest of the space would be for the meetings.

Asa walked around the town that afternoon telling people what he was doing. One man smiled, "we've been praying for two years for God to send someone. We'll be there on Sunday."

GOD LOVES TO GIVE

The first lady who walked into the building shook his hand, "thank you so much for coming here. God bless you." As she walked off Asa discovered she had left $10 in his hand. God had given him the rent that he needed.

By the time the service started there were 59 people ready to worship God. During the service Asa took up an offering which gave him enough money to feed his family for the whole week. God had been getting everything ready for Asa. Now God was helping him to stay there.

Asa couldn't help but smile at each person as they left. God still had one more surprise for Asa. "God told me to give you $12," one lady said on her way out. She did not know that was the exact amount that Asa needed to pay for his car.

Of course God could have given them a big offering to pay for food, the rent and the car. By sending three people with three different amounts to cover the three different bills God was showing them that he was in charge. God really wanted them there. They needed to know this, because not everything in their life was going to be easy.

MOVE ON

Asa was busy chopping wood. The church had not grown. In fact, there was only one family left in the church. God spoke to Asa, "*Now* it is time for you to go to New Meadows."

Asa put down his axe and ran to Lexie. "God says it's time to go darling so let's pack."

The one church member decided to join them. In the first meeting five people were saved. Every single service someone else was saved. God was doing a great work. Not only that, he was giving them what they needed. The manager of the local food store had been holding meetings in his home. He wanted to bless Asa so he gave them their food for free! They were blessed.

Before long the room they were meeting in was too small. So they moved to a larger cabin. And more people kept coming. "So many of us are following God now! We need to start a church."

When the manager of the store heard about it he was furious. "I am the only leader around here. I am the one in charge. I've been running meetings much longer than Asa Allen has."

The revival had started in a building owned by the manager. They were living in a home that belonged to the manager. So they had to listen to him when he came to them one night. "God says your time here is over. You have to move on." He told them bluntly.

Asa was not so sure. They were happy to move if God told them to, but they didn't think it was God speaking. Asa and Lexie asked God what they should do. God showed them very clearly that the manager was not a pastor or a leader in the church. He never had been and he never would be. God wanted them to stay.

They would have no food and nowhere to live, but if God wanted them to stay they would.

Asa spoke to each of the new Christians and told them what was happening. If you want us to stay we will stay, if you want us to go we will go. The Christians voted that night. Every single one of them felt God wanted them to stay except the manager.

Asa and Lexie moved out of their home into a new one. They lived off the small amount that the people could afford to give. They were poor, but happy, and people were being saved.

The church grew so much that they had to build a new building. God was using them in New Meadows, just as he promised he would.

CHAPTER 11

SOMEBODY'S GOT TO HELP HIM

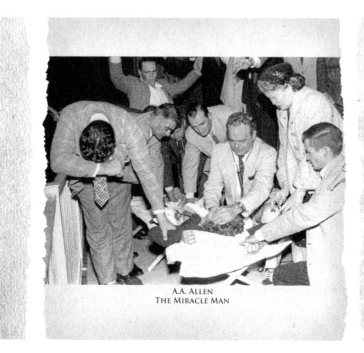

A.A. ALLEN
THE MIRACLE MAN

A sick lady is prayed for

GETTING COLD FEET

It was Sunday morning. And it was cold. Outside a white blanket of snow covered the ground. Asa got up early to light a fire in the church. He wanted the building to be warm when the people arrived. He left the fire burning and went back home.

Fifteen minutes before the service began Asa came back to the church. Next to the fire stood a boy in rags. His clothes were torn, his shoes had huge holes in them and his feet were frozen. He had walked the whole way.

Immediately Asa recognized the boy. His dad was a drunk. Even standing next to the fire, the boy was still cold. He took the child home and Lexie warmed him up. When he came back he was wearing a pair of warm socks. His shoes were back in the house drying out.

During the service Asa couldn't take his eyes off the boy's feet. The poor boy would have to walk home through the snow again. His shoes were falling apart. Asa remembered the kind man who had given him his first pair of shoes when he was a child. Surely somebody would help this boy.

Two people in the congregation were rich enough to help. Neither of them did. One lady drove off in her car before Asa had a chance to ask her if she would take the boy home. She lived near to his house and it would have been easy for her to help. But she didn't.

WE HAVE THE ANSWER

Lexie brought out the boy's shoes. She bent down to put them back on his feet. As she did so she glanced over at her own son's feet. They were the same size! She compared the shoes. They were warm and cozy. "Jimmie take your shoes off," she said.

Asa looked on. They had just had a baby and could not even afford clothes for the baby. How would they give away Jimmie's clothes? But he knew that he could not let the boy walk in the snow as he was.

"What will I do for shoes, Mama?" their son asked.

"You don't need them as badly as he does. Besides Jesus said 'Give and it will be given to you,' so Jesus will give you another pair."

Jimmie took his shoes off and gave them to the boy. Asa couldn't watch any more. He had to go and pray. "God, why didn't you get someone else to give them? You know we can't afford it." By the time he had finished praying he knew that they had done what God wanted them to do.

GOD SENDS THEM MONEY

The next morning a letter came in the mail. Inside was $20. "Mama, will there be enough there to buy me new shoes."

"There sure will," she smiled. Then she paused. Asa knew what she was doing. She was listening to God. He also knew what God was saying because God had just spoken to him too.

"Let's give half of it to our friend the evangelist," he said.

"Let's give ALL of it to him," she replied.

They both knew that God had spoken. They both knew that their friend really needed the money.

Asa rushed to the evangelist. "Here is $10," he said.

"I can't take that from you Ace," the man said. "I know how much you need the money yourself."

Asa was relieved. But then he knew he had done something wrong. God had told them to give it ALL to this man. He had only offered half.

"Please!" he cried out, "Please take it all. God told me to give you all $20. I have to do it."

The man smiled and started to praise God. It was just what he needed. If God wanted them to give it, then he knew God wanted him to take it. All that day Asa wondered how they would survive. All day they had peace because they knew that they had obeyed God.

The next morning another letter arrived in the post. Inside was a check for $50. Asa had never seen so much money. The note said, "I couldn't sleep tonight. God told me you would need this money in the morning. I planned to wait until then but God told me to get up and send it straight away."

They had given away a pair of shoes and $20 to people who really needed it. Now God had sent them $50. God had an even greater to gift to give them. The next Sunday a man staggered forward. He was the father of the boy with cold feet. As he came forward his friend joined him and several members of their family. All of them knelt and gave their lives to Jesus.

"Brother Allen, I hate preachers," the man said. "I always have. I've said all kind of bad things about you. But when my son came home last week I saw God's love for the first time. You took the shoes off your own son's feet and gave them to my son. I could stand it no longer. I had to come."

That Sunday Jimmie and the drunkard's son sat side by side. Jimmie held his feet out.

"Look at my new shoes," Jimmie said. "Mama said Jesus would give me new ones if I gave you mine and Jesus did it!"

Because of that one action many people were saved. That one act of love was bigger than any miracle of healing. That one action showed God to people who would never have come near a church. That one action also built up young Jimmie's faith as he learned that it is better to give things away than to receive.

CHAPTER 12

THE LIST IS NOT COMPLETE

A. A. Allen praying for the sick

LIFE CARRIES ON

Asa carried on serving God. Every four and a half years God moved him and his family on to start a new church.

Asa began travelling around the country to preach the Gospel. Life did not get much easier. Often they did not have much money. Asa travelled by himself and was away from his family for long periods at a time.

Back at home his children sometimes didn't even recognize him.

Other evangelists were stopping to get regular jobs. There was a war on and nobody could afford to look after them properly. But Asa kept going.

As he preached his voice felt tighter and tighter. Soon it was nearly impossible for him to preach. He definitely could not sing. He was only young and he had not done everything that God called him to do. He started to worry.

"I don't know how much longer I can do this for. If I can't speak I certainly can't preach." Every sermon he preached could have been his last one.

Finally he went to see a doctor. The doctor looked in his throat, "Preacher, your preaching days are over!" the doctor announced. "Your vocal chords are totally ruined. Find a job where you do not need to talk otherwise soon you won't be able to talk at all. Go and live in Arizona or somewhere dry and work for the defense department."

That was just what Asa feared. His preaching days were over. But Asa was not going to give up that easily. He went to see a second doctor. The doctor looked in his throat. "Preacher, your preaching days are over!" the doctor announced. "Your vocal chords are totally ruined. Find a job where you do not need to talk otherwise soon you won't be able to talk at all. Go and live in Arizona or somewhere dry and work for the defense department."

Asa went to see a third doctor. "Preacher, ..."

Asa interrupted him. "I know what you are going to say. But I am not going to stop preaching and I am not moving to Arizona. Nor am I going to work for the defense department. I will preach until I cannot talk and then I will write my sermons up on a board for people to read."

The doctor was amazed. How did Asa know what he was about to say? Asa didn't know who would want to listen to him. How could he preach about the sick being healed if he couldn't even talk himself! But he was not going to stop doing what God had called him to do.

As he walked home he was scared. The same fear he had felt as a child now started to take over his life again. What would happen in the future? The fear was so strong that he could hardly breathe.

At that moment a Bible verse popped into his head: 2 Timothy 1:7, "God has not given you a spirit of fear." So fear was a spirit.

He went to see a pastor. "Please pray for me and cast out the spirit of fear."

As the pastor prayed Asa was set free from fear. He started to praise God. As he praised, he found he could shout louder than he had shouted for months. God had healed him.

TORMENTED

Asa had been the pastor of a church for a while now. The church had doubled in size and they had built an extension to the building. God was really blessing them. Lexie was happy. Asa was not travelling around as much; they had a stable salary from the church and a nice home to live in. Their life was still busy as any pastor's home is, but at least their life was more normal.

Asa was not satisfied. Sure there were hundreds of people coming to the church, but there were millions of people who were not. If only he could reach all of them.

It was then that an idea popped into his head. Nearly every home had a radio. If he could speak on the radio loads more people could hear the Gospel. He raced to the church leaders and told them his plans. They felt tired just thinking about it.

"We've grown fast, pastor and that is good. Now let's take a bit of time to settle down. We don't think we should be doing any radio programs at this time."

Asa felt like he had been punched. He had so much desire to serve God and now he had been told no. Maybe they were right, but he wasn't happy. He started to sob uncontrollably. Sometimes he would cry out.

"He's having a break down," the leaders said when they saw him. "Let's pay for him to have a long holiday." They wanted their pastor to get better as soon as possible. Asa and Lexie drove to the mountains. All the way there Asa felt in pain. At night he could not sleep. When they got to a house in the middle of nowhere he could not rest.

"Let's go home and be around our people again," Asa said. And so they got in the car for the three day journey home. But it did not help! There was no way forward.

"I just feel so tormented. I wish I could sleep properly," Asa wept.

He was a grown man acting like a small child. He was a mess. Asa pulled the car over. Lexie turned to him. "Lexie, pray for me. Cast out this tormenting demon." Lexie put her hand on his shoulder and prayed, "In Jesus name I command you GO!" When she prayed he felt something disappear from his stomach.

For three whole days and three nights Asa slept and slept and slept. When he woke up he was ready to serve God again. He did not know what God had planned for him.

I MUST PROTECT MY FLOCK

"These men are making history."

Stories of a new breed of special preachers were going around the churches. Thousands were flocking to hear them preach. These men were not the best speakers ever, but when they prayed for the sick, the sick were healed! Asa read about them and laughed. There were stories of deaf people being healed and cancers falling out of bodies. Every known sickness was being healed.

"These people are a bunch of fanatics. They are religious loonies," he thought.

Asa had always preached that God could heal, but did God really heal people from cancer today? He had been told by God what he had to do if he wanted to see these miracles. In fact God had given him a whole list of things to do. But he had been so busy building a church that he had missed what God was doing in the rest of the church.

"These evangelists are probably just trying to get a crowd. It's only a publicity stunt," he thought to himself. "I must protect my people from these men."

When some of Asa's friends were going to a meeting, he decided to go along to see for himself. The evangelist was a man called Oral Roberts. As Asa walked into the tent he thought about the list God had given him. He still kept the list in the Bible and he had marked off every single item except the last two.

As Asa sat in the tent he was convicted by what he saw. Oral Roberts was doing what God had called Asa to do. Oral had obeyed God. Asa had not. He had not paid the price. He saw there watching the miracles and the crowds. His heart was stirred as he saw hundreds rush to the front in tears to give their lives to Jesus. At that moment Asa knew that this was not a fanatic. This was a man who was serving God. He was a man who wanted to see people saved.

Asa wept.

God spoke to him, "My son, eleven years ago you asked me to show you what you had to do to move in miracles. I showed you 13 things that you had to do. You have only done 11 of them. Eleven years ago I called you to the same ministry, but you have only done part of what I called you to do. I told you the price but you have not paid it. You have failed to do what I called you to do."

"I'll do it Lord, I am so sorry, I'll do it."

As soon as Asa got home he resigned his job as pastor. God had called him to preach the Gospel with signs and wonders. God had called him to be an evangelist. Asa was going to do what God had called him to do.

CHAPTER 13

THE REAL WORK BEGINS

Crowds at a service in Cuba

SIGN AND WONDERS

Asa looked out at the crowd. Last week he had left his church. This week God had opened the door for him to be an evangelist. All over the place pastors wanted him to come to them. God was moving across the nation. Now Asa was a part of that move. He was seeing more people healed than ever before. But still some people were going away disappointed.

One campaign took him to California. While he was in the middle of the campaign he took out the list to look at it again. There was only one thing left on it. He had tried but he could not beat it. He knew other pastors who struggled as he did, so he was no different from them, but he knew that God was calling him to live for him 100%. God had told him what he had to do. Surely he should be able to do it.

Asa spent time praying and finally gave the last area over to God. He took out a pen and crossed the last item off the list. He was ready.

As Asa went into the pulpit that night he knew that God was going to do something. God's presence was on the congregation like he had never seen it before. Night after night God came with his power. Many people were healed without anyone even praying for them. They sat in their seat and were instantly healed. Anyone watching could see the miracles.

Tumors fell off people. Crippled people were made whole. Goiters, swellings in the throat, disappeared. Blind people started to see. Not only that, but people came back night after night to tell what God had done. Some brought with them reports from their doctors and X-rays that proved that they had been healed.

Night after night people were healed, delivered and best of all more people than ever were getting saved. Asa had done what God had told him to do. Now God was doing what he promised he would do. Asa saw that some people needed help so that they would come ready to be healed. So he wrote a book to help people: God's guarantee to heal you. Thousands of people were healed as they read it.

ONWARD AND FORWARD

Asa was travelling more and more. Lexie longed to be with her husband, so they bought a trailer and travelled together. Their children were schooled in the trailer and travelled everywhere with their parents.

The more they travelled the bigger the crowds got. They realized that they needed a tent. They didn't tell anyone what they were thinking, instead they prayed about it.

One day a lady came to see Asa. "Brother Allen, God told me to give you this."

"What is it?" Asa asked.

"It's an offering that God told me to give you. It is to help you buy a large tent. Your ministry should not be limited to small buildings. God has shown me that you will preach to thousands at a time."

Asa was so excited; God had given him the first $600. He couldn't wait to share the news with the pastor of the church he was ministering in. That night Asa was surprised when the pastor stood up to take an offering. "God is telling Asa Allen to buy a tent, so let's give money to him to do that." Asa walked away from the meeting with another $500.

Asa never asked anyone for money, but people kept giving him money. Before long he had $1500. Now he just needed to find out how much a tent would cost.

"You'll need $6000, if you want it big enough to fit everyone in," a tent maker told him. "Don't forget you'll need to buy seats and a PA system too."

Asa knew they still had a long way to go. God had helped them so far. He was leading them. Surely, he would make a way for this to work. When Asa heard that a minister was selling a huge tent, complete with all the equipment he would need for only $8500 he knew God was in it.

But he still only had $1500.

Asa picked up the phone. "I've only got $1500, but you can have it all as the first payment for the tent."

The owner had been offered cash for the full amount from someone else, but he told Asa he would pray about it. The next morning the man called, "You can have the tent and all the equipment. Pay me $1500 now and $100 every night you use the tent until you've paid it all."

Asa was not surprised. After all if God wanted him to have it, it was his. Now all he needed was two large trucks to carry the equipment around. After he preached that night the crowd heard what he needed. One after another gave him money for the trucks. By the end of the meeting the trucks were paid for.

The A. A. Allen Revival Tent was ready for action. On July 4, 1951 in Washington DC Asa held his first tent meeting. The ministry was growing fast. Asa knew it needed a good structure to handle the money. He set up an organization and paid himself a small salary. Every other penny people gave him would go back to the ministry.

SPREADING THE GOOD NEWS

All through the summer of 1951 Asa preached and the tent was filled. He could not preach in the tent in winter, it would be too cold. If only he could take the tent to Latin America. It was warmer there and he longed to see many people saved. The only problem was that these people there were too poor to pay for the cost of the tent.

God knew what was on his heart. By the end of the summer God had given him enough money to pay for crusades through the winter. Asa and his tent set off for Havan in Cuba. That winter thousands of people came to Jesus.

The local priests were not happy, but the people were delighted to be meeting with the real Jesus. And so Asa had a pattern. In the summer months he travelled through North America. In winter he travelled to Cuba. But he still wanted to reach even more people.

Asa remembered his dream of preaching to people on the radio. It was time for that dream to become a reality. In November 1953 the Allen Revival Hour started on radio. In 1954 Asa was taking his tent around Cuba. As he travelled God spoke to him: "You reach people by radio in the United States, why don't you do the same here in Cuba."

And so his radio program was translated into Spanish and listened to across Cuba, the Caribbean and down into South America. By 1955 the radio station was on 17 Latin American stations and 18 American ones. The work was still growing.

CHAPTER 14

TO THE GLORY OF GOD

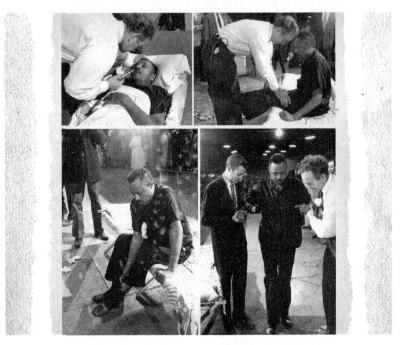

A man starts to walk after prayer

GOD IS REAL

So many people mock God. They don't believe he is there. Or if they do believe in him, they don't believe he can do anything to help them. God wants every single person to know about him. He loves people so much that he will do anything for them to see that he is God. He even sent his own son to die for us—that's how much God loves us!

There are some people who will never believe in God. Jesus said even if someone came back from the dead in front of them they would not believe in God. They know that if they believe in God then he will be in charge of their lives. They want to stay as god of their life. They don't want to give that up for God. If you talk to them they simply mock you.

But most people are waiting. They are waiting for someone to show them that God is real. If God is real, and we really are his followers, then miracles should follow us. After all Mark 16 tells us some of the signs that follow people who believe in God.

Miracles are great gifts from God because they point people to God. It's great when someone is healed because they are no longer in pain and suffering, but that's not the only reason God heals people. He wants people to see that he is real.

As we tell people about Jesus, God calls us not just to talk about Him, but to show Him to people by our love, by our lives and by His supernatural power. When people saw God working through Asa they could all see that God was alive and well and ready to help them. That's why thousands were saved in his meetings.

AMBULANCE MEN AMAZED

One man was brought to the miracle meetings by ambulance.

He was dying from lymphoma. He was so weak he could not even move. The doctors knew that it would not be long before he was dead.

The man did not want to die. He wanted to live. So he got the ambulance men to carry him into the service.

As Asa started to pray for him, the man felt strength flow through his body. By the time Asa had finished praying the man was jumping up from his bed and walking away.

The ambulance men could not believe it. When they brought him to the meeting he could not even sit up. When they took him home he sat in the front of the ambulance chatting to them the whole way home. He was perfectly healed.

BRAVE BOY BLEEDING

Little Timmie Dodge was just five years old. For two months now, he had bruises all over his body. His parents had 10 other children and none of them had needed a doctor before. They didn't think it could be serious. After all lots of boys get bruises as they play around.

Then Timmie started to bleed. Blood came out of his mouth and his nose. And it did not stop. Blood poured out for two hours at a time. Timmie's whole face went whiter and whiter as the blood left his body. His parents now knew something was seriously wrong.

That night he bled for four hours straight. Timmie needed a doctor. "Your child has thrombocytopenia. His blood can't clot," the doctor said. "Usually we can help people like this, but your son is too weak. He is going to die."

Timmie's parents were devastated. "Please give Timmie to me and I will look after him in the hospital," the doctor said. He was trying to be kind, but they needed more than kindness. They needed a miracle.

Rushing home they quickly found out where Asa was preaching. He was 1,800 miles. The whole family jumped into the car and started driving to him. As they drove Timmie started to bleed again.

"He needs a blood transfusion, or he is not going to make it to the meeting." his parents said. Let's stop and see another doctor. The other doctor could not help them.

"There is nothing that can be done to help him. Give him to me and I will look after him in the hospital until he dies."

The family did not want to give up on Timmie yet. They wanted God to save him. With 250 miles to go Timmie began bleeding once more. His whole body went pale and he almost passed out. But they kept going.

When they arrived he was still alive. They carried Timmie out of the car and burst into the tent. There was no meeting going on at that time. Asa was just about to leave. He prayed for Timmie and the bleeding stopped.

Timmie and his family were ready when the afternoon meeting began. He had bled so much that he was too weak to move. "Bring him onto the platform," Asa called. "We will pray for Timmie."

His small five year old body was easy to carry. Timmie's body seemed stiff as they carried him up. The whole congregation prayed for him. Three minutes later he sat up and spoke. "Please can I have an orange?"

Someone found an orange and Timmie ate it up! That night he was back in the meeting, sitting up and looking well. His parents stayed at the revival for the next few weeks. Timmie had been healed and they wanted everyone to see it.

Each night Asa looked over at Timmie. Soon his white face was a nice rosy pink color. A few days after he had been prayed for they took him to some doctors. They knew God had healed him, now they wanted the medical proof.

When the doctors had finished all their tests they smiled. "We can tell he did have thrombocytopenia, but there is no trace of it or any other illness in his body. It can only have been God that healed him."

CREATIVE MIRACLES

Mrs. Liscomb could hardly breathe. She had had TB and the doctors had found that one of her lungs had been destroyed. It was completely missing. The other lung was very badly damaged. Whenever she walked she had to stop every two steps to get her breath back. She could not do any work. She could not even bend down to pick up a piece of paper.

When she arrived at the tent, people had to help her fill in the card for healing. She was so out of breath. The stewards sat her in the emergency section and she waited. As people came forward to be prayed for, Mrs. Liscomb stood to pray for others. When she did she realized she could breathe. She did not have to fight for each breath. Her lungs were clear. BOTH her lungs were normal.

"I'm healed! Thank you, Jesus."

Mrs. Liscomb told everyone what God had done for her. Then she showed them by running around the tent. The lady who came in with half a lung left with two.

SUPERNATURAL SIGNS

But it wasn't just healings and salvations. God did lots of other miracles. Asa knew God could do miracles. Jesus fed 5000 people from one packed lunch and walked on the water. Jesus is still alive today and working through the church. Asa had seen God do miracles for himself. One time when he needed $300 God had turned $1 bills in his wallet into $20 bills. He wanted everyone else to know God is real.

Mrs. Alvester Williams was obese. As she sat in a healing service people watched her shrink. That night she lost 200 pounds in one go! That's the weight of a normal person. God had done a strange miracle in front of everyone.

In some meetings oil appeared on people's hand. Male and female, people from every race, children and adults all found oil on their hands. God was showing people that he could use anyone, not just the people who stood on a platform.

One evening a camera man was filming the oil that had appeared on his hands. As Asa lifted up one hand the camera man saw a bloody nail mark on the man's hand. Asa saw it too but God told him not to say anything for a few minutes. When he called for the man, the man had gone. The people had seen him, but he had completely disappeared.

They watched the film from the camera. It showed the man's hands, but the person's face could not be seen. Could it be that Jesus himself had stood with them? It seemed that God was doing more and more through Asa and his team. At every meeting people were healed, saved and set free to live for Jesus. Now it was time for the next stage of growth in the ministry.

CHAPTER 15

MIRACLE VALLEY

Inside a tent crusade

WE NEED A BASE

As people listened to the radio and came to the crusades there was more and more work to do. People wrote letter after letter asking for prayer. Asa started a newsletter to tell people what God was doing. Soon thousands of people wanted a copy each month.

It was clear that Asa needed to have a base. He was travelling all over the place, but he needed a new center to work from. A rancher gave him 1250 acres of land and Asa bought another 1250. Asa renamed the whole area Miracle Valley.

In the 1960s Asa built a church to seat 4000. He also built homes for his staff of 211 people and their families. Miracle Valley became a center for training missionaries and from there radio and television outreach could spread across the globe. The A. A. Allen ministry was now established and ready for the next stage.

MIRACLES BY RADIO

Gloria Macias had had warts all over her face since she was 8 years old. She was used to people staring at her and laughing at her, but she wanted to be free. One day she was listening to Asa on the radio with her family. When the program ended they looked at her. Your face is smooth. Your warts have gone. God had healed her.

Oscar Park had been very sick. He had cancer. Without an operation he would die. But the operation was very serious. Oscar had lost a toe because of the cancer. Now doctors cut out some of his lung, three of his ribs and some of his breast bone. They wanted to cut out every trace of cancer from his body. The doctors had saved his life.

One evening Oscar sat listening to the radio. Asa was preaching. "Reach out to God. He can do anything!"

As Oscar sat there he thought about his body. "God, when I come to you I want my body to be whole. Please can you sort my body out?" As he prayed, he reached over to the radio and put his hand on it. At that moment his chest bone, ribs and lung grew back.

The next morning when Oscar woke up he looked down at his feet. Both feet had five toes on. A new toe had grown overnight. Even the toenail on the new toe was perfect! God had done an amazing miracle.

On January 13th, 1952 Oscar went back to the surgeon who had cut out the cancer. It was only three months ago that he had had the operation.

"Can you do another X-ray of my chest please?" Oscar asked the surgeon.

"Sure," the surgeon said. But when the X-ray came he was puzzled. "I've either got the wrong X-ray or the wrong patient!" He knew he had cut out three ribs. No ribs were missing from the X-ray he was holding, so he took another X-ray. It was the same as the first one. The lungs were complete, the breast bone was all there and no ribs were missing.

"But we cut these out," the surgeon said. "I don't understand. They are all back again!"

Oscar understood. God had done a miracle. Doctors also knew he had a toe missing. But they could not argue with him when he took his socks off and showed them that his toe had now grown back.

GOD HEALS CHILDREN

Sammy was ten years old. He had polio.

Since that time his whole body had become useless. He could not even lift his head up by himself. Instead he had to wear special braces to hold his head in place. He had more braces on his legs. And the rest of his body was covered in leather and metal so that he could be kept standing.

His body was so twisted that he had to wear the braces all day. He even had to wear them when he slept at night. Sammy loved life. He just wanted to be able to run and join in with the other children when they played. When Sammy heard that Asa was coming near his town he wanted to go.

"Please let me go, Mum. I've heard about Asa, but I want to see him for myself."

So on March 24, 1959 Sammy went with a family friend to the meeting. When Asa got there, Sammy was ready to be prayed for. Asa picked him up and put him on his knee. Then he prayed, "God, come heal this child. I command this body to be whole in the name of Jesus."

Sammy felt something strange happening. For the first time ever all the pain had left him. He knew God had healed him. Sammy took the braces off with help from his friend. They used a screwdriver and pliers to get rid of the special shoes and the leather and metal around his body. Sammy stood up straight and walked across the platform. The crowd cheered—God had done a miracle.

When Sammy walked into his house he held his head up high. "How are you doing that? Where are you braces?" his mum asked. "How are you even walking?" She knew it was impossible for Sammy to walk without help. But with God all things are possible.

CHAPTER 16

CAUGHT IN THE ACT

A. A. Allen's tent from above

HE'S A DRUNK

Rumors started to go round the country.

Asa Allen was the son of a drunk. Now Asa Allen was a drunk. People heard of his past and nodded their head, "Of course it must be hard for him. We all have our demons that we have to fight. This must be his battle."

Sometimes it can be really hard to know what is true. Many people didn't believe the rumors. They knew that the devil will do anything to try and stop people from serving God. If he can't do that he will try to stop people from listening to servants of God. They saw this as a plot to ruin Asa's reputation. Other people believed the rumors. One thing was certain—his enemies were happy to help spread the rumors.

In the middle of the 1950s Asa was holding a crusade in Knoxville, Tennessee. Some of the pastors wanted Asa to hold the meeting in their church buildings. They knew that Asa would give them 10% of the offerings if the meetings were held in their church. They had big plans as to how they could use the money.

But because he held the meetings in an auditorium 10% of the offerings would be given direct to the denomination. They would not get any of the money they had hoped for. Every night Asa would drive himself and a couple of his workers to the auditorium ready for the meeting. Each night he would stop off at a café to have a glass of milk.

One night he stopped off as usual. Kent Rogers was with him in the car. "Rog, that milk tasted funny," Asa said. Kent shrugged, "Maybe it was sour."

Asa got in the car and started driving, but he felt really dizzy. "I better let someone else drive," and he pulled the car over to the side. At that moment the police arrived. When they tested him they found alcohol in his blood.

Amazingly the media and the pastors who were against him turned up with the police. What were they doing there? How did they know that Asa was about to be stopped by the police? Someone must have told them what was going to happen. Which means someone must have known it was going to happen.

Someone must have put something in his drink. Allen was given a ticket. The next day the newspapers screamed out their headlines: "Evangelist Allen was arrested for driving while drunk."

I'M CALLED TO PREACH NOT FIGHT

Allen could have stopped to fight, but he felt that the pastors only wanted to stop him. He was not going to be stopped from doing what God wanted him to do. Instead he paid the fine and carried on preaching the Gospel.

Asa wasn't drunk. His friend, Robert W. Schambach was in the car with Asa that night. Robert had been with Asa all evening. Robert was there when the police arrested. Robert was very clear, "he has not been drinking all night. If he had done I would have seen him."

When the police arrested Asa that was the final straw. The Assemblies of God could not take it anymore. They asked Asa to stop preaching. "I'm not going to stop preaching the Gospel. Thousands of people are dying without Jesus. I'm not going to stop preaching just because of this little thing. If you won't let me preach then I will leave your denomination."

They did not change their mind. Asa left them. God kept blessing the ministry and it kept on growing.

In 1968 they received 216,000 letters a day from 90 countries. 9,000 people were ordained ministers by Asa's ministry. 340,000 copies of the miracle magazine were sent out each month. 58 radio stations and 43 television stations showed his weekly broadcasts. Asa had been to 24 cities in America and two in the Philippines that year. God was doing much through him.

All this came at a great cost.

PERSECUTION AND SEPARATION

"I don't imagine that people are persecuting me everywhere I go," Asa explained. "But what else can you call it? So many times people have tried to destroy my ministry and stop me from preaching. It is persecution."

Wherever he went it seemed like the newspapers would write against him. Governments tried to slow him down with extra paper work. They accused him of not paying enough tax. Local leaders tried to persuade radio and television stations to stop showing his programs.

But Asa kept on fighting. He did not give up.

He started to speak out against certain churches and he focused more on giving money to God as his ministry grew. Asa raised lots of money. Some people thought he loved money, they did not know that he put it all back into the ministry. He didn't even own miracle valley, it all belonged to the ministry.

Was he being pulled away from what God had called him to do? Or was this a new phase of his ministry?

In 1967 Asa and Lexie stopped living together. God was using Asa, but his marriage was falling apart. It was a sad day for those who followed his ministry. Something bigger was about to happen in Asa's life that would get the whole of the church and some of the world talking. Asa would never know how it would affect people on earth. By the time people heard about it he would be dead.

CHAPTER 17

THE LAST DAYS OF HIS LIFE

A. A. Allen waves goodbye

TRAGEDY STRIKES

By 1969 Asa was not well. He had arthritis in his knee and was always in pain. Sometimes the pain was so bad that he asked others to take the meetings for him. Asa knew that he could not carry on like this. He went to the doctors and asked them to help him. When they suggested he should have an operation, Asa eventually agreed.

On June 11, 1970 Asa went to San Francisco. He had had one operation. He was going to see his doctor the next morning to see if he needed more surgery. Asa checked into his hotel around lunch time. He settled into his room. That evening he called a friend. Nobody knows what Asa said, but his friend was worried.

He rushed over to Asa's hotel. When he got there he spoke to the hotel manager. The manager got a spare key and they rushed up to Asa's room. When they walked in they found Asa sitting in front of the television. He was not breathing. That night, at 11:23 he was pronounced dead.

Strong medicines were scattered around the room. The coroner opened up Asa's body and did lots of tests. No drugs or medicine were in his blood. But he did have lots of alcohol. On his death certificate Asa died from a heart attack. Around his liver were fatty deposits caused by alcohol.

When you add this to the report of drink driving years earlier, it looks like Asa Allen died like his dad had—an alcoholic. It got everyone talking. "He had been an alcoholic when he was younger, it looks like he was never healed," some said.

"Is that why he didn't turn up to so many meetings in the last few years," other commented. "When you drink too much it makes you miss things you know."

"Did you know they found drugs all over his room? His friend Don Stewart cleaned them all up before anyone got there."

"He was only 59 years old. Just shows how dangerous alcohol is."

How do you think people felt? Many people had been saved as he preached the Gospel. Others had been healed. Now it seemed that the man who had helped them meet Jesus was an alcoholic.

But that's not the only version around.

THE LAST DAYS OF HIS LIFE (VERSION 2)

God had obviously used Asa loads in his life. Those closest to him said he never touched alcohol and he never smelt of it. They simply did not believe the reports.

In fact their version was very, very different.

We won't really know which is the true version, but a lot of things about the story of his death that you have just read didn't make sense to his friends. This is what they said happened.

Asa had been suffering from arthritis. His doctors had given him strong medicine to help with the pain. The doctor gave Asa very dangerous medicines to take. With these medicines you could end up needing more and more of them. Asa hated the medicines. They made him feel drowsy and stopped him from thinking clearly.

If you use these medicines with alcohol it is very dangerous. No doctor would give these medicines to someone who drank too much. Doctors are very good at telling who drinks too much. Alcoholics can hide their drink problem from their family sometimes, but not from their doctors. Even by looking at a person's hands they can tell if someone is drinking too much alcohol!

Asa had drunk lots as a child and a young adult. He had been brought up in a house full of alcohol. Now he used alcohol to take away the pain. Many other people used alcohol in the same way. In fact the doctors did not find the liver full of disease. Anyone who drinks lots of alcohol for a long time will start to kill their liver. Doctors call this cirrhosis. Asa's liver did not have cirrhosis.

Instead there were some fatty deposits around the liver. This is what happens when you drink lots of alcohol in a short period of time. When you stop drinking the fat goes away again.

So the doctors found that Asa had been drinking a lot for a short time. This agrees with Asa's friends' story—he had been using it to take away pain. We know he hadn't taken the medicines because when the coroner checked his blood he did not find any medicine there.

Asa was not an alcoholic; he was a man in a lot of pain. Asa was flying to see his doctor. He was desperate because he was in so much pain and he drank so much alcohol that he died. We don't know why God didn't heal his pain, but we do know that he was suffering.

IS SOMEONE TRYING TO SET HIM UP?

After he died lots of stories went around. Many people said that the room was full of empty bottles. But those who had found Asa did not find any bottles.

The story that Don Stewart had cleaned up drugs from his room surprised all his staff as they knew that Don was not in the same town as Asa. If he had been using other drugs the coroner would have found it in his blood. But he didn't.

When the friend went in with the hotel manager, they both found Asa together and called a doctor immediately.

How could any friend have cleaned up the room without the manager noticing?

In 1972, a couple of years after he had died a very strange thing happened. One lady was working in Miracle Valley. She was opening letters when out of one fell a check for $10,000. The check was not for the Allen ministry. It was for the person who had sent it.

The lady thought it must be a mistake until she read the letter.

"I was the coroner who examined Asa A. Allen after he died. I want to ask you to forgive me. I told lies to the media. I told them that he died from acute alcoholic poisoning which caused him to have liver damage. I am sending this check that was given to me to tell these lies. Please forgive me."

The check had been written by a group of churches who did not like Asa Allen. The lady gave the letter and the check to the directors. They read the letter and decided that one of them should go and meet the coroner. Before they could go to see him, the coroner was dead. He had killed himself.

Now they were not sure what to do. They got on well with the people from the other churches now. On Asa's death certificate it said he had a heart attack. They did not think the rumors of him drinking would carry on. So they decided not to do anything more about it.

Even today we still have these different stories about his death. Remember no one really knows what happened. The story from his friends seems to fit the facts we do know for sure. We know that men who serve God do mess up sometimes.

We also know that the enemy wants to shame men of God so that he can shame God. He loves to make up lies to make God's people look bad and so keep sinners away from God.

What we do know is that God used Asa in his life to lead many people to Jesus and to do great miracles.

ASA WAS A HUMAN BEING

Asa Allen made lots of mistakes in his life. But God still used him. God spoke to Asa and told him what he needed to do. But it took Asa years before he did it. Asa had a lot of fear, but he didn't let his fears stop him from serving God.

Near the end of his life he spent a lot of time talking about how bad other people were. Near the end of his life he was becoming bitter against other people. He should have put all of his energy into helping people meet with God instead of tearing people down. God calls us to love our enemies. At the end of his life Asa didn't seem to be doing that.

But we can learn from his successes and his mistakes. When God asks you to do something do it. Don't wait a week, act straight away. When you step out for God people will try and stop you and attack you. That's what they did to Asa. Jesus said this would happen to us in John 15:20: "Remember what I told you: 'A servant is not greater than his master.' If they persecuted me, they will persecute you also."

You don't need to worry about this. Instead we need to trust God. Almighty God knows what he is doing with our lives. Our job is to follow Him. If you make mistakes put your focus back on to God. Asa was not a superhuman. He was a human being just like Elijah and King David and the apostle Paul. He was a human being just like you.

If God can use all these people, God can use you too. He is just looking for people who are willing to pay the price to follow Him. When Asa paid the price, as God told him to, he started to see amazing miracles happen through his life. Many people were helped to find God and were set free to follow Him. God can use you to do supernatural things to help people know God.

Are you willing? What is God asking you to do today to follow him?

Don't worry about what has happened in the past, but decide to aim to follow God with all your heart today and into the future.

BIBLE STUDY FOR YOUNG GENERALS

Read Luke 6:39-40

1. If we follow someone who is not following God where will we end up (verse 39)?
2. Who is the teacher that we are following?
3. Write a long list of what Jesus is like (make sure these are not your own ideas but they are based on what the Bible tells us he is like)?
4. In what ways was Asa like Jesus?
5. In what ways would you like to become more like Jesus?
6. Think about how we can be trained to be more like him?

A. A. ALLEN —ACTIVITY SECTION

REMEMBER THE BOOK

How much of the story can you remember? Test your memory by answering these questions.

Answers are given on page 118.

1. Where did Asa receive the gift of tongues?
2. What did Asa and Lexie do when, after two weeks of preaching, nobody was responding to the Gospel?
3. How many people were saved the next day?
4. How many things were on the list that God gave to Asa?
5. What did Asa do when he saw a boy whose shoes were falling apart?
6. What was Asa's book on healing called?

CHOOSE THE RIGHT ANSWER

Answers are given on page 118.

1. What was Asa's childhood like?
   A. Very happy
   B. Okay
   C. Awful

2. How quickly did Asa stop drinking and smoking after he met Jesus?
   A. Immediately
   B. After one month
   C. After a year

3. How old was Asa when he first ran away from home?
   A. 5
   B. 11
   C. 14

4. What happened in Asa's home on Saturday nights when he was a young man?
   A. Bible studies
   B. Parties
   C. He watched TV

5. In what year did Asa hold the first tent meeting?

    A. 1934

    B. 1945

    C. 1951

6. What did Asa use to tell people about what Jesus was doing?

    A. A newsletter

    B. The radio

    C. Television

ANSWERS

1. In a Pentecostal camp, 2. They stayed up all night to pray, 3. Twenty-three, 4. Thirteen, 5. He gave his son's only pair of shoes, 6. God's guarantee to heal you.

1. C, 2. A, 3. B, 4. B, 5. C, 6. A, B & C.

AROUND THE WORLD

A. A. Allen travelled around America a lot. Time yourself to find out how quickly can you find these places in America *in the order they are written.* Can you spot the one place that is not in America?

1. Arkansas
2. Idaho
3. Cuba
4. Texas

5. Arizona
6. California
7. Colorado
8. Tennessee

Write down your times here.

Date	Time Taken

PUZZLE IT

Find the names of all 12 people in the 'God's Generals for kids' series in the grid below. Their first name and family name will be near to each other. Choose a different color to color in each person's name. Have you read the whole series?

1. Kathryn Kuhlman
2. Smith Wigglesworth
3. John Dowie
4. Maria Woodworth-Etter
5. Evan Roberts
6. Charles Parham
7. William Seymour
8. John Lake
9. Aimee Semple McPherson
10. William Branham
11. Jack Coe
12. A. A. Allen

C	K	A	T	H	R	Y	N	M	A	R	I	A	W
H	U	W	L	J	O	H	N	C	E	T	U	I	O
A	H	I	S	L	A	K	E	P	L	O	O	M	O
R	L	G	K	O	N	L	Y	H	T	O	J	E	D
L	M	G	E	D	S	U	S	E	M	P	L	E	W
E	A	L	J	O	H	N	S	R	T	H	E	O	O
S	N	E	N	W	E	W	H	S	W	O	B	E	R
P	A	S	M	I	T	H	G	O	I	W	J	A	T
A	A	W	N	E	O	U	R	N	L	I	A	F	H
R	A	O	A	I	T	H	A	N	L	L	C	O	E
H	L	R	O	B	E	R	T	S	I	L	K	D	T
A	L	T	M	A	V	K	E	S	A	I	I	T	T
M	E	H	B	R	A	N	H	A	M	A	P	E	E
R	N	F	E	C	N	T	S	E	Y	M	O	U	R

When you have found all the names, write down the remaining letters below, reading from left to right. Start in the top left-hand corner of the grid.

Answer is given on page 124.

— — —   — —   — — — —   — — — —

— —   — — — —   — — —   — — —

— — —   — — — — —   — — —

— — — —   — — —   — — — — —

— —   — — — — — — __. (Hebrews 12:2)

FIND IT OUT

Regrow leftovers. When it feels like we have nothing but rubbish left in our life, God can turn it into something good. See if you can use these leftovers to grow new plants.

1. Green Onions

Cut the green onion to leave around 2 inches by the white root base (you can use what you cut off in your food). Place the root base in a glass with enough water to completely cover the base and place it on a sunny windowsill. Cut off what you need as they'll grow back fast.

2. Celery

Chop off the base of the celery and rinse it in water. Place the base in a bowl of warm water on a sunny windowsill. Change the water every couple of days and keep the top of the base moist. Leaves will start to grow in the middle of the plant.

3. Basil

Take a few stems from a basil plant. They should be around 4 inches long. Remove all the leaves from the stem except for the ones at the top of the stem. Put the stems in a glass of water and place in a sunny spot. Change the water every other day. Roots will form after a few days. Once the roots start to grow, transfer the plants to some soil and watch them grow.

4. Garlic

Take one clove of garlic into a container full of soil. Bury the garlic to twice its depth. Water well and wait.

ANSWE TO PUZZLE IT

Let us look only to Jesus, the One who began our faith and makes it perfect. (Hebrews 12:2)

QUESTIONS TO THINK ABOUT

1. What were the differences between the way the different plants grew?
2. What did all the plants need to grow?
3. What do we need to grow spiritually?

FOR FURTHER RESEARCH

Find out what other vegetables you can grow from scraps.

YOUR TURN

Hebrews 12:1 tells us that, because we are surrounded by people who have lived their lives fully for God, we should do the same.

Who has encouraged you to live fully for God?

1. People from the Bible. (You can read about some of these people in Hebrews 11).
2. People from the God's Generals for Kids series.

3. Members of your family or church.
4. Other people whose stories encourage you to follow God more.

Get hold of photos or pictures for each of these people and create a picture collage out of them. Put the collage up in your room to encourage you to keep living for Jesus.

GET CREATIVE

Imagine you are A. A. Allen and you are about to hold a crusade in a town that you have never been to before. Create a poster to put up around the town to tell people that you are coming and what you are expecting God to do.

AUTHORS' NOTE TO READERS AND PARENTS

Like A. A. Allen, I believe that God can cure people miraculously today. I do not believe that this is the only way that God will work. God gives wisdom and knowledge to us to help us fight disease. Medicine continues to advance and medical care can actually be part of God's plan for bringing relief and healing to His people. However, medicine still does not hold all the answers. I am in favor of both competent medical treatment and the power of prayer. I would not encourage anyone to neglect either of these at their time of need.

BIBLIOGRAPHY

Asa A. Allen, *The Price Of Go♦'s Miracle Working Power* (Public Domain)

Asa A. Allen, Miracle Magazine: Various editions of magazine (Dallas, TX: A. A. Allen Revivals inc, 1955-1958 and Hereford, AZ: A. A. Allen Revivals inc, 1958-1965)

Paul Asa Allen, *In The Sha♦ow Of Greatness: Growing Up "Allen"* (Tuscon, AZ: Paul Asa Allen, 2008)

John W. Carver, *The Life An♦ Ministry Of A. A. Allen as Tol♦ By A. A. & Lexie Allen* (Westminster, MD: Faith Outreach International Publishing 2010)

David Edwin Harrell Jr., *All Things Are Possible: The Healings An♦ Charismatic Revivals In Mo♦ern America* (Bloomington, IN: Indiana University Press 1978)

Roberts Liardon, *Go♦'s Generals: Why They Succee♦e♦ An♦ Why Some Faile♦* (Tulsa, OK: Whitaker House 1996)

AUTHORS' CONTACT INFORMATION

ROBERTS LIARDON

Roberts Liardon Ministries, United States office:

P.O. Box 781888, Orlando, FL 32878

E-mail: Info1@robertsliardon.org

www.robertsliardon.org

United Kingdom/European office:

Roberts Liardon Ministries

22 Notting Hill Gate, Suite 125

London W11 3JE, UK

OLLY GOLDENBERG

BM Children Can, London WC1N 3XX, UK

info@childrencan.co.uk

www.childrencan.co.uk

GOD'S GENERALS FOR KIDS (SERIES)
Roberts Liardon & Olly Goldenberg

This series has been growing in popularity and it focusses on the lives and teachings of great Christian leaders from times past. These books are written for children between the ages of eight and twelve. Newly released and enhanced, each book now includes an updated study section with cross curricular themes, suitable for home schooling groups. Kathryn Kuhlman (Vol. 1), and Smith Wigglesworth (Vol. 2) begin the series. Also available: John Alexander Dowie, Maria Woodworth-Etter, Evan Roberts, Charles Parham, William Seymour, John G. Lake, Aimee Semple McPherson, William Branham, Jack Coe and A.A. Allen.

EVIDENCE BIBLE
Ray Comfort

Apologetic answers to over 200 questions, thousands of comments, and over 130 informative articles will help you better comprehend and share the Christian faith.

ISBN: 9780882705255

SCIENTIFIC FACTS IN THE BIBLE
Ray Comfort

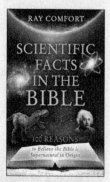

Most people, even Christians, don't know that the Bible contains a wealth of incredible scientific, medical, and prophetic facts. That being so, the implications are mind boggling.

ISBN: 9780882708799

HOW TO KNOW GOD EXISTS
Ray Comfort

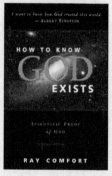

Does God exist, or does He not? In this compelling book, Ray Comfort argues the case with simple logic and common sense. This book will convince you that belief in God is reasonable and rational—a matter of fact and not faith.

ISBN: 9780882704326

SCHOOL OF BIBLICAL EVANGELISM
Ray Comfort & Kirk Cameron

This comprehensive study offers 101 lessons on thought-provoking topics including basic Christian doctrines, cults and other religions, creation/evolution, and more. Learn how to share your faith simply, effectively, and biblically... the way Jesus did.

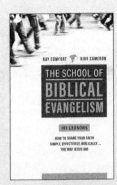

ISBN: 9780882709680

WAY OF THE MASTER STUDENT EDITION
Ray Comfort & Allen Atzbi

Youth today are being inundated with opposing messages, and desperately need to hear the truth of the gospel. How can you reach them? Sharing the good news is much easier than you think... by using some timeless principles.

ISBN: 9781610364737

FOR A COMPLETE LIST OF BOOKS, TRACTS, AND VIDEOS BY RAY COMFORT, SEE

LIVINGWATERS.COM

BEAUTY FROM ASHES
Donna Sparks

In a transparent and powerful manner, the author reveals how the Lord took her from the ashes of a life devastated by failed relationships and destructive behavior to bring her into a beautiful and powerful relationship with Him. The author encourages others to allow the Lord to do the same for them.

Donna Sparks is an Assemblies of God evangelist who travels widely to speak at women's conferences and retreats. She lives in Tennessee.

www.story-of-grace.com

www.facebook.com/
donnasparksministries/

www.facebook.com/
AuthorDonnaSparks/

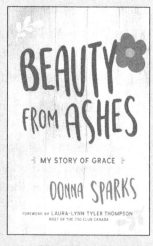

ISBN: 978-1-61036-252-8

ALSO AVAILABLE FROM BRIDGE-LOGOS

ALL THE WILD PEARLS
Heather DeJesus Yates

Every pearl has a story to tell. Join lawyer, speaker and author Heather DeJesus Yates as she creatively guides our generation through the transformational hope of the Gospel using both her own redemptive stories and those of an unlikely companion...a wild oyster.

Heather DeJesus Yates is a wife, mama, business owner, speaker, blogger, occasional lawyer and legislative advocate, and author. Out of a passion to see women walk in freedom from shame, Heather woos women into God's wide love through her disarmingly real-life stories, balanced with Gospel-centered hope.

Facebook: @amotherofthousands
Instagram: @amotherofthousands
Pinterest: @amotherofthousands.
www.facebook.com/amotherofthousands
www.amotherofthousands.com

ISBN: 978-1-61036-991-6

BRIDGE-LOGOS

OUR GOOD FATHER
Pierre M. Eade

Jesus said, "No one knows the Son except the Father, and no one knows the Father except the Son". He went on to give one exception, "and those to whom the Son chooses to reveal him."

If you desire a revelation of God the Father, you only have one place you need to go, listen to his son Jesus. Our Good Father takes the words of Jesus to bring a fresh understanding to the person of God the Father. Through the use of personal stories, analogies and humor, Our Good Father uses the words of Jesus to paint a picture of the true nature of God.

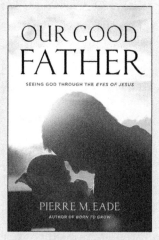

ISBN: 9781610361774

Printed in Great Britain
by Amazon

43368360R00086

LET ME TELL YOU M

Revd Neville Barker Cryer

First published 2009

ISBN 978 0 85318 329 7

All rights reserved. No part of this book may be reproduced or transmitted in
any form or by any means, electronic or mechanical, including photocopying,
recording or by any information storage and retrieval system, without
permission from the Publisher in writing.

© Neville Barker Cryer 2009

Published by Lewis Masonic

an imprint of Ian Allan Publishing Ltd,
Hersham, Surrey KT12 4RG.
Printed by Ian Allan Printing Ltd,
Hersham, Surrey KT12 4RG

Code: 0908/B

Visit the Lewis Masonic website at www.lewismasonic.com

CONTENTS

Introduction

When a Polish Freemason wrote to me recently from Warsaw, with thanks for the opportunity of reading the previous two books in this Craft series, I was newly reassured. This was just the kind of help that I had hoped to provide to fellow Masons. It was rewarding to learn, as I did from this recently raised brother, that not only did he now better understand what he had experienced during these three degrees but he would also enjoy them more because he could grasp what he was taught by the more surprising parts of the ceremonies.

Readers might be forgiven for thinking that by now I had covered all the subjects that Masons in their early years in the Craft might find relevant to their progress. What I am finding is that it is not only newer Masons but those with some decades of experience who appreciate whatever light I try to shine on what might be considered very well-known passages or customs in Freemasonry.

Indeed, many of the subjects included in the present collection are there precisely because they are so well-known. About half of what you can read here is the result of that common query: "We mention this constantly but what is it all about?"

Understanding what we are asked to learn, or invited to do, in our ceremonies is not merely for the benefit of being better informed. It also helps us to be more effective and believable in our delivery, even more animated in our performance. When we can see clearly the point of what we are doing this creates a new atmosphere in our meetings. Instead of just going through our time-worn ceremonies or repeating well-worn phrases we can begin to inject a fresh expectancy and drama into our degrees. Knowing why we prepare candidates as we do – and have done so for nearly four centuries – appreciating why we do have a second degree, knowing where Wardens come from and who Hiram Abiff represents and really was can, I believe, inject new interest in Masonic ritual for ourselves as well as our candidates and guests.

It is for these reasons, as well as others that you may discover for yourself, that I have the pleasure and the privilege of presenting *Let Me Tell You More.*

Preparing the Candidate for Initiation

For many of us, the preparation of a candidate for his entry into a Lodge is something that we have either completely forgotten since it happened to us, or have begun to so take for granted that it requires a real effort of memory to consciously recall just what was involved. Whilst that may often not be a matter of great importance because we have an efficient Tyler or a Past Master who supervises the preparation admirably, there is still one aspect of this important part of our practice that ought to matter to us.

By this I mean the understanding of why this preparation was done in the first place and why it is done in this particular manner. When we tackle this subject we shall find not only that we will better recall what has to be done but will also be able to explain it to anyone who still has questions about it. After all, if the preparation is important we ought to be able to explain why it takes place, and in this manner, whilst if it is not important then we ought not to be doing it anyway.

So let us look at the six points that make up a true preparation of a Candidate for Freemasonry on the occasion of his Initiation. They are:

1. *His being deprived of all metal objects.*
2. *The rearrangement of his clothing.*
3. *The provision of a sandal or slipper.*
4. *His being blindfolded.*
5. *Having a cable tow placed around his neck.*
6. *His encounter with a sharp instrument.*

We shall consider each of these actions in turn, looking at both the origin of their adoption and also the purpose which they currently serve in teaching a Mason about the Society that he is now about to join.

1. Making sure that the Candidate has neither metal nor valuable items on his person. This is one item of his preparation about which mention will be made in the ceremony that follows and hence it may seem to need less explanation than the others.

What is behind it, however, can only be fully appreciated when we recognise the situation in which this practice first appeared in Freemasonry.

It was in the days of a Mason's Guild Lodge when the Candidates were those who were not ordinary working men but Freemen of a city or borough and who qualified as Fellows of some trade. They were, because of that very status in society, men who already had the means to run a business, could employ apprentices and qualify for the offices of government in the local community. We are not with men in the setting of a working lodge on a building site but in a finely furnished room of a guildhall or better-class inn.

These men come in some of their best clothing expecting to be admitted to what they are sure is the company of their equals, who are also the established tradesfolk of the locality. They already know that to join this company is a not inexpensive business and they are prepared and able to pay their dues. They have therefore to learn an early lesson. Entry to Freemasonry is not something you can buy. If you are to be admitted to this Fraternity the most important asset is yourself and not your bank balance, your jewellery or your gold watch. It is therefore essential that on your initial entry to a Lodge, you should be seen to be "*without your normal possessions*" and relying on your own character, as a man "*of good report*", for your acceptance.

There is also something else.

Just as you cannot buy your way into this company, neither can you force your way into it. If you were accustomed to wear a sword or carry a dagger, as a gentleman might by the latter 17th century, then this too has to be removed so that you will not be tempted to rely on that part of your normal attire to assist your entry.

It is when we consider this background to our practice that we fully appreciate the words at the North-East corner: "*to evince to the Brethren that you had neither m...y nor m...c substance about you, for if you had, the ceremony of your initiation thus far, must have been repeated*".

We can now see why this procedure is essential, because any variation in this requirement casts doubt over the attitude with which a Candidate has entered our midst.

2. In considering the rearrangement of an applicant's clothing we touch, of course, on what is generally regarded as the most unusual, as well as the most distinctive, aspect of becoming a Freemason.

The outside world may see fit to use this part of our preparation as a ground for trivialising our whole involvement, and there may well be moments when we ourselves pause to wonder whether such a procedure is really necessary. Indeed, unless we again appreciate what is behind such a requirement as having an open shirt, a bared knee and a cord to retain our trousers, if a metal belt or braces are denied, we might well think that this is a requirement too far. Whilst, of course, most outsiders do not have the benefit of knowing what happens with a bared breast and a bared knee, the origin of how we come, somewhat dishevelled, to the door of our Lodge room is much more important.

What we are being asked to represent here is a working mason of the late Middle Ages. He came to work with an open shirt, knee breeches and a cord around his waist and it is that impression which the Candidate is now to offer.

May I remind you that when, in what were now ex-guild Lodges, Candidates who had not been apprentices in the stonemasons' trade presented themselves, the working masons present required that the least that the Candidate could do was to come in the age-old manner of working mason apprentices.

It is this that we now attempt to reproduce.

Because in the first Accepted Lodges there was only one ceremony and one obligation, the Candidates came with both knees bare, representing the normal condition of his dress. It was only later that the idea of dividing up the ceremonies led to one leg being exposed in the Entered Apprentice degree and the other in the Fellow Craft.

If we are ever challenged in future about the apparently strange dress arrangement when we entered Freemasonry, a short history lesson may be in order.

3. Yes, but you may be wondering why, if what I have just said is true, do we have this next preparation of a slipper on one foot?

Surely, this has nothing to do with the way in which working masons were dressed?

No, it hasn't. This practice was begun in the days when there was a Lodge attached to the mason's trade guild. This was from the time of Queen Elizabeth I when what we call "symbolic ritual" was beginning to be created. All this early ritual was based on stories and events taken from the Bible which, let us remember, was now translated into what was then modern English and was much more available for families, schools and individuals to read.

The story from which this incident of a slipper comes is in the Book of Ruth, which, by the way, was also the portion at which the Bible was eventually opened when a Lodge met in a separate Apprentice degree. It was also the book that spoke about Boaz, which was again appropriate as that was the eventual password for the First Degree.

The story goes that when Boaz decided to take Ruth as part of his family he made his way to the gate of the town where the heads of the families traditionally met. There he took off one of his slippers and handed it to the head of the family of Naomi, in which Ruth had become a member. When the head of the family accepted the slipper of Boaz, it meant that he approved of the person named leaving her present family and joining that of the person to whom the slipper belonged.

So Ruth became the wife of Boaz, or probably one of his wives.

A slipper given was the permit to join another family and that is what now happens to a Candidate. The Lodge hands over a slipper and the Candidate by accepting it agrees to become the member of his new family, the Lodge.

The slipper also means something else, as some early rituals show.

The question was once asked: "*What is that which you are wearing?*" The answer was: "An old shoe of my mother's" and the meaning of that exchange was that the Candidate was recognising that from the start of his Masonic career he was indebted to his Mother Lodge for something needed in his Initiation.

He is at once reminded of the bond that is being formed between him and his new Masonic family.

You can now see that what we do by way of preparation is not just playing at games or haphazard. It all has a meaning but unless we understand that meaning it may seem pure foolishness.

That is why people outside Masonry are so puzzled at grown men doing such things.

4. The reason why the Candidate is also hoodwinked or blindfolded follows naturally from what has just been said.

It is true that some say that the blindfold is necessary so that the Candidate should not see the interior of a Lodge, or the members gathered there, before he has committed himself by an obligation to confidentiality.

That may have been one of the original reasons, though nowadays, when possible candidates are invited to Ladies Evenings or meetings with the Lodge members and ladies present for a lecture, that is hardly a good enough reason for the continuing practice.

The main reason for a blindfold is so that from the very outset we can both test and create the Candidate's full reliance and trust in persons whom he cannot see and almost certainly cannot know.

The Candidate is asked, at the very outset of his journey into the Lodge, in whom he puts his trust. The answer expected, and which this author believes should be able to be given freely and without prompting, is "In God". Yet, we cannot see God and our very trust is therefore being tested.

In exactly the same way, the Worshipful Master tells the Candidate that he may with confidence follow his leader, whom he cannot see, and nothing will happen that he need be afraid of.

This is the first step in becoming a trusting member of the same Lodge that has given him his slipper. Even before many words are spoken we are teaching our Candidate the lesson of what being a Brother really means.

5. He also has a cable tow placed around his neck. Here, we may feel a little more certain as to what this is meant to teach. After all, there will be a moment before long when the Worshipful Master explains that such an item around his neck "would have rendered any attempt at retreat equally fatal".

Yes, it is true that the cord around his neck does link up with the old type of penalty, which is not now administered but only explained.

What interests me is that it is not called a rope, a cord or a halter. It is called a cable tow, which is a maritime term and seems so out of place in a society, which derives from men who built structures on land.

Medieval masons used ropes and cords for moving stones and halters for their cart animals, so why should we now have a cable tow put around the neck of an Apprentice Freemason?

The answer is very significant.

It connects with the same reasoning behind the use of doves on the top of most Deacons' wands. What we see here is a very ancient connection with the Bible story of Noah and the Ark. Without going into great detail, we should know that ancient Freemasons were called the sons of Noah because all the knowledge acquired by Adam was supposed to have been kept in the Ark when the Flood came, and so those who were able to receive the ancient knowledge were the sons of Noah after the flood subsided.

The idea of the Ark as the ship that carried all those who obeyed and trusted God to safety was strongly believed in the Middle Ages. That is why the main part of the church buildings that masons constructed was called a nave, which comes from the Latin word for a ship.

Moses too created an Ark to contain the things that conveyed divine knowledge, which brought the Israelites from Egypt in safety, and that Ark was placed in King Solomon's temple.

Perhaps you can now see the connection with us as Freemasons.

The idea of Noah as the father of knowledge and trust in God, was thus continued. That is why we have a cable tow from his Ark and why, also, the old form of the penalty spoke of being buried in the sands of the sea, a cable tow's length from the shore. The cable tow around the neck of the new Mason is to teach him that he is setting out on a journey into the unknown, as Noah did and if he should fail then he will be lost at sea.

The doves of Noah on the top of the Deacons' wands are meant to be messengers of hope and new information for the members of a Masons' Lodge.

6. As he enters the Lodge room for the first time, the candidate is gently prodded with the point of a sharp object.

This is part of another ancient practice which required that any Candidate for the trade of a mason had to have all his faculties. To test these faculties we ask first whether the Candidate can see anything.

We test his hearing by asking a question and making knocks. We know he can walk because he is asked to follow his leader and we know he can feel, because we now touch his flesh.

In older days, as in some Scottish Lodges still, he would have smelt incense on the central pedestal. Thus is his preparation complete. He is clearly a "FIT and proper person" to be admitted into a Lodge of Brother Masons whom he can trust and who trust him.

The practices we follow are not meaningless or odd. They are ancient and significant. Let us keep them but let us also explain them.

What do I say after my Initiation to those who ask about it?

No one should be surprised that you, members of my family or friends, want to know what happened to me this evening (or today, if a daylight Lodge).

What may surprise you to learn is that until quite recently it was expected that a new member would say nothing to anyone about the experience. All that is now changing and so I am able and glad to tell you what I am able to. Of course, it is all so new to me that I can't remember everything but I will tell you what has stayed with me.

Members greeted me when I arrived at the Masonic hall and they found me a place to sit until their meeting began. When the other Masons had put on their clothing and signed in, which is something you always have to do, I was shown into a small room where a Mason called the Tyler told me that I had to make some adjustments to my clothing as everyone does before they are Initiated. This is an ancient tradition to show several things that may appear silly to the outside world but are very relevant to what is about to take place, because all the things we say and do in our ceremonies have a symbolic meaning.

In the Lodge I have joined we don't wear a special suit for Initiation, as they do in some Lodges, but you do have to take off your jacket and tie, turn down your shirt neck to show that you are a man, roll up your right trouser leg so that you can kneel on a bare knee as the old masons did, and take off one of your shoes and put on a slipper. I now know that this last action is because of what we read in the Bible where a man called Boaz wanted to marry a girl called Ruth and so to claim her he took off his shoe and gave it to one of her family. In this way Ruth became part of the family of Boaz. In the same way, by accepting their slipper, we become part of our Mother Lodge.

Oh yes, they also take away all your keys, your cash, a belt with a metal clasp if you have one, anything else of a metal kind, even pens, tiepins, rings and spectacles. It seems a bit like going on an aircraft and the reason is partly the same. You are not allowed, when you start, to go into a Lodge room with anything that could be a weapon and you are also to represent someone "poor and penniless".

You learn why later.

Well, you may be poor and penniless when you enter the Lodge but the Treasurer comes out before then and asks if you still wish to join. If you say "yes" he then asks you to sign the Lodge register and he asks for a cheque to cover the Initiation fee and the first annual subscription.

The last thing that happens before you enter is that you are blindfolded. This is done so that, until a certain point, if you don't wish to go on with being admitted you can withdraw and you will not have seen where and with whom you have been. Halfway through the ceremony the blindfold will be removed.

Thus prepared, you wait until someone opens the Lodge door and asks who is there. The Tyler answers for you and when this has been reported to those inside you are taken by the arm and led into the Lodge room. Having a blindfold on makes it hard to concentrate but you are asked to kneel for prayer, which is what you do at the start of every meeting, and then you walk round in a sort of circle with people asking your guide questions. At last you stop and are led forward to a low desk where you are told that you have to kneel and make a solemn promise to abide by the rules of the Order, and to keep private some of the signs and words that are now shared with you. You do this by repeating words that you are told by someone in front of you. It is not easy to concentrate when you are still in the dark.

When you have finished the repeating, you are asked to seal that promise by kissing the Bible that is in front of you. The Bible is always open in all Lodges, in front of the Master, whilst the Lodge is meeting. You then get up and at last the blindfold is removed. After a few moments, having become accustomed to the light, you see someone on a big chair or throne in front of you and others on his left and right. The man in front of you now tells you that he is the Master of the Lodge and he begins to share the words and signs that you have promised to keep private. Even if I told you what they are, they would not make sense because even I still have a lot more to learn about them. They are the signs and words used by the ancient masons to prove their standing as craftsmen.

I then seemed to go round the room as I did before but this time I was questioned, but was always prompted about the things I had been told. When that was over I was given an apron as a new member. This apron belongs to the Lodge and it is only later that I will have to buy one for myself so that I can take it wherever and whenever I visit another Lodge.

There were other things said to me before the ceremony was over regarding my duty, as a Mason, to God, my neighbour and myself, but to be quite honest it was all such a lot of words that I shall have to go a few more times before I will be able to take it in. Finally, I was shown a place to sit in the Lodge and was then congratulated by the brethren around me.

The Lodge concluded all its other business and then I saw how they close a Lodge, which is always done the same way. When that was done, and the Bible was closed, we all left the Lodge room and went for drinks before we gathered for food in the dining room.

I had been warned that I would have a toast in my honour and whilst everyone else stood for that I remained seated. I had also been told that I must say a few things including a thank you to my proposer and seconder, and to the Lodge for accepting me.

I hope I did that satisfactorily.

After the toasts were over, the dinner ended and we were free to stay and chat or come home. The whole ceremony took just over an hour and I am really looking forward to seeing another person go through it, so that I will be able to enjoy and appreciate even more the making of a Mason. Of course, as I am now a Freemason, I can go to any other Lodge in the UK as a visitor but I may be examined there and I must always sign their register with my Lodge number.

Do we really need the Second degree?

In the light of modern practice, the question with which this section begins is a very proper one.

When a Candidate has experienced the incidents of the First Degree, his reaction to the Second must seem much less intriguing. He is not blindfolded, he knows what a Lodge looks like, he can now recognise the men who accompany him, he knows where he is going when he processes round the Lodge, he has begun to hear and learn the ritual, he even knows some of the faces around him and having his clothing rearranged is no longer a puzzle. He has a new word and grip to learn as well as steps and a shorter obligation and charge to take or to hear, but as compared with the surprises of the Apprentice degree it really is rather unimpressive.

The tools are presented in a similar manner, there is no address after being Passed as there is after Initiation and he certainly has no more books to receive. Isn't it really a bit unnecessary?

Well, I appreciate the feeling but let me give you a bit of history.

English Freemasonry of the 18th century had developed from what we call guild Lodges that had been attached to the masons' guilds that had started at least in the early 1400s. In those guilds there were no apprentices because if you wanted to be a Fellow, which was how a guild member was described, you had to have become a Freeman of the local city or borough, and the word, Freeman, meant that you were now free of your apprentice indentures or being controlled by a craftsman.

You had to be a master mason, or master craftsman, and you usually had to have the financial status to be able to employ an apprentice, or apprentices. When Lodges began to be attached to the Guilds, usually in the 1500s, there was therefore only one degree, that of Fellow.

By the way, I do mean Fellow, because the Scottish term *Fellowcraft* was not used until the next century.

What it is important for us to realise, however, is that when the Guild Lodges finally lost their link with the trade guilds, as they began to do in the late 1600s, the Lodges had then to run themselves and so three things happened.

Firstly, they copied the old guilds and began to have a Right Worshipful Master and two Wardens. Secondly, they also had to have a Secretary and a Treasurer. Thirdly, they had to think who were to be their members.

As they were no longer attached to a Guild, they could of course, choose people who may not be Freemen. They could invite members of the nobility, gentlemen, military men and others who had no connection with any trade. That did in fact begin to happen but then the working masons who were still members of the Lodges started to insist that if someone who had never been an apprentice joined such a private Lodge they must be put through at least a ceremonial form of Apprenticeship.

That led to different kinds of development.

One kind of development found in the Grand Lodge of All England at York, that had started before 1705 and lasted until the 1790s, was that there was only one degree for ordinary members, that of Fellow, and if someone had to be admitted to the grade of Apprentice it was done in the degree of Fellow.

You could say that it was like having two degrees on the same day but the really important ceremony was that of Fellow, and in that ceremony for example, both B... and J..... were the words given and explained. There was also only one obligation for both grades.

The other kind of development was when the Premier Grand Lodge of London and Westminster began from 1717.

It was agreed that if Lodges wanted to have a ceremony of entering a person as an Apprentice then each Lodge was to do it privately.

Soon, however, the Grand Lodge made it a rule that there had to be a separate degree of Apprentice for everyone whatever their status, and in order to create a ceremony for the new type of Initiation they split the old Fellows degree and so Accepted Freemasons began to have a practice more like that with which we are familiar today.

You can now perhaps appreciate why the Second degree ceremony seems to be a paler reflection of what happens in the First. You may also appreciate why the obligation and the Charge at the South-East corner are shorter and refer to what happened on the previous occasion.

As a result of what I have told you the reaction may be: "Good, let us make the Entered Apprentice degree the one that now matters and forget about the Second." Well, that might seem a right solution, but if we were in fact to do that there are some important items that we would have to deal with because they are also part of our long-standing tradition.

Let us look at six of these.

The first and most important are the tools of a craftsman – the square, the level and the plumb rule.

These are the tools of a Master Craftsman and it would be a severe break with inherited tradition if we were to replace the tools associated with the Apprentice degree with those of the persons who once taught them. In any case, if we could devise a way of introducing them as the tools to which an Apprentice might aspire we are still left with another problem.

Have you not noticed that these are the tools whose shapes often adorn the backs of the Chairs of the Worshipful Master, Senior and Junior Wardens?

They are there just because originally, as I told you, a Guild Lodge was held in the Fellow degree. You ought also to know that a Lodge on a working site was also held as a Lodge of Fellows and that is why, to this day, you have to open a Lodge in the Second degree before you can install a Worshipful Master.

That, by the way, would be the second issue. We have here a Landmark that you would have to get rid of, or newly incorporate, if you wanted to ditch the Second degree because there seems to be no way, at present, of starting an Installation in the current form of Entered Apprentice degree.

On the other hand, I suppose you could redesign the chairs that have Master Craftsman's tools carved into them and start an Installation in the Third degree, where it eventually finishes up.

That would be a real break with tradition.

The third issue is, of course, what was originally done in the Fellow degree, the explanation of both B and J on the same occasion.

Actually, this need be no great problem. We just need to explain, at some point, that the reason why two Deacons attend the Initiate on his entry, and as he makes his obligation, is because originally, there were no Deacons, and this duty was performed by the Wardens. They were associated with the two pillars, small copies of which are to this day on their pedestals. The Junior Warden represents B and the Senior Warden J, and the Deacons do likewise as their deputies, which is why they have what were once the Wardens' wands.

What is important is that any Candidate for Freemasonry does need to have an introduction to, and an explanation of, the pillars at the porchway or entrance of the inner temple of King Solomon.

Mention of the porchway leads me on naturally to the fourth issue – the steps taken by us in Masonry as we come to make our obligation. We take three in the First Degree, two more in the Second and two more in the Third. (I should point out here that those who think there is no connection between the Third degree and the Royal Arch should take note that we still only have seven steps there)

These steps can be better understood if we realise that they take us on our journey from the Eastern, or outer gate, of the whole Temple by one step, into the court of the non-Jews or Gentiles, one step into the court of the Women, and another step into the court of the male

Israelites. As an Entered Apprentice, we are therefore admitted to the family of B… but we are not yet allowed further.

The fourth step takes us into the Court of the Priests where the altar of sacrifice was set and the fifth step takes us into the porchway or entrance of the inner temple.

It is therefore appropriate to be introduced to J, the High Priest, for only priests were permitted into the areas just traversed.

The last two steps would then be the sixth that puts us in the middle chamber or Holy Place, whilst the seventh leads us through the West door into the Holy of Holies, where the Ark of the Covenant was found which appears on our Master Mason certificate.

The steps of the Second degree thus enable us to go to the place where the craftsmen received their wages in the middle chamber of the side rooms of the Holy Place. This, of course, was only done whilst the Temple building was being completed for after that time only priests were allowed in this inner part of the Temple. If the Second degree is discontinued would we not lose that meaning and, by the same token, would it matter that the staircase of 15 or more steps would be lost with all the symbolic meaning attached to that?

Therein, after all, we are taught more clearly about the Seven Liberal Arts and Sciences which we are encouraged to study by the Charge at the South-East corner. This recommendation to such learning was, by the way, retained in our form of Freemasonry because in the operative trade it was the men who were expert in the Seven Liberal Arts and Sciences, who were alone eligible to become Master Masons.

If we were to drop this stage would it matter?

When you discover that the basis for the story of the winding staircase was a medieval religious legend of how Mary the mother of Jesus, was, as a girl, encouraged to mount such a staircase to approach the court of the men, and this story was acted out in the pageants that the Masons' Guilds shared in, you realise that to remove it would be destroying a very long tradition indeed.

And then there is the matter of 'S'.

You may not know this but this Password is the only correct one for its degree, kept from ancient practice. The password for the Entered Apprentice degree, when it had been created, was originally TC, which fitted perfectly, as "the first artificer in metals", with the idea of Hiram Abiff being the creator of the pillars which were erected.

The Password for the Master Mason degree was at first a word that was later taken as the Grand Word used at Installations or as part of the entry to a Royal Arch Chair, so another Password had to be found and therefore TC was used in the Third degree.

The only Password that remained where it had been from Time Immemorial was this one of S, and so if there is a portion of the old Fellows degree that has a hallowed place, this is it.

You might almost claim that, using the term in its popular sense, this is something that you may find you would move at your peril; it is a real S, something that matters to people so much that they would be quite scandalised if anything happened to it.

I hope, of course, that you are all aware of how very perfectly it fits the features of this degree, an ear of corn beside a fall of water.

The word without aspiration is the present Arabic word for an ear of corn, 'siblet'; whilst the word with aspiration is an appropriate old Hebrew word for a flow of water, 'shibboleth'.

Can't you just hear the water run?

That the two words became associated with the story of Jephtha and his wars with the Ephraimites, because even in Bible days the use of such a Password was undoubtedly clever, is clear and so undoubtedly old, and if we were really to finish with the Second degree then a place for it elsewhere would certainly have to be found.

There remains, of course, the sixth issue of the Second degree that we would have to account for: the smooth or square ashlar.

This stone, very often seen in northern and older Lodges, on the South-East corner of a Lodge room floor, signifies the progress that a Freemason, like his operative forebears, has made in the science.

It has always been a symbol of the skill of the master craftsman.

On the other hand, some Lodges content themselves with combining this stone with the tripod or other lifting gear and associating it with the Third degree. Maybe that is how we could manage its disappearance along with the Fellow Craft. And that leads me finally to a suggestion that might horrify some of you but begin to make sense for others of us.

I have always believed that ancient Masonry was composed of three grades. Not degrees because degrees only came in with Accepted Freemasonry. The three grades of the working Craft were Apprentice, Master Craftsman and Master Mason.

What is so different in that, you may say, from what we have?

But wait a moment and let me finish. We have been pondering on the possibility that we could dispense with the present Second degree. I certainly can see the sense in doing that if we then changed the Third degree into that of a Master Craftsman and bring back to life the true Master Mason degree which, because of changes made by our Premier Grand Lodge forefathers, had to become what we call the Royal Arch.

I don't intend to go into the history of how that came about but what I do want to bring to your attention is the fact that though we say that we have the Master Mason's degree yet we don't have its secrets - the only degree in all English Freemasonry that doesn't give you what is promised at the beginning: and when you sit as Master Masons in the Third degree for an Installation you get turned out of your own degree because there are things going to take place that you have not been made privy to, even though it is still the same degree.

Doesn't that make you think?

What it convinces me of is that really those who are called Master Masons are no better than Craftsmen, though to make things seem better I would prefer to call them Master Craftsmen.

My suggestion for a change, if the Second degree were to be dropped, would be to make our present Third degree the Master Craftsman degree and then make that Supreme degree in which Masons are exalted the new Third degree, so that they were properly the ones who should be Masters of their Lodges.

Does that seem very revolutionary?

Just imagine how it would give Master Masons the real status they deserve, ensure that all Craft Masons had the essential knowledge that at present means you have to join another Order and, oh yes, paying fewer fees.

Well, it is just a thought if we are seriously saying: "Do we really need the Second degree?"

Of course, there is another path we could take and that would mean retaining the Second degree but returning to it the whole Mark story that was at least once part and parcel of what was done in *Antients'* Lodges. If we did that we would be able to have a rather richer obligation, an historical section such as we have in the present Third degree and a cipher alphabet to learn about.

We could have a new role for Deacons, a reporting on members' welfare that some of us only enjoy in the Order of the Secret Monitor, and the benefit of knowing what on earth the keystone was all about. I dare say that is still wishful thinking but I hope at least that I have reminded us all of one thing. If you don't know about the history of English Freemasonry you cannot appreciate what we have, or where we might better go in the future.

Our heritage is very precious but if it could help us to create something even more fitting for our times in the future, then it is not just a valuable heirloom, it is also an invaluable guide.

What inducement have you to leave the East and go to the West?

Does that question still surprise you, as it probably did when you first heard it? Or have you heard it so often that you take it for granted and just let it flow over you without any further thought?

For me, it provides a constant fascination every time I hear it and in 58 years of Freemasonry, that has been a lot of occasions. I want to now share some of that fascination with you and let you into the secret of why such sentences as that in our title keep me attracted to Masonry and to writing about it after all these years.

The first thing that fascinates me here is why that question is there at all. For just consider, if you compare this form of opening with what has gone before, you have to wonder why there is a change. In the Second degree opening, having ensured that the Lodge is properly tyled and the Brethren are standing to order as Apprentices, the Master rightly enquires of a Warden how he would prove himself a Craftsman before he requires that same proof of all present. That proof given the Worshipful Master calls for prayer and then opens the Fellow Craft Lodge.

Initially, the same exact procedure takes place in opening the Lodge in the Third degree until all the Brethren prove that they are Master Masons. But then the Worshipful Master starts a new catechism with both the Wardens.

Those familiar with early ritual, and not least that of the Royal Order that dates from pre-1730, will know that the ancient practice was for the Candidate to be obligated and invested and then seated with the Brethren whilst a catechism, instructing him in the degree to which he had been admitted, was conducted between the Worshipful Master and Wardens. It is clearly part of such a catechism, which is now entered into here but why is it engaged in during this part and not later in the ceremony?

There are two possible answers.

The first, is that nowadays the manner of doing ritual is different and we no longer use the catechismal form, so there would not be a place for this sort of enquiry. Whilst this is largely true there is still the question of why, if the nature of our ritual has changed, this kind of catechism is included at all. If it is replaced by another form of ceremony, which is more dramatic and descriptive then surely any residue of the older style of teaching ought to have been left totally aside, as outworn and out of date. The fact that this is not what has happened suggests that there probably has to be some other explanation.

That is where a second answer fits.

The reason why this short catechism between the Worshipful Master and the Wardens takes place, is because even though it cannot be used as it was originally in the body of the ceremony, it is too important to be left out and therefore it has been reinserted at this point. If this explanation is the correct one, however, there are two further questions to be answered.

Firstly, what is it that is so special about this catechism that it needed to be retained in this form, even if it was to be used at what might appear to be an unexpected point and in what may seem such an odd manner?

Secondly, why could not the content of this catechism be included in the course of the ceremony that is to follow?

The first thing to be said here is that in fact the placing of the catechism, if it was to be used at all, is not in the least odd. As was mentioned earlier, the pre-Union form of instruction was for the Candidates to be seated and for the Worshipful Master to exchange questions and answers that formed the main content of the teaching in this and any other degree. If what is in this catechism relative to the Master Mason degree could not be communicated in the course of the rest of the ceremony, then what better way could be used than the ancient one of a dialogue between the Worshipful Master and his

Wardens. As some form of such a dialogue has been retained at the opening and closing of each degree in Lodge, then it would seem that this was obviously the point at which any teaching contained in a catechismal form was best given.

The fact that what we have here is in catechetical form, tells us that this part of the ritual was obviously of pre-Union origin and yet was regarded as so essential to retain that a place for it had to be found. It was, as it clearly had been, so important for the Master Mason degree that it had to appear somewhere. Even if it broke the mould of the new Sussex or Emulation working, it had to have a place found for it.

The strange thing today is that by being inserted where it is, it has become simply a brief adjunct to the business of opening a Master Mason's Lodge and has not been given the attention that the post-Union ritual creators intended.

The second query that results from the earlier answer, means that we have, of course, to be absolutely clear as to what the catechism is saying, and that includes an understanding of the question at the start of this section: "What inducement have you to leave the East and go to the West?"

In case it has never before seemed a question to ask, which East and West are we talking about?

Is it the East and West of our Lodge room, the East and West of the globe, or is it some other location?

This is precisely the kind of mystery that the sudden insertion of this catechism creates in our present ritual. There is no doubt that the wording we have is a shortened section of a much longer presentation that would almost certainly have provided us with the context, and hence the correct setting, for this exchange.

As it is, we have to do some detective work.

It becomes obvious that the directions cannot apply to the present Lodge room. If the present Wardens are going anywhere it is from the West to the East as they progress to the Chair of King Solomon.

Yet the words of this catechism tell us that they are bound in the opposite direction. In the light of this fact I once used to imagine that what the Wardens were representing were men who came with the wisdom of the East so as to impart that wisdom to the people of the West. That indeed was their inducement, to share this knowledge they had with fellow Masons, ourselves in the West. Didn't that make sense and didn't it concur with the Christian origin of Freemasonry in that we have three wise men coming from the East to the West to bring the greatest knowledge of all, the best of all presents, the presence of the Most High amongst us.

Well, logical as that argument seemed to me for a time, it had to come to terms with the rest of the catechism.

The inducement that is plainly stated here is that of searching for that which was lost and which had been lost because of some event that had happened in a specific place and time, long before the events of Bethlehem. Moreover, there was no concept of bringing new knowledge from East to West because an important secret has not only been already known but has been temporarily lost.

So it was not the global points of the compass that were being spoken about.

What then occurred to me was that as Hiram Abiff is here referred to, it could be the Temple at Jerusalem that was the setting for this catechism. If that was the case then how did that help to explain what was being said?

The answer was that it helped a great deal.

The Temple at Jerusalem was situated along the opposite alignment to that of our Masonic Lodge. Indeed I recall looking at a pre-Union ritual at this time and there it was stated: "The West End of the Temple shown from between the Pillars in the East".

It is against such a setting that the words of the catechism have now to be understood. They refer to the pilgrim who enters the Temple precinct via the golden gate in the East and proceeds to the inner temple in the West. He then enters that inner temple through the two pillars, moves into the Holy Place, where the legendary history states that Hiram Abiff was slain, and his sharing in the ultimate secret was thus lost until another took his place.

The Masonic pilgrim, however, is not meant to rest here as the present Third degree, with its substituted secrets, might suggest. The catechism rather implies that that is not the ultimate goal of this degree.

"What inducement have you to leave the East and go to the West?" and the reply is clear: "To seek for that which was lost, which, by your instruction and our own industry, we hope to find."

These words deserve some careful reflection.

Let me remind you that the ritual does not say: "To seek for that which was lost but which, even with your instruction, we cannot hope to find and certain substituted secrets is all we can hope to achieve."

No. Even though substituted secrets is what the Senior Warden regretfully reports at the close of this ceremony, that is not what this opening catechism promises.

The plainly specified objective of a Master Mason's path, is that along with the Worshipful Master's greater knowledge, and his own efforts to acquire that knowledge, it is expected that the genuine secrets will be found by the Master Mason.

This surely prompts the renewed question.

Why did the post-Union ritual composers, who knew that only substituted secrets would be found in this ceremony, take the trouble to include this old catechism in the opening of the degree they approved?

To reinforce what has already been a suggestion, but now is manifestly the only conclusion, the catechism was included because the ritual formers knew that, whatever a Candidate in this form of Master Mason's degree might imagine, he had NOT completed his journey as a Mason by receiving the substituted secrets.

It might seem, as some of our Brethren are now saying, that the present Master Mason's degree seems complete in itself but the ritual creators knew that this was not the case. That is why they had to include what might otherwise seem an anomaly right at the outset of this ceremony.

If you really want to share in the original, and total, aim of being an Accepted Master Mason then there is more than what we have here for you to learn, and it is not just the opening catechism that makes this point.

In the latter part of the present ceremony, the Worshipful Master informs us that those substituted secrets shall designate all Master Masons throughout the universe, UNTIL time or circumstances SHALL restore the genuine.

There is not the slightest question here of this degree being the end of the story. There is more that the Master Mason has to discover and receive.

That is why, on a Sunday afternoon in 1732, a Past Grand Master of the Premier Grand Lodge, the Reverend Dr. Desaguliers, introduced three noblemen to those further secrets, in a ceremony held in the home of the Duke of Montagu.

Dr. Desaguliers was one of those who had decreed that ancient Masonry consisted of three degrees only, so whatever he did that afternoon to make those noblemen Super Excellent Chapters, must have been part of the three degrees and was, presumably, the completion of being a Master Mason.

If, therefore, to return to the main topic of this section, we would know what is the inducement that would lead you or me to progress through the Temple until we reach that Western point where the Holy of Holies stands, it is because in that centre spot, from which a Master Mason cannot err, the lost secret of all our Masonry is at last revealed, on a plate of gold where the Ark of the Covenant stood.

It is there that we uncover the fulfilment of our whole Masonic journey, through what is now called the Holy Royal Arch. That is why the catechism was felt to be so important that it must be preserved and introduced as our guide.

For me, the fascination is not simply that the mystery of this part of Freemasonry is now solved but that its interpretation begins to reveal and enhance the whole story of our fraternity.

An alternative presentation of a Grand Lodge Certificate

It is with a sense of privilege that I respond to the request of the Worshipful Master to present to you the Certificate that you are entitled to receive on having attained the Third degree in Masonry.

Such certificates are the descendants of a practice in operative masonry by which an apprentice signed a paper, an indenture, attaching him to a master mason for a period of seven years. At the successful conclusion of that period his indenture was returned to him countersigned by the master mason and assuring any who needed to know that he was now a fully-fledged journeyman mason or master craftsman.

In Accepted Freemasonry the practice was adopted but slightly changed.

Initially, it was when a Brother had become a Fellow of the Craft that he received a certificate from his Lodge to inform anyone concerned that he was now a Mason in good standing with such a Lodge.

In the latter part of the 18th century the certificate idea was adopted by national Grand Lodges and it was now Master Masons who could receive such a certificate permitting them to be accepted in Lodges abroad as well as at home.

I now present you with your certificate in a folded form emphasising that this is a private document that is not to be publicly displayed. Please open it and let us examine some of its contents.

This is not the first type of certificate to have three pillars or columns even though the name *Three Pillars Certificate* is now generally given to this document. Earlier forms of this document showed the pillars with three characters, who stood upon their apex; *Solomon – King of Israel, Hiram – King of Tyre*, and *Hiram Abiff*.

That is why to this day the present pillars, whilst having vacant tops, are still associated with those persons. It was, incidentally, the custom in ancient Judah for an incoming king to be stationed briefly beside a pillar of the temple so that he might be identified, and as an indication of a semi-priestly status. That is how the associations began.

It is the presence on the certificate of the black and white pavement that confirms that the Order is connected with the Temple of Solomon, since this feature was adopted when the first illustrated English Bible of 1560 showed the floors of the Tabernacle and Temple in this manner.

Symbolically, it is with the construction of that latter edifice that the working tools are displayed and of their speculative significance you have already been made aware in the degree ceremonies.

Below the arms of the Freemason who is the Grand Master for the present, there appear the details concerning yourself, which details ensure that this certificate is unique. The document is signed by the Grand Secretary for the time being, thus again probably distinguishing your certificate from mine.

On the left of the certificate is the seal of the United Grand Lodge of England that was formed in 1813 by the union of two former and rival Grand Lodges, known as the *Moderns* and the *Antients*.

The seal bears the imprint of the most holy item in the original Solomon's Temple, the Ark of the Covenant, and beneath it are the Hebrew characters that spell out the words "Kodesh Lo Adonai" meaning "Holiness to the Lord".

These characters were originally inscribed on the triangular jewel fixed to the mitre of the High Priest, who was the only person in Israel permitted to enter this place where the Ark of the Covenant once stood. The words indicate again the type of life that Freemasons are expected to display and the Ark, as the object that bore the Mason Word that was the ultimate secret of the Craft, was that to which all Masons were meant to direct their steps.

That the Holy Royal Arch is the goal of your Masonic journey is further shown by the absence of an important tool at the very centre base of this certificate. There you will see the VSL open and on it the square. There are no compasses. That is because you have a further step to take. The compasses enable you to draw and form an Arch, and Masonry is therefore not complete until you are a Royal Arch Mason.

I now invite you to go to the Secretary's table where you will sign this certificate with your normal signature. I wish you well in your Masonic membership and may you live long to serve, and enjoy, your Lodge and its members.

Stewardship

The notion of Stewardship derives from a longstanding English practice, which was followed by the land-holding gentry from at least Anglo-Saxon times.

Just as they had an agent responsible for the management of their acres and animals, so they also had an officer whose sole care was the fabric, finances and maintenance of his house or houses.

That man was called a Steward, which name comes from the Anglo-Saxon words; stig (meaning hall) and weard (meaning care). Stewardship therefore means, in any context, looking after the affairs of the household.

That is why, as early as 1720, the new Grand Lodge that was called into being in 1717, decided that it would entrust the organisation of its quarterly feasting and other special occasions of feeding, to a group of specially chosen brethren whose task was to provide for and financially underpin those occasions of dining.

They were to be called Grand Stewards and they were to be drawn from a limited number of appointed London Lodges. As the dress of these brethren was to be the usual lambskin apron bordered with deep red, the Lodges from which they were chosen became known as Red apron Lodges.

To this day, the responsibilities of the Grand Stewards have been retained and in addition, the reigning Masters of those Lodges perform the ceremonial task of attending the Investiture of Grand Officers each April and escorting those Brethren to and from their seats. In that sense, they are also serving the members of the Grand Lodge household.

The extension of the office of Steward to private Lodges occurred quite soon. There were a few such Lodges, like Royal Cumberland in Bath, where they introduced Stewards under the direction of the

Director of Ceremonies after the Union, and these Stewards not only wore miniature red aprons of the same design as those in Grand Lodge but sat, as they still do, in a phalanx on the north side of the Lodge.

Elsewhere, the office of Steward was also adopted but the Brethren wore normal blue aprons and sat in the south west part of the Lodge room. Their duties varied according to how much assistance was required at the festive board. In some northern and country Lodges they still actually serve the dishes at table and clear the tables later. In most other Lodges they are actually wine waiters or raffle ticket salesmen.

One aspect of Stewardship that can easily be overlooked is a description of the Junior Warden as the ostensible Steward of the Lodge, though it may be a surprise to learn that the first known appearance of that phrase in a ritual was not until 1890. The care of the Lodge by the Junior Warden, by the vetting of visitors or any itinerant masons, dates from the 1600s but it was not until the 1770s that in the Installation ceremony there is the description involving those duties.

When, after the Union, the custom was followed of restricting the Wardens to their seats, the necessity of having other officers who could attend on visitors and the members at table became obvious. Today, the Junior Warden might be required to examine a visitor, especially from a foreign Constitution, but his one other duty as an ostensible Steward, is to propose the toast of the guests for the evening.

Stewardship is not simply confined in Freemasonry to the matter of helping the Brethren to be hospitable and to wine and dine. Stewardship is also extended to the whole charitable field.

In the support of a national Masonic appeal, there are very special places reserved for those who are willing to cap their normal contributions to the good cause concerned, by reserving a place at the special Festival banquet. In doing so, the Brother becomes a Steward of the Festival and he may even acquire another place as Steward for any partner that might accompany him to the occasion.

Here, the term obviously means that one is caring for the general well-being of the Masonic household by supporting its provision of care for the sick, the aged or the orphaned. It might be Stewardship expressed in terms of a financial commitment but it is hoped that besides the gift that is made, there will also be a recognition of how the family welfare is being served.

Being a Steward in a Lodge can, of course, teach one a great lesson.

It is, that as a step in our progress we need to start afresh at the bottom and be willing to serve our Brethren. It was a sad experience to discover not long ago that a fresh member of a Lodge who seemed so full of promise refused point blank to accept the office of Steward because, he said, that would require him serving some members who were junior to him in his profession. When it was pointed out to him that this was what all the rest of us had done, or would be expected to do, in whatever form of Masonry we joined, he resigned saying that it was beneath his dignity to perform that sort of service.

By preserving this kind of office, Freemasonry is perhaps teaching its members how very equal we are all meant to be. Nobody is too lowly to be served; true dignity is found in the willingness to serve anyone. The VSL confirms this.

Another general aspect of Stewardship amongst us relates to our use of the talents that we have been given, even if at first those talents are not clearly perceived.

It is as we take our part in the ceremonies and activities of the Lodge that we perhaps begin to recognise the particular gift that we can contribute to the well-being of our Institution. There are going to be natural ritualists amongst us, there are going to be orators and teachers, there are going to be fund-raisers and there are going to be secretaries. In a whole range of tasks there are going to be those with noticeable talents, and wise will be the Lodge that can exercise Stewardship and allocate amongst its full members, such tasks as they can best fulfil.

In this household of the Masonic fraternity there is not just one Steward but a place for many.

Stewardship of the earth was what the VSL tells us was entrusted to mankind. In Masonry, using well "those talents wherewith God has blessed us", is enshrined not just in our ritual but in our practice.

Let us aim to be good Stewards out of the Lodge, as well as in.

The ancient office of Warden

It has always been a very real privilege to talk to those who have had the opportunity, which was never mine, of sharing the distinguished office of a Provincial Grand Warden.

What my time in Surrey as a Provincial Grand Master did, was to give me the chance to observe many aspects of Freemasonry and the time to ask myself why we do what we do, and from where our various practices have derived. For me, that has been a source of never ending interest and one facet of that is the origin and practice of the ancient office of a Warden.

The origin of the term is undoubtedly medieval and was almost certainly introduced, like my own family name, by the Norman conquerors of Britain.

Certainly, the Norman kings introduced the idea of Wardens, as the major noblemen who were responsible for the protection of the realm on the edges of the kingdom. Hence, the Warden of the Welsh Marches or, and this office is still in existence, the Warden of the Cinque Ports.

The word is an English adaptation of the Norman French word *warder* (pronounced WARDAIR) and thence *wardien* and thus, *warden*. It was a person who kept "watch and ward" and this applied to those who watched over castles, as well as the kingdom's borders.

It also began to be used in church circles to describe the office of the one who looked after the material affairs of a parish church and as a sign of authority in that office, the Warden was given a "princely token of status"; a staff or wand.

A churchwarden to this day has both the right and the duty to bear such an item.

In the church situation another development also occurred. Because in every place the king or monarch had a right to be heard, and if need be to act, it became the practice that in every church there should be two Wardens, one representing the church in the "person" of the rector, hence the origin of the term "parson", and the other representing the Crown and the people. That is why, to this day, every parish church is expected to have two Wardens. The names now may no longer be the same as they were but the reason for this duality of the warden's office is clear.

It was not only kings and churches that had Wardens.

Because most of our oldest institutions found their origin and pattern in ecclesiastical and courtly practice, it is not surprising that when the guilds of tradesmen in our oldest towns and cities were formed, they had two Wardens to assist the principal officer of the guild or company.

If you like, the Master of a Guild was like a king or ruler, or as the priest used to be in a local church, and hence he needed these men to assist him. In the guild, the office of Warden was usually an indication of progress in the company and usually meant that when the reigning Master retired he was followed by the most senior of the Wardens.

That is why they began to have names like Upper and Lower Warden, or Senior and Junior. These men were of course not elected to office by all the members of a company but only by the members of the ruling body called the Court, in which the present Master and his predecessors sat.

By the middle of the 14th century in England, this was very much how all guilds or companies were ruled and no doubt you can begin to see a similarity between this practice and that of our present day Lodges.

Before I come to any connection with ourselves, however, I think you may find it interesting to have a look at the old stonemasons' practice on a building site, as opposed to what happened in the guild.

Something rather different took place there.

On such a site, the stonemasons would construct a sturdy but temporary lean-to against the side of whatever was being built and they named this an *allogement*, from which Norman French word comes our more familiar word, a Lodge.

Here, the craftsmen gathered to carve and prepare the stone before it was taken out and set up in its proper place. Here, they would refresh themselves, talk about any matters of common concern and even rest, after breaking their fast at midday; Le noon-jeune, which we came to call luncheon.

To keep order in this lodge, especially when matters concerning the admission or training of apprentices, wage rates or their well-being were to be discussed, the craftsmen elected a Warden to preside over them.

As the craftsmen who occupied this lodge were in England called fellows, the tradition was that you had to be a fellow to be a warden, and it was the fellows who elected and witnessed the choice of the one who was called warden, to preside over them.

What we now have to notice is that in the medieval working lodge there was only one warden and there was no master.

Indeed, the remarkable thing is that, as the extant 1350 records of the York Minster workyard show, the master mason in charge of all work on the building site was not allowed into the lodge on any occasion. If he wanted to consult the foremen or overseers of the craftsmen he would call them to his own design room and there convey his plans or introduce them to the apprentices that he had chosen but whom they were to train. The only time that the master mason may have approached the lodge was to knock on its door to summon the craftsmen after the midday break.

When after 1350, stonemasons entered the guild system and formed companies of their own trade, they discovered that the usual practice was for there to be not just one Warden in charge, but a Worshipful Master and two Wardens, as has already been mentioned. Moreover, they soon realised that it was not permitted for all the members to elect the Master but purely the members of the Inner Court, and they also found that you could not be a member of the guild just because you were a trained and expert craftsman. You had also to be a "Freeman" of the city or borough in which the guild was licensed. This meant that you had to be wealthy and well-known enough to be allowed to apply for the "Freedom" unless your father had also been a Freeman member of a guild in that place.

So, not all craftsmen became members of a guild. The other stonemasons were just men employed on a daily basis, and as daily in the old language was journée, they became "journeyman masons".

It is from the customs and practice of a guild that much of what we now do in the speculative Lodge of today, derives. This was because the Freeman Masons who formed a City Guild decided to add to their guild a unique body called "A Lodge", and in that Lodge they naturally decided to copy some of the ways of the guild for organising how things were to be done. That is why, though we have a Masons' Lodge we have a Worshipful Master and two Wardens, rather than just one Warden.

Yet, the office of a Warden is so old and has acquired so much esteem that what we still need to do is to look at how the old distinctions have been preserved.

Notice, for example, that to be the ruler or Master of an Accepted Lodge today, you still have to have been a Warden with a share in the ruling of a Fellow Crafts' Lodge.

In Bristol, we see how, when the Senior Warden departs from the Lodge with the Past and Installing Master, to take part in his Installation elsewhere, the Junior Warden sits on a stool below the Master's place and wears his hat as the ostensible ruler of the Fellow Crafts, who are left behind. He only moves from that position when the newly installed Master re-enters to occupy his chair.

The old distinction between Fellows and true Master Masons is clearly demonstrated.

Or again, has it ever struck you as odd that though a Worshipful Master would surely be able to open a Lodge by a direct order to the Inner Guard, he does not do so.

Why is this?

It is all the more odd when you see a working in which after the Junior Warden has addressed the Inner Guard, the latter responds directly to the Worshipful Master. If he can do such a thing, why is the Junior Warden the first to be involved?

It is, of course, because there was a time before the 19th century when no post of Inner Guard existed and the person who had to get up and see that the Lodge was tyled, was the Junior Warden.

More than that, however, is the fact that it was a warden in operative days who opened the lodge for business. That is why a Warden is still so addressed.

The same is also true at the closing of a Lodge.

The Worshipful Master could close a Lodge directly but he does not do so. He defers to the Senior Warden because that is the maintaining of what was the practice in a working site lodge.

In operative times, his job as warden was to pay the fellows the wages that "were due" to them before they left the site and so he is the one who has to confirm that all have indeed "had their due".

Notice, however, that this proves that originally there was no opening or closing of the lodge in an apprentice grade, because they did not receive wages but were given food and board by the master mason for whom they worked. The ancient office of Warden is yet again distinguished and honoured.

There is more to be said, however.

Notice that the Worshipful Master carries on a catechism with the Wardens in all the opening ceremonies of the three degrees and these catechisms become more and more involved.

In Ireland to this day, the Brethren who assemble in a Lodge are individually questioned as to the password of each degree before the

Worshipful Master can continue with the opening ceremony. In the 18th century this was the task of the two Wardens and that is why, in our shortened English form, the Wardens are asked about "what is the next care" and then required to prove the Brethren Masons by signs.

In Ireland, the questioning of the Brethren today is done by the Deacons but that is because, after 1813, this office was generally introduced and the wands that had belonged to the Wardens, as in church to this day, were now lent to the Deacons to show that they acted on the Wardens' behalf.

Incidentally, the Worshipful Master's wand was lent to the new officer, called a Director of Ceremonies, for a similar purpose.

The further catechisms that the Wardens respond to are of ancient origin.

The earliest practice we know of ritual in England was that which was conducted round a table after the Candidate had been obligated in the appropriate degree. He was then seated and the Worshipful Master proceeded to ask the Wardens to give the answers to a series of questions, which explained the part of Freemasonry into which he had just entered. Those who belong to the form of Freemasonry known now as the Royal Order of Scotland will confirm for you that that is still the way instruction is conducted there.

Since I am here addressing particularly those who have had the honour of being Provincial Grand Wardens, I wonder if any have ever questioned why it is that in the opening of any Provincial Grand Lodge, as indeed in the Grand Lodge in London, the Wardens are said to occupy Mount Tabor and Sinai?

Where do such references, of course originally taken from the Bible, find their Masonic origin?

Well, it puzzled me for years and then I came across a ritual of two Lodges that met in London in the 1730s, and in which a Right Worshipful Master conducted a catechism in which just these two features occur.

Mount Sinai, we are there informed, was where God first revealed his glory to the people of Israel in giving the Law to Moses, and Mount Tabor was where God revealed himself again in a revelation to three chosen disciples.

These Lodges were eventually excluded because they taught more than the Grand Lodge wanted to be known by third degree Masons, and they kept this knowledge to themselves. That is why the Grand Lodge also frowned on the growth of the Holy Royal Arch, but that is another story.

There, in a ritual that dates from the earlier part of the 18th century, the Grand Lodge knew that the original basis of English Freemasonry was still communicated. They retained it for their meetings, combining the Old and New Testament revelations, and when Provincial Grand Lodges began to open in their own right, instead of being held as part of a private Lodge, they were allowed to use the same ritual. What Wardens used to say was part of some of the oldest English ritual we know and this once more confirms that the office of a Provincial Warden is rooted in the very foundations of the Craft.

The Place and the Role of the Master in the Lodge

In any civilised society we depend on knowing just who people are and what they do. A pharmacist is expected to give sound advice on treatments, a judge to give impartial sentences, a grocer to sell sound fruit and a banker to give, well, not good but reliable interest.

Knowing such things helps enormously.

In Freemasonry, the same rule applies. It is good to know what a Grand Master and a Provincial Grand Master are for, and at the Lodge level we know what a Warden, a Deacon and a Tyler have to do.

But now, let us think of a position in Masonry about which there is often either ignorance or a lack of understanding. We may take the position of a Worshipful Master for granted but how many of us really appreciate just what it is that we are aiming to achieve as a Worshipful Master, or may have had in our possession when in that position.

If we don't really know what being a Master means, then it is no surprise if we fail fully to act properly when the time comes for us to do so. If, on the other hand, we did not fully grasp what it meant to be a Master when we were in the Chair then we are likely to have the wrong opinions about such an officer when we are called Past Masters.

The question then arises, are you and I truly proper Past Masters?

The whole matter does really deserve some careful thought. As I recently had the privilege of being in the Chair of my Mother Lodge for the first time after 55 years in the Craft, and have also had the experience of having been in nine such Craft Chairs previously, I ought to have some useful and practical thoughts about the matter.

In order to assist with this subject, I want to dwell for a short time on the historical background to the office of Worshipful Master and then consider some of the very practical issues that face any holder of that office today.

Originally the ruler of an operative, working lodge on a working site was a warden, or senior fellow, and he was elected by other fellows, this title being the correct English term for a master craftsman, whilst Fellow Craft came from Scotland after 1717.

It is because this was the original practice that we have to be in the Second degree before an Installation can begin, and it is also the reason why the Worshipful Master allows a Warden to invest a new Mason with his apron and also to close a Lodge.

Old traditions really do linger.

Where then does the idea of a Right Worshipful Master come from? Well, it derives from the time that more well off masons who became Freemen of their local city or borough, obtained a charter to hold a trade guild. Such a guild was organised on the pattern of a local parish church which had a Rector and two Wardens.

Incidentally, all these officers were supplied with wands or rods to indicate their authority and that is why the Director of Ceremonies now has the Master's wand and the Deacons have those of the Wardens.

By the late 1500s these Masons' Guilds began to have a Lodge attached to them and whilst only stonemasons could join the Guild Freemen, members of other trades could apply to join a Guild Lodge.

At first, these more ceremonial Lodges were ruled by a Warden which is why we see Elias Ashmole enter such a Lodge in 1645, with a Warden in charge. By the end of the 1600s the situation had changed. The stonemasons started to have a new guild just for their trade or one shared with bricklayers and blacksmiths. The Lodges that had belonged to the old guilds now had to rule themselves and they adopted the form of the Guild Court, with a Right Worshipful Master and two Wardens. That is how we came to have what we are now familiar with.

There is, however, something else.

Though the earlier master masons of operative days were a class apart who never came into a working lodge, but had their own separate tracing room and house, when the guilds were formed both master masons and master craftsmen or fellows, could become members as long as they had enough money to become Freemen.

What seems to have happened, however, is that because the master masons were the wealthier and more socially prominent in a town or city they usually became the Masters of the guilds and the idea of a Right Worshipful Master being like the previous master masons of the operatives still continued.

What is now clear from the evidence we have, is that the ruling Master of a Lodge was regarded as a Master Mason.

One fact that shows this very clearly is that when the occasion arose in 1717 that someone had to be appointed as the next Grand Master in London and Westminster they chose, from the four Lodges then combining, a man who, though he was not a stonemason, so the title could not have been a trade one, was yet *"the senior Master Mason among them"*.

This proves that there was a grade of Master Mason before what we are usually told was its appearance in 1726.

Such a grade obviously marked out men who had been rulers of their Lodges. It was because Anthony Sayer, a bookseller, had been a ruler of a private Lodge that at least he could be considered for the post of superior ruler, especially as he was the most senior and experienced among them.

We also know that there was a ceremony of making such a ruling Master, though some of those then present were not aware of what that was. We are not too clear about its details.

This means, therefore, that as far as ancient Freemasonry was concerned there were indeed three grades; Apprentice, Fellow or Master Craftsman, and Master Mason, this latter being the grade of a ruler.

To prove that was the case we only need to hear the ritual revealed by Prichard in 1730.

In the Master Mason degree we have the question: "*What are the three Lights in your Lodge?*" Answer: "*They represent the sun that rules the day, the moon that rules the night and the Master Mason who rules his Lodge.*"

In addition, the password of that degree was then the word that is now the word given to an Installed Master in the Inner working. That, of course, explains why, to this day the Installation of a new Worshipful Master takes place in the degree of a Master Mason and why those who think they are Master Masons are asked to leave.

It also explains why the *Moderns* Grand Lodge always insisted, as today, that an Installation ceremony is not another degree. That is, of course, because only Installed Masters are really Master Masons.

We can now, therefore, start to look at the place and the role of the Master in the Lodge today. He is elected, by those who are in the degree of Fellow, to be the ruler of the Lodge and it is in that degree, let me remind you, that this post is defined for the Brethren, and the Master-elect is also questioned before being obligated.

The words used are very important.

The Candidate for this office is to be an "*experienced Craftsman*" so that he can "*preside over them*" and to be presented to a Board of Installed Masters "*the better to qualify him for the discharge of the duties of his important trust*".

So, immediately, there is a clear indication of two things.

1. The person who undertakes this office has to be knowledgeable about the Craft.

May I remind us all that as soon as the Candidate has been Initiated, he is told that he is expected "*to study more especially such of the liberal Arts and Sciences as may lie within the compass of your attainment*". That is a direct link with our operative past because the only way by which you could become a working master mason was to be expert in those liberal Arts and Sciences. Skill in those was what distinguished a man from a mere master craftsman. That distinction is still meant to be there.

Whilst the Fellows may elect a man to be Worshipful Master, they cannot bring his Installation about.

The only people who are fit and proper persons for that task are those who are themselves qualified Master Masons in the full sense. We call them a Board of Installed Masters because they represent the Past Masters who were once left at the board or table in the centre of the Lodge room. In my mother Lodge, the Master Elect even has to know a new Password to be admitted.

2. The post of Worshipful Master is clearly regarded as being not just an honour but a place where there are specific duties, and where the person selected is being trusted to be able to discharge them.

It is therefore right that the Master-elect is at once reminded of what he is supposed to be able to undertake. His character is important as one of *"good report, true and trusty"* and *"held in high estimation among his Brethren and Fellows"*.

He is, further, to be an example in conduct, courteous and able to speak easily whilst also being firm in carrying out all those matters which Masons regard as important.

That, of course, requires something more than a pleasant and reliable person. It requires knowledge.

A Worshipful Master has to be *"well skilled in the Ancient Charges, Regulations and Landmarks of the Order"*.

To a question asking if the Master-elect can meet all these demands he is somehow expected to say: "I can."

Well, can we?

How skilled are the Masters of today in the Science of Freemasonry? I do not ask simply whether they can conduct the ceremonies of the three degrees before they take on the Chair. I mean how much do they really understand what they are doing? What are these Ancient Charges to which reference is made? How much do Masters know of the Regulations contained in the Book of Constitutions? How many Past Masters could tell their Brethren what are the essential Landmarks of the Craft?

If we are really serious about the response that a Master-elect is supposed to make, how sure are we of our Worshipful Master's knowledge? For what is the main task of the Brother who is put in the Chair of King Solomon?

Well, the answer is plain at every opening of the Lodge: "*The Master's place?*" "In the East." **"Why is he placed there?" "…to open the Lodge, and employ and instruct the Brethren in Freemasonry."**

There you have it. The reigning Master of a Lodge is not just someone who has put in the time and effort to come to Lodge meetings and steadily risen through the ranks from Steward to Senior Warden. He is meant to be a person who has been fully instructed in the background, the history, the significance and the purpose of Freemasonry over a period of years, so that when he sits in that Chair he is indeed able to do so with the confidence that he knows his powers, can explain its work, correct error and lead others to the same level of understanding as he also received.

There is, however, another factor that must never be lost sight of. When the new Worshipful Master is placed for the first time in the Chair of King Solomon, he is handed the tool of his office, now a gavel, though I have just been in two Lodges where it is still the original English tool, a mallet.

As this implement is given to him he is told that he is now in charge of the Lodge and he thus has the tool that will enable him to keep order in the Lodge. His authority is confirmed, his presidency demonstrated and his responsibility underlined. It is believed that with his knowledge and force of character, the Lodge can benefit under his care.

Let me illustrate the need for this quality of work in three areas.

The preparation needed before a meeting.
The protocol to be followed in exceptional areas.
The proceedings at the festive board.

These do not exhaust the matters requiring a Worship Master's attention but in looking at these we will begin to see just how important more than just ritual ability can be.

1. Does a Master just leave everything to the Secretary and the Preceptor or Director of Ceremonies? Has everything been talked out sufficiently in advance so that what appears on the summons is already expected by the Worshipful Master? Is the relationship such that he will be able to cope with any mishap; a Candidate who cannot come, an officer who falls ill, an objection to a possible Candidate, a death that needs an obituary?

The Master is the one who needs to make sure that all will be well on the night. He may be grateful for help to deal with a matter but his is the ultimate responsibility for the night's programme. He needs to have done all the preparation necessary to ensure that when he at last sits down in Lodge, he knows all that is likely to happen. He is truly in charge.

2. Of course, the Craft has assisted Masters since the Union by creating the office of Director of Ceremonies, and in dealing with most unusual or exceptional occasions his help will be valuable.

But the Worshipful Master is the person in charge and it is therefore his responsibility to know how to receive the official visitor, to conduct a discussion if some point of order arises in the Lodge, to know what to do if a ballot goes wrong (and sometimes it does), or to know how to manage matters if someone in an unrecognisable regalia or from another Constitution presents himself.

It may not be often that such occasions arise but it is unquestionably the Master's place to know what needs doing and to instruct the appropriate officers accordingly. That does mean knowing the Book of Constitutions.

3. The whole matter of conducting the arrangements at the festive board is part of any Master's task.

If there is one conviction that I have acquired over the years, it is that there is too much control at this point by the Director of Ceremonies. Of course I have heard WMs suggest that as the DC knows what to do, it is easier to let him do it.

In the north of England many DCs actually take the gavel themselves and act as if they were the Worshipful Master.

I believe that is contrary to ancient and good practice.

The Worshipful Master should be sufficiently instructed in the matter of Masonic table etiquette to make his own announcements and sound for order.

Who is in charge here? What I am contending for is already illustrated in the ceremony of Calling Off and Calling On.

This ceremony is the last remaining reminder of the days when Lodge members met around a table in the centre of the room, and upon the table there were both Masonic tools and furniture as well as food and drink, though in modest amounts.

When the Master felt that it was time to have a break from a ceremony he would Call Off and the Brethren would literally eat, chat, smoke, drink, spit or even relieve themselves in pots from under the table. When the Master called the Brethren from social intercourse, he would Call On. He does that to this day and no DC has to get up and warn the Brethren that the Worshipful Master is going to Call Off or On.

Why, then, does he have to do that at the separate dining table? Of course he can discreetly suggest to the Master that now is the moment for some wine taking or toasts but the gavelling, the announcement and the calling for replies is the responsibility of the Master.

My DC is relieved not to have to keep getting up and down.

There is also the whole matter of speeches. The WM needs to set an example as to what his Lodge expects. That will mean more preparation so that we do not speak overlong, do not repeat banal phrases, decide on two or three points that one wants to get over at each meeting and choosing either before the meeting, or early into it, who the responder for the guests shall be.

If the Junior Warden is to give that toast, then he or the proposer also need to know early who is responding. As a WM, I would expect to decide just how many speeches there were to be. On a very personal note I also request that anyone who might want to tell a joke will first try it out on me in the interval before dinner. Neither I, nor the Lodge, need to be embarrassed.

All such control, of course, requires preparation and training. If a Worshipful Master has come to the Chair too soon, and that is a present danger, or if he has come without the necessary instruction for Lodge room or dining table, then of course he cannot preside, instruct, influence or relax the Lodge as he should be able to do.

Being a Master is a big job. It is meant to be one of the highlights of any Mason's career. Perhaps we Past Masters have a bigger job still, in making sure that our future Masters are better prepared than we were.

Or do we think that being a Worshipful Master is just being a figurehead of no real consequence?

I think what I have just written should already have dispelled that thought.

Finding the truth about Hiram Abiff

Whilst doing the research that was required for this subject, I have been reminded how easily we can take certain parts of our traditional story so much for granted.

To have been able to look afresh at this symbolic and central Masonic character and what can be known or claimed about him, has given me hours of real pleasure. Let me now share with you the results of my searching.

What I have first to share with you is the possibly surprising fact that whereas we might imagine that what we have to examine is a straightforward, single theme, namely the tale that we constantly repeat as Freemasons, the facts as they unfold reveal two, three, four and even five other themes.

If what we were examining here were a piece of music instead of an historical narrative then I would have to say that what we have here is not a simple melody but a fugue – a set of variations on the initial theme. It is only as we uncover these variations and assess their contribution to our understanding of the Hiram story, that we are likely to arrive at the truth about Hiram Abiff.

I naturally start with what we are all familiar with, the events of which we are made aware during our progress through the three basic, or so-called Craft degrees.

We soon learn that the ruling officer in a Free and Accepted Lodge represents King Solomon, sitting symbolically in the chair, or throne, of that monarch. Under his sway we are then engaged in the task of helping to build the temple that he, in place of his father David, was allowed by God to undertake so that the sacred contents of the Tabernacle, first erected as a movable place of worship in the wilderness by Moses, Aholiab and Bezaleel, could now have a fitting and permanent place in the capital city of the Hebrews. To achieve this aim Solomon readily accepted the help of another king, Hiram of Tyre, a non-Jew, who agreed to supply timber from the cedar forests of Lebanon and stones quarried and cut by the skilful Gebalites.

In the course of these arrangements King Solomon sought help from artisans skilled in making bronze furnishings and King Hiram despatched another Hiram of Tyre, who, however, was the son of a widow of the Hebrew tribe of Naphthali, and whose father had also been a skilled worker in bronze. In the second book of Chronicles, chapter 2, we further learn that he was called Hiram Abiff and that he was expert in working gold, silver, iron, stone and wood, as well as purple, blue, crimson and fine linen. His working place for casting the temple vessels were the well-known clay grounds that lay between Succoth and Zerathan [sic].

All these facts are confirmed for us in the VSL, as well as in our ritual, but then we are informed, as Accepted Freemasons, of a few more non-biblical details.

This Hiram Abiff was not just a skilful craftsman. He was the master mason, or architect, of the whole temple project and was admitted to the exclusive company of the two other Grand Masters, Solomon, King of Israel, and Hiram, King of Tyre. They shared a secret that required all three of them to be together if they were to disclose it. That secret was the key to the essential knowledge required to become a fully qualified master mason.

Not surprisingly, there were some craftsmen who, tired of waiting for the secret to be granted to them, took desperate steps to secure what they mistakenly thought they could obtain from just one Grand Master. Hiram Abiff was thus attacked, injured and killed and then hurriedly buried in a makeshift grave. The rough interment was discovered and the body of Hiram was decently interred beneath the Holy of Holies, whilst his attackers were suitably punished.

The place of Hiram Abiff as a Grand Master was then taken, we are told, by Adoniram, another man of Tyre.

Such is the traditional and straightforward account of Hiram with which we are familiar. But we have to note that whilst the first part of the story is based on scripture documents acknowledged for three millennia, the latter events are only of about four centuries existence and are clearly part of a very private tradition. In one sense our apparently continuous story has already become two separate themes and that immediately raises questions about how correct the latter half of our knowledge about Hiram Abiff may be.

That there was such a person the VSL seems to confirm. Whether he was an architect with Grand Master status, whose life was forfeit as a result, is rather more questionable.

Let us look again, however, at that part of our Hiram story which has firm backing from the biblical accounts. It was in 1931 that a Warwickshire Freemason, A. W. Adams, published a well researched booklet entitled: *"The story of the 2 Hirams: Hiram the king and Hiram Abi."*

In 1 Kings, chapter 5 he reminds us that *"Solomon's and Hiram's builders and the Gebalites fashioned the stones and prepared the timber to build the house."*

The Gebalites (in Hebrew, Giblim) came from a town called Gebal (now called Jubeil) and since those who formed our ritual knew the tradition that only Jews were allowed to work on the Jerusalem site, they used the term *Giblim* not to describe those who actually came from Gebal but all the expert stonesquarers or master craftsmen employed on the temple work.

In 1 Kings, chapter 7, verses 13 and 14 we meet Hiram, the son of a widow woman, whose previous husband from Tyre had been a worker in brass or, more correctly, copper. This Hiram was filled with wisdom and understanding and was *"cunning"* (an old word that meant "having special knowledge") to work all works in brass.

There is then a list of all the work on ornaments and vessels which he cast for Solomon in the work ground between Succoth and Zarethan (see v.46). There is no other such craftsman mentioned in 1 Kings. He is then mentioned in 2 Chronicles, chapters 2, 3 and 4, and in chapter 2, verses 7 to 14, a very different story is told from that in 1 Kings.

This writer, Adams, claims that as 2 Chronicles was a much later work, written after the Babylonian exile, the idea that King Hiram sent a competent architect is a fabrication with no historical basis. In other words the craftsman, Hiram Abiff, was only brought in later to create copper and gold ornaments and vessels.

For the record, these ornaments included not only the two great pillars of B and J, but a large molten basin and some smaller ones, in which the sacrificing priests could wash themselves and the people's offerings, and also shovels and pots that helped with roasting meat and storing it.

These were the items in the priests' court but there were also the gold items for the Holy Place: the altar of incense, the table for the shewbread, the Menorah or seven-branched candlestick, other assorted implements and even the hinges on the doors.

It was a very extensive assignment of craftsmanship. These facts help to explain why Freemasons now use TC as the Third degree password.

In 2 Chronicles the two pillars are said to be twice as high as those described in 1 Kings, and Hiram is also said to have made the altar, the cherubim and the veil of the Holy of Holies. We are thus faced with two quite different descriptions of Hiram's tasks. What Brother Adams concluded was that Hiram was a skilled metal smith introduced by Solomon to make a large number of articles, great and small.

That then leaves us with the important question: *Where did the rest of the Masonic story of Hiram Abiff come from?*

First, though, we must look at more of what Brother Adams tackled.

He raised the question: *"Why is Hiram the craftsman called Hiram Abiff?"*, and to provide a satisfactory answer he asks his readers to consider two key sentences in 2 Chronicles.

The first one is verse 13 of chapter 2 which can be translated as: *"I (Huram, king of Tyre) have sent a cunning man, endued with understanding, of Huram my father's."*

If this is the correct meaning it implies that the man from Tyre had already been employed by the king's father there, someone also called Huram.

But the compilers of the books of Samuel, Kings and Chronicles recognise only one king Huram, the one to whom Solomon wrote. A Jewish historian, Josephus, does mention king Huram's father but he calls him Abibaal, never Hiram.

As this translation *"of my father's"* does not seem helpful or correct, it is worth noting that the King James Bible at this point has an alternative rendering which reads: *"I have sent a cunning man, endued with understanding, even Huram my father."*

Here a name, Hiram Abiff, is given to the visiting craftsman and since the author of the book of Chronicles would, of course, know the earlier verse in 1 Kings chapter 7 where *"Solomon fetched Hiram out of Tyre"*, it seems more likely that this is the true meaning. But why is the craftsman, Hiram, then called "my father?"

So as to help us unravel that query Brother Adams asks us to consider a second verse in chapter 4 of 2 Chronicles. This is: *"The pots, and the shovels, and the flesh hooks and all the vessels thereof did Huram his father make for King Solomon."*

We are, therefore, faced with two variations. In the previous verse the King of Tyre calls the craftsman *"my father"* while here the Chronicler seems to call him *"Solomon's father."*

To resolve these variations, Brother Adams looked at what might be the meaning of 'father' in the Old Testament, when the person referred to was not the natural father. He mentions Genesis chapter 45, verse 8 where Joseph says to his brothers: "*God has made me father to Pharaoh and lord of all his house and ruler over all the land of Egypt.*"

Here, the word "*father*" meant the chief adviser or chief minister, and from other verses it now seems clear that in Israel it was customary for the title of '*father*' to be given to a capable official or trusted friend. If that idea is applied to our present study it is not surprising if the Chronicler naturally attaches the words "*my father*" first to someone associated with the King of Tyre and afterwards to someone serving King Solomon.

It is at this point that Brother Adams raises the matter of Hebrew grammar. He notes that in that language possession is indicated by adding letters after a noun and not in front of it as we do.

So, if AB means "father", then ABI (pronounced ABEE) means "my father", ABIHA means "her father" and ABIV is "his father".

In the early 18th century, it was thought that the letter V was pronounced F, so hence we have Hiram ABIFF.

Also, 15th and 16th century scholars who first translated the Bible into what we would call recognisable English could make no sense of "Hiram his father" because the man clearly could not be Solomon's father, so they left ABIV, supposing it to be the craftsman's full name.

That is how we get Hiram Abiff in the Old Charges, but it has now been realised that this was a mistake. What has to be noted is that in Matthew's and Taverner's English Bible versions, the name is given as HIRAM ABI. After 1550, the second part of the name is not given but translated "of my father" without any explanation.

Brother Adams concludes this part of his study with these words: "The traditional account of the two Hirams now current among Freemasons is not, except to a small extent, derived from the Bible. Whence it came is unknown. Presumably it was introduced into the ritual of the operative masons' guild in the early part of the 16th century ... (All that we are to) bear in mind is that the significance of the word ABIF is 'the trusted assistant, the right-hand man' of King Solomon."

With such a detailed and carefully reasoned study at our disposal you might be forgiven for thinking that all that could be said on this subject had been said.

But you would be wrong.

In 1963 a Jewish rabbi, the Reverend Morris Rosenbaum, produced a paper for Quatuor Coronati Lodge that raised a totally new question. He revealed that in a Hebrew commentary on the books of Kings and Chronicles, a 19th century rabbi, Meir Lob Malbim, suggested that a father and son (both called Hiram Abi) were employed in building Solomon's temple. There had to be two men called Hiram Abi, he claimed, because one was the son of a woman of Dan and the other was the child of a widow of Naphthali.

The man mentioned in 2 Chronicles, that king Hiram was asked to send, was to be a skilled all-round craftsman who worked in timber and stone and was an engraver and master of device, an architect, whereas the man mentioned in 1 Kings is just a brass smith. In 1 Kings chapter 5 there is no mention of a skilled workman and only timber is asked for which is why in the next chapter we read of the cedar wood temple framework that was covered with gold. In chapter 7 we read of Solomon and his palace and it is then (verse 13) that Solomon sends for "Hiram out of Tyre" who is the son of a widow of Naphtali, a worker in brass whose work is then described.

The all-rounder, says Rosenbaum, had been sent before any work began, while the worker in brass came in the middle of the temple erection and made the two pillars, the huge brazen bowl and the lavers.

Josephus, in his book, Antiquities viii/iv, seems to confirm the view of Hiram, the cunning man from Tyre, as a later arrival. Moreover, this later arrival was "a widow's son", so he could have been the child of the architect Hiram who had been slain, and hence his mother was of Dan, making her a widowed mother.

This idea, said Rosenbaum, is reinforced when you recall that the first Hiram was skilful in brass and so, if he had not died, why did Solomon send for another brass worker?

Brother Rosenbaum then asks, what does Abif/Abiv mean?

The second book of Chronicles chapter 4, verse 16, states that "Hiram his father" made pots, shovels, etc. Some, as we have seen, think that this means "adviser to Solomon" and this is a possibility for the Hebrew can be interpreted in that way.

Another unquestionable interpretation, says Rosenbaum, is that it is simply his full name, Hiram Abiv, and even Luther called him Huram Abiff.

So, Rosenbaum argues the case from the Bible, that whilst a first Hiram made the pots and instruments of "bright brass", it was a second Hiram who finished off the work with the pillars and lavers because this next Hiram was especially clever at this craft.

The name "Hiram Abiv" refers first to being "the father of Hiram 2" and in the case of Hiram 2 it meant "son of his father".

He also suggests that the father was Huram and the son Hiram. (A final note on this shows that 2 Chronicles chapter 4, verse 11, in Hebrew reads: "And CHURAM made the pots, etc. and CHIRAM finished the work") In 1 Kings. 7/40 we have "CHIROM made the pots and CHIRAM finished the work."

The King James Bible also points out the changes in the names in the Hebrew.

Rosenbaum goes on to say that some authors have suggested that the traditional history is a copy of several classical legends but is devoid of historical truth. He refers to Dr. Oliver's Freemason's Treasury, lecture 45, where the Doctor questions the exhumation of Hiram Abiff's body because "the celebrated artist was living at Tyre many years after the Temple was completed".

In Lecture 47, Oliver also points out discrepancies in Masonic history, including the assertion that the Scriptures have no reference to the death of Hiram Abiff.

Rosenbaum, as we see, questions that.

Why, he asks, did Hiram 1 not finish the work? Surely it was because he, the father, had died on the job and so his son was the son of a widow. Furthermore, Solomon sent an escort to accompany the son to the site of the temple. Rabbinic legend in several places speaks of Hiram going into "heaven alive", like Enoch and Elijah.

If the death of Hiram 1 was mysterious, then it is not surprising that popular rumour might suggest an unusual passing into the hereafter. It seems, Rosenbaum concludes, that there could be a substratum of truth in the death-story of Masonic tradition.

What more is there to consider from others?

Well, in 1925 a Reverend J. S. M. Ward issued a 250-page book with the title: *Who was Hiram Abiff?*

It is clearly not possible to cover in any detail the whole of what is presented there but let me sum up for you the main points that distinguish Ward's thesis.

Having already recognised that we might have two, three or even four Hirams to think about, Brother Ward has one chapter entitled: *The 5 Hirams in the Bible.*

By this he means (1) Abiram who became Abraham; (2) the Abiram in the Sinai wilderness, who suffered a terrible death; (3) Hiram the king; (4) Hiram Abiff; and (5) Adoniram.

In each of the cases he shows in great detail how each of these leaders were involved in death by sacrifice, as Hiram Abiff was. He therefore claims that Hiram Abiff was a chosen sacrificial victim following very ancient tradition.

What he inserts, however, before he ends this catalogue of Hirams, is the following passage:

"As every initiate in Freemasonry represents Hiram ... it naturally

follows that in taking on his character an initiate takes also the title of 'Son of the Widow' ... In this latter form the candidate then becomes the representative of the Saviour whom the Gnostics, like orthodox Christians, considered to be Christ. Thus, in the course of time, by a perfectly natural process of religious evolution, it comes about that it is today quite legitimate to regard the candidate as a humble representative of Christ. Just as Christ sacrificed himself, so must every candidate, and in the 3rd degree the manner of advancing from W to E, emphasises the manner in which Christ died on the cross." So speaks Brother Ward.

There are three other viewpoints that we need to look at in order to appreciate the full range of the thinking about Hiram Abiff.

A paper by the Reverend C. J. Ball made its attempt to clear up some of the mysteries. The possible confusion over Hiram Abiff's mother is solved, he says, if we think of her as one of the daughters of the city of Dan in the tribe of Naphtali, whilst this Hiram's father was an inhabitant of Tyre, rather than a Phoenician by birth. The name Hiram comes from Ahiram, a clan of the tribe of Benjamin. The inference he draws is that whilst Hiram, like his father, may have come from Tyre they were emigrant Jews who were perfectly suited to work on the temple site.

The same attempt to show the Jewishness of the characters involved is repeated in the case of Adoniram.

Referring to a 1768 book of ritual entitled: "*Solomon in all his glory*", Brother Ball shows that whilst Adoniram is usually regarded as a kind of clerk of works, over the timber workers in Lebanon, in this ritual, as Adoniram Abinu, that is, Adoniram our father, he replaces Hiram Abiff in the story.

It is pointed out that in 1 Kings chapter 12, verse 18, he is called Adoram and in 2 Chronicles chapter 10, verse 18, the name is Hadoram. He is killed by rebels whom he has sent for work at the start of the reign of Rehoboam, Solomon's son.

Ado, Adon or Hado is a divine title which points to an Aramean or Galilean origin. This is confirmed by the name of Adoniram's father, Abda, which is the Aramaic form of the Hebrew word obed, which meant a slave. What Ball finds of peculiar interest is the fact that, although there is no reference in Bible sources to the tragic death of Hiram Abiff, there is the record of the murder of this Hadoram or Adoniram.

Brother Kellner, in his 1905 *Explanation of the Hiram Legend* concentrates on the fact of classical parallels that we have already noted in Rosenbaum's paper. Hiram, he writes: *"signifies the height of intellectual life and liberty. The legend, without a doubt, teaches us how the intellectual man is always assailed by ignorance, brutality and vice; a strife that dates from the beginning of the world; it is Abel slain by Cain; Adonis by a wild boar; Osiris by Typhon; Orpheus torn to pieces by the Bacchantes; Moses left to die in the caves of Pisgah; Socrates made to drink the hemlock; Pythagoras expelled, and so on in never ending succession even unto this day."*

The fact of such parallels, which also appear in Ward's book and the more recent work *The Hiram Key*, does not prove that they are therefore of any special significance.

It only remains to direct your attention to a now long forgotten article by a Brother Hayter Lewis in the very first volume of the Q. C. Transactions.

He refers to an Arabic manuscript probably written in the 14th century but using Hebrew letters.

The work, of which there are said to be copies in both the Bodleian and Cambridge University libraries, was very likely an introduction to the Sunnah, an originally spoken commentary on the Qur'an.

What particularly struck those who first heard this paper, and may still prove to be a surprise for Masons today, is the explanation of three Hebrew letters that appear in this presentation of the Hiram story.

The letters form the word M A CH (CH pronounced as in Scottish loCH) explained as:

M tsanu = We have found
A rabonu = Our master
Ch uram = Huram/Hiram

which thus enables us to understand the words used in the Third degree and which some have always regarded as bogus Hebrew:

Mach-abon = We have found our Master Hiram the builder.
Mach-benach = We have found our Master Hiram slain.

It would not be surprising if, with all this gathered information, we are left with a sense of bewilderment.

So, in trying to discover the truth about Hiram Abiff, then it is time for a few clear conclusions to be drawn. Having had an opportunity for reflection on these various studies as they arose it is my own conviction that certain clear statements can be made but I must preface these with the proviso that they are but my own conclusions, and so they are therefore open to challenge and amendment by anyone who can show that a more satisfactory exposition can be given.

For me at least, after nearly 60 years in the Craft, the Hiram legend, as I now understand it, makes sense and fits into my personal pattern of belief.

I start from a conviction that Masonic ritual and history were formed in the guild Lodges and that from at least 1550 to the early years of the 18th century its nature and form was of an wholly orthodox Christian kind. Anyone who is familiar with examples of ritual or Masonic history during this period, will be aware that the Hiram legend as we know it had hardly begun to surface.

In the Dumfries Ms of 1710, we have the following from a very long set of questions and answers:

Q.   Who was master mason at the building of the temple?

A.   Hiram of Tyre.

Q.   Who laid the first stone in the foundation of the temple?

A.   The above said Hiram.

Q.   What did he say when he laid it?

A.   Help us, O God.

Q.   What was the greatest wonder that was seen or heard about the temple?

A.   God was man and man was God, Mary was a mother and yet a maid.

Q.   What was meant by the brazen sea that Hiram framed?

A.   It was appointed to bathe and wash the priests in at that time, but now we find it was a type of Christ's blood whose blood was to purge sin and to wash the elect.

In a book of 1722, entitled *Long Livers*, we also have: "*Thus suffered our Great, our immortal Master, who came into the World to do the Will of his Father which is in heaven and whose Brethren we are (as he says himself) if we do so too. If you ask me what this Will of his Father is, I answer, it is Christ's will.*"

The first mention of a dead body being found in a grave: "*almost consumed away, taking a grip at a finger it came away ... so they reared up the dead body and supported it setting foot to foot, knee to knee, breast to breast, cheek to cheek and hand to back*", is not for Hiram but for Noah and he was the acknowledged Old Testament parallel with Christ.

All this is in the Graham Ms of 1672 where, when Hiram is later mentioned, he comes fifth in an order that has *Christ* as first; then *Peter, called Cephas; Moses; Bezaleel; and only then Hiram who was filled with wisdom and understanding.*

For reasons that I have tried to explain in a chapter on the changing role of the Master Mason in these 200 years, in my forthcoming book

Royal Arch Journey, the degree bearing the title of Master Mason was refashioned to admit Masons who had not passed the Chair, and the further roles of sacrificial victim, an exemplar of moral courage and Masonic fidelity, are transferred to an otherwise quite authentic and identifiable craftsman whose name was Hiram Abi. It was this form of the name because whether the name is translated or not, he was Hiram, the son of his father by the same name, or Hiram as named after his patron, the King of Tyre.

Of course, when his name is used by others they would refer to him as Hiram Abiv, the Hiram of his father or Hiram Abiha, Hiram her son, that is, of the widow.

That is why I persist in calling him Hiram Abi.

The reason why our Masonic Hiram Abiff is elevated in a legend to the rank of Grand Master is because in operative tradition there was a need for three such officers, especially as guardians of the great trade secret.

That this was actually the case in Solomon's time is most unlikely, not only because there is no evidence of such an arrangement but also because there must be real doubt as to Solomon and a non-Jewish king being so associated. Help with practical materials was fine but being co-Grand Masters on a sacred Jewish project was a quite different matter.

Lastly, and this is probably the most controversial point of all, I do not believe that the real Hiram ever died in the service of King Solomon.

That there was the operative masonic tradition of a need for a sacrifice, even a human sacrifice, before a noble edifice could be completed is not in question. It is that tradition that our Hiram's story seeks to preserve and that is all.

Consonant with the written evidence that we have from non-Masonic tradition, I believe that when Solomon summoned the chief artist to his side, as he was showing the completed temple to his guests, it was Hiram Abi, now called Adoniram or the Lord Hiram, whom he honoured. This Hiram duly returned to the land of Tyre and was, sadly, put to death by those rebels of whom the Bible speaks.

Believing this to be the truth does not in any way make me less appreciative of the important legendary history and practice that make up our present Third degree. There is a very great lesson being taught here, of supreme fidelity and trust, but there is a yet greater lesson than the one that we presently offer.

It is that which involves that Bright Morning Star, "*whose rising brings peace and salvation to the faithful and obedient of the human race*".

What I set out to do on this occasion was to present the truth about Hiram Abi. That, to the best of my ability, is what I have sought to do. It is there that I rest my case.

Our Debt to Antients and Moderns

In a few years time we shall be celebrating a very important Masonic bicentenary.

In 1813, the two previously London-based Grand Lodges, which were formed in 1717 and 1751 respectively, came together in a Union. From that act there resulted the United Grand Lodge of England. For all Masons in England there has never been any other kind of Freemasonry and it is not therefore surprising that we take it for granted. Nearly 200 years is quite long enough for most Freemasons to be quite unaware of anything that was earlier.

But why did that Union settlement come about and what are the elements of that Union that we owe to the two participants.

To explain why a Union was necessary is really very simple. Great Britain was developing industrially at an increasingly rapid rate and not least in its trade ventures overseas. With that development went greater mobility of population and a greater exchange of ideas.

As Freemasons travelled about much more in the United Kingdom and abroad, especially with trade, the Army or Navy, so there arose problems of recognition between those who gave allegiance to the Premier Grand Lodge, by now called the *Moderns*, and those who subscribed to the Atholl Grand Lodge, more often called the *Antients*.

Though some local English Lodges turned a blind eye to the credentials of any stranger visiting them, so long as he was known to be a Mason, this was by no means general and if a Mason overseas was refused admission it could cause embarrassment, if not anger, especially where a Mason was too far away from one of his own Constitutional Lodges. The military Lodges were, not surprisingly, more strict about who attended them when in a civil situation.

In particular, the constant encounter abroad of Masons from the three Constitutions caused difficulties.

The Irish Grand Lodge had always tended to favour the *Antients'* members whilst the Scots looked more favourably on those who belonged to the *Moderns*. By the beginning of the 19th century, it became more and more essential that there should be agreement as to whom each Constitution could regard as regular. That meant deciding what kind of Grand Lodge could represent England to the other Constitutions, and especially overseas, for example in the United States of America and Canada.

A union of the two existing English Grand Lodges was the only viable option. That is what led to the founding of the body we know.

But achieving such a union was a far from easy undertaking.

We know that from the late 1780s there was a growing recognition of how much better a Union would be for the Craft but, as we now know, it was to take nearly 30 years for the merger to happen.

Freemasons have a developed sense of loyalty to their Order and for the *Antients* a mere 40 years after the inauguration of their Grand Lodge was not a long enough time for them to be willing to forego the claim to be the legitimate practitioners of what had been guild or ancient Masonry.

Even though the *Antients* forms of ceremonial practice were also creeping into a few *Moderns* Lodges, the *Antients* might have been forgiven for thinking that, because members of the Royal Household mainly attended *Moderns* Lodges, a Union would favour the customs that they practised but which the *Antients* dared to question.

That is why it took nearly 30 years to bring the Union about.

Only the formation of a Lodge of Reconciliation, with an equal membership of both *Moderns* and *Antients* members, could hope to make progress. For historians, the sad fact is that the documents recording the discussions, and the no doubt heated disagreements of that body, are either inaccessible or not in existence.

All we have are the proposals made by the body that then followed the Union, the Lodge of Promulgation, whose task was to convey the combined styles of ceremonial and ritual which had been agreed to the Craft at large. If you wonder why there are so many private Lodge variations in England to this day, it is because the means by which the agreed forms were made known were so much less effective than they later became.

A comparison with the way in which the recently proposed changes in the Royal Arch have just been circulated can show how comparatively primitive were the former channels of communication. It was all by word of mouth with a few hastily scribbled notes made on the occasion of one demonstration, and no written guidelines to take away.

All that accepted, the main elements that we still have today, and which owe their existence to what our forebears insisted on keeping, can be divided into five sections.

The first of them has to do with the layout of the Lodge.

It might never occur to us that there could ever be anything of consequence regarding the exact positions in which the three principal officers in a Lodge might be placed and it may therefore be something of a surprise to learn that if you enter a Lodge room in Scandinavia or on the mainland of Europe, where the Lodge assembling does not owe allegiance to the United Grand Lodge of England, then you will see the Worshipful Master sitting in the East and the Wardens facing him in the South-West and North-West.

If indeed you only go as far as the Canongate temple in Edinburgh, you will find the same arrangement. That is because this was the form of the Lodge adopted by the members of the Premier Grand Lodge of 1717, and thereafter transferred and copied in France, Holland, the German states and finally Sweden.

This form, derived from the idea of the rule of King Solomon and the lay-out of the Inner Temple he built, symbolised the King sitting on a throne where the Holy of Holies was usually placed, and the Wardens having their positions alongside the two great pillars at the other end of the space. The retention to this day of those pillars in miniature by the Wardens underlines this old way of thinking.

For the adherents of the *Antients* Grand Lodge, this was a sure sign that the Premier Grand Lodge had forsaken a feature of truly ancient Masonry. For them the positioning of the one who ruled a Lodge and his assistants had to be determined by a much older method, the places occupied by that trio of truly ancient, and more early, biblical elements; the sun, the moon and the law giver himself.

The sun that rules the day, the moon that governs the night and the instructor in true knowledge, who directs a mason's lodge.

What has to be recognised is that, originally, Solomon sat in the West, where the Sanctum Sanctorum was placed, and the pillars were in the East.

The working stonemasons met with the ruling warden placed in the West and his assistants in the North and East so that they could effectively mark or observe the sun at its meridian, at its setting and at its rising.

In the 18th century, all Lodge rooms were rearranged in the manner of Christian places of worship, as they are today, and so the ruler now sat in the East.

However, the *Antients*, who pleaded their form's antique origin, secured the layout we have adopted, meaning of course to represent a square, the working craftsman's implement, with a Right Worshipful Master at its apex.

As an acknowledgement of the *Moderns* custom, the position of the main officers at the dining table was in the form of their earlier seating in the lodge room, representing a pair of compasses, the tool of the architect or ruler mason.

The second section of the Union agreements concerned the ceremonial.

As we would expect this was a particular source of interest for Masons but it was especially so for the *Antients*, since it was in this area that they had from the outset, in the 1740s, begun to question the way in which these features were presented in the new Lodges that were formed under the Premier Grand Lodge. There were at least four very distinct areas of usage in which a difference would have been noted.

The first, was that particular care was taken over the preparation of Candidates and ensuring that any who attended the Lodge were adequately proven as legitimately entitled to be present. Not only were written or spoken testimonies on behalf of the Candidates to be produced in open Lodge, but also all who attended would be asked by the Wardens individually, for the grip and password during the opening of the Lodge, as is still the custom in the Irish Craft.

The *Moderns* were less insistent on such enquiry, regarding this as petty and demeaning in a fraternity that included gentlemen whose word and presence were not to be doubted. In this regard, the *Moderns* had had a shock in the 1730s when exposures of the ritual had revealed the existing passwords of the first two degrees.

The *Moderns* promptly reversed them and so, during the rest of the century, ensured that those attending a meeting from the other Grand Lodges would be at once discerned. The *Antients* retained the order of words that we use to this day.

The *Antients* were insistent not only on care at opening a Lodge but on a Candidate being properly paraded round the Lodge on every appearance for a new degree and on his being constantly tested before admission to the next stage. This was considered by the *Moderns* to be again fussy and unnecessary.

If a man was considered to be "fit and proper" for membership, then this needed to be proceeded with as soon as possible. He would be brought by the two Wardens to the foot of the table, questioned as to his qualifications, and then led to the adjoining floor drawing, advanced to the Master in the East and then obligated.

It can be seen that in this regard, the form of constant perambulation and testing preferred by the *Antients* largely won the day.

After his investiture with an apron, the Candidate was, in both procedures, seated at the table as a newly recognised Brother. There then began the lectures or catechisms that were conducted round the table, with the Worshipful Master asking questions and the members replying in turn.

A difference here was once more a matter of length.

The *Moderns*, as the Prichard Exposure reveals, kept their lectures to very modest limits, whereas the *Antients* seem to have steadily extended the catechisms, as time went by.

Those familiar today with what is called the Royal Order of Scotland ritual will have some idea of the extent to which catechisms of the mid-18th century could reach, and the 108 or more questions as used in some American constitutions, for a Candidate seeking another degree, show the influence of the 18th century *Antients* practice.

It is here that the effect of the Union can be most vividly seen, for it was then decided that, apart from the occasional or optional use of the approved Emulation lectures, there was to be no explanation of the ceremonies or their furniture in the new United Grand Lodge units.

The general unawareness, even today, of the Emulation Lectures shows how this Union decision had a lasting effect on our Craft. Had there been no such decision then meetings for real "instruction" might not perhaps have been necessary and I, and others, might not have had to write as much as we have.

The last aspect of ceremonial use that we might mention here, apart from the Installation usage which will be dealt with shortly, is the rather more explicitly Christian nature of the *Antients* ceremonies as compared with the *Moderns*. So specific were the *Antients'* prayers that they ended with a clear reference to Jesus Christ.

This was claimed by them as being part of true ancient Masonry but it is to their credit that from the 1760s they were prepared to allow any Jewish candidates (and more were now joining), to use a Hebrew form of prayer at their Initiation. The *Moderns*, whilst retaining some plain Christian references in the catechismal lectures, were already moving in the direction taken after the Union, the universalist approach to the Craft, so that persons of any religion in the growing Empire might feel at ease in joining this fraternity.

They were especially accused by the *Antients* of allowing Lodges to neglect the part played in the Masonic year by the two festivals of St John, and an increasing failure to open the VSL at the first chapter of St John's Gospel.

The familiar symbol of two parallel lines flanking a circle was described as the figures of Moses and Solomon guarding God's revelation and they replaced the earlier John the Baptist and John the Evangelist. The fact that this feature was to largely disappear after the Union was precisely an example of where, as they could not agree on its interpretation, they tacitly left the matter for each Lodge to decide.

An *Antients* practice of reading a piece of Scripture when a Lodge was opened is a further example of a difference in this area which has persisted in not only many Northern Lodges but doubtless elsewhere.

The failure to keep the two St John's days as those for Installation or Consecration, leads us naturally into the next section of difference – the matter of appointing a new Lodge ruler.

This is, of course, a subject that could well merit a whole book to itself, so I must be selective in dealing with it.

Let me start by recalling that in ancient guild Masonry the choice and installing of a ruler was carried out by the Past Masters alone. For the *Antients* it was regarded as a separate step and in the 18th century was called the degree of Past Master.

It was therefore performed with a grip, token and word in the presence of other Past Masters. It became a formal act at a definite time of the year, on 27th December. It was called a Festival, it was linked to a service in the local Anglican church, and the meal provided was more like that to which we are usually accustomed. It was a very special event and not least because, as you may know, it was linked with another degree.

For the *Moderns*, certainly during their first 50 years, much of this was totally unnecessary. Election of a Master was a matter which each Lodge could decide for itself, and in some cases it was not even an annual event since the Master could continue if acceptable to him and the members.

The ceremony was one that was carried out in the course of ordinary Lodge business, much as in the Rose Croix to this day, with the ordinary Brethren withdrawing behind the Wardens' chairs, the Past Masters forming a huddle in the East (the origin of the turning to the East, as still known to us) and the few secrets of the Chair being communicated in a low voice.

As there was no recognition of any degree beyond that of Master Mason, the only importance of being a Right Worshipful Master was that of being the present holder of King Solomon's place.

Differences then, can be seen, and the distinction between what we today call the normal and extended working of a Board of Installed Masters.

Anyone who wishes to learn more about these variations can do so by reading my book *What Do You Know about Ritual?*

Having spoken about one office in the Lodge it is only natural to mention two others that mark the difference between the two traditions.

Beginning with the *Moderns*, it was not long before there had emerged the distinctive office of Stewards who assisted at the Premier Grand Lodge Festivals. They began by assisting the Grand Wardens in arranging the annual feasts but it was soon clear that they were able, and willing, to carry out this task on their own. The idea spread to the local Lodges and if you visit Royal Cumberland Lodge No. 41 at Bath, you will see the Director of Ceremonies sitting in the mid-North side, with his cluster of Red aproned Stewards around him.

The *Antients* did not have Stewards but, with their more Christian emphasis, introduced Deacons in some of the Lodges. Like Stewards, these were regarded from the outset as assistants of the Wardens when Lodge memberships grew in number.

To this day, that aspect of the office is retained in describing their work at every opening of a Lodge. They were not at the beginning floor officers in a ceremony, and it is only when they are now being formally invested at an Installation that their duties in this regard for a ceremony are outlined.

At the Union the Stewards were accepted as table assistants but because the practice now began of not allowing the Wardens to leave their places, someone else had to do their previous work on the floor. The Deacons were given the Wardens' wands as a sign of delegated authority and they thus began to perform as we are accustomed to see them do today.

Once again a compromise of traditions was achieved.

There remains only one other section to describe and that relates to the limits of work permitted under the Lodge warrant. For the *Moderns* this was restricted closely to the three Craft degrees as known and practised by us. That, by the way, is why they were adamant that the Installation step was not a degree.

For the *Antients*, the Lodge warrant permitted the practice of any recognised degree and, having from the start an Irish connection, there was at once what we would now describe as a Royal Arch and a Knightly Red Cross Order tradition, that was to be permitted and practised. Whatever may or may not be the full facts about the prevalence of other degrees from the outset of the Grand Lodge of the *Antients*, the fact remains that as far as they were concerned the

Past Master, Arch and any other existing ceremonies were separate degrees able to be used and promoted in their Lodges.

It was only the insistence of a figure like Thomas Dunkerley who could persuade the *Moderns* Grand Lodge to accept the Royal Arch, and even then the ceremony had to be conducted on a separate occasion in a body called a Chapter. It is noticeable that even after the Union, the Royal Arch, whilst being accepted, was yet to be performed in a separate Chapter and not the Lodge.

Here, then, were the main elements of what had to be considered and combined if a Union was to be effective. That it has lasted so long without major alteration is a tribute to the Duke of Sussex and his advisers. That it revealed the sure touch of British compromise, with a blind eye for many minor variations across our land, is almost a mark of pure genius.

What we have to do is to value the various strands of our heritage and help new generations to do the same.

The Sources of Masonic Practice

During the last few years I have been seeking to unravel the course by which the now commonly recognisable form of the English Masonic Lodge took the shape that it did. It has been a journey based not on a preconceived or formally determined theory but on the increasingly persuasive evidence of such records, artefacts and social circumstances as existed in, or from, the period of at least 1350 to 1730.

Whilst that story has been unfolding, and must stand or be amended by the data that has been assembled, I have been studying another strand in the same period.

For what needs to be looked at and examined, as I once learnt in a cogent paper by Brother Michael Baigent, is not simply the form of the emerging English Lodge but the content of its ritual and practice. Whereas we may now be able to see how the grades of the working stonemasons' craft developed into the three degrees (with the Holy Royal Arch) of the Free and Accepted system, there still remains the query: *"From where did we get our Masonic history, our signs and symbols, our use of allegory, our forms and penalties of obligation, our passwords and types of recognition, our early types of catechism and instruction, our clothing and our titles for the various offices?"*

We take these matters for granted but what do we really know about where they originated and why? It is as an introductory attempt to answer this somewhat heavily laden enquiry that I proffer the following for consideration.

Anyone familiar with Harry Carr's *The Freemason at Work* or Bernard Jones's *Compendium of Freemasonry* will be only too well aware of how previous Masonic instructors have sought to grapple with such matters. Foolish indeed would anyone be who ignored what they and others like them have suggested in days past.

Yet, whilst it is essential to give due attention to such earlier suggestions, one overriding and as yet apparently unrecognised query, fails to have been addressed. This is, *"Have we uncovered what was the overall and truly original source and means by which such material came to be adopted?"*

For the sake of clarity as to this enquiry let me put my proposition in another, and more specific, form.

By 1738, a form of official Masonic history had become accepted by its being included in the Book of Constitutions, compiled by Dr James Anderson for the Grand Lodge of London and Westminster, hereafter referred to as either the Premier or Moderns Grand Lodge.

This edition was a revised version of that which had first appeared in 1723, which was itself based on material drawn to Anderson's attention by those, such as Grand Master Payne. He had produced a copy of the Old Charges, previously used in the latter's home city of Chester. Brother Payne's familiarity with a copy of these Old Charges was almost certainly due to his father's encounter with them in the Lodge that had emerged in that city during the 17th century.

For many, that is a quite sufficient answer to the query as to the provenance of a form of Masonic traditional history. The question that I believe is still not answered is, from where did the Old Charges get their form of the history?

It is here that we begin to enter what is new territory for many.

Held in the library of the oldest Lodge in York is a facsimile copy of the very version of the Old Charges which Brother Payne drew to the attention of Anderson. Inserted in the text of the narrative we come across a plain reference to its source. This compilation of ancient events comes, says the text, from the source called *Sir Ranulph Higden's Polychronicon*, which we know was compiled in the early 14th century because its author, Higden, died in 1346.

In those days, monks as well as knights were addressed as *Sir*, and this learned monk of St Werburgha's Abbey, Chester, produced an account of world history from ancient times up to his own day that is still regarded as among the most notable of all medieval historical works. It is hardly surprising that it should be the quarry from which the stonemasons, no doubt guided by some ex-monastic adviser, should draw the information to support their claim to be of ancient foundation.

What more authoritative source could there be for Chester guild Masons to quote in their request to the Crown for a charter, than this acclaimed work, created in their own locality? When, moreover, we learn that King Edward III, in the late 1300s invited Sir Ranulph to his court to discover more about his history, its influence was enhanced, especially as it was that king who required of the guilds, including the masons, that they produce a history to justify their guild claims to antiquity.

In this case, it is therefore possible to trace in a direct manner the initial source of what might otherwise have just been imagined to be a masonic secular invention. Indeed, it has sometimes been suggested that it was precisely because this historical narrative was devised by somewhat less educated craftsmen, that it contained so many curious statements.

This now proves not to be the case.

The Chester guild stonemasons and, through their initiative countless others of their day, were using the best and most reliable material that they had to hand. The monastery of St Werburgha might eventually be destroyed but its heritage through the Polychronicon lived on.

What similar routes can we uncover as we search for the original practice or knowledge that led to other aspects of the Craft? Might it even be that here was a more common source than we might otherwise have expected?

Let us, therefore, continue by looking next at what we might call signs and symbols.

Their presence and indeed their necessity in our Masonry does not need underlining, so let us go back beyond the 18th century and see what the situation was in the 17th. We are assisted here by Dr Plot, who, though not a Freemason, was a close associate of Elias Ashmole and one who made specific reference to the manner in which Freemasons in Staffordshire, and indeed across the whole country, were able to communicate with one another.

This is what Dr Plot says: "*Into (this) Society when any are admitted they call a meeting (or 'Lodg' [sic] as they term it in some places) which must consist of at least 5 or 6 of the Ancients of the Lodge (and) they proceed to the admission of them, which chiefly consists in the communication of certain secret signs ... ... by which means they have maintenance whither ever they travel; for if any man appear, though altogether unknown, that can shew any of these signes to a Fellow of the Society, whom they call an accepted mason, he is obliged presently to come to him.*"

Elsewhere, he explains that workers on a site can communicate from the top of a steeple or at a fair distance by using the appropriate signs.

It is of course true, as I pointed out in my book, *Arch and the Rainbow*, that there were Strasburg Steinmetzen in the 14th century who had a range of signs and symbolic acts that show us the earlier history of what we do.

Yet, I again ask, where did they get their ideas from?

Another Freemason first pointed me in a direction that I have steadily pursued ever since. That is the use of various agreed signs as a means by which the monks of several Orders, and the Cistercians in particular, communicate with each other. I mention the Cistercians, or their even more mute descendants the Trappists, because in these communities of monks there were more extensive periods of complete silence, not least at mealtimes when the tongue was otherwise used, but life had to go on.

Let me give some examples of the signs that were not only used in the Middle Ages but are still used in their houses today. Certain of them may seem very familiar to us. Fingers on the lips for silence, pointing upwards or downwards for heaven or hell, or pulled across the throat for death.

If you wonder what this has to do with stonemasons, may I remind you that the Orders I have specially mentioned were occupants of houses in such remote locations, that in order to have their own special workforce for extension, repair and maintenance they were the only monks to have their private, on the spot, bands of stonemasons and carpenters. Those craftsmen formed part of the lay brothers who also lived in their monasteries.

Do you now wonder how they learnt sign language and adapted it to their purposes?

We next turn to an early form of Masonic practice called *"catechismal instruction"*.

We still retain this in some sense by what occurs after a Candidate has been obligated and then entrusted by the Worshipful Master. The new member of the Craft is led to the two Wardens who proceed to question him about the events that he has just undergone. This is of course but a pale copy of what took place in much earlier times. As anyone who is a member of the Royal Order of Scotland will be aware, the more ancient practice was to seat the Candidate at the table after he was obligated and to begin a catechismal interchange that was conducted by the reigning Master or Past Masters of the Lodge with the two Wardens, seated as if at a table.

Indeed, in that Order the places at which the Master and Wardens sit are as we are used to seeing them at the festive board in the East, South-west and North-west.

We thus, have in the one form of procedure not only an old type of material but also an old type of communication. When we go 40 years further back from the reaffirmed Royal Order ritual of the late 1730s to the Edinburgh House Ms. of 1696, not only do we find traces of the same instruction but we have exactly the same catechismal method.

What we learn from evidence in York and Ireland at the same period is that this alternate questioning was done not just with the Wardens but involving all the members seated around the Lodge table.

From whence, we must now again enquire, does this method of communicating knowledge derive?

Some of us with memories still of earlier instruction in religious matters might at once respond, from the church catechism style. Is this really its ultimate source? Where did this type of instruction have its birth?

One point of view is that it derives from the form of dual communication that was part of all monastic worship. The singing in their choirs was done by exchange. One side of the choir made a statement and the other side came back with a response. They even had special names. One side was called Cantoris and the other Decanus, Chanter and Deacon in English.

This gave rise to the idea of so communicating knowledge, with the professed novice Master asking the questions and the one or more novices supplying the correct replies. I surely do not need to spell out the similarity to the priest or schoolmaster adopting the same method as that being the one with which the Accepted Freemasons who attended the first Grammar Schools would have been very familiar.

The catechism style of instruction seems to have had a monastic origin.

Yet it was not just this form of instruction which we inherited. There was something even more important for our Lodge practice. I mean the exercise of memory.

To pursue this side of our culture could occupy us a very long time, so let me therefore give you four pointers to the way in which I believe that this aspect of our practice arose.

When two years ago I asked the Grand Master of Pennsylvania if I might acquire a book of their ritual he fixed me with his eye, asked what kind of obligation I had once taken and then said that his men learnt all their ritual by word of mouth, and face to face with their predecessors in office.

For them, memorising was, and always had been, their practice from the 18th century.

The Freemasons who came into the guild Lodges in the post-Renaissance period of the 17th century would have recognised the cult of memory, as Dr Frances Yates has made clear in her many books, as an essential requisite of any trained scholar at school or university.

Memory was part of the skill that any craftsman needed for his trade and when the guild masons put on their mystery plays it was required of them, without demur, that their parts had to be learnt by memory and had to be word perfect, or they were fined.

But the ground of all this emphasis on memory as an art was culled from the monks of old.

In a recent book devoted to the subject of *Memory in Medieval Culture*, Mary Carruthers has the following to say relevant to our subject:

"It is my contention that medieval culture was fundamentally memorial, to the same profound degree that modern culture in the West is documentary. That is why the fact of books in themselves, which were much more available in the late Middle Ages than ever before, did not profoundly disturb the essential value of memory training until many centuries had passed. A book from the Cistercian library of St Mary's, Holme-cultram, makes a particularly interesting study of mnemonic technique (because being) in Anglo-Norman indicates that it was for the 'pueri', or novices, of the monastery, many from noble families, beginning their studies. I think one will find the traditions of memorial art not in separate treatises but in the practices of monastic prayer. The way in which these practices were translated for the pious laity of the late Middle Ages, the same audience that read the medieval arts of memory addressed to lawyers, merchants and other gentlemen, may illustrate a neglected source of early humanism."

I hope the indication is clear. Monastic custom and method again seems to have been the first basis for another part of our Masonic practice.

As the last of the elements in the formation of our ritual, I turn to that term which is part and parcel of our own definition of the Craft.

We say that it is "veiled in allegory and illustrated by symbols".

Where did these ideas come from? No one doubts that we have them from the earliest days of Accepted Masonry for the allegorical meaning of many things that we say or see in the rooms or on the tracing boards of our Lodges, appear at the earliest moment of recorded ritual. But yet again, I must pose the question: "From where did those early ritual formers get these things?"

Could it possibly be from a similar source to that which we have already seen being used?

The answer is: "Yes, it can."

I had occasion recently to read again a book of the Reverend Dr Oliver, regarding the elements of Masonry in his time, of 1847. Merely to restrict myself to two of the items that he mentions we read as follows regarding the candlestick in the Holy Place (which, incidentally, appears on many Second degree Tracing Boards today):

"The seven lamps are emblems of the gifts of the Spirit; the knops and flowers, the graces and ornaments of a Christian life. As the candlestick gave light to the tabernacle, so we must remain in darkness unless Christ shall enlighten his Church."

He then turns to the table of the shewbread, which also figures on some of our Fellow Craft boards:

"Some understand by it the holy scriptures, and interpret the four rings by which it was carried, when removed from one place to another, as the four evangelists, by whom the gospel of Christ was carried, as it were, from nation to nation."

From where did he get all this allegorical interpretation?

Believe it or not but his words are a remarkably close repetition of what was written by the Venerable Bede, the Monk of Jarrow, just 1150 years previously.

In one of Bede's works, the one called "On the Temple", we find the following:

"The seven lamps are the seven gifts of the Holy Spirit. The cups, bowls and lilies are aptly ordered under the branches because the hearts of the elect are upheld by the Lord's gifts, commandments and promises ... It is a lampstand because it has shown the path of light to those who have gone astray."

And then later:

"For surely the 4 golden rings are the 4 books of the gospels of the evangelists, through faith in which it has come to pass that all Sacred Scripture is read and understood throughout the whole world."

When you consider that what Bede wrote and taught had made such an impression on the monastic curriculum that it was copied and communicated through the ages, so that it was in time written, as it were, in stone is it any wonder that as the mason craft that served the monks, and then created the guilds in which Accepted members could share in the new forms of teaching by ritual, that these by now well-worn and tried ideas continued to be employed?

There was no need to create new allegorical meanings. They were already to hand. Nor was this the case only for symbols from Christian antiquity.

In the age of the Counter-Reformation from the 1580s a new body of monks appear, the Soldiers of Christ, otherwise known as the

Jesuits, and from them we take one of their most potent and treasured emblems, the All-Seeing Eye.

The monastic source of Masonic usage seems to be underlined in its most modern form.

What I have outlined here needs of course to be both tested for its widest possible application and examined still further in detail to ensure its reasonable acceptance. For myself this continuation of a tradition that in England looked as though it had been almost obliterated, is both evident and natural.

When I again consulted that fascinating book, *English Monks and the Suppression of the Monasteries* by Geoffrey Baskerville, and was reminded that so many Abbots became Deans or Bishops, and the monks became parish priests or school masters, why are we surprised that both they and the laity whom they served should have acquired the monastic wisdom of the ages and brought it into one of the social groupings, the new guild Lodges that begin around 1600?

When you think about it, the wonder is that it should have been so long before we have realised where our true ceremonial origins lay.

This, I suggest, could be the real Masonic, not the Hiram, Key.

Why and how has Freemasonry survived?

Accepted Freemasonry, in a form that we would recognise as such, has passed through at least seven major challenges to its happy progress.

In making such a claim I am, of course, assuming that we all recognise that Masonry in its Accepted form started at least a century and a half before the four remnants of that earlier, ancient Craft in London and Westminster decided to request the aid of a new kind of Grand Lodge, in 1717.

Had there not been "survival" at least twice in the century before that landmark event, it is quite possible that there may not have been even those four Lodges seeking a new future, or Accepted Freemasonry would have developed in other places and in another fashion.

In an attempt to answer the why and how, the accumulated wisdom of some 500 years of experience has to be taken into account.

Freemasons may not always have profited as fully from the experience of their predecessors as they might but there have always been some lessons taught that have been taken to heart and then applied with benefit in the next generation.

That is the first answer in our quest. Freemasonry has been willing to adapt and learn from its past.

The next answer that I would submit to the question why Accepted Freemasonry has survived, is that it has always been aware of its ancient roots and I would continue that theme by claiming that ours is a tree that has so far had very firmly established roots. Some call them "landmarks".

It is no coincidence that a newly made Mason is told that he has now become a *"member of our ancient and honourable institution. Ancient no doubt it is, as having subsisted from time immemorial"*.

Even if this does not mean that we are somehow the direct descendants of the Egyptian, Greek and Roman builders, there are some aspects of ancient wisdom that have been preserved by the Craft through the ages, and which have been transmitted using the symbolism of the builder's art. It is that core of sacred knowledge and moral direction, based not least on the teaching throughout of the Holy Scriptures, that has given Freemasonry an acceptable, recognisable and unshakeable base.

As we are so properly reminded: *"Our Order is founded on the purest principles of piety and virtue."*

One indisputable fact is that the working stonemasons' trade in England underwent a traumatic shake-up in the Tudor period. Along with the demolition of not only holy buildings but sacred parish and social guilds, it was the masons' guilds with their own special traditions, even with a diminished operative membership, that were a main focus for those non-mason Fellows in the local community, who had lost their own means of social intercourse and charitable concern.

That change is the root of our whole history.

Meeting under the canopy of an apparent trade association a welcoming hand was extended to, and accepted by, those who were seeking fresh fellowship and purpose in what remained the masons' long established, saintly and social unit.

Accepted Freemasonry at its outset met a real social need.

During the next 300 years it repeatedly did the same. From the end of the 17th century and for the next 50 years, the Grand Lodge of All England at York provided a place where Roman Catholics and Anglicans, Jacobites and Loyalists could all meet.

In the 18th century Huguenot refugees made an increasing contribution to the Masonic Craft as well as English commerce. You only have to mention Desaguliers, a Grand Master, Foulkes, a Grand Warden, and Villeneau, the printer of the first Constitutions, to realise how true that was.

In that century too, there came a new influx of Jewish refugees from Eastern Europe. Establishing their foothold in English society was a perilous and quite difficult business but one of the openings that they rightly seized on was that of becoming members of Masonic Lodges, even if after entry they might soon be aware that Craft Masonry still bore many marks of its Christian origin.

To be accepted as a Brother "on the level", when in the rest of society you were treated as second class, was worth any amount of toleration to a Hebrew citizen.

There was also the military story.

Soldiering prior to the year 1700 was not an honourable undertaking. Apart from such members of the nobility as were expected to lead their own local detachments of men to war, or were given high command by their monarch, the ranks and their subordinate leaders were regarded as disreputable as travelling actors and stage players.

It was John Churchill, later Duke of Marlborough, who in the early years of the 18th century created the change. His stricter discipline, regular pay and encouragement of career service, started a new appreciation of the military life and his fabled victories, smart uniforms and regimental pride provided the basis for a modern army.

I like the story of what happened in Chester in 1720. The old guild Lodge there, that had recovered from the time when the Civil War was over, had by the late 1600s lost any connection with the operative craft so that it had no recognisable controlling authority. It continued to grow, however, and by the early 1700s was so large that it was becoming unwieldy.

The help was sought of the Duke of Richmond, a leading Mason, and his advice was taken. He recommended that the now private Lodge should be divided up into three new Lodges, one for the nobility, gentlemen and military officers, one for professional men and one for craftsmen and tradesmen.

Not only does this reflect the new status of at least military commanders of all ranks, but it usefully illustrates how the Freemasonry of the time was able to adapt to social custom and status whilst yet retaining the sense that, as Brethren, they all gathered on the level as members of one fraternity. Not only did three such Lodges appear in Chester but they were soon to be enrolled on the books of a new Grand Lodge.

It was precisely because of the serious change brought about in the late 1600s by the creation of brand new guilds for the operative building trades, that the Lodges previously attached to their late medieval guilds began to look around for a new authority to guide their activities. This is why in York the old guild Lodge, now a private Lodge, adopted a new guise by becoming a Grand Lodge from at least 1705 and probably before.

In London, as we know, four now private Lodges determined to establish an overarching body as the new Grand Lodge for London and Westminster, in 1717. It is no coincidence that this Grand Lodge should be so designated because whereas under the operative guild system, one of the seven divisions of England was called York, north of the river Trent, so the division south of that river had been termed London and Westminster.

Traditional terms and practice still persisted.

What was new about the 1717 Grand Lodge was that it formed an association in which, whilst each private Lodge was left free to manage its own day-to-day affairs and ceremonies, it could benefit from the opportunity to confer with those from other Lodges on matters of constitutional policy, social involvement and wide charitable ventures. It gave the Accepted Craft a new sense of identity, the strength of coordinated effort when required, and a sense of control over those who might want to become members.

It was precisely because Freemasonry now had a new and recognisable place in society, approved by the Government, that drew the nobility into its ranks and its leadership, whether in York or Westminster. It was past being merely a local phenomenon and became a national one.

It was in making this transition that a new difficulty arose in the south.

Just because the Grand Lodge of London and Westminster was a new body prepared to create clear, workable systems but with officers reared with different backgrounds and experience (from ancient guild Lodges, from Scottish practice in operative Lodges or from acquaintance with other and non-masonic societies), it is hardly surprising if in their plans these rulers overlooked or disregarded what some Lodge members regarded as essential landmarks.

These included fixed saints' days for an Installation, the irreversibility of some passwords, the failure to acknowledge the significance of the Old Charges and the reduced status of an Installed Master. All these and several lesser points soon led to a feeling in some quarters that "ancient St John's Masonry" was being lost or overridden.

As early as the 1730s, a steadily growing tide of feeling had built up that might have caused serious division in the still new Grand Lodge's ranks.

But certain safety valves were to avert any disaster.

One was an occasional lack of stability amongst the rulers of Grand Lodge which prevented steadily effective discipline being in place between 1730 and 1750. This meant that alternative and old forms of ritual were being practised without any serious restriction, even in the capital.

The other development, by 1751, was the emergence of a rival Grand Lodge of the Old Constitutions, more familiarly known as the *Antients*. This restored to regular usage precisely those features which were believed to have been neglected and which, incidentally, were still at this time part of the Grand Lodge of All England at York practice.

That is why the *Antients* later called themselves "Old York Masons".

It is instructive to note that even with three Grand Lodge systems in operation for the rest of that century, Accepted Freemasonry did not seem to falter or suffer unduly. Whether this was due to what was still the comparative isolation of different parts of the country, remembering the unpaved roads and the need for Masons to travel on moonlit nights, dependence on the horse and the constant delay of coaches if you could afford them, or whether the varied styles of Freemasonry were practised in different places, or parts of a large town, has, I believe, never been properly studied.

What we do know from a most interesting paper written for Quatuor Coronati some 35 years ago, is that Brethren found a practical solution. In many areas, whether it was constitutionally permitted to visit a Lodge of another type or not, *Moderns* are known to have incorporated into their ceremonies *Antients'* practices which suited them.

As one of our greatest freedoms in English Freemasonry has been to be allowed to perform any ceremony that complied with the general landmarks, this could well explain why there was not more antipathy or aggravation at this time. Though in some places there may have been a refused entry to a Lodge of another tradition, the division was not so deep or widespread as to fracture the fraternal image of the Craft.

There were other survival features of 18th and 19th century Masonry.

The first was that the Accepted Craft was integrated into society as it had been from its outset. Not only had the Mason Guild Fellows taken their share in local government but processions of robed Masons along the streets on their way to church for an Installation sermon and invites to the City rulers, and sometimes their ladies, to attend the subsequent banquet were common in the 18th century.

When the 19th-century building explosion occurred, Masons were constantly seen in regalia at the foundation stone laying of a church, a bridge, or a hospital.

Details of Masonic meetings or charity bazaars appeared in the local newspapers while the activities of Masonic notables such as Princes, Dukes, peers, Bishops and Deans were sure to get ample coverage. To be a Mason was to have a recognisable place in society and even for some a chance for a move up in social level.

That Freemasonry was an acceptable addition to English social behaviour was unquestioned. It was a part of the Establishment.

Another survival feature was the requirement that no religious or political discussion was allowed during Masonic meetings. That this was, and still is, a major ingredient for preserving harmony is unquestioned. The fact that adherents of differing Christian traditions, Jews and Muslims, Sikhs and Parsees, Hindus and some Buddhists, as well as Radicals, Socialists and Traditionalists, have all been able to take their seats together in one Lodge room was why the Craft was able to find a natural place in the expanding British Empire.

The "Mother Lodge" poem by Kipling eloquently expresses this aspect of the Craft.

To this landmark requirement there has to be added the determined process of steadily removing from the basic Craft degrees any explicit references of a strictly orthodox Christian character. This process developed more swiftly in *Moderns* Lodges and was, of course, directly tackled at the time of the 1813 Union.

Whilst *Antients* Lodges had from the 1760s followed the custom of providing a special Hebrew prayer at Initiation for Jewish Candidates, this was discontinued and a common prayer, which avoided any specific religious association, was introduced.

Mention being made of the Union of the two then extant Grand Lodges in 1813, reminds us that this at last enabled the Craft to enter upon a period of new growth without the burden of divided Masonic

style of Lodges that we see the results of today. There appear school and university Lodges, research and lecture Lodges like Quatuor Coronati and the Dormer Circle, Installed Masters and Provincial Stewards, legal and medical Lodges, Bisley marksmen and caravanners.

The list is apparently endless.

All tastes and fancies appear to have been catered for, yes, even dining Lodges in which the quality of the food and drink provided was more important than anything else they met for. It is only a few months ago that I was invited to lecture in such a Northern Lodge because the Provincial Grand Master had told the members that if they did not do more than meet to dine well, then he would request their warrant.

But is all this relevant to our main theme of "survival"? Well, I think it is.

Along with the prospect of "promotion in rank", a need to retain interest by creating Lodges of like-minded folk was recognised and, until recently, so-called "closed" Lodges were not only allowed but encouraged.

Yet, if this very significant increase in Lodges appeared to be ensuring the prosperity and future of the Craft we now know that it was survival (in a century of clubs), at a price. Every Mason who helped to found this special kind of Lodge and swell the Grand Lodge list and coffers, was thus expected to support two Lodges whilst those who were Initiated in the new Lodges may have been depriving existing Lodges of new Candidates. Whilst it could be claimed that this was using a fresh incentive to ensure the continuance of our Order the truth, as we now know, was that it was a survival measure at a cost.

The creation of Lodges for those who had experienced comradeship of a high order in two Great Wars clearly met a need. Whether new Lodges were the answer, is the question.

Such relationships die, literally, and then the original inspiration of the Lodge dies also. Perhaps we have to recall the experience of Lodges in the earliest days.

Lodges were formed; after some 20 or 30 years they dwindled; they closed and their warrants were sold to another group of men, some of whom were Masons but others were Initiated on the day of "warranting" the new Lodge, and so Accepted Freemasonry resumed its path.

What was crucial was not that some men wanted to meet regularly but that they had a desire to practise the Craft. That is the cornerstone of our whole system.

Are we really interested in what is the distinctive core of Freemasonry? Not its adjuncts, our dining, charity, visiting, promotion or pomp... but the ceremonies, ritual, the teaching, principles, tenets and their history.

What has to be mentioned is that period of apparent withdrawal from society which was encountered by those of us who joined the Craft 50 to 30 years ago. Reticence about our membership, utter silence about our activities (save for mention of senior Masonic appointments in the *Daily Telegraph*) and certainly no involvement in public events, were the accepted order of the day.

With hindsight, some have thought it to have been a mistaken approach but I would contend that it may have been a less questionable policy at a time in the 1960s and 1970s, when most principles and tenets that we treasure were being questioned if not overturned in the England around us. We were rudely shaken out of that privileged privacy that may have looked like secrecy by the churches that suddenly felt threatened and wanted scapegoats, by a Press that exercised new freedoms to question everything, for nothing was sacred anymore, and by those in the seats of authority who revelled in what was called "political correctness".

If we were to cope with these serious challenges to the Craft that some of us have witnessed in our lifetime, those from half-informed secular journalists, church leaders and national or local government officials, then we had ourselves to be firmly anchored in, and much better informed about, the great and ancient Society to which we say we belong.

For make no mistake, we do seem to have surmounted those storms of the 1980s and 1990s that looked at times as if they might threaten our very survival. We have recognised that we are in a new era and a different kind of society from our forebears and fresh strategies to aid our members, as well as inform our non-Mason friends and neighbours, are needed.

Let me, however, proffer a word of caution.

If we are to be effective in assisting the survival of Freemasonry, then we have to be very clear as to what it is that we are defending.

I believe that the words of a new Freemason need to be heeded. This is what he wrote in an early MQ magazine:

"I would not want to see Freemasonry become more open, nor would I want to change Lodge ritual or the structure of the festive board. Freemasonry is as valuable now, in its current guise, to the current generation, as it has ever been. I really hope that we start to realise and appreciate that the system, ethos and artefacts we already have are the best blueprint for our success in the future."

"That's what Freemasonry is all about, isn't it?"

Anyone who has heard a great many Masonic after-dinner speeches, as I have – and you will notice that I said "heard" and not "suffered" – will be more than familiar with the above phrase.

On a great many occasions speakers use it as a kind of rhetorical shorthand, going on about some matter of personal or Lodge concern, trying to show how important it is and then, imagining that they can clinch their argument or finally convince their hearers, they say:

"Well, that's what Freemasonry is all about, isn't it?"

Often I am left with the feeling that the speaker is not saying what he really means but is merely using this phrase as a device which he hopes will have its own inbuilt magic; just as when it is suggested to us clergy that *"if your argument is weak then thump the pulpit ledge harder."*

On the other hand I do occasionally hear these words delivered with such emphasis and sincerity that I am actually led to believe that the speaker does see his particular interest in the Craft as the real and only purpose for which Masonry exists.

What I then find myself doing, is asking whether what he is claiming for the Craft is what I would say was its fundamental purpose.

So it is to deal with both these approaches, what I will call the casual and the serious, that some years ago I decided to offer a paper on this well-worn phrase. My hope was, and still is, that if I can give some generally acceptable content to those words, then perhaps we can correct others when they use the words too offhandedly, whilst enabling us all to accept the words with much more understanding of what they are trying to express.

In order to do this, I must obviously begin by trying to see how the words of my title fit some of the aspects of Freemasonry to which they are sometimes attached.

I begin with Benevolence and Charity.

Indeed I would have to say that it is in this sort of context that I most often hear them. The proposer of a Candidate, for example, is offering the toast to the Initiate at the festive board, reminding him of the dish or charity box that was placed before him at the North-East corner, and seeking to make clear in the new member's mind the essential obligation to practice generosity towards all the charitable causes for which a Mason may be liable.

He may quote the appropriate phrases in the First Degree Charge or extol the second feature in the well-known triple motif of Masons – *Brotherly Love, Relief and Truth* – but then, with a flourish that is meant to embrace every Brother in the room he will conclude:

"That, Brethren, after all, is what Freemasonry is all about, isn't it?"

Well, is it?

Forgive me, Brethren, if I disappoint some of you by saying that it is not. Of course charity has its place but that is not what Freemasonry is all about. If it were, then I would have thought that the Craft was both misguided and misleading in its true purpose. Whatever can anyone with any practical sense think of an Institution that claims charitable support as its fundamental and major purpose and yet persuades men of some substance in the world, to divert some of their hard-earned money into the cost of regalia, dining fees, ladies evenings, entertainment of visitors, hours of learning ritual, joining appendant degrees and ceremonial rehearsals, not to mention the scrutiny of Candidates, and – wait for it – the payment of not inconsiderable Grand Lodge and Provincial Grand Lodge dues.

If, in fact, Freemasonry is really established so as to be a charitable institution then I would have to say: *"Stop this drain on members' purses and let us divert all that good money into the causes that Masonry is all about."*

We don't say that and we would not be terribly happy about anyone who really meant that, not because we do not want to help charitable work but because we instinctively know that Freemasonry is not initially, or finally, about giving donations to those in need.

It is part of our Freemasonry, and there is not a genuine Freemason anywhere who cannot be relied on to give constantly and generously to those who can properly benefit from his kindness and concern. Yet the very fabric of Freemasonry is more than, and distinct from, the many acts and occasions of benevolence.

So, what next?

Well, the second claimant on this phrase, at least in my experience, is one that may not take as long to deal with, but it is a very persistent suggestion all the same. This one takes account of the other aspect of our fraternal practice – the importance of hospitality, or entertaining guests and enjoying their company in the temple or at the festive board.

Though it may be in desperation at the difficult task – and make no mistake, it is a difficult task – of proposing yet again the toast to the guests, I must confess to a strong dislike of the suggestion that this is somehow the very root and marrow of our whole enterprise and that if there were no visitors somehow Freemasonry would fall apart. Even more do I find it hard if the speaker goes on to assert that without visitors the ceremonies would lose some of their sparkle or even real meaning, and then concludes by saying: *"but, of course, Brethren, having the chance to share all this and our table with our guests is what Freemasonry is all about, isn't it?"*

Again, with deference to every generous impulse that there is in all of us as Masons, I have to say:

"I beg to decline."

If this really were the case, then it may interest today's Masons to know that in the 18th century the number of guests was exceedingly small, if any, at more than special meetings of a Lodge and that it was only with the development of the "dining club" approach to the Craft in the 19th century that this emphasis on the outsiders being entertained really started to grow.

If hospitality were the heart of Masonry then we would not, presumably, have got to where we are today. Moreover, I am bound to express my deep concern about any Lodge that somehow thinks that guests are essential in order to improve the way in which ceremonies are conducted. Do forgive me but I thought the working of the degrees was primarily for the benefit and enlightenment of the Candidates and not the onlookers. After all, it is the Candidate who pays good money for the privilege and he is coming into our midst to experience the best of the work that we can offer. If you are doing all this for the benefit of the visitors, then you may be culpable under the terms of the Trade Descriptions Act.

But to be serious, the substance of Freemasonry has nothing, but nothing, to do with the presence of guests and any who are privileged to be the real visitors from the Province are only too well aware – and I speak from experience – that such a presence is more likely to detract from the best concentration on the work than enhance it.

As a Worshipful Master said to me on one occasion, and after the minutes were read:

"Please, Sir, will you help me to try and forget that you are here."

The third and most obvious misnomer is to apply the title of this section to the sheer business of dining as the real purpose of Masonry.

Whatever the future of this practice in the Craft may be, I would only have to take you to some private meetings of Lodges in the far West, the North, or in Scotland today, to convince you that to think that sitting down to a three, four, or five course meal is essential to Masonry, is completely unfounded.

We may like our custom, we may still be able to afford it, and we may see its value as a strengthening of ties within and beyond our Lodge but it is far from being essential and the future may indeed make many more Masons realise that this is, *"Not what Freemasonry is all about."*

A fourth contender for the stakes of being what *"Freemasonry is all about"*, is that it is a *code of life.*

I am not always absolutely clear what a speaker means by this phrase but one thing is certain and that is, that we have had renewed statements in various Quarterly Communications of Grand Lodge against anyone who attempts to erect Freemasonry into a religion or the substitute for a religion.

If by a *code of life*, anyone is really saying that they find in Freemasonry the whole of what any form of religion can provide and that there is really no need for anything more, not only would he be starting up that very kind of controversy against which the Craft and its First Degree Charge steadfastly sets its face but also, he would be making a claim that is very hard to sustain.

What he may rightly assert, and it may be this to which most Brethren who talk of a Freemason's *code of life* are referring, is that in the words of the ritual and in the general tenor of Masonic membership there is a basis of practice and conduct that can be usefully held up as a pattern for imitation.

I mean, of course, the fact that a Candidate for the Master's Chair has to be one, *"held in high estimation among his Brethren and Fellows"*, or that we may so act that we may, *"live respected and die regretted."*

The Charges of a Freemason express the general requirements for living in harmony in the Craft, and the special facets of each degree, obedience, fidelity, confidentiality, the pursuit of science and the consideration of how to die well, are all admirable – but to try and rustle up these precepts so that they form a universal *code of life* will, I think, soon reveal significant gaps and some awkwardness in their application.

Following and practising Freemasonry is good as far as it goes but to claim that it is a complete code of life is less than the truth.

It is not what *"Freemasonry is all about, isn't it?"*

These then are some of the areas which, in my experience, people will stand up and claim, whether rhetorically or with passion, as the basis of *"what Freemasonry is all about."*

Each of them, I have tried all too briefly to show, is incorrect and can be misleading. If we are going to answer the claims of such contenders then we have to look at something else as the answer to the query.

It is to this proper question that I now bend my attention.

Clearly, my answer will not be concerned with a philosophy, charity, hospitality or dining. It will be something other than these whilst at the same time related to these, just because the real core of the Craft obviously draws these aspects to itself and incorporates them happily and naturally into its scheme of things. It obviously will have a great deal to do with the basic ingredient of all Freemasonry from its earliest recorded days – the ritual and the ceremonial – and it will also be intimately linked to the "landmarks" of our ancient institution.

Take away the working of a degree, the delivery of a Charge, or (and this is just as ancient as the former) the giving of a Lecture and some explanation of our work, and you will not have Freemasonry.

You can still give to charity, you can dine with your friends and others' friends, join religious and moral organisations dedicated to some special and honourable purpose, and even learn by heart how to proclaim prose and poetry at great length for your own and others' entertainment. Yet not one of those things by themselves is Freemasonry.

However, I would want to reassure those who are not natural matchbox deliverers of Emulation ritual, that failure to achieve that great feat does not mean any failure on their part to be part of, or to understand, Masonry. That only means that you are different from those Masons who can do these things.

So, where then are we left?

I would put it like this. Freemasonry is the heartfelt sharing, by men who have their own personal religious and moral convictions, of certain insights into the nature of what it is to be alive that can only be communicated by ancient and agreed formulae that require careful reflection and constant explanation. I could, of course, have compressed the whole of this book thus far, into a commentary on the precise question addressed to a Candidate for the Second degree.

He is asked: *"What is Freemasonry?"* and his proper, memorised and considered reply is to be:

"A peculiar system of morality, veiled in allegory and illustrated by symbols."

The reason I did not take that route was because I wanted to flush out some of the more inadequate expressions used to answer that question, by people who have clearly not reflected on what they were taught in their progress through the degrees.

In any case, that well-used phrase is so pregnant with meaning that just to use it is not enough. It needs to be unpicked section by section to mean anything.

For example: Masonry is not a code of life or guide to morality but *"a peculiar system"*.

What does that mean?

I can only tell you what it means for me – a carefully constructed progression in, and introduction to, some of the main facts of life that touch my common living with the rest of you. It is not, nor is it meant to be, another set of Ten Commandments or even the Noachic Laws.

It is something other than those, something distinctive or *peculiar* (and that doesn't mean ODD), something that is worth having though not necessarily, as some would claim for a religion, that without which you will suffer eternal loss.

Since Freemasonry is not a religion or a substitute for religion such limitations on it are of no consequence.

What speculative Masonry can do and what for many in my experience it has done; what in fact I believe it was designed to do in the beginning (and I believe at last that we are almost at the point of clarifying when that was in England), is so to form and stimulate the minds and hearts of men that they will be generous to the needy, love their Brethren, pursue truth and honour their God.

When you have so learnt and understood the ritual we use, and taken the steps that are suggested, then you are entitled to get up and say:

"That's what Freemasonry is all about, isn't it?"

INDEX